THE
Dragon King

THE ALARIS CHRONICLES
BOOK III

MIKE SHELTON

The Dragon King
Copyright © 2017 by Michael Shelton

ISBN: 0-9987935-1-5
ISBN-13: 978-0-9987935-1-1
Library of Congress Control Number: TBD
Greenville, North Carolina

Cover Illustration by Brooke Gillette
http://brookegillette.weebly.com

Map by Robert Altbauer
www.fantasy-map.net

For More information about Mike Shelton and his books
www.MichaelSheltonBooks.com

Acknowledgements

This series has been so fun to write. I couldn't have done it without the help of my wife Melissa, the editors at Precision Editing (Heather, Crystal, Julie, and Lisa), and wonderful cover and maps by Brooke Gillette and Robert Altbauer. These people do amazing things in fine-tuning my story and keeping me straight on events and timing.

I love all the wonderful feedback I get from my readers. This, along with my joy of writing, pushes me forward in creating new stories and new worlds.

-Mike-

Books by Mike Shelton

WESTERN CONTINENT BOOKS:

Books of the Realm:
The Cremelino Prophecy:
The Path Of Destiny
The Path Of Decisions
The Path Of Peace
The Blade and the Bow (A prequel novella to The Cremelino Prophecy)

Dragon Rider Books:
The Alaris Chronicles:
The Dragon Orb
The Dragon Rider
The Dragon King
Prophecy Of The Dragon (A prequel novella to The Alaris Chronicles)

The Dragon Artifacts:
The Golden Dragon
The Golden Scepter
The Golden Empire

GEMSTONES OF WAYLAND BOOKS:

The TruthSeer Archives:
TruthStone
TruthSpell
TruthSeer
The Stones of Power (A prequel novella to The TruthSeer Archives)

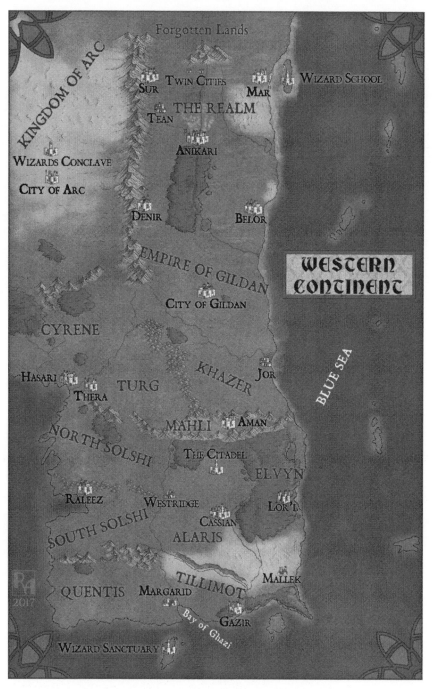

See Color map at www.MichaelSheltonBooks.com

CHAPTER ONE

Bakari circled high above the Elvyn city of Lor'l atop the back of his growing dragon, Abylar. The Blue Sea to the east, sparkling with the sunlight of early spring, enhanced the deep blue of Abylar's jagged scales. They had spent almost four months together, but the bond between the two still grew deeper each day. The depth of feeling Bakari had for his dragon was only rivaled by his affection for Kharlia Attah, the young woman he had met just weeks before Abylar had hatched.

"It's amazing, Bak!" Kharlia shouted from behind him. She held on tight, with both hands wrapped around Bakari's waist.

Bakari couldn't help smiling. He had been attracted to Kharlia at first sight. It wasn't just the similarity of their dark skin tones. Her willingness to help everyone and her genuine concern for him had been immediately apparent.

Her dark brown hair now hung past her shoulders, and he thought he could sense her brown eyes looking at his back. So Bakari turned his head.

Kharlia cried out. "Hey, watch out!" she said. "Those braids are getting longer."

Bakari laughed and resumed looking forward. She had been the first to ever braid his dark hair. The previous winter, the braids had barely been a few inches long; now, they hung down past his chin. Wearing his hair in braids was characteristic of his Mahli heritage.

Thinking about his ancestral land put a frown on his face. After growing up in Alaris, he'd known nothing about that part of the world. But he'd been to Mahli three times now: first, as a new dragon rider; second, after the war in Alaris had come to an end; and most recently, when he had returned to discuss things with the regent there once again—this time with Kharlia at his side.

"Don't worry, Bak," Kharlia whispered, tickling his ear with her breath. "They will work it out."

Bakari was amazed at how well she could read him.

His second visit to his homeland had been the most difficult. He'd had to inform Regent Nagasi that his son, Kolo, had died. The regent had taken it well enough, but many who had sided with Kolo did not. Ever since meeting Bakari, Kolo had been jealous of him and had wanted to be a dragon rider himself—and, eventually, the Dragon King. Then Kolo had been manipulated into stealing a dragon egg by a man they called the Chameleon—so named for his ability to take on the form of another person—and this pursuit had led to Kolo's death.

The most recent visit had gone better, but there were still those in Mahli who didn't believe that Bakari was the prophesied Dragon King—a prophecy that Bakari was still not sure about himself.

Descending over an empty field between the sea and the Elvyn Forest, Bakari sent a silent message to Abylar to land. Upon doing so, they saw a contingent of elves approaching, who bowed to Bakari and offered to bring food for Abylar.

I like these elves! Abylar said to his rider.

Because they give you food?

Yes, why else? Abylar's stomach growled. *That is a sign of respect toward our race.*

Bakari laughed and hopped off of his dragon, then turned and offered his hand up to steady Kharlia as she climbed down from the growing dragon. Bakari rubbed his hands over his dragon's snout, and their bond flared stronger. Bakari felt his tiredness diminish and his strength return. It had been a long ride from Mahli.

"Greetings, oh mighty Dragon King," said a man with a laugh, coming up to Bakari's side. Bakari winced at hearing the title, and a few of the gathered elves gasped at the informality of the man's greeting. If prophecy was to be believed, Bakari, as the first dragon rider in recent memory, was also destined to become a king.

"Roland!" Bakari said, putting out his hand to shake. But he was pulled into a hug instead. Then, stepping back, he surveyed his friend.

Roland Tyre, at seventeen years old, was a year older than Bakari. They were polar opposites in nearly every way imaginable. Roland had chin-length, blond hair—flopping down over his forehead—bright blue eyes, and a smug confidence, proclaiming himself to be the most powerful wizard around. While Bakari had dark skin, brown eyes, and a more reserved attitude as a scholar wizard—at least, until Bakari had become a dragon rider. Now, he was forced to make decisions quicker than he would like and to lead others.

"Nice to see you again, Kharlia." Roland took her hand in his and brought it to his lips for a kiss. "Are you keeping our dragon rider in check?"

Kharlia blushed at Roland's attention but stayed standing next to Bakari, her other hand in his.

"How goes the Citadel?" Bakari asked.

Roland groaned. "I never knew administration could be so tedious, Bak. But we are getting new apprentice wizards all the time."

"You did proclaim yourself High Wizard, Roland," Bakari reminded his friend. "And with that comes responsibility, not just power."

"I know. I know." Roland slapped Bakari on the back. "So, how did the trip to Mahli go? I haven't seen you since the coronation of Mericus deGrande as King of Alaris."

Bakari shook his head with a laugh. "*deGrande*. Leave it to Mericus to give himself such a name. I still find it hard to believe Alaris has a king now. After one hundred and fifty years of hiding behind the magic barrier, with judges ruling the land, it will take some getting used to."

A group of elves motioned for Roland, Bakari, and Kharlia to follow them into the giant tree city of Lor'l. As they passed a table of food, Roland reached his hand out, easily calling a plate of fruit to himself. He grabbed a piece without slowing his pace and shoved it in his mouth.

"You were the one that brought down the barrier, Bak," Roland said with a full mouth. Then he wiped juice from his chin. "This is all *your* doing."

Now it was Bakari's turn to moan. He had indeed found the Orb, a dragon egg that—through the power of guardians giving their life-sources to it—had sustained a barrier around Alaris for one hundred and fifty years. Bakari had been taught that the barrier was there to protect Alaris from other kingdoms, but he had found out later that it was actually put up to protect the other kingdoms from Alaris.

"How is King Mericus doing?"

Roland smiled. "Not half bad. He broods around a lot and complains about the work."

"Like you?" Kharlia piped in.

"Yes, like me." Roland laughed. "He is doing well, though. The old Chief Judge, Daymian Khouri, has actually been acting as a type of ambassador for Mericus by reaching out to other kingdoms."

"I'm glad to see that Daymian took this so well," Bakari said. "It could have started another war on the tail of the first one."

They reached a grouping of enormous trees. Pulleys and vines held a platform that was being lowered to the ground to pick up the visitors. They climbed onto the platform and, at a signal from Bakari, they were lifted up, zooming at a rapid pace through openings between branches.

The Elvyn city itself was amazing in its scope. Giant trees of all kinds had been made into houses, and buildings filled thousands of acres of the Elvyn Forest. Looking up, Bakari could see the largest tree to their right. In this was the king's quarters. Memories of visiting him before came to Bakari's mind now.

The last time was to talk to the old, dying king, Arrowyn Soliel. In his ancient wisdom, Arrowyn had shared with Bakari the secret of the dragon eggs. With that knowledge, Bakari had found others to become dragon riders with himself. Though, in his heart, he still felt there was one more rider needing to be found—a quest that tugged at his mind, even now.

When they reached the top position of the platform, a dark-haired young woman approached. Dressed in battle attire, looking ready for trouble at any time, Alli, Bakari's short friend from Alaris, greeted them.

"Bak, you look well," Alli said. "The braids are longer."

Bakari smiled and gave her a hug. "Alli, it is good to see you. I didn't know you were coming."

Roland rolled his eyes. "She said I needed to be protected. But she's a year younger than me!"

"And twice the battle wizard that you are." Alli laughed, hair bouncing at the top of her shoulders. Her green eyes met Roland's with affection. "He thinks being the head of the Wizard Citadel means he knows everything."

Roland's eyes widened. "Me? Well, of course I know everything. I *am* magic."

The four friends laughed. This claim was something that Roland had always said. Bakari had verified this was indeed true: that in the ancient histories, most of the High Wizards of the Citadel were not only powerful in one of the magical disciplines but had abilities with all. Roland had been apprenticed as a counselor wizard but also held many abilities that scholar or battle wizards held.

Then, out of a doorway in front of the group of teenagers walked a middle-aged man, and the mood turned more somber. His long, dark hair hung over his pointy ears, and his eyes held a look of sadness, but he smiled genuinely at the group. Approaching Bakari, he reached out his hand for a hearty shake.

"Lan…or should I say *Prince Lanwaithian* or is it *King* now?" Bakari stumbled and then added, "Greetings."

"Dragon Rider," Lan said and then paused with some emotion. "Good of you to join us. There is food waiting for you inside. The ceremony will commence this evening. Until them, *Prince* or just *Lan* will do." The prince's father had passed away recently, and a private ceremony was to be held to confirm Lan as the next king of the elves.

"Any word from Breelyn?" Bakari asked, looking at Lan.

The prince seemed conflicted, and his mouth tightened. "She is, apparently, on your errand, Dragon Rider."

Bakari glanced down for a moment. She was indeed on his mission, and he too hoped she was well. Breelyn was the beautiful, young protector of the elves who had become the second dragon rider. She was also engaged to the prince.

"She flew north to Gildan," Bakari explained, "to let them know about the barrier falling. She should have returned by now."

"So I have been told," the prince said.

Bakari walked up closer to Lan and pulled him aside as the others entered to find food and rest.

"Have I offended you, Lan?" Bakari asked. "We are still friends, aren't we?"

Lan's shoulders slumped, and his head fell. After a moment, he gazed back up into Bakari's eyes. "I am just worried for her, that is all. And, with the king's passing…it has been…hard." The prince's eyes looked moist now.

Bakari nodded. The elves lived long lives, and their relationships with the land and with each other were deep. Lan's father had been king for one hundred and fifty years, a long reign even among the elves.

"We are still friends, Dragon Rider," Lan started and then stopped. "But, once I am king, what will that make us?"

Bakari understood this question all too well. At the end of the war for the rule over Alaris, Roland had proclaimed Bakari as High Dragon King, a king over all other kings, and as the only person whom Roland—and, by default, the other wizards—would need to answer to. Mericus, the new king of Alaris, was also a wizard and would be beholden to Bakari through that relationship.

"We will face that when it comes, Lan. For now, we are friends, and my purpose is to establish peace among the lands."

The prince nodded and then motioned Bakari to follow the others inside.

Then they heard a loud roar up above them. So they ran to a nearby platform, where the two of them could look up into the air. Circling above them were two colorful dragons: a yellow one, with orange tips on its scales, carrying a beautiful, blond-haired elf maiden and a bright green dragon, carrying a fifteen-year-old boy with a long, dark ponytail flying in the air behind him.

"Breelyn! Jaimon!" Bakari yelled out loud, but he also spoke their names through the dragon bonds. They both waved, and a mutual feeling of joy was carried through their bonds to Bakari.

Lan laughed out loud with a quick expulsion of air and then said, "Breelyn."

Bakari patted the prince on the back. "She will be your queen someday, Lan. Don't worry."

The prince turned to Bakari and smiled. "I can hardly wait for that day, Dragon Rider. Have you ever been in love?"

Bakari felt himself blush and knew that his dark cheeks were going even darker.

"Ha!" Lan punched Bakari in the shoulder. "You are in love, aren't you? With that lovely young woman you came up with." Lan motioned once again for Bakari to join the others as he added, "Well, don't let me keep you waiting. I know how fond the heart can grow when we are away from those we love."

Lan left to ride the lift down to meet Breelyn, and Bakari walked through the open door to join the others. As soon as he entered the room, Kharlia was at his side. Bakari's heart lifted but then grew sad. He hadn't told her yet, but he would have to leave her for a while. For he needed to fly north to find the next dragon rider.

CHAPTER TWO

L ater that evening, mage lights and candles adorned the great Elvyn hall high up in the trees. Bakari caught the sweet aroma of the lilacs, roses, and gardenias placed throughout the front of the room. The elves had the ability to grow flowers like these any time of year it seemed.

A raised dais held everyone's attention in front. Seated on one side were Prince Lan, Breelyn, a younger cousin of Lan's, and an older aunt and uncle. The other side held three senior council members and a scribe.

Bakari stood in the back of the room with Kharlia, surveying the others who were present. The heads of a dozen or so of the largest Elvyn houses were seated on two long benches. Next to them sat a smattering of ambassadors and other government officials. This would be a private ceremony tonight. A formal coronation would occur in three months, after the allotted time for mourning and for making preparations.

Then Bakari saw Lan motioning for him to join Lan on the dais. Bakari let out a deep sigh, knowing that this was now his lot in life. There would be few rooms where he wouldn't be recognized or honored.

Go on, Rider. Represent us well, Abylar voiced through the bond. He and the two female dragons, Miriel and Cholena, were feasting by the sea on some food the elves had prepared for them.

Bakari took strength from Abylar's words and stepped forward, toward the dais, leaving Kharlia to sit with Roland, Alli, and Jaimon, the only others in attendance—an honor that was given to few individuals that weren't elves.

As Bakari sat down next to Prince Lan, the man put a hand of encouragement on Bakari's knee.

"Thank you," Lan said. "I feel better knowing you are here."

Confused, Bakari leaned over and whispered, "Are you worried about something?" Bakari glanced around the room but didn't see anything out of place. They shouldn't be expecting any trouble from any of the elves. Lan was well-liked by his people and had been trained his entire life to become king after his father's death.

"I hope not." The prince shook his head, his long hair flying softly to each side. "But something seems off."

Bakari reached out with his own heightened senses, though they hadn't been very strong until combined with his dragon's bond. He didn't sense anything at first but kept searching. Though not the strongest of magic users, elves were the most sensitive to detecting its use. Most elves had some type of magical ability, even if they weren't called *wizards*. They were also more in tune with nature than other races in the human kingdoms were.

After the doors in the back were closed, the chief council member stood and approached the podium. "In recent days, we have grieved the unfortunate passing of our beloved and long-reigning king, Arrowyn Soliel."

Heads bowed in respect for the old king, and eyes glistened with memories of his fair rule. Then the council member cleared his throat and continued, "During times of grief, we must still move on. And so today we bring forward the heir to the throne of the elves, Prince Lanwaithian Soliel."

The prince stood, his face looking serious, but his eyes seemed alert and bright. He took a few steps toward the front of the dais, to stand next to the councilor. Then the councilor nodded to another man, who stood and brought forth a small crown. Interlaced with gold and silver, the crown reflected the bright lights in the room.

The prince knelt down. A slight breeze could be heard outside the room, rustling through the great trees. Bakari watched in amazement. This was the second coronation he had seen in recent months: the first being for Mericus in Bakari's own land of Alaris.

"All gathered today do witness this occasion," began the councilor. "The crown of faithfulness doth now bless thy head, Lanwaithian Soliel. Ye are now consecrated in this sacred duty: to be the servant of all the elves in this land. As I place this crown on thy head this day, may your heart be graced with love, your mind be infused with clarity, and your body be filled with strength from the earth you touch, and may ye reign in honor and fairness with justice and mercy. Do ye accept this burden of your own free will?"

As Lan lifted his head, his green eyes were glistening. "Yea, I do accept this crown with all the burdens it holds, to be the servant of all. I will rule in fairness and walk in the light all my days."

Bakari glanced over at the assembled crowd and caught Kharlia wiping her eyes. As their eyes met, he smiled at her. Even Roland appeared moved by the solemn occasion. Bakari moved his gaze around the room, noticing that most of the elves seemed to be at peace. But a few hung their heads low, and Bakari could not discern their thoughts.

Then the crown was placed on Lan's head, and the chief councilor bade him to rise.

"May I present, to those assembled, our new king, King Lanwaithian Soliel. Long live the king!"

"Long live the king!" the crowd repeated.

Lan stood at the podium and, with a voice thick with emotion, began to say a few words. "In recognition of my father, we will forgo the celebratory coronation for three months. During that time, I will meet with the council and heads of houses. May our kingdom continue to be a place of peace, and may our people live within the light and within the strength of the earth and its great trees." Lan seemed to be struggling for the appropriate words. He turned to Breelyn, then to Bakari and added, "I am honored to serve beside these great dragon riders and thank them for all their service to Elvyn and to the lands around us. May our peoples live in peace."

With that, the councilor directed the heads of houses to come forth and give their fealty to their new king. One by one, each elf came forward, elegant with their long hair and silk robes, to greet their new king. Bakari stood with Breelyn off to the side and marveled at this serious reception. In the six months that he had known the elves, he had found them surprisingly humorous and full of laughter in their daily duties. Today, however, marked a solemn occasion, one that did not occur often in the Elvyn kingdom—the last time being over one hundred and fifty years previous.

Then Roland, Alli, Kharlia, and Jaimon moved closer to the front of the room, on the opposite side of the king from where Bakari and Breelyn stood. Alli, with tight leather armor hugging her fifteen-year-old body, stood with a hand on her sword's hilt, her eyes flickering around the room. She looked ready to pounce at a moment's notice. Roland appeared relaxed, but Bakari could tell by the clenching of his jaw that Roland too was worried about something happening.

As the line of elves dwindled, Breelyn put her arm on Bakari's shoulder and leaned in, whispering, "Something is not right here, Master."

It felt strange to Bakari for Breelyn to refer to himself as her *master*. She was twice his age and had served as an Elvyn protector for many years. But he did know, in regards to their relationship to each other through the dragon bond, he was indeed her master.

Bakari agreed with Breelyn's assessment and sent a thought through the bond to his dragon, Abylar: *Be vigilant in watching for trouble.* Aloud, Bakari said, "Breelyn, as a protector of the elves, do you know everyone here?"

Breelyn's eyes swept around the room carefully and then returned to Bakari. "Most. I know all the councilors and other officials, but the heads of houses can change."

Bakari signaled for Jaimon to watch the back door. Still not quite fifteen years old, Jaimon Schafer hailed from Quentis, a kingdom to the south of Alaris. Being the last rider to receive a dragon and not a magic user like Bakari or Breelyn, Jaimon was still getting used to the bond with his dragon.

Roland came around front, closer to the king, and caught Bakari's attention. Then he tilted his head toward the last elf in line. The man had long, dark hair falling over a light cream robe with gold bands running at its edges. He didn't look any different than the rest, except that he kept his head down. Given the solemnity of the occasion, that action hadn't brought any undue attention to him until now.

Lan finished accepting the fealty of the second to last elf, lifting the man from his knees and giving his thanks. Then he glanced over at Bakari, his face still grim. Even though Lan had been trained for this day for many years, Bakari knew that it was still hard for Lan to lose his father, the old king.

As the new king held out his hand, to beckon the last head of house forward, the man still did not look up but took two steps closer. The other elves had gathered at the side of the room, and Bakari could hear the light laughter of one of them rise over the otherwise quiet moment.

Bringing his hands up, the last elf pushed back his long, dark hair and brought his face up to glare at Lan.

"Bakari!" Roland yelled. "It's him, the Chameleon."

Bakari's eyes widened as he too saw what Roland did: the same green eyes that had looked at him months ago from multiple faces—including that of a new black dragon.

Before Bakari could say anything, the Chameleon pulled a shiny and black blade out of his robes and struck at the new king. Bakari would swear that he had seen wisps of black smoke rising off it. But Bakari rushed to Lan's side, pushing Lan away from the danger; however, the blade still scraped along the side of Lan's arm.

As the king yelled out in pain and tried to pull his own sword with his other hand, Alli jumped across three rows of benches in a flash, spinning in the air, and then pulled the Chameleon backward by the back of his robes, sending him stumbling into the benches. But he somehow remained upright and then jumped up onto one of the benches.

The others in the room either pulled out their weapons or rallied around the king to protect him. Bakari saw that Jaimon hung at the back, for he was the one least trained to fight.

Breelyn knelt down next to Lan as Bakari stood up to face the menace. In front of them all, the Chameleon's hair shortened, his ears rounded, and his face, as well as his body, took on a new look—even his eyes took on a yellow glow. He had now become a humongous warrior.

Bakari paused as the man grew even taller in front of them.

"You cannot defeat me, you pathetic magic users," the Chameleon said. "We will rule you all."

"We?" Bakari asked, trying to keep the Chameleon's attention as Alli moved back behind the man. "I don't see anyone else here with you."

"The thrones of all the lands will be ours," the Chameleon continued as he waved his hands in the air, a dark magic pulsating through the room.

Alli screamed, and Bakari looked over at her.

"My magic," the young battle wizard said, "is gone."

"All the magic is gone. From each of you." The Chameleon smiled and changed his shape again. This time he appeared as a scholar wizard.

Bakari glanced at Roland for confirmation. He nodded his head at Bakari. The other elves confirmed that they too had lost what little magic they had possessed. Bakari sensed two things about himself then: He had lost his normal wizard magic, as weak as it had been. But, he still retained his powers as a dragon rider—extensive abilities that he could pull from the power and might of his dragon. With a quick glance at Breelyn and Jaimon, Bakari could see in their eyes that they too still felt the power of their dragons.

"What do you want?" Bakari took a step toward the Chameleon.

"Want?" The Chameleon's golden eyes flashed, and he put his finger on his chin as if thinking. "I want you all dead." With this, he brought his hands up in front of him and called forth a ball of black fire.

Alli threw a knife at the Chameleon's back, but it seemed to bounce off of some invisible shield.

Then the Chameleon said, "And you will be the first, Roland Tyre," as he tossed the fire at Roland and, once again, changed shapes—into Roland himself now.

Bakari moved quickly, pulling on the power of his dragon, and blocked the ball of fire with a shield of air.

The Chameleon turned to him, his surprise written all over his face. "Incredible," the Chameleon said, still looking like

Roland. "I guess I underestimated the power of the dragon riders."

The real Roland reached into his pocket and pulled out a small vial. "Breelyn," he called out, tossing it into the air and saying, "I can't use it right now, but you can. It is powerful magic."

Breelyn grabbed the vial from the air and took off its top. Black tendrils rose out of it, winding their way around Breelyn. The elf maiden took a deep breath and then stretched her hands forward, toward the Chameleon.

But before Breelyn's power could leave her fingertips, the Chameleon had changed again, now looking like an exact replica of Lan, the new king. "You wouldn't kill me, would you?" The voice was Lan's, and Breelyn faltered.

From the ground, the real king groaned as he tried to sit up. So Kharlia rushed to Lan's side to help.

"It's spreading, Bak!" she screamed out.

Bakari glanced over. Along the king's arm a thin, spidery trail of black was extending out from his knife wound.

Breelyn turned back and gathered her strength. "You will die for what you have done." She brought forth all the power she could muster from her dragon and, with the help of Roland's vial, she pushed it all at the Chameleon. The black ball of fire only slid around the man, vanishing in the air.

"You cannot use my own powers against me, girl." The Chameleon laughed deeply.

Breelyn's face grew darker, and her eyes became black.

"Good, good. Feel the rage, the power," the Chameleon encouraged. "That's what I feel. Isn't it wonderful?"

"Breelyn, no!" shouted Lan. "Don't do this!"

"He tried to kill you!" Breelyn said, raising her voice, a mass of black fog encircling her.

From outside of the hall came a giant roar of despair that was heard and felt by all. Then the walls rattled and the lamps swung widely, and the Chameleon stumbled and began to fall off the bench.

Bakari felt Abylar's terror through the bond.

She is going to kill us, Abylar shouted to Bakari's mind. *The power is dark and evil.*

Bakari turned to Breelyn. "Stop, Breelyn." He reached his hand out to her. "You must stop or you will kill the dragons."

Then Jaimon bent over and held his head in his hands. Bakari almost doubled over in pain as well. He suffered from the foul power of what Breelyn held and what the Chameleon commanded. The power was filthy and gross.

"Kill me, elf maiden," the Chameleon taunted.

Bakari forced himself to concentrate as he pulled all the pure power from Abylar that he could. He hated to pull rank on one of the other dragon riders, but there was no choice.

"Breelyn," Bakari said, "as your master, I command you: Stop. Let go of the power." The voice he had spoken with was Bakari's own, but deeper, nobler, full of power. A command from the dragon master.

He flung out his power toward her, finding the full might and authority of the Dragon King at his disposal. His power wrapped around the black tendrils and held them at bay.

Slowly, Breelyn's eyes returned to their clear, sparkling blue, and she shuddered, taking in a long breath.

With a nod of her head to her master, Breelyn brought her hands down, dropping the container and releasing the evil power. Then she fell, slumping to the ground, and cried. Bakari wanted to go to her, but he knew that the Chameleon was still a threat.

Then the Chameleon changed appearances again. This time, into a nondescript young elf. He pulled a cowl up over his head, hiding his eyes—the only characteristic that Bakari had found to distinguish the Chameleon from anyone else. Then he pulled a small box out of his pocket and opened the lid.

"You will bow to me one day, Dragon Rider, Elf King, and High Wizard," the Chameleon said to them, his body starting to vaporize in front of them. "My brothers and I will rule the western lands under my father—the real wizard king."

Soon, only the Chameleon's head and torso were left. Bakari was too spent to bring forth any more magic, and Breelyn had stayed sprawled on the ground. But Jaimon still stood by the back of the room. Fear spread across his face, but then a determined look set in. Through the bond, Bakari could feel the power of the dragons being pulled into the youngest dragon rider.

Right before the Chameleon would have disappeared completely, Jaimon threw a bright ball of pure dragon power at him. As the power hit, the Chameleon shrieked, then disappeared.

"Is he gone?" Alli asked. "I hate not having my powers." Her features showed she was furious, and she clenched her sword's hilt in her hand.

Jaimon shook his head. "I did not kill him. I was too late." The young man lowered his head. "I hesitated too long."

Bakari could feel the boy's shame. "Jaimon, you did well. None of us were able to disarm or kill him, and you did what you could."

Jaimon nodded but didn't look convinced.

A loud wail came from the floor, and all eyes turned back toward the king. Lan's arm was now almost completely black.

CHAPTER THREE

When Bakari took charge, no one challenged his authority. He sent most of the elves out into the tree city of Lor'l, to make sure no other damage had been done.

Roland moved over to Lan's side and was putting his hand on Lan's darkening arm. Roland closed his eyes for a few minutes. Then he shook his head and said with almost a wail, "I can't sense my magic anymore." He stood up and began pacing the room. "It's impossible. I won't let that maniac take my abilities away." Then the High Wizard mumbled under his breath, "I *am* magic."

Kharlia grabbed her bag and pushed Bakari gently out of the way with a grim smile. "Magic isn't always around to heal," Kharlia said. "Let me see what I can do." She dug into her pack, pulling out small bags of herbs and jars of ointments.

Bakari knew Kharlia had learned her craft well from her mother and could heal many things, but this injury was done with magic—evil magic. So Bakari didn't know if she could do anything for Lan, but he would let her try nevertheless.

Breelyn was sitting on the floor about ten feet away, her head in her hands, only looking up whenever Lan moaned. He was conscious still, but just barely so. His face looked red and hot, as if a fever were moving in rapid waves over his entire body.

Bakari sat and then scooted over on the floor next to Breelyn. She was the first elf he had ever met and, actually, the first person to step foot into Alaris in over one hundred and fifty years. She had found Erryl, a young guardian of the Orb, an orb that had really been Abylar's egg. These two had then found Bakari and had helped him to find the Orb and release his dragon from it.

Breelyn's long, blond hair hung to her hips, and her skin, normally pale, now appeared a shade darker.

"Breelyn." Bakari didn't know what else to say.

She glanced up at him, her bright blue eyes rimmed with red and brimming with tears, but still as beautiful as ever. "Bakari, I...I...I'm so sorry," Breelyn said weakly, her pale lips quivering.

Bakari shook his head, his braids swinging from side to side. "It's fine, Breelyn. I didn't want to do that either. It wasn't right of me."

Breelyn's voice strengthened as she said, "It was right, Bakari. You are the master of the dragon riders, the Dragon King. You have all the right to command us in anything you wish, and we have vowed to obey."

Bakari wondered how they could all treat him with such respect. He was only a sixteen-year-old boy, a weak scholar wizard, who had hardly left the library until six months earlier. He shook his head with wonder.

Breelyn's voice softened as she said, "It is true, Bakari." Then she put her soft hand on his arm. It looked paler against his dark skin. "I know what you are thinking," Breelyn continued. "You are young, Bakari, but you are the prophesied one. The Dragon King."

"I don't feel much like a king today."

That brought a smile to Breelyn's lips. She peered over at Lan. "Kings are not always invincible, Bakari. You did what you could do. You brought me back."

Bakari nodded his head toward Lan. "Let's see what we can do about your king."

Breelyn raised her eyebrows at Bakari. Then they moved back over next to Lan. Roland, Jaimon, and Alli were gathered around him, watching Kharlia at work.

"I have given him yarrow and peppermint for the fever," Kharlia said. "Garlic may help against the infection, but the injury is caused by magic, so I'm not sure."

Lan moved his hand over and grasped Breelyn's, saying, "Garlic, huh?" His voice was weak and hoarse. "Still going to kiss me?" he asked Breelyn.

Bakari smiled. From the first moment he had met Lan, he had been surprised by the man's sense of humor.

Breelyn leaned down and, with tears in her eyes, gave him a kiss on the lips.

"I see you have grown bolder among the dragon riders." Lan laughed.

"I will stay and take care of him," Breelyn voiced. "My healing magic is already returning."

Bakari hadn't noticed. But, once he checked, he too felt a little of his magic once again. He looked at Roland and Alli, but they shook their heads.

"It must be due to the dragon bond," Bakari said. "But I am sure it will return."

"I hope so," Roland grumbled. "I would be the shortest reigning High Wizard in history."

"I have never read anything about a wizard's magic disappearing totally," Bakari said. He scrunched his face up and then mumbled off a few instances where magic had been only temporarily immobilized. As long as he could remember, Bakari had had the amazing ability for remembering everything he had ever read. This skill had come in handy many times.

"I trust your memory, Bak," Roland said, seeming to relax with Bakari's words. "And I'll hold you to it."

Breelyn placed her hands on the spreading blackness on Lan's arm and tried to heal him.

But Lan batted her hand away and shouted out in terror, "What are you doing?" Lan's voice sounded gruff. "I thought you were going to heal me, not kill me."

Breelyn's lips went tight. "What do you mean? I was pushing my healing power into you, you stubborn man."

"That wasn't healing power, Breelyn." Lan glared at her. "I have been healed before. So I know what it is, and that's not it! You were pushing more of that wretched evil into me."

Breelyn opened her eyes wide and turned to Bakari.

But before he could say anything, Alli spoke up.

"The Chameleon did try to get you to use the power of the object that Roland had given you." Alli glared pointedly at Roland, who only shrugged. "I have told him to stay away from the dark powers and artifacts in the basement of the Citadel—they are locked away for a reason."

"Power is not good or evil, only the user or intention of it is," Roland stated firmly. "That is what we have always been taught."

Bakari held his hand up. "But," he said and then paused, "maybe the magical items held in the Citadel were kept there because they were infused with black magic—something evil. Or, if not the magic itself, then the intention of whoever infused them was for an evil purpose."

"So I'm infected now with this evil magic?" Breelyn asked, raising her voice as she added, "I can't use my own magic anymore?"

Just then, a few of the elderly elves returned to check on the progress of their king's healing. One elf stepped forward.

"There doesn't seem to be any other damage to the city, sir," the elf said as he looked back and forth between Lan and Bakari, as if he were not sure whom he answered to.

"And the magic?" Bakari asked the elf.

"The removal of magic was limited to only this room. We have healers that can now see to our king." Behind the man came a group of Elvyn healers, their white robes trimmed in red, signifying their occupations.

"I will stay with him also," Kharlia offered. "Like I said, not everything can be cured with magic."

Bakari nodded and pulled the rest of their group away from Lan. Breelyn reluctantly followed as they moved out to a deck area overlooking the considerable tree city. A slight breeze blew across their faces, the tangy scent of the Blue Sea hanging in the air. Bakari could even see Abylar, who stood ready with the two other dragons below, next to the sea.

"We need to find out more about this dark magic and the Chameleon—" Bakari started to say, but he was interrupted by Jaimon.

"Dragon Master," the young dragon rider said, then looked hesitant to speak. "I have something that might help."

Bakari motioned for Jaimon to proceed.

"At the end, when I sent the magic of the dragons into the Chameleon," Jaimon said, "I think some of it went with him."

"You're not making any sense," Roland said, resting his hand on a wooden railing.

Bakari glared at his old friend, but his look was only met with a look of stubborn annoyance.

Then Roland waved his hand at Jaimon, for him to continue. It seemed like such a kingly gesture that Bakari almost laughed despite the precarious situation they were all in.

"As you know," Jaimon began, "I do not have magic like the rest of you." Jaimon seemed to shrink in front of them, and then he rushed his words out. "But I do have the bond with my dragon, Cholena. Since using the dragon power against that man—or whatever he is—I have felt something in my mind. It is faint, but I think I can tell where he is or, at least, in what direction he may be."

Bakari smiled, the first real smile, it seemed, since the Chameleon had shown up. "That's great, Jaimon," Bakari said. "That's a start at least." A plan was now forming in his mind. "Jaimon, I want you and Alli to try and follow the Chameleon. Keep an eye on him, and try to limit any damage that he may be doing. Until we figure out how to defeat him, we need to know where he is."

Alli looked to Roland for confirmation.

"Gonna miss me, sweetheart?" Roland quipped.

"Errr," Alli growled. "You are insufferable, Roland Tyre."

The two had met in Alaris six months earlier, just prior to being taken with the Chief Judge to the Citadel, to meet the former High Wizard, Kanzar Centari. At that time, both were powerful apprentices who were disgruntled to be given such low ranks. Since then, Roland had risen to a level four wizard, had proclaimed himself High Wizard, and had granted Alli her wizard test. Now she stood as the Battlemaster of the Citadel.

The whole group laughed now at Alli's remark. Roland had indeed been insufferable at times. His arrogance had angered many wizards. But the one thing that was different about Roland's arrogance was that it wasn't egotism: he truly was the most powerful wizard around.

"Roland," Bakari continued, "you will return to the Citadel. Send word out to all the other wizard schools. We need more information about this Chameleon's magic and how to beat it."

Roland opened his mouth but then closed it again and just nodded. Bakari knew that it was hard for Roland to not be in charge.

"What about me?" Breelyn asked with an uncharacteristic frown. "I don't trust my magic."

Bakari sighed. "Hopefully we can find a cure for it along with banishing the Chameleon. For now, you are still a dragon rider. Fly west, to Raleez, and warn the kings of North and South Solshi of the Chameleon."

"What about Lan?" Breelyn asked.

"He's in good hands here with the healers. There is nothing else you can do here, Breelyn."

"And you, Bak? Where are you going?"

"I feel pulled to the north. There is another dragon rider and dragon egg somewhere up there," Bakari explained, pointing in that direction. "I will go there."

Everyone nodded and then stood quietly for a moment. Then, one by one, they bowed to Bakari and left on their missions.

Once they were gone, Bakari stood quietly on a platform, looking out over the tops of the trees toward the Blue Sea.

After a short time, Kharlia came out from the room and put her hand on Bakari's arm. So he turned toward her.

"Kharlia, I really don't know what I am doing," Bakari whispered.

"But they follow you, Bak," she said. "They trust you."

Bakari nodded his head. "I know. And it frightens me terribly."

Kharlia leaned into him, resting her head against his shoulder. He turned his head, looking down toward her.

"You did great today with the king in there," Bakari said. "I wish I could take charge like that."

"The man was dying, and Roland and Breelyn's magic wasn't working," Kharlia stated. "I just did what I had to do."

"You are a talented healer," Bakari said.

Kharlia moved back a few inches away from him and peered down at her feet. "But I don't have any magic, Bak. All of you are so powerful: Roland, Alli, Breelyn, and even Jaimon, who has the power of his dragon."

Bakari put his hand under her chin and brought her face up so that her brown eyes met his. "Kharlia, you don't need magic. You are wonderful without it. I...I—" Bakari faltered for a moment and then said, "I liked you from the moment we first met—before all the dragon riders and before the barrier came down. You don't need magic."

Kharlia put her hand on the side of his face and said, "Thank you, Bak." She paused, then moved her fingers with a gentle touch over his eyelids. "Your eyes are beautiful. The whites turn blue now when you use your magic. Quite exotic."

He laughed and took her hands in his. "I don't know what I am becoming, but I want you next to me as I do." Then he leaned down and gave her a soft kiss.

Her full lips molded to his perfectly, and her fingers tightened around his. But Kharlia gazed back at him with tears in her eyes.

"What's wrong?" Bakari asked.

"I want to be with you too, Bak. I really do." Kharlia struggled to hold back more tears and then added, "But I need to stay here with Lan—to learn from the healers. That is my *magic*."

Bakari nodded and let out a brief sigh. He would feel better knowing that she was safe with the elves while he flew north. They stood in a comfortable silence, looking over the trees to the Blue Sea.

A moment later, a few of the healers emerged from Lan's room. One healer nodded in respect to Kharlia.

"Thanks to the quick actions of you, Healer," he said to Kharlia, "his fever has broken."

Bakari squeezed Kharlia's hand to remind her again of how special she was, even without magic.

"I will be staying here to learn from you," Kharlia said.

The healer smiled at them both. "Our knowledge is open to any healer that is a friend of the master dragon rider. However, the blackness stills spreads on the king's arm. We have slowed it but cannot stop it yet."

"We will find a cure," Bakari said, trying to reassure them. "The High Wizard and all the dragon riders will continue to reach out to all the lands until a cure is found."

The healer bowed to both Bakari and Kharlia and left.

Bakari put his arm around Kharlia as much for his own comfort as for hers and said, "I will return as soon as I can."

Kharlia didn't say goodbye but only stood up on tiptoe and gave him one more kiss on the lips.

Then with one last hug, Bakari left, calling out in his mind for Abylar to ready himself to fly north. Bakari took the lift back down to the ground, gathered some supplies, and met Abylar back out on the flat land.

Mounting his blue dragon, Bakari then held on tight as Abylar lifted up into the sky. As they glided over the trees, Bakari could see Kharlia growing smaller down below. Bakari waved down to her, then turned Abylar northward. There was one more dragon rider to gather in.

CHAPTER FOUR

After a brief break later that night, Bakari continued northward on the back of Abylar. Soon the spring morning dawned, bright and clear over the Blue Sea, bringing with it the promise of better things ahead.

Abylar dipped closer to the water, dragging his right wing along the top of the rolling waves, causing a light spray to cover Bakari.

Hey, you're getting me wet! Bakari thought through the bond.

Abylar roared in delight and flew faster.

Bakari laughed and then said out loud, "You're playing like a child!"

I am not a child! Abylar said to Bakari's mind. *But I do like to play!*

The giant blue dragon turned his head back toward Bakari, his yellow eyes flashing playfully. Then, without warning, he rose straight up in the air. As a few seagulls scattered in front of him, Bakari grabbed the leather strap in front of himself and hung on for dear life.

As they flew on, Bakari was amazed by all of the water. Having grown up in Alaris—landlocked and behind a magical barrier—Bakari had only recently seen any body of water larger than the Dunn River.

Looking westward, Bakari could see all of Elvyn, covered with a canopy of green. Looking northward, Bakari saw the ring of mountains that separated Mahli from the other northern kingdoms. The mountains were approaching swiftly, with the city of Jar—the capital of Khazer—spreading out from the bay.

"Abylar!" Bakari screamed out loud and said through the bond to Abylar's mind. The dragon had reached his apex, high in the sky, and then began his dive back toward the sea. Wind rushed against Bakari's face, and his growing braids flew around his head like out of control snakes.

Don't wear yourself out, Bakari told Abylar. *We have a ways to go.*

Can you sense it, Dragon Rider?

Sense what?

The other dragon egg. Abylar's mind was filled with glee.

I feel the pull northward, but it is unclear whether the egg and the rider are together or not.

As Bakari opened himself up more to the power of the dragon, the power of the spirit, he felt his soul fill with sweet delight. This made him laugh out loud with joy. He was so excited to find another dragon rider. After Kolo and the Chameleon had turned the last dragon evil, they'd had to kill it. The Chameleon had taken its form, for a brief time, before continuing to cause havoc in Elvyn.

Passing by Jar, Bakari could see the people below, looking up in the air and running with loud shouts to tell others what they had seen high up in the blue sky. Spring flowers bloomed along the coast of Khazer, its meadows leading right up to the sandy shore of the Blue Sea. Yellow daffodils filled acres and acres; their contrast to the bright Blue Sea was amazing.

I can't believe how fast we can travel, Bakari said.

Do you want to go faster? Abylar asked.

Oh, no, no, no, my friend. Bakari laughed. *This is fast enough. I am not as strong as you are.*

That is true. Abylar shook with what Bakari felt was laughter. *You are a weak and puny race.*

We may be small, but remember who your master is, Bakari teased his dragon.

Abylar leveled out and roared, spitting flames of blue fire in front of himself, the edges bringing warmth back to Bakari's face.

So Bakari patted Abylar and reassured him of his love through the bond. Then he asked, *Can you slow down a bit?*

Later that day, they landed somewhere near the border between Gildan and the Realm, where a picturesque river ran through meadows of new grass and then splashed hard into the sea.

Bakari dismounted, stretched his arms over his head, and tried to walk off the stiffness of his legs. The day was warm, so he removed the light cloak he had been wearing. Underneath, he wore dark leather pants and a green shirt. His wizard robes were in one of the pouches on the sides of his dragon saddle, along with a few of the wooden discs, should he meet with any danger.

His thoughts went immediately to Kharlia, and he missed her already. He even picked a few colorful flowers and thought about how they would look in her dark hair.

Then Abylar flew off, in search of big game, while Bakari opened up his pack and pulled out some bread and meat. The broad meadows made him feel so small, and he shook his head at the wonderment of it all.

He was amazed that he now stood in yet another kingdom. Growing up in Alaris and spending most of his time in the library—either at the Citadel or in Cassian—Bakari had read many of the old records and books about the rest of the world. But he had never thought he would actually see them himself.

It had been one hundred and fifty years since any new information or books about these lands had made their way into Alaris. What if the facts that he knew about these lands had changed? A few books in Mahli and in Elvyn had updated him on some of the more recent events outside Alaris. One of those events was the acceptance of wizards and magic in the Realm, beginning about fifteen years earlier with the rise of their wizard king.

Bakari wondered where the closest library might be from here. Clearing his mind, he brought up the most recent map that he could recall. Just to the north of here was the ancient city of Belor. He grinned, thinking about what treasures a library *there* might hold.

Soon Abylar came back with his belly full. And Bakari climbed up on his bulky, blue back and instructed him to fly north to Belor.

We need to find the other dragon egg, Abylar reminded him.

I know. But we have to stop somewhere for the night. So it might as well be where they have a library! Bakari said through the bond.

A roaring laugh ensued. *Just one night, Rider. Time is short.*

Soon they spotted buildings with tall domes just inland from the Blue Sea. A bright, white wall surrounded the sizable city.

Bakari took a deep breath. He didn't know if these people had ever seen a dragon before or had heard of himself yet. Breelyn had visited Gildan, just to the southwest of here, but that was as far north as she had flown.

They landed between the Blue Sea and the walls of the city. Before Bakari even dismounted, a group of soldiers surrounded his dragon. The largest man—and, presumably, the captain—approached them with his sword drawn.

"We mean you no harm," Bakari said. He couldn't imagine that he appeared very threatening to them. The captain was looking more at Abylar than at Bakari, though, and Bakari realized that he had grown so accustomed to having his dragon around.

Bakari dismounted and took a few steps toward the group, saying, "I am Bakari, scholar wizard of Alaris and a dragon rider of Mahli." He intentionally left off any mention of his status as the Dragon King—one title that he still wasn't even quite sure of himself.

The captain ordered some of his men to encircle Abylar. But the young dragon growled, and they backed away.

"Abylar, be good," Bakari said in his mind but also out loud, for the benefit of those gathered.

They look good for eating, came Abylar's reply to his mind.

Bakari tried not to smile. He knew that his dragon was joking—at least, he hoped he was.

"The dragon will obey you?" asked the captain, his language the same as Bakari's but his accent somewhat different.

"He will," Bakari said.

Abylar lifted up off the ground with silent words to Bakari that he was going in search of more food.

The captain gave a short bow to Bakari. "I'm not one for magic, sir, but our king is. And it so happens that his best friend, our governor, Kelln El'Han, is here today. I will take you to him."

Bakari nodded. "I would like that."

Bakari followed the soldiers through a gate and into the city. Not as spacious as Cassian, Belor was of good size nevertheless. And the city was bustling with evening activities. Vendors hocked their wares, and people were gathering for their evening meals. Meat roasting somewhere grabbed at Bakari's senses.

As a dark-skinned teen, Bakari stood out against the predominantly pale-skinned and red-haired Belorians. Bakari knew they were part of a kingdom called *the Realm*, but he didn't know much else about their heritage.

But I bet they have a substantial library! he thought to himself.

The captain led Bakari into a palace with a sizable dome in the center and four smaller domes around it. Inside, the walls were tall, and the floors were a smooth marble.

Servants eyed him carefully, but soon Bakari and the group of guards stood before a polished wooden door. The captain excused himself for a few moments before returning to usher

Bakari inside while the rest of the guards stayed out in the hallway.

Sitting behind a desk was a man in his mid-thirties not much taller than Bakari. He had red hair, a thin build, and a smile that immediately put Bakari at ease.

"Welcome to Belor, Stranger," he said. There was a glint in the man's green eyes, which seemed to be holding back secrets. "I am told that you brought a mighty dragon with you."

Bakari bowed his head to the man. "My name is Bakari, Scholar Wizard of Alaris and Dragon Rider. And, yes, I did bring a dragon; Abylar is his name."

"That's fantastic!" the man said as he stood up, clapping his hands together. "My name is Kelln El'Han, governor of Belor." The governor led Bakari over to a small sitting area. "Have a seat. You must have a tale to tell, and I do love a good adventure story."

Bakari took a seat and immediately felt at ease with the governor—a man Bakari believed he could trust. So, after partaking of some refreshments, Bakari told the governor all about Alaris, the barrier, the dragons, and the problem with the Chameleon.

After Bakari had finished, the governor sat in silence for a few moments.

"You do believe me, don't you, sir?" Bakari asked, knowing that the tale sounded tall. But Bakari would need the help of all the surrounding kingdoms to rid the land of the Chameleon and his so-called brothers.

Kelln smiled and waved his hand in the air. "Oh, yes, yes. Of course I do. I had quite magical adventures myself, at your age. Of course, we don't have dragons here in the Realm. Darius will be excited to learn about them, though."

"Darius?"

"I'm sorry," the governor said. "I forgot that you were closed off behind the barrier. King Darius DarSan Williams, a wizard of the heart and my best friend."

"Ah," Bakari said as he thought back. "I remember that one of my dragon riders met Emperor Mezar Alrishitar of Gildan, and he mentioned to her that your king was a wizard. We may have need of his services to help us against the evil powers of the Chameleon."

"Yes," Kelln continued, "Mezar and Darius go way back. Not as far as he and I go, but... well, we are all old friends. If we have time later, I will tell you my story. But, for now, what can I do for you?"

"I would like to see your library," Bakari answered.

"Ah, a scholar you said, right? I think that's what Emperor Alrishitar is—a wizard of the mind," Kelln said. "Not me, I haven't had much use for books. I prefer real-life adventures."

"Daddy," a young boy said as he came running through a side door and grabbed the governor's legs.

The governor blushed, his face almost turning the color of his hair. "Excuse me," he said. "This is my three-year-old son, Caeden."

Bakari laughed and smiled at the young boy.

A woman followed him into the room. Her dress looked comfortable and serviceable, but she wore it with a regal bearing. She gave the governor an adoring smile.

"Sorry, Kelln," she said. Turning to Bakari, she greeted him and explained, "I am Marianna El'Han, the governor's wife." As she gave him a brief curtsy, her auburn hair swished around her head, framing her soft face and pert nose. Her lips smiled generously with the greeting.

Bakari stood and said, "Ma'am." Then he gave a short bow.

Kelln stood also and put his arm around Marianna. "The only lady that could ever get me to settle down. And now we have a young one running under our feet and another one in the oven." He winked at Bakari.

Bakari was confused for a moment, until the governor patted Marianna's stomach.

"Oh!" Bakari gasped, understanding his meaning. "Congratulations."

"Now, about that library, Bakari," Kelln said as he moved toward him. "It's not very extensive, but you can read whatever you like. The best library has been established on White Island, the home of the wizard school."

Bakari felt hopeful that he could find information to counter the Chameleon's magic in one of the libraries.

"It's north of here, off the coast of Mar," Kelln said.

With those words, Bakari felt a definite tug inside him. A pull on his powers. "That is where my dragon and I will go next. I am here to find another dragon rider."

"Amazing and fantastic." Kelln smiled again. "This reminds me of the old days. We didn't have dragons, though. We had Cremelinos."

"Cremelinos?" Bakari's eyes opened wide. "The magical horses?"

"Yes, yes," Kelln said. "You will find a lot of them on White Island. That is where the herd is raised."

Bakari could hardly contain his excitement.

"You're not thinking of going there, are you, Kelln?" Marianna said.

"Well...I...uh," Kelln stammered in response to his wife's question. "We'll talk about it later."

Marianna rolled her eyes at her husband. "Kelln is a wonderful governor," she told Bakari. "But he does love going off and causing a bit of mischief now and again."

Turning back to Bakari, the governor laughed and said, "Nothing wrong with having some excitement in your life, right, Bakari?" He paused and then got back to business. "Now, let me get someone to take you to the library. Then, you will meet with me for dinner. I will have rooms prepared for you this evening."

Kelln began barking out orders to nearby servants. Then he asked Bakari, "What about your dragon?"

Bakari sent a quick thought to Abylar then answered, "He will go and hunt, then return for me in the morning."

"You can communicate with it?" Kelln asked.

"Yes."

"Just like the Cremelinos," Kelln said, almost jumping off the ground with his apparent excitement. "You have to meet our king, Bakari. You really do!"

"Maybe I will," Bakari said. "First, I need to go north."

With that, Bakari left, walking with a steward to the library.

CHAPTER FIVE

Once Bakari had reached the library, he studied in it up until dinnertime. Then, after a pleasant meal with the governor and his family, Bakari returned to the library to see if he could find anything else on dragons or on the power that the Chameleon had used against them.

Soon he found that the more he studied, the clearer his mind became. He let out a great sigh.

"My powers are back," Bakari said in a whisper.

"Sir?" the head librarian asked, turning toward Bakari.

Bakari waved his hand in the air and said, "Oh, nothing. Just talking to myself."

"It is getting late, sir." The librarian yawned. "I am sure that you don't want to be flying up in the air on that dragon tomorrow and fall asleep."

Bakari chuckled at the librarian's attempt to get him to leave. The mention of Abylar prompted Bakari to reach out through his bond to the young dragon—somewhere to the west. Abylar had hunted and taken his fill and was now flying over a range of huge mountains, trying to find a good place to rest for the night.

Bakari had noticed that dragons liked heights and enjoyed staying in caves whenever they could. *Silly dragon!* he let slip through the bond.

Even at this distance, he felt Abylar's humorous chuckle.

Bakari stood up from his chair and moved over to a window. Even though he couldn't see much outside—other than a few late-night lanterns, scattered throughout the dark streets below—Bakari did enjoy looking in the direction where Abylar was. Leaning on the sill, he took comfort in their bond.

Without warning, he felt another presence, intruding into the bond. It was quiet and small, scarcely discernible there at all. At first, Bakari though it could be one of the other dragons.

Abylar, great dragon, the voice whispered, c*ome to me.*

Bakari stood up straight.

"Everything all right, sir?" the librarian called out.

"I don't know." Bakari put his fingers on his forehead to concentrate more deeply. "There is someone else out there."

"Out where?" the librarian asked, walking up to join him at the window.

"Someone is intruding on my bond with my dragon," Bakari said.

"I have only heard about the bond with the Cremelinos." The librarian seemed more awake now. "Is it like that?"

"I'm not sure." Bakari shook his head. "We can share thoughts and feelings over a great distance, and he shares his power with me."

Abylar? Bakari reached out to his dragon.

I feel it, Abylar whispered back into his mind. *It's up ahead, in a great cave.*

Feel what? Bakari couldn't feel anything.

Something powerful, Abylar said. *It must be the other dragon.*

Bakari tried to concentrate harder. Was there a dragon to the west? He didn't think so. He still felt a pull northward. So he reached his mind out stronger within the bond.

What are you? he called out to the stranger.

There was no answer.

Abylar, where are you? Bakari asked.

Somewhere in a large mountain range, in a deep cave. There is great power here. It was made for dragons many, many years ago.

Abylar, don't go in any farther. There is no other dragon in there. Bakari had a bad feeling about what might be happening, for his young dragon was sometimes impetuous. *Come back, and we will go check it out together tomorrow.*

It's beautiful, Dragon Rider, Abylar said, his voice growing weaker.

What's beautiful, Abylar? Bakari asked, fighting to keep the bond intact. *Stay with me.*

Come to me, you beautiful blue creature. Feel my power, said the unknown voice again, just strong enough for Bakari to hear the words.

Abylar! Turn around now! Bakari yelled in his mind. He felt the dragon stumble and stop. A command from the master dragon rider carried a lot of weight. *Come back to me.*

I am here, closer to you, Abylar, the other voice said. *Come to me, and feed upon my power,* reiterated the stranger.

Bakari merged his eyesight with Abylar's and found himself standing next to a beautiful underground lake inside a spacious cavern. The depth was lost in shadows.

"Sir, are you all right?" The librarian grabbed Bakari by the shoulder. "You've been staring out the window. Did you fall asleep?"

"What did you do?" Bakari reeled around, staring at the librarian. "I've lost the bond." He tried to establish the bond again but couldn't find it.

"I can't find Abylar," he cried out with dismay.

"I'm sorry," the librarian whispered from next to him and then took a step back.

The lamps in the library had all burned out except one. How long had he been connected to Abylar?

"It's dark in here," Bakari said. "What's wrong?" Bakari flicked his hand out, and a mage light appeared. "Something was calling Abylar away," he said to himself.

Bakari closed his eyes and concentrated, digging deeper into the bond, searching along the lines of magic—pushing west, where Abylar had last been. Bakari jumped once, his mind brushing up against something else, something wrong and evil. But he pushed this aside with some work and then continued looking for his dragon within the stream of magic.

Abylar! he called once again, pushing as much magic as he dared through the bond. A flicker flashed inside his mind. Then he was seeing through his dragon's eyes once again.

Ahead of Abylar was a churning lake. Bakari could hear a rumble, and then rocks collapsed into the water. Abylar turned his head and roared but couldn't seem to break away as a dark presence filled the cavern, emanating from the lake itself.

Abylar took another step, bringing himself closer to the water. He was so thirsty after eating, and the water looked inviting to drink and maybe even to rest in until morning.

Come closer, and rest your weary bones, said the voice again. It was louder now, as Bakari's mind was melded with the dragon's. There was a strange compulsion in the words. Bakari felt Abylar moving forward despite Bakari's warning and pleas to turn back.

Even in the murky gloom, Bakari could still see the water somehow through Abylar's eyes. The dragon took another step forward, his front feet splashing into the cool liquid. As he did, burning pain scorched Bakari's mind, and Bakari cried out.

He steadied Abylar's mind and tried to dig deeper into Abylar's intellect. There were times in the past when Bakari had taken control of animals. Once, with Abylar himself, when the guardians of Celestar had died. But Bakari had taken control then to keep Abylar's sanity.

He tried it again now, but this time it didn't work. Something else was pushing against him. Bakari gritted his teeth and pushed harder.

"Dragon Rider!" the librarian yelled as the mage light blinked out, plunging the library into darkness.

Bakari paid no attention to him and pushed more magic into the bond. The building shook with his efforts, books falling off of the shelves. But Bakari had barely registered this havoc in a far corner of his mind.

He needed to get to Abylar.

The dragon took another step forward into the water, his rough skin feeling its cool touch. But Bakari's mind blazed once again, and he had to pull back from taking control. He was losing the bond.

Abylar knelt down at the edge of the water, the slight waves lapping against the side of his body. Then he gazed ahead, into the water.

Sleep, said the soft, deep voice. *Sleep.*

Bakari felt the dragon's eyes closing, so he shouted one last time for Abylar. But the vision in front of him was shrinking as the dragon's eyelids drooped. Just before they closed, a light flared within the water, and Bakari gasped.

"No!" Bakari screamed, grabbing his head. As the bond broke, he crumpled to the floor. Then he heard a loud crash outside the room and voices yelling.

"Sir! Are you all right?"

Bakari could hear the librarian's voice but couldn't open his own eyes yet. It was too much. The bond was gone.

"It's him," Bakari whispered.

"What?" the librarian said, trying to get Bakari to sit up. "What did you see?"

"Him. I saw the eyes of the Chameleon or someone like him," Bakari said in despair as he opened his eyes.

The librarian gave him a look of confusion. "The Chameleon? Who is that?"

"Someone trying to bring an evil magic back into the land. He stole the bond with my dragon!" Bakari screamed, and the building shook again.

Then a group of guards entered the library and formed a circle around Bakari. They wore armor of leather and steel and had their swords drawn and ready. The apparent leader reached down and brought Bakari to his feet.

"Captain, this man must be the cause of the destruction," another guard said as he helped the first. They held Bakari between the two of them, the second one bringing out a rope and tying Bakari's hands behind himself.

Bakari was confused. "What?" he asked. His head was killing him, and he was mourning the loss of his bond.

"Lamps blinking off, buildings shaking," the captain said. "People are afraid. So they are blaming the dragon rider for bringing destruction to our city."

"I...I didn't mean to," Bakari stuttered, trying to stay conscious. He was having a hard time concentrating. Echoes from the dark cavern filled his mind. The power there had felt like the Chameleon's—but so much more powerful. Bakari felt unclean after being in its presence.

The captain moved forward with Bakari in tow. "You will be taken to the dungeon until a meeting with the governor can be arranged. Magic is too dangerous to be flinging around the city without any regard."

"No! Let me go!" Bakari struggled free. "I have to go after my dragon. He needs me!" He brought his hand up to form a ball of fire, and a few of the guards stepped back.

The captain wasn't frightened so easily. Before Bakari could react, the captain had brought his fist back and slugged Bakari in the side of his face. Blackness spread across his vision, and he felt his legs weaken.

"Oh, Abylar," Bakari muttered and then everything went dark.

CHAPTER SIX

On their way south, to Quentis, on the back of Cholena, Jaimon's dragon, Alli and Jaimon stopped in Cassian to inform Mericus deGrande, the new king, of what had transpired in Elvyn. They were escorted into this capital city of Alaris by an honor guard. Upon entering the castle, the king himself greeted them.

Dressed in his signature black clothes, his cape swirling around him, and his dark hair slicked back on his head, the king took Alli's right hand softly in his. Bringing her hand to his lips, he locked eyes with her.

Alli blinked twice, trying not to be mesmerized by his dark and brooding eyes. Mericus had earned Alli's respect by the end of the war, but he seemed to want more from her.

"Battlemaster, good to see you again," the king said, his slick words rolling off his tongue.

Alli pulled her hand away from his and gave a short bow as she said, "My king."

Mericus laughed. "No need to be so formal, Alli."

"But you are the king of Alaris now, Mericus," Alli said with a grin.

Kanzar, the former leader of the wizards, had instigated a rebellion against the Chief Judge of Alaris—attacking a system of leadership that had reigned since the barrier around Alaris had first gone up. The man had meant to set himself up as king. In the end, however, Kanzar had been killed, and the choice was put to the people for a vote.

Ultimately, Mericus, a wizard and a former judge, had been elected as the first king of Alaris. And, now that the barrier had been down for the past few months, Alaris was once again establishing relationships with its neighbors.

"Come join me, and tell me why the Battlemaster and a dragon rider honor us with a visit this day." Mericus led them to a group of chairs and had refreshments brought in.

Jaimon sat down tentatively. He was so young and was the newest dragon rider. And Alli knew he was still nervous in the presence of wizards and magic.

Turning to Jaimon, Mericus asked, "And, how is your dragon master?"

As Jaimon blushed at the attention and stumbled on his words, Mericus seemed to be enjoying himself.

"Bakari bids us here today," Jaimon finally said. "There has been trouble in Elvyn."

Alli let Jaimon tell the story. Among the dragon riders and wizards, they were still trying to figure out who ranked higher. The dragon riders were beholden to Bakari and were gathered from multiple kingdoms. The Citadel in Alaris, ruled now by Roland, also called apprentices and wizards from all lands and also had sworn allegiance to Bakari. As a wizard himself, Mericus, even though he was king of Alaris, was tied to Bakari too.

After Jaimon recounted what had happened at King Lanwaithian's coronation, Mericus sat back and put his finger on his lips.

"And you say your powers were taken away?" Mericus asked, turning to Alli.

For some reason, Alli had to control her blushing in Mericus's presence. The man was insufferable, flirting almost as bad as Roland.

"They were," Alli finally said. "But they are slowly returning."

Mericus nodded. "It wouldn't do to have our esteemed High Wizard be without his powers. What kind of a leader would he be then?"

"He will be fine," Alli said, tightening her lips.

"Ah, you and he have developed feelings for each other, I see." Mericus gave a short laugh.

Alli jumped up, her reflexes moving her hands toward the two swords at her sides. Jaimon stood and moved next to her.

Mericus waved his hand back and forth in the air and then stood to join them. "Don't get all angry now, my dear. I just wanted to make sure the High Wizard had things under control. The Citadel does sit in my kingdom."

"But Roland does not report to you."

Mericus frowned at that. "Either way, I do have concerns about it. Many of my citizens live around there and work there."

"He is fine, I am sure," Alli said. "Be careful where you set your sights, Mericus. Is being a king not enough for you?"

"Oh, Alli, my dear. You misunderstand me." Mericus reached for his goblet and, while taking a long sip of wine, moved up very close to Alli and said, "I would never do anything to jeopardize our relationship."

The man was so arrogant. Alli had helped Mericus to secure the throne of Alaris, but only because there wasn't a better alternative. She had found herself admitting, many times over the last few months, that Mericus had indeed done a fair job at ruling. After narrowly avoiding an all-out civil war, the people needed a strong king to rally behind. Mericus's flashy ways had provided them that. He was also fair and a strong administrator. But he had been trying to court Alli the entire time—and she was not interested.

"We do not have a relationship, Mericus." Alli flipped her hair behind her and turned to Jaimon. "Dragon Rider, it's time we left."

Jaimon nodded and began to walk to the door. But before Alli could move, Mericus put his hand on her arm.

She felt its warmth and glanced up into his eyes. The man was at least fifteen years older than her, but a fire seemed to burn behind his eyes when he looked at her. She couldn't help but be flattered—to some degree.

"A king needs a strong queen by his side," Mericus said, leaning in with a breathy whisper.

Alli's eyes went wide. What was this man saying? It was scandalous. She was too young to be married.

"Just think about it," Mericus said as he removed his hand. Turning to Jaimon, he said, "Tell Bakari that we will watch out for any trouble here in Alaris and will let the dragon riders know if we see signs of this Chameleon. You have my full support."

Jaimon nodded his thanks.

Alli headed to the door and began to turn around to look at him one last time before exiting. She knew that she shouldn't. It would show Mericus that she was interested in his proposition. So, halfway around, she turned her head back toward the door instead and continued out with Jaimon.

But she heard a small chuckle in the background as the door closed behind them.

Men!

* * *

A few hours later, Cholena, Jaimon's dragon, took the two riders across the southern divide toward Quentis. Plains of early spring grass greeted them as they flew farther south toward the Bay of Ghazi. As the sun set to their right, they saw the beautiful ocean city of Margarid rising in front of them on the Quentis side of the bay—a city that Jaimon said was known as the Pearl of the Coast. Its white-domed buildings rose multiple stories into the air, a bright contrast to the Blue Sea behind them.

Over time, the city itself had spread from the coast, along the bay, and up next to where the Mahli River fed into the water. Leafy palms were the predominate plants, growing high above all the buildings. Rolling meadows of grass blew in gentle waves along the river's banks, leading into the city.

This is where Jaimon landed his green dragon. Her red eyes took in their surroundings, and then she turned her head to her rider.

A silent conversation ensued, during which Alli took out a waterskin and drank deeply. It was warmer down south—and humid.

Jaimon walked down to the edge of the river and crouched down, his long hair hanging in a ponytail behind him. After washing his face, he stood back up and walked over to Alli.

"He is here somewhere," Jaimon said. "I can feel him closer now."

Alli gave him a questioning look. "Do you know *where* here? It's a big city."

Jaimon shook his head. "Sorry."

Alli let out a deep breath. "I know this is all new to you, Jaimon. I'm sorry. Not having my full powers has made me feel cranky. But, the farther we have flown from Elvyn, the better I am." She closed her eyes, reached inside, and smiled. "My wizard powers have almost fully returned."

"That's good," Jaimon said. "I'm still not much for fighting."

"You'll do all right if it comes to that," Alli reassured him. "Your training is going well. I've heard you are quite good with a staff."

A broad grin spread across Jaimon's tanned face. "I'm all right, I guess."

Alli laughed. She had been training and fighting since she was ten. As a battle wizard, fighting was second nature to her now. Alli had recruited a young apprentice to help train Jaimon over the past few months, and this young rider, two years younger than her sixteen years, had done well enough.

"Anyway," Alli added, "you have a hungry dragon at your back."

At mention of her, Cholena, the female dragon, turned her head toward the two and gave a small roar.

Alli walked over and patted Cholena. "We girls can take care of danger, right?"

Jaimon joined Alli by his dragon and asked, "So, what now?"

Before Alli could answer, Jaimon frowned, and then his expression turned into a blank stare. His dragon's expression did the same.

Alli reached over and shook him. "Jaimon, what's wrong?"

Jaimon groaned and scrunched up his face, putting his hand up, but he didn't say anything else for a solid two minutes. Then he fell to the ground. He held his face in his hands and took deep breaths. After another minute, he looked up at Alli with pain in his light blue eyes.

"It's Abylar," he groaned.

"What? What's wrong? Is Bak all right?" Alli said, rushing him for an answer.

Jaimon shook his head. "I don't know. Abylar went into a trance. I could feel Bakari calling him, but he couldn't get through. Then I felt something evil through the bond—a power that broke the bond between Abylar and the dragon master."

Alli paced for a few minutes.

"We must go and help him," Jaimon said, standing back up. "On Cholena, we can find them. They went northward."

"No, Jaimon," Alli said, though she too wished they could leave and go to help her friend. "The mission here is too critical. Bakari would want us to continue. Maybe it's connected. All of this."

Jaimon's expression grew dark. "He is my master, not you."

Alli understood Jaimon's allegiance, but Bakari would have to take care of himself for now.

"Your master sent us here on a mission—your first real mission, Jaimon—to find this Chameleon. You saw what that man did in Elvyn." Alli paused and then lowered her voice. "I know that you want to help Bakari. I do too. But I think the best thing we can do is to help him here."

Jaimon put his hand on Cholena and stood quietly for a moment. Finally, he sighed and said, "You're right, Alli. I'm sorry."

"No problem, Jaimon. Let's go find this Chameleon and take care of things here. Then we can go and help Bakari and Abylar."

Jaimon smiled again, and they began walking closer to the city.

"So, did Cholena convince you to stay?" Alli asked, glancing at Jaimon from the corner of her eye.

"Maybe." The young man smiled, looked over at Alli, and then laughed.

"Well, I told you we girls can take care of things."

Soon they approached the city walls. The people of Margarid had seen Jaimon and his dragon before on prior visits, but, as they arrived, people still pointed and cried out for others to come and see. Cholena would stay outside of the walls, as the streets of the city were too narrow for her to walk in.

Upon reaching the gates, they met a local guard, who gave a bow to Jaimon and then yelled out to some other men, "Escort the dragon rider and his beautiful friend wherever they need to go."

Alli blushed at the compliment, and Jaimon laughed.

"Ever been to the bay before?" Jaimon asked her.

"No," Alli said, wrinkling up her nose. "Smells different here."

Jaimon took in a deep breath. "I know. Isn't it great? I remember my first time here a few months ago. Margarid is so much bigger than the small town where I grew up, in the hills to the north."

Alli didn't know whether the smell was all that great, but she couldn't help getting caught up in Jaimon's enthusiasm. This would be her first time outside of Alaris or Elvyn. After being locked behind the barrier in Alaris for almost her entire life, it was hard for Alli to imagine an entire world out there.

She would like to see more of it, but she didn't know if the Citadel could do without her for long. There, she was the Battlemaster and had trained other battle wizards. And Roland needed looking after too. The man had become more moody lately and was spending more time in the basement with the old magic artifacts. Alli hoped his powers were coming back like hers.

Alli recalled how she had been shocked to suddenly be without her powers. She was sure glad that the Chameleon's spell was only temporary, and maybe that meant he wouldn't be that hard to catch. She hadn't been able to use her weapons in a while and was looking forward to a good fight.

As Jaimon pointed down a broader thoroughfare, they turned, with guards trailing behind them. The city was quiet, with few people roaming the markets. Passing out of the market district, Alli noticed the smell of fish growing stronger, and she almost had to plug her nose. Oversized warehouses filled the street to either side.

Looking up on a nearby hill, she could see larger homes and taller palm trees. Small palm bushes and ornamental grasses graced the front of each mostly white stucco home. Then the salty scent of the sea grew stronger, and they soon came to a grouping of docks. Going down to one that held small boats, Jaimon walked up to a thin but fit man.

"Are you going to the Sanctuary, Dragon Rider?" asked the man.

"The Sanctuary?" Alli frowned.

The man gave her only a cursory glance, then turned back to Jaimon.

So Jaimon said to Alli, "The Sanctuary is on a small island. It's where the wizards of Quentis, Solshi, and Tillimot train. The island is not governed by any kingdom but by the Sanctuary commander."

Turning back to the man, Jaimon said, "Please prepare a boat for us."

The man led them to a bright, white boat. Its crew consisted of three men, including its captain. They hoisted the sails, tacked out of the bay, and soon were heading south, toward an island that Alli could see in the distance. It appeared lush and green, with its palms and other tropical plants waving in the ocean breeze.

After tying up next to a small dock, they walked to the Sanctuary's gates. From the inside, a man approached them at the iron gate. He had dark hair and wore a blue robe over his thin body. His blue eyes pierced theirs intently.

"Welcome to the Sanctuary," he said, his voice softer than Alli had expected.

Jaimon bowed. "I am Jaimon Schafer, dragon rider, and this is Allison Stenos, Battlemaster of the Wizard Citadel of Alaris."

The man's eyes widened as he looked Alli up and down, no doubt wondering what kind of battle wizards their northern neighbors might have, if some slip of a girl led them. So Alli gave him her most disarming smile and released some of her magic to glow around her—glad she had it back—and then nodded at the man. Having been raised to a level three wizard about four months earlier, Alli's powers manifested themselves closer to a level four now.

"I am Leopold, and I greet you on behalf of the Sanctuary," the man said more formally. "You are both most welcome here. Would you like to see someone in particular?"

Jaimon glanced at Alli, then turned back to the man. "For now, we would like a place to stay for the evening. And then, tomorrow, we would enjoy a tour of the grounds. I have heard that their beauty is unmatched."

Leopold nodded and took them to the housing quarters to get cleaned up before the evening meal. The main complex seemed eerily quiet, and Alli noticed people giving quick glances in their direction and then scattering off out of their way.

Jaimon exchanged a worried glance with Alli. His look mirrored her own thoughts. Things did not seem right.

CHAPTER SEVEN

The next morning, Leopold woke Alli and Jaimon in their separate rooms. After a hurried breakfast of pastries and fruit, Leopold led them out to the gardens of the Sanctuary. The man's hands continually fidgeted at his sides.

Colorful tulips lined the walkways, and hundreds of flowering trees and bushes grew among fountains and statues of marble. Enormous palms spread their fronds like a canopy high over their heads. Walking to the edge of the Sanctuary's grounds, they beheld the Blue Sea to the south. Cholena was flying up high in the sky and gave a short roar while tilting her wings at them. So Jaimon waved and smiled.

Leopold glanced around and then said in a lowered voice, "I am glad you are here, Dragon Rider. Things have not been the same lately." The lanky man rubbed his hands together and peered around him again. Then he pulled them down a short path to a more secluded area.

Alli gave Jaimon a questioning look, but he just shrugged as if to say that he didn't know what was going on either.

"Lately, wizards have been sent out from the Sanctuary to other cities. Friends of mine have left, and I have not heard from them. A delegation was also sent, yesterday, to the king in the city. He hasn't been seen in public lately, and there are rumors he is sick."

"What can we do?" Jaimon asked.

"I don't know," squeaked Leopold. "Ever since our Sanctuary commander became ill last month, strange things have been happening."

Alli turned to Jaimon. "Do you think it's *him*?"

Jaimon nodded. "It could be. He is here on the grounds somewhere. I can feel it."

"Who, Dragon Rider?" Leopold asked.

Alli didn't want to give too much information out. They still didn't know for sure who to trust. This could be a trap.

"Just a man we are looking for."

Leopold didn't question this response.

Before they could say anything more, they heard voices from down toward the dock. From a small garden hill, they could see the dock area. A boat had landed, and coming out of it were a half dozen guards from Margarid, who seemed intent on looking for something.

Leopold motioned Alli and Jaimon down another path as he said, "This way."

They followed the old man, not knowing what else to do. Alli continued to glance behind herself. But they had not been discovered yet.

Then Leopold led them to the back of one of the Sanctuary's buildings and in through a back door. There were few windows inside, and Alli sneezed from all the dust in the air.

Where is Leopold taking us? Alli thought, her senses on full alert.

Hearing sounds from outside of the building, the three hurried faster down a flight of stairs. At the bottom, a few old, lighted lamps were staggered down a hallway, casting eerie shadows on the white stucco walls.

Jaimon stopped.

"What is it?" Alli asked.

"I feel him," he whispered.

Angry, Alli turned to Leopold and said, "Where are you taking us?"

The man's face reddened. "To safety. You must trust me."

"I don't trust anyone easily," Alli said. "It's not in my nature." Alli drew one of her swords and held it out in front of her. "If this is a trap, you will regret it, Leopold."

The man's eyes opened wide. "It's not a trap," he said. "I am taking you to someone you can trust."

Jaimon gave a grave look to Alli.

She nodded and drew out her second sword. "Who are you taking us to?"

Then Leopold smiled, but his forehead was beaded with sweat. "We have been waiting a long time for you, Dragon Rider."

Behind them, and up the stairs, they heard the guards entering through the back door.

"Someone is here," one of them said. "I see footprints."

Alli pushed Leopold forward with a growl and said, "Hurry then. If you can bring us to safety, let's go. If not, then I will have your head first."

Alli heard the man swallow hard. As he turned down two more hallways and then led them down another flight of stairs,

Alli extinguished the lamps and smoothed out the footprints in the dust behind them. They were underground now, and the air felt even cooler. She hoped her efforts would be enough to fool the guards.

At the bottom of the stairs, they came to a dead end with a door in their way. But Leopold reached forward and knocked with a peculiar rhythm.

Alli turned to Jaimon and put a hand on his arm. The boy was clearly frightened and was almost shaking.

"Is he in there?" she asked Jaimon.

Jaimon shook his head. "I don't think so. He is somewhere above us."

Alli relaxed only slightly.

Then the door in front of them opened, and the three of them were admitted into a small, lighted room. Then the door was closed behind them.

In the center of the room sat a table that was about six feet square, and around the table sat eight men and women. Alli reached out her senses. Some in the room were wizards, but not all. Her swords remained in her hands, and she took note of where her knives were hidden inside her clothes.

"I have brought him to you," Leopold said to the group.

As one, they arose and, after bowing, they spoke in unison: "Hail the dragon rider."

Alli felt Jaimon jump behind her. She turned and motioned him forward. "Looks like they like you, Jaimon."

Jaimon took two steps forward, gave a short return bow, and asked, "Who are you?"

A middle-aged woman in the middle of the group smiled and brought her hands out to encompass the group as she said, "We are the Followers of the Dragon, a secret ancient society that protects dragon lore and prepares for the next dragon rider. We have waited a long time for you, Dragon Rider."

Jaimon put his hands on the table in front of him, to steady himself. "But...But..." he said as he struggled to find the words. "But how did you know I would be here?"

One of the men motioned toward the back of the room, and another door opened up on its own. A brighter light poured in from the new room. Then the group began walking, and Leopold led Jaimon and Alli behind them.

Alli gasped when she entered the new room. She could sense power in the room. On a table against one wall sat three books and a few figurines, and empty shelves filled two of the other walls.

Jaimon walked to the table and picked up a small carving. It was of a green dragon and his rider. The artifact was only about six inches tall, but the detail was amazing. In silence, he turned it around in his hand. Then his eyes went wide, and he almost dropped it.

"It's me," Jaimon said as he showed the figure to Alli.

Looking more closely at it, Alli saw that sitting on the dragon was a dark-haired young man with a long ponytail.

"How can that be?" Jaimon asked.

Alli moved to protect Jaimon, her swords still in her hands. "What do you want with the dragon rider? What is he to you?"

The woman who had spoken earlier took a step forward. "Allison, isn't it? We have heard of the famous young Battlemaster from Alaris. You have made quite a name for yourself already."

Alli opened her eyes wider, but she stayed quiet. Had people in Quentis truly heard of her?

"My name is Lea. You honor us with your presence, as a companion of the dragon riders," the woman said and bowed her head to Alli. "We mean you no harm. The dragon rider has been prophesied for hundreds of years. During a time of great need to our kingdom, a prophesied dragon rider would rise out of Quentis, the first from our land in five hundred years."

A man stepped forward and prostrated himself on the ground toward Jaimon and then said, "Dragon Rider, we have protected the prophecies and awaited this day. We are at your command."

One by one, each man and woman, including Leopold, knelt with their heads to the floor.

Jaimon looked at Alli, tears forming in the corner of his eyes. He shrugged his shoulders at not knowing what he should do.

Alli sheathed her swords and patted Jaimon on the back. "Looks like you are famous already, Jaimon. Maybe they can help us."

"Of course." He cleared his throat and, with a reddening face, said to the group, "Please rise. No need to bow to me. My name is Jaimon Schafer."

The group rose from their knees and approached Jaimon with apparent awe. They repeated his name and gathered him

The Dragon King

in their arms, leading him over to a dark brown, stuffed chair in the corner of the room. They offered him this seat and then sat on the floor in front of him.

Alli almost laughed at the deference they were giving the young man. Jaimon was hardly more than a kid and very much untried in the ways of the world. But he did have a good heart, and Alli couldn't bear to see him suffer any more under their scrutiny.

Clearing her throat, Alli directed their attention back to her. "People of the dragon," she began.

"*Followers* of the Dragon," interrupted a man.

Alli controlled herself by not rolling her eyes as she said, "Followers of the Dragon, then, we are on a special mission from Bakari, our dragon master."

With that statement, the group held their tongues and paid attention.

Alli continued, "We are searching for a man who is very dangerous. Based on what we have heard of what is happening here and on Jaimon's ability to track him, we believe that man is here, in the Sanctuary."

"What does he look like, Battlemaster?" Someone from the group said.

"That's the problem," Alli said as she shook her head. "He is like a chameleon. He takes the form of different people. So we must be very careful."

Then Leopold spoke up. "The city guard is here, looking for the dragon rider and his companion."

"Why would they be looking for us?" Alli asked. "If need be, we can hide until this is all straightened out... But you can't hide a dragon," Alli said, turning to Jaimon. "What do you think, Dragon Rider?"

As the group turned their attention back to Jaimon, awaiting his words, Alli hoped the poor boy could deal with all the attention.

Jaimon seemed to be thinking for a moment and then looked around the room. "You seem to have gathered a few magical artifacts here," he said. "I am not a wizard, but I can guess that some of you are. What powers are contained in this room?"

A man in the back stood up and said, "I am Devin and am the keeper of the artifacts for the Followers of the Dragon. Over centuries, we have searched for and collected what artifacts we could find. We know there are more—records say there were more artifacts that disappeared about five hundred years ago. These are all we could find. But we have protected them with our lives. They are all at your disposal. They are intended to be used by a dragon rider to augment his or her powers."

Alli knew about the dangers of magical artifacts from those stored under the Citadel. She hoped they would fare better with these, for they might need that help to face the Chameleon.

CHAPTER EIGHT

Breelyn Mier was flying her dragon, Miriel, over the Elvyn Forest and into Alaris. She had stayed in Elvyn a few days, making sure that Lan was being taken care of. She wiped a few tears from her eyes, trying to get control of her feelings and thoughts. She couldn't forget the pain she had caused Lan, her betrothed. She had always been talented at healing, but now her talent was tainted by the darkness.

Breelyn, what is wrong? Miriel asked through the bond. She had the ability to discern Breelyn's thoughts, and, after four months together, they understood each other well.

The darkness, Breelyn said to her dragon. *It's always at the edge of my vision now. I can't shake it.*

Breelyn felt Miriel push some dragon power into her, and she gasped. Everything around her became clearer. Looking down at the meadows of central Alaris, Breelyn could even discern each blade of grass and sense the smells of early summer wafting up to her.

You are amazing! Breelyn said as she patted Miriel's back. And the darkness had subsided somewhat.

Passing over the Citadel in the evening, Breelyn decided to stop and take her evening meal with Roland. She wanted to make sure the High Wizard's powers were returning. The man was resilient, if anything…unless he was just putting on a good front.

Breelyn took her dragon down and landed in the courtyard. And the guards on the ground bowed to her and were more than happy to take her to see Roland.

Soon she sat with Roland at a private table in the corner of the Citadel's dining room. Other wizards in the room tried not to look in their direction, but Breelyn knew that they were by the small whispers that circled the room.

Spreading some jam on more freshly baked bread, she watched Roland dig into a second piece of seared beef. She scrunched her nose up in distaste.

"And how are your powers?" she asked.

"Bakari said they will return, so I trust him," Roland said. "The farther from Elvyn I got, the more I could feel my powers deep down inside me."

"So you blame Elvyn?" Breelyn spat out. Then she shook her head in apology. She didn't know what had made her say that.

"I blame the Chameleon," Roland said. "Are you all right, Breelyn?"

"I'm sorry. I am not very good company tonight." Breelyn stood up from the meal. Others in the room, along with Roland, also stood up, in respect for her station as a dragon rider.

"I just need to sleep," she explained.

* * *

Dark dreams plagued her the entire night, and Breelyn woke up feeling more tired than when she had gone to bed. Walking outside, to meet her dragon and continue her trip to Solshi, Breelyn blinked in the bright sunlight. The glare was giving her an immediate headache.

Walking to the edge of the practice yard, Breelyn observed the numerous apprentices and wizards training now in the Citadel. The number was much more than they had in Elvyn, and Breelyn worried about the growing power of Alaris in the region. Historically, their wizards were hungry for power, and their current leader, Roland, was no exception.

Thinking of the High Wizard seemed to bring him to her. For Roland walked out of the Citadel right then, his gold cape billowing around him and a contingent of wizards and apprentices attending to him. Breelyn wondered if this seventeen-year-old would be satisfied with *only* running the Citadel. She shook her head to clear away the darkness gathering at the edges of her vision.

"Breelyn." Roland waved and walked toward her. "Leaving so early?"

Breelyn didn't know why she didn't trust Roland. Everyone else did. He was Bakari's best friend, and the Battlemaster, Alli, hadn't left his side in the past three months. Breelyn shook her head once again—it was that creeping darkness inside her now, making her suspicious of everyone.

"What was in that vial?" she said to Roland, sounding harsher than she had intended.

Roland stopped short, standing for a moment with a small frown. Then he waved away those with him and continued the last few steps to Breelyn by himself.

"What is wrong?" he asked.

"That vial that you gave to me. Whatever was in it is in my head now, and I can't shake it. What did you do to me, High Wizard?"

"I…I…" Roland said, stumbling on his words, something that was not common for him. "It was all I could think to do, Breelyn. The Chameleon had taken our wizard powers away," he explained. "I was trying to help," he added with more of an edge.

"Well, you shouldn't play with things that you don't understand." Then Breelyn waved her hand around at the area as she added, "Magic can be dangerous. Maybe you shouldn't be running things if you don't understand that."

Roland's face reddened. "Breelyn, this is not like you. We all did the best we could. It's that evil man that is doing this to us. We must catch him and take *his* powers away, not blame each other."

A loud noise ensued overhead as Miriel landed in the practice yard, sending a puff of dust into the air. Her yellow and orange scales glowed in the morning sunlight as she took a step toward Roland and Breelyn.

Roland rolled his eyes and asked, "Trying to bully me with your dragon?"

Breelyn let out a deep breath. *What's wrong with me?* she wondered. She put her hand on her dragon and felt an immediate release of stress. Her thinking also became clearer.

"I am sorry, Roland," she said. "I don't know what got into me."

Roland winked at her and said, "Forget it, Breelyn. Someone as beautiful as you can get away with a lot."

Breelyn had forgotten how her pure Elvyn features affected the humans around her. "I am more than my looks, Roland Tyre."

"Of course you are." Roland coughed, having the decency to look embarrassed at his slight, and then added, "You are a powerful dragon rider."

"Now you mock me?" Breelyn laughed, and it felt good.

"Just trying to get you out of your funk, elf maiden." Roland smiled wide. "Isn't that a lot better than pestering me?"

Miriel growled and moved her giant dragon head closer to Roland.

Roland took a step back and said, "No offense, Miss Dragon. Just trying to help out your rider. I don't think she slept well last night."

Breelyn saw a flash of black again at the corner of her eyesight. Then her heartbeat picked up and her head began to ache. "She is very protective of me, Roland. You might be more careful."

Roland put his hands up in the air and shook his head. "Breelyn, Dragon Rider, I will never understand women— especially elf women. You are crazy, you know that?"

Miriel growled again, and a small puff of steam flew out of her nostrils. So Breelyn climbed up her scales and slid into the saddle behind her long neck. Looking down at Roland, who was once again joined by other wizards, she tried to breathe in deeply and not leave things in a bad way.

"How is your power?" she asked Roland for the second time since her arrival the night before. She tried to show compassion, which she didn't feel but knew that she should.

"Better than yesterday," he grumbled. "But not yet to its fullest glory."

Breelyn raised her eyebrows and flicked her hair behind her pointed ears. "You think magic is about the glory?"

Roland shrugged. "It's who I am, Breelyn. I *am* magic."

Breelyn gave a silent command to Miriel to lift off.

The dragon's wings whipped up a strong wind, almost knocking over Roland and the others in the yard. But Breelyn needed to get away. Now! Her head was killing her, and she knew she was acting irrationally. Doubts and dark thoughts about Roland and his Citadel wizards plagued her mind. She was a dragon rider, but she also was a protector of Elvyn—and Alaris better not attack them again.

She flew due east, heading into Solshi as Bakari had requested, but her own mission was to find something that would heal Lan. When Breelyn had left Elvyn, their healers had stabilized Lan, but the darkness remained on his arms, creeping in spidery lines still—although very slowly—up and down his arm. That same darkness now crept into her own heart and mind.

Breelyn screamed with a deafening howl in the afternoon air as they were crossing over the Mahli River.

Dragon Rider, use my powers to comfort your soul, Miriel offered.

Tears burned in Breelyn's eyes. Her dragon's suggestion was out of pure caring and love. Breelyn closed her eyes and breathed in the power deeply. It was so pure and clean and powerful.

Running her hand over Miriel's scales, Breelyn opened her tear-filled eyes and noticed a slight blackness on the tips of the ones she had touched. She wondered what that meant. Did dragons change color?

Also, where would she go to find an antidote for Lan? North and South Solshi didn't have wizard schools. These were sparsely populated lands that sent most of their promising wizards to the Sanctuary in Quentis. The capital of both lands, Raleez, sat on their shared border, high up on a hill, overlooking the waters of a bay to the west. The city had palaces for both kingdoms' kings and—though each half was referred to as North or South Raleez—it was one city in reality.

Breelyn decided to go there first and try to find her answers.

The city itself, originally built on a large hill, now spilled down the hill's sides and sprawled out into the surrounding countryside and over toward the bay. More people lived here now than in the rest of Solshi altogether. The people of Solshi were quiet, generally, and stayed out of regional politics and confrontations. It was a mostly flat land, except for the mountains in the north and south, and the two kingdoms were known for their textiles and intricate weaves and unique dyes.

Breelyn landed on the outskirts of Raleez, much to the surprise of many workers, who were out tending the fields and working on the spring plantings. Their clothes, a mixture of yellow, orange, and bright green articles, upset Breelyn's Elvyn aesthetics.

Miriel went back up into the air to go and hunt for food. As soon as the dragon had left, Breelyn once again felt the darkness begin to creep back into the corners of her mind. She gritted her teeth and tried to will it away with her own significant powers. However, the more she used her powers, the more the darkness advanced. Giving up, she let her powers recede and then walked toward the gate of the city.

Wearing her signature white cloak, her blond hair flowing down her back, the dragon rider strode up to the guards and presented herself.

"I am Breelyn Mier, dragon rider, Elvyn protector, and the betrothed of King Lanwaithian Soliel."

That should give them enough titles to not restrict my entrance, she thought.

"I request the presence of the northern and southern kings," she continued. "Please inform them I am coming."

"Miss," a guard said as he bowed, "we are…uh…*honored* by your presence, but the kings are not in residence at the moment."

Breelyn furrowed her eyebrows and asked, "Where are they?"

"They were summoned recently to Quentis by the Sanctuary commander," the man stated. "They left just days ago."

Breelyn thought for a moment. Using Miriel, she could catch up to them quite easily. But she could do that at anytime. "Who is in charge while they are away?" she asked the guard.

Maybe they could direct her to the libraries where she could find an answer for Lan.

The guard appeared troubled and asked her to wait there a moment. Then he walked back to a small shack. Soon another man came out and strode in her direction.

"I am Commander Orsen. How may we help you, Dragon Rider?"

"I have a message for your kings from Bakari, my dragon master." Breelyn tried to keep her patience, but it was becoming difficult. She rubbed her forehead with her fingers. "I have been told that they are gone, and so, I would like to see whoever is in charge in their stead."

Commander Orsen glanced down the broad street, then leaned in and whispered, "We have heard of the famed dragon riders and respect what you represent. But, I will tell you, it would most likely be better for you if you left the city."

"I am getting tired of your stalling, Commander." Breelyn pulled herself up straight, and, even though it hurt her head, she let some of her power show forth, creating a glow around her. A glow that used to be bright white, but now was duller.

The commander's eyes pleaded with her once again as he said, "I don't mean any disrespect." He paused and peered around once more. When he seemed sure that no one else could overhear their exchange, he continued in a whisper, "The man who has taken charge is not a very nice man. He is evil, ma'am. Just leave us be."

Before Breelyn could answer, a small troop of soldiers walked up to the gate from inside the city. They wore bright red outfits and tall red caps. The man in front stepped forward. His hair was jet black, and his mustache hung over each side of his mouth, dropping below his chin.

"Commander, do we have a problem here?" the newly arrived man said to the gate commander.

The commander looked at Breelyn pointedly, as if to say, "I told you so."

Breelyn stepped forward and said, "I was asking to see whoever is in charge in the absence of the kings."

The man in the red uniform stood up straighter and narrowed his eyes at Breelyn. "And, who might you be?"

Breelyn put on her best smile and shook her hair around her face. "I am a dragon rider, who can destroy this entire city in two swoops on my dragon." She reached her slender fingers to the captain's red jacket and touched one of his bright gold buttons. "But I would hate to do that, you must understand. I bet a strong soldier like you knows who's in charge, don't you?"

The man coughed and stepped back. Blushing hard, he stammered, "Y...Yes, of course, I understand. You would like to see General Trevis."

"Good." Breelyn let out a deep breath. "He speaks for both the North and the South?"

"He most surely does."

Wrapping her hand around the man's arm, Breelyn motioned him forward. "Then take me to him now, please."

Turning her head around, Breelyn looked back at the gate commander, who slightly shook his head. She wondered what the man was trying to warn her against. Besides her own powers, she had the might of a dragon behind her. So she feared nothing.

With a sly grin, she walked forward with the soldiers. The darkness tickled the edge of her senses once again, but she did nothing to push it back. She had needed the power to do what she had just done and would need more of it to get the answers that she sought.

CHAPTER NINE

Bakari awoke the next morning to the sounds of distant voices. Before opening his eyes, he reached out to Abylar. Then he gasped and sat up straight. He had forgotten that the link to his dragon was gone.

His heart began to beat quicker. He felt hollow and empty inside. How had he ever lived like this before? Abylar seemed to complete him like no other. *Well, there was one other.* He grabbed onto thoughts of her. *Kharlia.*

Bakari looked around for her, but then he remembered that she had stayed behind in Elvyn, to help care for the king, and learn the healing arts of the elves. Placing his hands on his head, Bakari tried to steady his mind.

What will I do without either of them?

Soon, Bakari heard the sounds of boots on stone. As the sounds got closer, torchlight filled the passageway outside of what he now realized was his cell. He stood up and walked to the bars that covered one side of the cell. There, Governor El'Han stood in front of him, frustration evident on his face.

"Dragon Rider, I am sorry about this." The governor seemed legitimately apologetic. "The captain was only doing his duty, and they didn't want to disturb me last night. I assure you, I mean you no harm."

Bakari nodded and tried to regain his composure. "I understand. My dragon's bond was broken, and I must have done some damage."

The governor smiled broadly then. "I remember the king's agony when the Cremelinos lost contact with his wife." He paused, as if reliving this memory, before continuing, "The people of Belor do not have a good history with wizards. About sixteen years ago, an evil wizard ruled the city."

Bakari, as a student of history, was intrigued by the chance to hear this story. "What happened?"

"I killed him," the governor said matter-of-factly.

Bakari surmised that there was much more to the story than that, but he let it drop. The governor motioned for the guards to release Bakari, and together they returned to the governor's rooms.

"Where is your dragon?" the governor asked, once they were seated. He poured Bakari a glass of water.

Bakari drank the cool liquid and tried to let his mind get working again. Then Bakari shook his head. "I don't know what to do. He is somewhere in the mountains to the west."

The governor nodded. "The Superstition Mountains. A very sizable mountain range. Are you planning to go and find him? I can send men with you."

Bakari hated what he must now do, but he shook his head and answered, "I can't." He was doing all that he could to keep from breaking down; though, a single tear had leaked out of the corner of his eye. He wiped it away discreetly. "Duty calls me north, to find another dragon rider. There is a time for every egg, and I can't delay any longer."

Bakari wondered if what he planned to do was right. *What would Abylar think of me?* Sometimes Bakari hated duty and doing what was right. He clenched his fist and shut his eyes tightly for a moment.

"Some king I am," Bakari mumbled under his breath.

"King?" The governor's loud words made Bakari open his eyes back up. "I thought you said you were a dragon rider?" He stood up and stared hard at Bakari. "We have only one king—King Darius DarSan Williams."

"It's complicated," Bakari said. "Please sit." He wanted to say more, but his thoughts were too lost at the moment.

The governor complied but didn't look happy. His face reddened as he said, "I can't have someone that is proclaiming himself a king travel through our kingdom, you must understand. Now, tell me what you mean about *being a king*."

"It all starts with a prophecy," Bakari began.

"It always does." The governor smiled, losing his anger. "Those pesky prophecies."

Bakari proceeded to tell the governor about the prophecy of a dragon rider from Mahli becoming a dragon king. He told him about breaking the dragon orb, the barrier coming down, and the struggles for power in the southern kingdoms.

"The rise of the dragon riders comes at a time of great need," Bakari explained. "There are three of us so far, and I plan to go north to find another one."

"Here, in the Realm?" the governor asked.

"I believe the rider is here. The egg may be farther north. I am not entirely sure without my dragon." A hollowness settled once again inside his chest, and Bakari breathed in deeply.

After a moment of silence, the governor cleared his throat and peered deeply into Bakari's eyes. "And, are you this dragon king?"

That's what it all came down to, wasn't it? With or without his dragon, was he the prophesied Dragon King? Was he the one to bring peace to the land? Bakari turned his focus inward and tapped into his own wizard power. Weak though he may have once been, the bond with his dragon had augmented his powers, and he realized, for the first time since the bond was lost, that he still held some of the shared power from the dragon within himself.

Drawing upon that power, Bakari reached out and felt the other dragons: Cholena, with Jaimon, far south in Quentis, and Miriel, with Breelyn, in Solshi. *Though...* He paused a moment there. Something wasn't right, and he would need to figure out what soon.

Digging deeper, Bakari felt his connection to Roland, in the Citadel. The High Wizard had sworn allegiance to him. He also felt Mericus, in Alaris, and suddenly realized that he could *always* sense those who had sworn allegiance to him as the Dragon King.

A melancholy joy filled his breast, and Bakari joined into the stream of magic, brought to him by the dragons, and took a deep breath—a calming, potent, mighty breath of magic.

"Bakari?" the governor prodded him.

Bakari opened his eyes, and the governor gasped.

"I *am* the prophesied Dragon King," Bakari stated firmly and stood up. Striding to a nearby wall, he surveyed his own image in a mirror there. He had grown a few inches taller in the last few months since the barrier had come down, his braids were longer—below his chin now—and his face was looking more like a man's. But the eyes staring back at him now were what shocked him most.

He turned and studied the governor, who sat in silence. Then, looking back at the mirror, Bakari once again stared at his dark brown eyes—the whites were now a speckled blue a few shades lighter than his dragon was. Bakari turned back to the governor again, who had stood up and had walked a few feet toward Bakari.

After a moment, the governor said, "This is fantastic! Oh, I haven't had this much fun since I was your age."

Bakari shook his head a few times and then said, "Governor, I don't know what being a king means. I don't expect I will rule any lands…except for maybe Mahli. But I have indeed been declared the High King, the Dragon King, by our High Wizard in Alaris."

The governor clapped his hands. "I believe you have a good heart, Dragon Rider. I will keep your secret for now—not good for men around here to hear about another king. I only ask that I be allowed to tell my king. He is a powerful wizard of the heart and knows more about magic than anyone in our kingdom."

"Thank you, Governor." Bakari nodded. "I will need to find transportation north…" He swallowed hard, thinking about leaving Abylar farther behind. "To White Island, I believe. I need to visit the wizard school you said was there."

The governor nodded in apparent understanding. "I will provide a ship to take you up the coast. If the weather holds, it shouldn't take you more than a few days," he explained. "In fact, I think I may travel with you. I hold no small influence in the Realm, and I will make sure you find your answers on White Island. Then I will travel personally to Anikari to discuss these events with Darius. Maybe he can find your dragon for you?"

Bakari smiled broadly. This was the first hope he had felt since losing the bond with Abylar. "I would appreciate that very much, sir."

The governor rubbed his hands together in obvious glee. "I've been itching to get out of the palace for a while. This will be fantastic!" Then his face dropped a bit. "I just have to figure out a good way to tell my beautiful wife."

CHAPTER TEN

Two days after Breelyn had left the Citadel, Roland strolled around the gardens alone in the evening. The gardeners had kept the grounds cultivated during the war, and now fresh spring flowers scented his walk along the winding cobblestone walkways. A few cardinals chirped up in a blossoming tree to his right, and a gurgle of water sounded farther off to his left.

It wasn't often these days that Roland was left alone. With naming himself as High Wizard a little over three months before, he wondered if he had bitten off more than he could chew. It had been relatively easy, leading apprentices around, when Kanzar and his men were gone. But now many of the wizards throughout Alaris had returned to the Citadel. It was time to regroup and to determine their next course of action.

But the barrier around Alaris had kept them in for so long that relatively few wizards remembered a time without it. And the war between the Chief Judge and Kanzar had split loyalties among the wizards: feelings had been hurt and many felt betrayed. So, it was a time to rebuild.

A new sound intruded upon Roland's thoughts, and he turned toward the source of it. Coming around a side path was Tam, a recently raised level two battle wizard.

Roland sighed and thought, *I guess my short time of solitude is over.*

"Sir," Tam said, once he was a few feet away from Roland, "the delegation from the Sanctuary in Quentis has arrived."

Roland nodded. "Have them shown into the gathering room, and ask the servants to bring them refreshments. I will be there soon."

Tam raised his eyebrows but said nothing.

Roland knew what Tam was thinking. "I know, Tam." He put his harm on the man's broad shoulder, which stood a few inches above his own. "You are a battle wizard, not an apprentice or an errand boy."

"I would never think to counsel you, High Wizard," Tam said with wide eyes but a slightly teasing tone to his voice. Tam gave a short but flourishing bow, moving his hand up to his dark locks of hair as he did so.

Roland laughed. "It's just that I still trust very few here, and, with Alli gone…" Roland let the statement trail off.

"You're smitten with her, aren't you?" Tam's lips turned up into a mischievous grin.

Roland stood straighter and said, "That's none of your business."

"I've seen that one in action, sir. She is quite the fireball. I hope you don't get burned."

Roland joined in with a grin of his own. "Don't I know it." He lightly punched Tam on the arm and winked. "Now, off with you, and make sure the delegation is gathered."

Tam was a good-natured man, a few years older than Roland. Even though Tam wasn't the strongest battle wizard, he was levelheaded and organized. Roland had learned to rely on Tam more and more and was thinking about rearranging the

Wizard Council to include a few of the younger men and women, like Tam.

As Tam was walking away, Roland called after him one last time, saying, "How many are there?"

Tam turned his head around and said, "Five, sir. All wizards."

Roland nodded for Tam to proceed but stayed behind himself for a moment. Five foreign wizards in the Citadel would be cause for some alarm among his own wizards. But he had sent a call out to all nearby kingdoms, to join with him in creating a greater school for wizards.

Most that came were young apprentices, who needed training. But Quentis had its own prestigious school, and so, when he had received their missive by rider a few weeks ago, Roland had wondered what they wanted. Now he would find out.

Closing his eyes for one brief moment, Roland pulled upon his powers. Blessedly, they had now almost returned to full strength. Having been trained as a counselor wizard, Roland felt more than that as he reached into the depths of his magic. Knowledge and skills as a counselor, battle, and scholar wizard coalesced within him. But there was still more.

Roland had reached out to Bakari when he had been trapped in the Citadel through some other power. He had ran across the lines of the true power—the power of the spirit—the power that the dragons and other magical creatures held. He needed to do more research on that. The true power could help him become the most powerful wizard not only in Alaris but maybe even in the southern kingdoms.

Walking back into the Citadel, Roland was greeted by a group of four guards, who instantly followed behind him. Grabbing his formal golden cloak from a hook in the hallway and running his hand over his chin-length blond hair, Roland made one last stop before meeting with the delegation.

If they had brought five wizards with them, he would bring more. It was, he anticipated, going to be a showdown of power between the two groups. So Roland sent guards to have three council members join him—one from each discipline of magic—Jandon, Analeyea, and Eryck.

Roland poked his head into the common room and called Gorn to follow him also. The man had said he was retired after the battle in Celestar, but Gorn had proven his worth and loyalty. And having someone as large and solid as him in the room wouldn't hurt either. Along with a young and promising apprentice, named Loreleigh, and Tam, who would already be in the room, Roland would have six other wizards with himself.

A servant opened the double doors, allowing Roland's guards to enter first. Then Roland took long strides into the room to meet the southern wizards. The additional wizards at his back had the intended effect, and all five of the visitors stood up at once. Though, one, a brown-haired man, seemingly in his mid-thirties and the youngest of the visiting group, did take more time in doing so.

Standing in the middle of the room, on an ancient but colorful rug, Roland spread his hands wide and said, "Welcome to the Citadel." Then he put on his best and broadest smile for his guests.

The brown-haired man stepped forward. His eyes were wide with surprise. "Younger than you thought, huh?" Roland asked him.

The man nodded slowly and then seemed to come to grips with the situation. "Sir, I am Caylb, and these are my companions. Greetings from the Sanctuary."

Roland stuck out his hand and shook Caylb's hand in the Alaris way, one-handed, but Caylb wrapped both of his hands around Roland's one. Roland felt a jolt of power, and a tendril of darkness was trying to sneak into his mind. Closing his thoughts off, Roland slammed a barrier in the way.

Then Roland took a step back and said, "Is that how you greet everyone, Caylb? By trying to get into their minds? You won't find that so easy here."

The man grinned only briefly, as if he had finally been caught, and said, "It is our way in the Sanctuary. There are no secrets there. Please excuse my ignorance of your customs."

Two women from Quentis stepped up beside their apparent leader. Roland surveyed them all, extending this moment of silence. The last two from Quentis, who looked to be a man and a woman, stood in the back, their heads bowed.

Roland reached his power out tentatively toward the two, barely scraping the edges of their powers. They were both extremely powerful, more so than the three wizards standing up front.

Pushing through to the two in the back, Roland stood in front of them until they raised their heads. He did all he could to not jump back as he surveyed their golden eyes. A power—not exactly the same as but definitely related to the

Chameleon's—shined forth from them. These were the dangerous ones in the group; Caylb was just a front.

Instinctively, Roland threw up a wall of magic between the two wizards and himself. Bringing up their own hands, the two called forth a dark power, gray mist flowing from their fingertips. The mist pushed against Roland's wall but did not penetrate it.

"I have felt the power of the dark before, Wizards," Roland said. "I will not fall prey to it so easily this time."

Roland motioned for the rest of his wizards to surround the group. But memories of being held in the rooms below the Citadel and of having his magic be taken away by the Chameleon rose up in Roland's mind. He was, admittedly, a little intrigued by their power, but he would not bow to it again.

"I know you feel a longing for our power, Roland Tyre," the woman with the golden eyes almost purred.

Roland strengthened the barrier between himself and them. Whether he was interested in the power or not, he wasn't going to be forced or manipulated by it.

So Roland replied, "We have more than enough wizards at our disposal to stop you, here at the Citadel." Roland ground his teeth with the extra effort it was costing him to keep their tendrils of evil magic away from himself and from the rest of the group.

Without their noticing, Tam had crept behind the two. Bringing out two daggers, he twisted them in his hands and with handle held out from him, hit both of the wizards hard in the head. Immediately, their dark magic retreated, and they slumped to the floor.

Caylb and the two female wizards with him moved to stop Tam, but it was too late. Analeyea and Gorn, two battle wizards with Roland, intervened and wrapped a spell of magic around the three visitors, stopping them in their tracks.

"That is enough!" Roland yelled at the wizards from Quentis.

The two wizards on the floor began to awaken, but Tam and Loreleigh tied them up and kept them from striking out. Then Roland motioned for Tam to haul them up onto their feet again, and he strode over in front of them.

"We accepted you here as our guests—one wizard academy to another—and this is how you greet us. Is this what wizardry has turned into while we were behind the barrier? Explain yourselves. Now."

The woman with golden eyes held her chin high, her short, graying hair framing her elderly face. "I am Deganya," she said with a slight accent that turned their vowels short. "And my companion is Hyam. You will bow to our master, Young Wizard, or we will wipe your Citadel off the face of the earth."

Roland was taken aback by the woman's boldness for a moment, then he let out a laugh and said, "Bold claims for someone in your position."

"Our master works through us and will deliver us," Hyam said when he spoke for the first time. His low, raspy voice did not fit his younger, smooth face as he added, "We are prepared to die for his cause."

Roland flipped his hand out. "Well, that's stupid of you. Why would you die for someone else's cause? You look hardly older than me. You are prepared to throw away your life for some master?"

Hyam opened his eyes wider and seemed to be thinking about what Roland had said. With less vehemence in his voice, he continued, "You do not understand the way of our master?"

Roland saw that he might be breaking down Hyam's resolve and decided to continue breaking down the man, but then Caylb spoke again.

"Our master rewards us for our deeds. His power is greater than yours." Caylb tried to take a step forward, but Tam held him in place.

Roland turned to regard the outspoken wizard. "And, what is your reward?"

As he watched Caylb turn and look into the eyes of Hyam and Deganya, Roland understood.

"Ah, I see, the eyes." Roland turned back to Caylb. "They are a sign of the power. You want eyes that glow."

Caylb smiled and nodded. "You don't understand the power."

Roland was getting tired of this conversation and of people telling him that he didn't understand power. He would show these renegade wizards what true power was.

Reaching deep inside himself, he found his reservoir of power. Briefly, thoughts of when it was taken from him by the Chameleon ran through his mind. But that just gave Roland a stronger resolve to show these wizards what he could do.

Then Eryck stepped up to Roland and put a hand on his shoulder. "Sir, this is not the time," the senior wizard whispered. Roland shook his head. Eryck had been a good advisor but was as timid as a mouse, never wanting to show forth the power at their disposal.

"Now is the perfect time," Roland said. "I will show these wizards and their master what they are up against."

As sweet power filled him, his senses expanded. Roland could hear the birds outside and the whispers of servants out in the hallways. His vision picked out every thread in the tapestries hanging on the wall in front of him. The ocean scene in one tapestry seemed to come alive in front of him. He smelled the dirt on the travelers' robes, identifying the regions they had traveled through to arrive here. He pulled this all up inside of himself.

His gold cloak floated around him with winds of power as Roland held his hands up in the air. Then golden light surrounded him, and he breathed in deeply. As he did so, the other wizards of the Citadel stepped backward, and those from Quentis watched him, their eyes wide open.

The golden power came out from Roland and wrapped itself around the five intruding wizards, bringing them tighter against each other. Hyam fell to the floor in obvious agony. And Roland could feel the evil in the man fighting and pushing against Roland's own magic.

"So much power," Caylb said in fear. "I never knew."

Roland nodded. "Your master is not the only one with power, Caylb."

"But how?" the man inquired, a desire to know shining through his eyes. "I thought our master and his brothers had the greatest powers."

Roland faltered for a second. "And his brothers? Who is this master of yours?"

When no one answered, Roland stepped closer to Deganya and squeezed his power around her mind. She grimaced and fought to stay in control.

"He is one of three," she finally said. "Brothers who will rule the world under their father, the true wizard king." Then Deganya spat at Roland.

Three? Roland thought. *The Chameleon must be getting around.* Was he only one person? Or, were there, in fact, three of them?

"Brothers, you say?" Roland asked.

"Three men of such enormous power that you will shrink in their presence," Deganya continued. "At this time, they are gathering followers—wizards and kingdoms all over the West."

Roland thought about his encounters with the Chameleon and paled, thinking about having three of them loose on the world. He pulled more power into himself and then opened himself up to the specific stream of power that he had felt one time before, when he had called for Bakari to come and help him.

Riding on that stream of power, Roland felt Bakari's presence farther north. A sadness enveloped his friend's soul at the loss of his dragon. But Roland could feel the dragon farther east of Bakari. Then Roland felt Alli's presence to the south, in Quentis. She and Jaimon were in trouble there. Roland ground his teeth in frustration, but he knew that he couldn't do anything about it at the moment. The last presence Roland felt was Breelyn's. She had just left him days ago. Breelyn was east, in Solshi. But, as Roland got closer to her presence, he noticed a flare of darkness around her.

Suddenly, in the room around Roland, an evil presence appeared. Hyam stood back up, his lips pulled back as if someone else were controlling his actions.

"Feel my power, boy," Hyam said.

Within moments, a black fog had surrounded the five wizards from Quentis and an evil presence was filling Roland's magical mind. Then Tam fell backward and let out a loud scream.

"Wizards, attend me," Roland ordered, to get the others to supplement his power. Additional white light filled his being, and he pushed back against the darkness. Then he pulled additional power from his fellow wizards and dug deeper into the stream of magic. He sensed others there also, other wizards in faraway places farther north: a king, an emperor, and a female wizard, who all flared brightly in the stream of magic. Their control of the mind, the heart, and the earth was amazing. They joined with Roland now to push back the evil darkness.

Yellow eyes flew into the darkness, trying to control his mind, and Roland felt a crack opening in his own power.

"Noooo," he yelled out loud.

In front of him, Hyam and Deganya broke free of the Citadel wizards' control. Bringing their hands up, Hyam and Deganya sent out evil tendrils of black power, as thick as ropes. These tendrils clung to Roland's legs and began to wind their way up his torso, enveloping his body in blackness. But his mind held strong.

Slowly but surely, Roland felt his body begin to convulse. His breathing slowed, and his heart began to skip beats. He realized that his body was dying, succumbing to the evil power of the Chameleon and his brothers. But Roland's spirit soared through the stream of magic, gathering as much power as he could.

As Roland's physical eyes began to close, Roland watched Tam stand back up and come to his aid. Tam tried to pull off the black tendrils that were encasing Roland's fragile physical body.

"High Wizard, no!" Tam yelled. "Fight it!"

But Roland knew that he couldn't fight off both the physical and the mental attacks. He had to choose one or the other. So, to not have his soul fall victim to the evil blackness, Roland had to let his body fail. He took one last deep breath as the dark gloom covered his body, then felt and heard himself fall to the floor among the screams of the other wizards in the room.

At the moment of his body's collapse, his mental and spiritual senses increased, and Roland knew exactly where the Chameleon and his brothers were—Quentis, the Realm, and Solshi. Their evil emanated from those points, and Roland felt fear creep through his soul as he realized that the dragon riders were there.

Running to a corner of the stream of magic, Roland burrowed himself in deeper and covered himself with layers upon layers of magic. He would have to hide from the evil until he could figure out a way to save the world from their mad plans.

CHAPTER ELEVEN

Bakari leaned over the back railing of the governor's medium-sized ship and watched Belor fade into the distance behind him. Not ever having been on this style of ship before, he only knew that it was a medium-sized ship because he had seen larger and smaller ones in the small port off of Belor.

"Rather than head straight up the coast," their captain informed Bakari, "we will be heading out east, into the ocean, and then turning around and heading back in a northwesterly direction to reach White Island."

Watching the water speed by underneath the ship reminded Bakari of flying on Abylar. He clenched his mouth tight and tried to push these thoughts to the side of his mind. This was the only way he could handle it. His pain from the loss of their bond was still too great.

He felt traitorous by moving farther away from his dragon rather than searching for him. But once again duty called. And, in the deepest pit of his stomach, Bakari knew that he needed to go north and find the other dragon and its rider first.

Just that morning, he had felt a lurching of the magic inside him. Letting his mind roam the magical stream, Bakari had felt the frantic touches of Roland, who once again appeared to be in trouble. A dark magic was chasing after

Roland. Bakari had wanted to help him, but then, at that moment, the captain had informed Bakari and the governor that their ship was ready to be boarded. Roland would have to learn to take care of himself, for Bakari couldn't help everyone at once.

Feeling a firm hand on his shoulder, Bakari turned to find the governor standing next to him. The governor's smile was infectious, and Bakari smiled back.

"Looks like you're lost in some thoughts," the governor said. "Your jaw was so stiff I thought it would break."

Bakari let out a deep sigh and glanced around. They were alone—well, as alone as you could get on a ship. "Sometimes, being a dragon king is not as glorious as it sounds, Governor." He stared down at the ship's deck.

Then the governor said, "Call me Kelln, Dragon King." As Kelln smiled, Bakari couldn't help laughing. The governor's attitude clearly brought out the best in people.

"Please just call me Bakari, or Bak, if you prefer. It's hard to be a dragon king without a dragon."

"You are not the Dragon King because of your dragon, Bak. You are a dragon king because your heart is as big as a dragon. I can tell... You are a good person who wants to do what is right."

A wave hit the side of the ship and sprayed a cool mist over the two of them. Kelln backed away from the stern's edge, motioning Bakari to follow him.

As they strode toward the passenger cabins, Bakari continued, "But I can't be everywhere and help everyone at once."

Kelln nodded his head. "That is a heavy duty you bear, Son. You can burn yourself out that way. You told me you stabilized Alaris, the rest will come also—in time. You say you are the answer to prophecy."

Bakari ducked his head as they went back down underneath the deck toward a small galley to find some food.

"I don't know much about prophecy," Bakari said. "Seems that I should have a say in things."

Kelln laughed. "That sounds just like my friend Darius. When he was younger, the Cremelinos had a prophecy about him—though, he didn't know it was about him at first. He wanted to make his own way and his own choices. But, in the end, it worked out well enough. He is the king and has been a good one!"

They found the galley and watched the cook scramble around for a moment, getting ready for the evening meal.

"You like fish?" the cook asked as he turned to Bakari.

Bakari turned his head toward Kelln then back to the cook again. "Sure. I guess so. I used to eat river trout in Cassian."

"Ever had ocean salmon, baked in an oven?" The cook's eyes twinkled, his oversized belly shaking with delight.

"No." Bakari shook his head. "I didn't know you could bake on a ship."

"Well, we didn't used to bring fire on a ship," the cook said. "You know, being wood and all. But our illustrious governor has a history of working with metals and invented a metal oven that works on a ship." The cook winked at Kelln. "I heard that his friend, the king, infused it with some type of magic, which keeps it from getting too hot on the outside and burning up the ship."

"It's nice to have friends in high places." Kelln laughed.

Bakari nodded his head, his scholarly mind beginning to calculate what would be needed for that kind of spell. "Seems like your king is a powerful wizard?"

"Aye," the cook said, pulling a large salmon out of a bucket of water. "Most powerful wizard in the Realm."

Kelln nodded in agreement with the cook's statement.

"And, has your kingdom done well with a wizard being the king?" Bakari knew about all the arguments in his own land of Alaris through the years, of whether a wizard king was the best or not.

The cook continued moving around the small room as he said, "It wasn't always that way. I remember sailing as a young lad on my father's ships, between Belor and Mar. Magic was not talked about in the open, though we all knew someone that seemed to have the spark. An evil wizard used to rule Belor— that is, until Governor El'Han and King Darius came along." He pointed to the governor.

Kelln blushed with the attention and added, "Since then, the king has opened a wizard school on White Islands, and more and more magic has become accepted."

The cook lowered his voice and looked around as he said, "Though, not all like it, I tell you."

"Oh?" A frown crossed the governor's face.

The cook seemed to have forgotten who he was talking to. So he stumbled on his words a bit as he added, "No offense, sir, to any of your friends… But some say the wizard school is getting too powerful."

Bakari was going to ask the cook more questions, but then another man came into the galley. It was the first mate, a tall, mustached man with corded muscles that wrapped around his arms like thick ropes. So Bakari and Kelln grabbed a few slices of bread and left the cook to his preparations.

The rest of the day passed with a cool breeze blowing into the sails as the ship continued out into the picturesque Blue Sea. As Bakari spotted some small islands dotting the horizon, the mainland disappeared completely behind them.

That night, Bakari lay down on his small bunk, and, despite the snoring of one of the crew, Bakari was rocked asleep by the gentle movements of the ship on the water.

The next day dawned bright and clear. But, throughout the day, distant clouds were billowing thousands of feet above the ocean's surface.

When the ship reached its easternmost point, it took a wide turn, heading northwest, toward White Island. They picked up speed as the wind blew faster—signaling an approaching storm. And the day ended with Bakari finding it harder to sleep now than on the previous night.

The next morning, something woke Bakari, and he sat up quickly, cracking the top of his head on the wooden bunk above him. Yelling out, he lay back down for a moment to gather his wits. Rubbing the top of his head fiercely, he got up slowly out of bed, only to be tossed back against it a moment later, when the ship lurched to one side.

A few of the crewmen swore and climbed out of their own bunks.

"I'm going to see what is going on," Bakari mumbled to himself, heading out of the door. Climbing the few steps to the deck of the ship, Bakari was buffeted by the strong winds that were blowing his cloak out around him. The governor joined him in the hallway, coming out of his own private room.

The wind pushed a torrent of rainwater into Bakari's face as he climbed up the steps to the main deck. He gathered his cloak around him. But, in seconds, it was soaked. Holding on to the side railing, he gazed out over the vast gray and churning water, only to find that he could barely see a few hundred feet in front of himself.

The ship's bow lurched up and down dangerously in the breaking storm. Lightning flashed off to one side, and thunder rolled through the sky. Bakari watched sailors scrambling along the deck, trying not to slip and fall, but with little success. A few looked his way with glares that seemed to ask for him to help or for him to get back down below.

But what could he do? The storm was huge, and Bakari knew he didn't have the power to control nature—that was more in line with being a battle wizard, who got their powers from the earth. Bakari's was the power of the mind. He dug deep into his thoughts and memories of all he had read. He couldn't do anything about the storm, but maybe he could help protect them through it.

Raising his hands up in the air, Bakari brought forth the powers of his young mind. He built up as much as he could, then went deeper. He thought of the power that Abylar used to share with him, and his own powers lurched with sadness. Grabbing hold mentally, he fought back the grief and found the stream of magic. Even though Bakari no longer could sense his dragon bond, his mind was still infused with much of the power that he had gained from Abylar. And he realized now that it was easier each time to go deeper and grab a hold of more.

One with the power, Bakari felt the stream of magic flowing all around himself. Out of his fingertips soared a blue flame that rose up into the storm, spreading itself out as an iridescent shield over the entire ship. The storm still raged, but their bodies would be protected from the worst of it underneath the shield.

Bakari heard yells and cheers around him. Still with his eyes closed, he afforded himself a slight smile.

"That was great, Bak!" the governor said and patted Bakari on the back.

Before letting go of the magic, Bakari reached farther into the stream. Something wasn't right. There was a darkness to it that wasn't there before—echoes of evil swirling around its edges.

Bakari, a faint voice said, floating to him on the currents of magic.

Roland? Is that you? The presence of his friend felt wrong: too solid in the magic stream.

Fight the darkness, Roland's voice said.

Roland, where are you? Bakari asked.

A faint apparition touched Bakari's mind, and Bakari saw the outline of his friend, the High Wizard. *I am here, Bak, in the magic stream. Stay away until I can find the evil.*

What evil? Roland, how are you here?

I have left my body, Roland's voice said, growing fainter. *He was too strong for me. But my spirit is stronger. I will find a way.*

Bakari began to lose contact with Roland.

No, Roland! he called.

There are also three more of them. Be careful. One is in the Realm. Roland's presence flared brighter for a moment and then fled away.

Bakari reached for Roland again but couldn't find him. So Bakari turned his power toward the other dragon riders and searched for Breelyn. But, just as he touched her presence, a dark evil pushed back against him.

No, Dragon Master, go back. It was Breelyn's voice, but not her tone.

Breelyn, are you in danger? Bakari tried to ask, but he felt an evil presence closing in around him.

I must save Lan, came Breelyn's only response.

Bakari had to jump away or be swallowed up by the tainted dark magic he felt around Breelyn. She was not well.

How can I handle all of this? Bakari asked himself as his shoulders sagged lower.

He felt Mericus and let him be—things appeared under control there. Then he searched for Jaimon and his dragon, Cholena, and found them in Quentis. Jaimon was still learning how to communicate through his dragon bond, but Bakari learned enough by touching Jaimon's mind to know that Jaimon and Alli were closing in on the Chameleon.

Be careful, Bakari said to Jaimon's mind. *Roland is in trouble, and so is Breelyn. Tell Alli to tread carefully. The evil of the Chameleon is spreading.*

We found some ancient artifacts that will augment our powers, Jaimon said, his presence barely within the stream of magic—his dragon carrying the weight of connecting them with her magic.

Be careful, Bakari said. Before Bakari could say more, Jaimon yelled out in pain and said, *He is here. He is close.* Then the connection collapsed.

Bakari saw the yellow eyes in the darkness again and fled. *The Chameleon again!* Bakari pushed back at the evil and felt his own powers waning. Suddenly, a flash of power screamed through the stream of magic. White, hot, and bright. In its presence stood a woman, about thirty years old. She had short, blond hair and exuded such strength that Bakari backed off.

The woman struck a magic staff to the ground of the magic realm, and the air shook, the evil retreating farther away. Then she turned and saw Bakari, a look of surprise on her face.

Who are you? Bakari asked.

I am High Wizard Danijela Anwar, leader of the Wizard Conclave of Arc. And, who might you be, young wizard? Her voice was soft and kind, but her eyes glowed with a power that was immense.

I am Bakari, he said, in awe of her majestic power, *a scholar wizard from Alaris.* Then he added more softly, *The Dragon King.* He didn't feel much like a king but wanted to appear as somebody important in her mighty presence.

The woman smiled. *Ahh, the prophecies are fulfilled at last. Welcome, Dragon King. Your abilities are needed. A great evil is trying to take over our western kingdoms.*

I have felt it, Bakari answered back. *The Chameleon—we have met.*

Bakari felt his strength waning. He felt a drop of water hit his face again. The barrier he had erected was failing. He was using too much of his power in the magic stream. Then High Wizard Danijela Anwar began to fade away.

We will fight with you, Dragon King, she said. *You are the prophesied one. I will gather others. Where are you?*

Bakari fell to his knees as he struggled to stay conscious. *I am in the Blue Sea and about to die!* The storm raged over him again. The magic was fading, and the thunder was deafening.

I will send help, she said.

Bakari nodded, grateful for any help. He needed to find the last dragon rider, then Abylar, then help Roland...and Breelyn...and Jaimon. It was all too much.

Rain splattered on his face once again, and his body sagged to the ground. Then Bakari felt Kelln's arms around his shoulders, helping him to sit up. He tried to hold on, but, without the strength of Abylar, he couldn't hold on any longer. The light of the woman had fled, and tendrils of darkness raced toward him.

As the full force of the storm hit him once again, Bakari screamed and then blacked out.

CHAPTER TWELVE

Liam DarSan Williams, son of the king of the Realm, sat on the southern coast of White Island, his Cremelino, Liberty, behind him, eating the newest growth of spring flowers. He sat about seventy-five feet above the water, on a high cliff. He kept a brooding expression on his almost sixteen-year-old face, as was usual, and his dark brown hair hung down over his ears on each side.

A dark storm raged farther out, over the water, and the wind whipped at his cloak, but he took no notice of it. Thinking of a small spell that required very little energy, Liam erected a shield over his head, to block out most of the rain. He enjoyed storms. He always had. The lightning and thunder, the destructive forces of nature—these matched his mood.

Liam didn't much care for the wizard school on White Island. He had learned all he wanted about wizardry by reading and studying—of course, he didn't have much choice. Born with a clubfoot that didn't work very well, Liam was never destined for the army or to do much with weaponry. He had learned enough of these to get by and used magic to his advantage, when needed, like keeping the rain off his face now.

His father, the king, thought it would be good for Liam to learn in a classroom setting. So Liam and his twin sister,

Breanna, had been sent to the school for six months each year for the past three years.

It wasn't such a bad place. But this year had been stranger than normal. Things were changing, people were quieter, and life there was just plain boring. Also, the headmaster of the school was eerily absent lately, yielding rumors of a sickness.

Behind himself, Liam heard his sister's voice, floating on the wind and over to him.

"Liiiiaaammmm," she called again.

Turning, he saw her galloping down a gently sloping green field. His sister rode with the grace and ease of her station. She was a wizard of the earth, and new flowers seemed to spring up as she passed.

With her hair flying long and free, Breanna looked very similar to their mother, Christine, with her same petite features and white skin. All that was different was the brown hair Breanna and Liam had both inherited from their father, Darius.

Breanna was everything Liam wasn't—successful, with many friends and having a bright personality—and, as the oldest, she was trained to take over as Queen someday. But he loved her dearly. She was one of the few people that could bring a smile to his face.

Liam stood up to greet his excited sister. "What is it?" he asked. "Is something wrong?"

"Auntie Danijela just communicated to me through the Cremelinos."

Liam smiled at their pet name for the High Wizard of the Conclave of wizards of the kingdom of Arc. A few years younger than Liam's dad, Danijela had helped their father, years ago, to establish peace in the Realm and had become like an aunt to Liam and his twin as they grew up. Danijela had visited often and taught them much about magic.

As a fellow earth wizard, Breanna had formed an easy relationship with Danijela. As a wizard of the mind, Liam had given her a few more problems. But Danijela was one of the only other people that could make Liam smile. And her optimism and happy personality had taken Liam out of his dark thoughts many times while he was growing up.

Breanna dismounted from her beautiful white horse—its back as tall as Liam's head—and stood in front of Liam, barely breathing from her short ride from the school grounds, a few miles away.

"She needs our help," Breanna said.

Liam stood up straighter. Maybe something *would* take them off this boring island. His Cremelino came up behind him and stuck his nose into Liam's arm.

Anxious for an adventure too, aren't you, Liberty? he said to the mind of his magical horse. Both twins had bonded with their Cremelinos in the first year after they were born. Almost sixteen years old, Liam recalled that the four of them had had many long rides together throughout the farmlands outside of Alaris.

"What does she need?" Liam asked.

"The storm has caught a young wizard out in a ship, and she needs us to rescue him." Breanna combed her fingers through her silky hair to get out the tangles that the ride had put in it.

Liam's thoughts went dark. "You know I can't swim."

"Oh, Liam, don't get so defensive," Breanna scolded him. "You need to lighten up. Your thoughts are always so negative."

Liam wasn't in the mood for her lighthearted banter. The dark storm had stoked his mood. "What would you know about enduring hardship, dear sister?" He limped a step toward her and then shook his lame foot at her, its half shoe wiggling at a strange angle.

As Breanna put her hands on her hips, she looked so much like their mother that Liam had to bite his cheeks to keep from smiling.

"Don't blame that foot for everything," Breanna said. "You can be a great wizard and do anything you want in life."

Liam rolled his eyes and tried to stay angry, but he couldn't. His sister had never made fun of him—ever—and had always made Liam seem more important than he was. It wasn't her fault that he wasn't anything special.

"All right then." He tried to smile, but worried that it probably came out more like a grimace. "How do we get to a ship that's miles out to sea?"

Breelyn grabbed his right arm in both hands and walked with Liam to the cliffs. She pointed out into the storm. "We can use magic to bring them to us."

Liam felt his eyes widen. "That's a lot of magic," he said, glancing around to make sure they were truly alone. "What if the school finds out? We aren't supposed to do that much magic alone, and Danijela doesn't have any authority here."

Breanna raised her dark eyebrows. "Not direct authority, strictly speaking, but she *is* the strongest wizard in the western lands."

"True," Liam said. Shielding his eyes, he peered out into the dark clouds. "I can't see anything out there."

Breanna motioned for him to sit back down, and Liam was grateful for it—his foot always hurt when he stood too long. This was another thing Breanna had going for her—her natural compassion for others, without making them feel bad about receiving it.

"I am a wizard of the earth," Breanna said. "And I have been learning to control nature—wind, rain, water. And you are a wizard of the mind, a *scholar,* in your own words, I believe, when you're bragging about it."

Liam actually blushed. "Go on."

Breelyn pointed to the Cremelinos. "And we can pull power from them. Between all of us, we should be able to figure out how to bring a ship in from the storm."

Liam let out a long breath. So far, only the edges of the storm had sprayed water around them. But it was blowing in harder now, and the wind was picking up.

"How are you always so optimistic, Breanna? You think there is nothing that we can't do."

His sister's lips curved up in a broad smile. "There is no limit to how high we can fly, Liam. Don't you just feel the power coursing through your veins? Don't you just want to jump up and float on the wind and sail over the earth?"

Liam grunted and then said, "I'll stay here on the ground, thank you very much. You can fly to the clouds all you want."

"We can do this," she said.

Liam turned his mind inward. This could be a good time to test his abilities and to show that he was ready to leave the school...

"Let me think a moment," he said.

Breanna patted his arm and put up a small barrier that blocked the incoming storm from them. The Cremelinos moved closer to the twins.

After a few minutes of thinking, Liam smiled. "There is something that I have wanted to try," he said. "And, with the clouds so low, it might work. I have been studying where the magic comes from and why some wizards are stronger than others."

"Quite the scholarly pursuit, for someone that doesn't think they can accomplish anything," Breanna teased.

Liam punched his sister lightly on the arm. Seeing the joy in her eyes, he realized he would do anything for her.

"Magic flows around us like a stream," he explained. "And, just like a real stream of water, some places are wider or deeper than others. So, if we can get ourselves into the deepest part of the stream, we will have more power to use."

Breanna just nodded.

"And, if we can join our powers together..." Liam continued.

"Which we have been doing since we were born," Breanna added.

Liam nodded. "Yes. But, if we use my powers to guide us to the stream and then your powers to shoot us forward, I think we can expand the reach of our powers. I also think we might be able to direct our powers between the water and the clouds to reach out into the storm."

"Oh, Liam." Breanna clapped. "That sounds wonderful. Do you actually think it could work?"

Liam grew more excited with his sister's enthusiasm. "Well, it is a big ocean out there, but we can try. Once we find the ship, you can use your power over the wind to push its sails our way."

"And the Cremelinos?" Breanna asked.

"That's what binds our powers all together. Their power augments ours. But, more than just increasing the power, the Cremelinos' powers help us work together better."

Getting so wise now, young wizard, thought Liam's Cremelino.

Liberty, will you help us? Liam asked.

Of course, Liam. We are always here for you.

Liam turned his head toward Breanna, who was listening through her Cremelino, Crystal.

"Why is it that, most of the time, I think they already know what is going on but are just waiting for us to ask?" Liam said.

Both Cremelinos snorted, but Crystal answered, *How would you learn otherwise?*

Breanna reached for Liam's hands. Hers felt much warmer than his own. They had done this many times in the past. They had learned as young children that, by touching each other, their powers worked better. But Liam didn't know if this was the case with all wizards or only because they were twins.

Liam closed his eyes, helping himself to concentrate better. Initially, there was only darkness. But, reaching inside himself, he felt the familiar magic burst from his mind. It blossomed, bright and blue. Then, soon afterward, he saw his sister's power—the power of the earth. This grew more rapidly and was dark green in color. Then the soft touch of the Cremelinos' magic wrapped around theirs in a soft white layer.

Still being shielded from the storm by Breanna's barrier, the twins stayed seated on the wet ground and faced the sea. Liam reached his mind outwards, trying to find the currents in the magic around them. With the wizard school so close, eddies of magic swarmed all around. Then a bright stream erupted in the corner of his mind, and Liam found the stream of magic— the stream that gives all magic users their abilities but that only a few wizards could actually see or touch with their minds.

Liam guessed that, due to his physical limitations, he had pushed his mind farther than others had. Or, maybe it was his connection to his twin. Or, possibly, that he was the son of one of the most powerful wizards in the western lands.

Whatever the reason, Liam had always been able to find this source of his powers. It had annoyed his teachers and made other wizards jealous. Still, he would trade it all to be able to walk normally and to train his physical abilities like others. For, even as the son of the king, he had been teased mercilessly his entire life. Even adults would sometimes give him a look of disgust when they thought he wasn't watching. But he always was watching.

Liam felt Breanna's magic touch his own, urging him on. She flew with him through the spiritual, magical stream. Their vision expanded and raced through the building storm. The farther out they went, the worse the storm got. Thunder boomed around Liam, and flashes of lightning seared his vision, but still he pushed on—trying to find one lone ship in the huge sea.

After an hour of searching, Liam's strength began to ebb. His Cremelino, Liberty, strengthened him, and he continued his search. He finally felt a small, but specific prick of magic. It was not from his sister or their Cremelinos but someone else. Someone out in the water. Liam narrowed his magical focus with his mind and pulled Breanna along with him.

Is it him? Breanna said to Liam through their bond with the Cremelinos.

It's someone with magic, Liam answered back. *But it's faint.*

He pushed himself to the limits of where he had ever gone before. He felt Breanna's magic weaken, and the barrier blocking the storm from them fell. As rain pelted their faces, they both struggled to keep their magic intact.

"There it is. I got the ship!" Liam yelled with delight. He directed his magic toward one man in particular and locked on to his magic.

Breanna followed Liam in.

"Now bring the ship in, Breanna. Hurry, before our power weakens any more."

As Liam felt his sister gather her growing earth powers, the ground shook where they stood and the wind went out from her fingertips, traveling at a tremendous speed miles out into the Blue Sea, until she grabbed hold of the ship. She wrapped her powers around the ship too hard at first, and it lurched even more dangerously in the mammoth waves. Then, drawing power from the earth deep below the ocean's surface, Breanna steadied the ship and began to pull it toward them, out of the storm.

Liam extended all the powers he could afford to give to his sister and almost giggled with delight. They were doing something that none of his teachers could teach them. The power was intoxicating—and real. Liam gripped Breanna's hand and let her pull the ship to safety.

CHAPTER THIRTEEN

Bakari woke up on the wet floor of the ship's deck. The barrier he had built over the ship to block the storm had collapsed, and he didn't have the physical or magical strength at the moment to reestablish it. The sails had all been brought down, and now they were at the mercy of the crew's experience to get safely through the storm. The captain was barking orders as the crew slid across the ship, trying to keep the boat's mast from collapsing.

"We need to get back inside," the governor said. "Can you stand?"

Bakari nodded and sat up. Kelln stood and then had to put his hand against a railing to keep himself from falling back down. The two helped each other up and toward the stairs. But walking down the steps to the rooms below was difficult. The rocking of the boat continued to throw them from side to side. Lightning lit the sky around them with an almost simultaneous boom of thunder. Slipping down the last few steps, they landed on the wet floor.

"Can't you do anything more?" Kelln asked. He was drenched himself, and his red hair was plastered to his thin face.

Bakari had been thinking the same thing himself. He was so tired, but he reached inside himself nonetheless, trying to find his magic. In so doing, he felt another touch of magic—as if a slight breeze of power flitted across his mind—and he dove deeper.

Bakari didn't know whose power it was, but it felt safe and familiar. As he focused on it, it grew stronger. Then Bakari saw the blurred face of a young man, not much younger than himself. It filled his mind, and he smiled inside. Once again, Bakari had been lead to the next dragon rider.

The young man's power shifted, and a larger force enveloped his. Then the boat leaned perilously to the starboard side.

The governor yelled out and grabbed hold of a railing. Then the rocking diminished, and Bakari felt the ship being pulled away from the brunt of the storm. He sensed a powerful magic at work and wondered whose it was. Was it from the woman he had seen in the stream of magic? He wasn't sure— but it was from someone with power over the elements.

The rocking slowed, and Bakari and Kelln went back out onto the deck. The captain glared expectantly at Bakari.

"It's not me, sir," Bakari said. "Someone else is helping us."

"I hope they are helping," the captain said in a gruff voice. "I don't like having the control of my ship taken from me."

The governor frowned at the captain. "Sir, have some respect for the dragon rider. He is doing all he can."

The captain nodded his head, obviously feeling chastised, but turned back to his crew.

Bakari and Kelln moved to the front railing. Peering through the dark clouds and rolling water, Bakari could see the sky light up ahead. It was still raining, but they were leaving the worst of the storm behind them. Bakari opened up his mind to his magic and reached out.

Up ahead through the storm was land: an island. And on that island, Bakari sensed a lot of magic—magic so powerful and deep that it felt similar to the dragons' magic. This brief thought made Bakari's stomach churn. He was still coming to grips with not being with Abylar. But he pushed that thought aside for now. He needed to focus.

Among all the magic he sensed, there were two humans with their powers directed at his ship. They were pulling the ship to safety. Bakari's magic touched theirs. A boy and a girl of tremendous power!

The captain yelled out, "We are coming in too fast! If you want to help us out, Rider—now is the time."

Opening his eyes, Bakari now saw the outline of land. The captain was right. The looming white cliffs of the island were growing closer—too close.

While keeping his eyes open, to help himself focus on the land, Bakari reached for his magic. The intensity of his need brought his magic quicker and clearer this time. He felt the others' powers and how these were wrapped around the ship and were pulling them in.

Powerful indeed, but untrained, Bakari thought and almost laughed. Wasn't he just as untrained?

Even though Abylar was far away and Bakari couldn't feel the bond, Bakari still had been given significant tutoring and power while he had been with Abylar. Reaching out into the stream of his power, he pulled it into himself.

He heard a gasp through the stream as a person on the other end fought Bakari for a moment before realizing what he was trying to do.

Grabbing the power of the earth that was pulling the ship, Bakari thought about how to refocus it to keep them all safe. Then another mind popped up by his—a mind like his own. This mind began using the knowledge in their minds to diminish the raging power of the wind around the ship. Then the sails of the ship seemed to rise up of their own volition. The crew and captain gasped, but the action had its intended outcome, and the ship began to slow down.

Bakari, however, realized that this would not be enough. There was only a small beach and then the looming white cliffs behind it. Bakari now did close his eyes to concentrate more as he summoned creatures in the sea beneath them.

A dozen dolphins and giant sea turtles swam up next to the ship. Bakari directed them to come closer. His ability to touch their minds had grown since his bonding with the dragon. Doing this wasn't wrong or evil—as had been taught for so long—it was natural, and the creatures had a desire to help. Touching the sides of the ship, they used their bodies to begin to slow it down.

"Bakari, it's working," Kelln yelled out. So Bakari opened his eyes.

"Never seen anything like this in my life." The captain's eyes grew round.

"It's beautiful," said another crew member.

The wind had died down, the storm moving away behind the ship, and, with the gentle nudging of the animals, the ship floated slower and slower across the water, until coming to a standstill a few hundred feet from the shore of the island.

As the crew cheered, the captain slapped Bakari on the back and said, "No one will ever believe me, Dragon Rider. Forgive me for my outburst earlier." The captain shook his head before yelling orders to his crew, to navigate around the island to a proper port.

"Sir," Bakari called back to the captain. "We would like to get out here."

"What do you mean, Bakari?" Kelln turned in surprise. "They have a port on the other side of the island."

"I need to meet the people that helped us."

Kelln gave a hard glance at Bakari for a moment. Then, turning to the captain, he ordered, "Do as the young wizard commands, Captain. I will go with him."

The captain's eyes bulged. "But, Governor, you can't. This isn't proper for you. Who will greet you here?"

Kelln laughed, and a bright gleam lit his eyes. "I will be fine, Captain. I will meet you at the harbor tomorrow. I have a great wizard to protect me." He slapped Bakari on the back, and the two of them headed to the side of the ship.

Soon the crew had lowered a smaller boat down into the water. Bakari and Kelln jumped inside. Then the two oarsmen began to take them in to the shore.

Bakari wondered what kind of man the governor was. He couldn't imagine any of the governors or judges in Alaris traipsing around like this—without all the usual pomp and circumstance.

As they approached the shore, Bakari noticed two people standing up on the cliffs and looking down at them. The two seemed to be about his same age. The young woman turned to the young man, and what appeared to be a brief argument ensued with the shaking of heads. The young woman disappeared, and then, as the boat neared the shore, she appeared again, climbing down a steep path from the cliff to the sand.

The small boat took them right up to the shoreline. Bakari stepped out ahead of the governor. He breathed in deeply. It felt good to be on land again. Though, he still felt like he was rocking.

Saying goodbye to the oarsmen, Bakari bade them give his thanks once again to the captain. Bakari took a few steps forward on the wet sand, then he gazed straight up. The white cliffs stood about seventy-five feet high above them, rainwater still dripping down their rocky surface.

"Amazing!" Bakari said.

"They certainly are," Kelln agreed. "I never get tired of seeing them."

Out of a crevice, a young woman emerged. Her light brown hair was long and wet, but her smile brightened up her heart-shaped face. She took a few steps toward them, seeming surprised.

"Breanna!" Kelln yelled and then grabbed her into a full hug. She stood a few inches shorter than him.

"Uncle Kelln, what are you doing here?" the young woman asked, her brown hair fluttering in the post-storm wind.

Kelln laughed and turned to Bakari. "This is Breanna DarSan Williams, the daughter of the king." He turned back to Breanna. "And this is Bakari."

Breanna opened her eyes wide, as if waiting for more of an explanation, but none followed.

"Where is the other one?" Bakari asked.

"Other one?" Kelln repeated, then laughed out loud. "You mean that scoundrel, Liam, is here too?"

The young woman frowned slightly and pointed up above them as she said, "He is up there."

"Liam is also the king's son—the two are twins," Kelln explained to Bakari. "Both wizards."

Bakari wondered why the young man hadn't come down to greet them also.

Breanna seemed to have sensed his question, for she said, "He has a bad foot and can't climb or walk well."

Her face held a serene sympathy that almost brought a tear to Bakari's eyes. He could tell that she loved her brother very much.

"But Liam is an amazing wizard," Breanna added.

Bakari smiled at that. "You are both quite amazing for your age; I felt your power."

"Our age?" Breanna smiled. "You aren't that much older than us—and I felt your power. A type of power I haven't felt before."

Bakari just shrugged. He wasn't ready to explain anything else yet—especially about the dragons. So he looked up the cliff and said, "I would like to meet your brother."

Breanna opened her mouth, as if to ask more questions, but was polite enough not to push. "Y...yes. Of course," she stuttered. "If you don't mind the climb."

After surviving the ordeal on the ship, Bakari and Kelln were exhausted by the time they reached the top of the cliff.

"I'm too old for this, Breanna," Kelln complained.

"Oh, Uncle Kelln, you need to get out more." Breanna laughed.

Nearing the top, Bakari noticed that the storm had continued blowing away and that the sun had begun to peek out around the receding clouds. Putting his hands on his knees at the top of the cliff, to catch his breath, he eventually stood back up. Then he noticed a young man, with dark hair and a brooding face, looking intently at him.

"Liam!" Kelln said as he reached over and slapped the young man on the back. "You've grown taller since the last time we saw each other. Are you ever going to stop?"

A smile lifted the corners of Liam's mouth.

"Liam, this is Bakari," Breanna added, introducing them.

Liam stared for a moment longer.

Then Breanna nudged him and said, "Liam, where are your manners?"

Bakari surveyed the two and marveled that they were twins. Then he took a step toward the young man and put his hand out. "Nice to meet you, Liam. Thank you for saving us. Your control was amazing."

The compliment had its desired effect, and Liam's lips turned into a full smile. He brought his hand out to shake

Bakari's and said, "Well met, Bakari. What you did with those animals was staggering. Where did you learn that?"

Bakari ignored this question for the moment and let himself feel Liam's soul. A magical whispering told Bakari that this young man from the Realm was the one.

Now, I just need to find Liam's dragon, Bakari thought to himself.

"Where are you from?" Breanna asked him.

"Alaris, though my heritage is Mahlian."

"Alaris?" Breanna clapped her hands together. "So it is true. The barrier is down?"

"Yes, it is." Bakari nodded.

"We need to tell my father that you are here," Breanna said. "Emperor Alrishitar told us, but my father was somewhat skeptical about the news."

"I am on my way to see your father," Kelln added. "Just had to get this young man here to White Island first."

"Tell him we are doing well," Breanna said.

"Are we?" Liam asked, brooding once again.

"So, who is the oldest?" Bakari looked from one to the other and couldn't tell.

"What you mean is who will rule the Realm next?" Liam said. His eyes were dark, and he stared down at his lame foot. "Breanna will be the next queen while I limp around and accomplish nothing."

"Liam!" Breanna exclaimed. "That is not true. *You* had the idea of how to save their ship today. What you did was wonderful."

Bakari smiled broadly and clapped Liam on the back—much to Liam's surprise. "I am glad for your power, Liam—and I wouldn't worry too much about not being a king or thinking you can't do much. I have a feeling that you will accomplish extraordinary things in your life that few others will ever experience."

As Bakari looked over at Kelln and smiled, the governor seemed to get Bakari's meaning but was fine with holding the secret in.

"Whatever," Liam said, though his frown had faded. "For now, I would just like a warm meal in a dry room."

"Now, that is one thing we can all agree on, I think," Kelln said. "I'm always one for adventure, but I am hungry." After a brief pause, Kelln clapped the twins on the back and added, "This is so fantastic!"

They all laughed together. Even Liam gave a brief smile.

Then Bakari noticed the two horses for the first time. So he reached his hand out to touch one.

"Be careful," Breanna said. "They are temperamental."

"Ahh, the famed Cremelinos," Bakari said. The closest horse stood almost as tall as himself and was pure white.

The twins turned toward each other in apparent surprise.

Bakari caught their looks and said, "I am a scholar wizard and read a lot."

"I thought I felt something familiar when our powers touched," Liam said, regaining a more jovial mood. "I am a scholar also, a *wizard of the mind* we call it here."

Bakari nodded and continued to reach out to the closest Cremelino. He rubbed his hand along its side and then smiled, saying, "Her name is Crystal."

Breanna's green eyes opened wide. "How did you know?"

"She told me," Bakari said matter-of-factly.

"She spoke to you?" Breanna almost whispered. "They usually only speak to their own rider."

"I am a rider too," Bakari said, though rather cryptically. "But let's get dried off first. I am here on important business, and you might be able to help me."

Liam mounted his horse, and the rest of them walked as they moved together toward a grouping of buildings off in the distance.

"We attend the wizard school here," Breanna said. "We have a place for you to change, get dry, and have a meal. Then you can meet the headmaster."

Liam frowned. "If he is well today."

Breanna nodded. "Yes, he hasn't been seen much lately."

Bakari felt a growing sense of unease in his stomach. Reaching out his mind toward the school, he felt around with his powers. Something dark approached him, and he pulled back. Stumbling on a walkway, he almost fell.

"Bakari, you all right?" Kelln put his arm around Bakari. "You look pale."

Bakari only nodded and tried to smile. But he sure wished that he had Abylar with him.

CHAPTER FOURTEEN

For two days, Alli and Jaimon stayed hidden from the men looking for them. The Followers of the Dragon, if anything, were overly protective of their dragon rider. Jaimon had sent his dragon away from the city so as not to attract any more attention than needed. Rumors were sent out of the Sanctuary, by Leopold and the rest of the Followers, that the dragon rider had left abruptly in the middle of the night.

It was now early in the morning of the third day, and Alli pulled a hood over her head and walked down a long tunnel, away from the rooms where they had been hiding. The tunnel went northward, under the short strait of water that separated the island from the mainland—an old safety measure for the Sanctuary. With the ease of using boats on the water, the tunnel was little used now, and she was able to walk the distance without meeting anyone else.

After emerging inside a small cave on the mainland, she continued walking up a road that led to Margarid itself. The sun had just risen, and only a few shopkeepers were beginning to open their stores. But things were still too quiet for a city of this size.

Hugging the sides of the buildings, the young Battlemaster moved with quiet steps toward the king's castle at the eastern edge of the city. A vendor selling hot pastries stopped her and engaged her in a running commentary on the benefits of his baking over his neighbors'.

But he had a strange accent that sounded like there were marbles in his mouth, so Alli had a hard time following everything the man said. Finally, she pulled out some local currency and paid the man for a sugared pastry.

A street later, Alli found herself licking her fingers. She had to admit that the pastry had been worth the money. Her stomach growled for something more substantial—she had left the basement of the Sanctuary before the morning meal had been brought in.

The look of the ornate gates, manicured yards, and multi-storied buildings let her know she was in the nobles' district. There were fewer people out this early in this part of town than in the merchant district in the morning. And, those who were out were servants, running errands for their masters.

Turning a corner, Alli ran into a rather bulky woman, who spilled a pot of breakfast porridge all down the front of Alli's clothes.

"Oh dear, I'm sorry," the woman muttered.

Alli froze for a brief moment, wondering what she should do.

But the woman took care of it for her. She grabbed Alli's hand and began dragging her along with her, saying, "My dear, I have ruined your clothes. You must come with me. I will get you all cleaned up."

Alli mumbled her thanks. As she tried to stop the woman from pulling her onward, she said, "I'm fine, ma'am."

The woman glanced over but never stopped moving. Even with her large girth she was quite quick, her short legs almost running along the cobblestone street. Then she said, "Oh, poor dear, you don't sound like you're from around here."

Alli felt fear prick her heart. She couldn't give away who she was. Luckily, she had kept her swords at the Sanctuary when she had left that morning. Oh, she still had weapons hidden all over her, and her magic was more powerful than most. She wasn't sure, however, how to respond.

Once again the woman made Alli's choice for her, saying, "You must be from Alaris. We've had plenty of young ones here, seeking the world around them now that the barrier is down. Is that what you are doing?"

As short as she was, the woman was still an inch or two taller than Alli. At times, Alli's height worked to her advantage, making her seem even younger than her sixteen years. Today might be one of those times.

"My father came to do business here, and we got separated." Alli hated lying, but the woman just made it so darn easy.

"Oh, you poor thing." The woman pulled her along still. "You must be no older than fourteen or so—about the same age as my master's daughter, I would guess. We'll get you all cleaned up, and then my master can help you find your pa."

Alli bristled at the mention of her age and blushed, but she kept her mouth shut. Let the woman wonder. Her size had given her the advantage before, as people seemed to underestimate her abilities—it was usually the last mistake they ever made.

Palm trees grew in pots around one particularly immense home. It stood at least four stories tall, covered with white plaster, and was one of the largest single homes Alli had ever seen.

They turned a corner and entered a side door of the formidable structure.

Seeing inside the small entrance, Alli could tell that the home was furnished with all the niceties that life had to offer. Artwork covered the walls, decorated golden vases lined the glass shelves, and a soft carpet sat under her feet.

The woman put down her pot in a back kitchen and then proceeded to bring Alli down a long hallway. Coming to a foyer, they had turned to the right, when someone yelled out from the left.

"Hannah!" a young but deep voice called out. The accent was from here but sounded more refined than Alli had heard before. "What have we here?"

Alli turned and looked, becoming self-conscious of the food stains on her clothes. She tried to brush down her dark black hair with one hand and, without thinking, stood up as tall as she could.

Standing in front of her was one of the most beautiful people she had ever seen. Olive skin, full lips, twinkling brown eyes, and brown hair that hung just past his collar. He was similar in height to Roland, but broader of shoulder. With a small breath through her nose, the light scent of cinnamon filled Alli's senses, and his white teeth showed a sparkling smile that froze Alli in place.

Taking a few steps toward her accentuated his style—his colorful blue robe swirling around his white shirt and dark blue pants. He almost made the grace and beauty of the elves seem merely human.

Alli was comfortable and at ease on a battlefield, but she was not prepared for this.

The man bowed low in front of her. Then, taking her right hand in his, he lifted her hand to his lips and kissed it softly. Alli knew she must have reddened profusely.

Hannah turned to Alli and said, "This is Kaspar Von Wulf, the teenage son of the Wolf."

"The Wolf?" repeated Alli, not knowing what else to say.

"My father, the minister of trade, has built quite a reputation for his fierceness in negotiations and was nicknamed *the Wolf* years ago by the king," Kaspar said and then laughed at Alli's reaction.

What must this man think of her? She shook her head and drew upon her magic to steady her thinking. Upon seeing Alli do so, Kaspar drew in a quick breath through his lips and tilted his head at her.

"This young girl is from Alaris—oh, what was your name?" Hannah asked.

"My name is Allison—or Alli."

"Well, Master Kaspar, I spilled porridge on her and only thought it right to bring her here and get her cleaned up," Hannah explained. "Her father is doing business here, and she got lost. Poor young thing."

Kaspar stared at Alli without blinking and cocked his head to the side again. "I don't think she is as young as you think,

Hannah," he said. "I see much in her eyes—and her soul is troubled."

Alli was taken aback. Who was this man? And what did he mean…that he could see her soul? He had no right to do that to her. Her mouth tightened, and she glared up at the man.

His looks almost made her back down, but Alli steadied herself and said, "I am sixteen years old and *can* take care of myself just fine. And you have no right to look into my soul, Kaspar."

A bright smile crinkled the corners of Kaspar's eyes. He nodded his head and then let out a small laugh. "Call me Kas." He turned and said to his servant, "See, Hannah—she has some spunk in her. I think she is more than she seems."

Hannah looked worried for a moment and then said, "I'm sorry, Master. Should I take her back out? I shouldn't have brought a stranger into your father's home."

"Nonsense." Kaspar waved a hand in the air. "I sense no danger in her—at least, no danger to us. Help her get cleaned up." He then turned to Alli and added, "I invite you to join me for our morning meal."

"N…no, that's fine," Alli stuttered. "I need to be somewhere."

"I insist," Kaspar said. "My father will be joining us, and I am sure you would enjoy meeting the minister of trade and heir to the throne of Quentis."

Alli gulped and barely kept her composure. She had been on her way to spy out the castle and the king, whereas now she could talk to his son. Then it dawned on her who Kaspar was.

"That makes you…" Alli said.

Once again Kaspar smiled with his pearly whites and stunned Alli by his beauty. "That's right," he said. "I am the grandson of the king and second in line as heir to the throne of Quentis. Welcome to our home." He bowed again to her and then bid her farewell.

Following Hannah back down the hall, where they had been originally going, Alli stumbled once.

"He has that effect on people." Hannah laughed and patted Alli's arm. "You are not the first girl to be smitten by his charms and good looks."

"I am not smitten by him!" Alli said with force. "And, what's all this about looking into my eyes and soul?"

Hannah took Alli into a room with a sink and a tub. She turned a knob and waited a moment, until hot water came out. Alli gasped in delight. The Von Wulf's were wealthier than anything she could imagine.

Hannah motioned for another servant, a girl younger than Alli, to help Alli disrobe, clean herself up, and find some new clothes to wear. Before Hannah left the room, she turned back to Alli, her face serious, and said, "Kaspar sees things others don't see, Miss. I hope you are not hiding anything that would endanger him or this household. They are good people and good to all of us."

Alli turned back to the young servant, and together they began to get Alli all cleaned up. The young girl gasped when she saw the assortment of knives and other weapons that came out from under Alli's clothes. Alli knew that, soon, all the servants in the house would know about them too. She put on her meekest face and explained them away as wanting to be careful in a foreign city.

After Alli was clean, she borrowed a light blue dress robe that cinched tight at the waist. A colored pattern adorned the hem and the end of the sleeves. Her hair had been washed and dried, now hanging just over her shoulders. Looking into a full-length mirror—another luxury she'd had a hard time believing—she enjoyed how the robe's color offset her pale skin and dark hair.

Soon Hannah came for her and led her into what Alli supposed was a private dining room. It was bigger than the house she had grown up in and almost as big as the full dining room at the Citadel or at the castle in Cassian. A long, dark-toned table sat in the middle atop a beautiful carpet. Clear glass windows adorned one wall, offering a view of the Bay of Ghazi and its clear blue waters. Tall, crystal chandeliers with hundreds of candles, unlit at this time of morning, ran the length of the room.

Alli was led to a table where Kaspar, a girl a few years younger than him, and an older gentleman—who Alli could only guess was their father—were already seated. Upon Alli's entering, Kaspar stood and took a few steps in her direction. Words caught in her throat for a moment as, once again, his beauty affected her.

"Welcome again, Alli," Kaspar said as he motioned Alli to a seat across from himself and next to the girl. "This is my sister, Gabriele."

Gabriele stood and made a small curtsy to Alli. Dimples adorned the olive skin on both sides of her face, and dark hair hung down her back to just above her waist.

Alli smiled back. "Nice to meet you, Gabriele."

"You can call me Gabby," the young girl said. "All my friends do."

Alli was touched by the simple generosity of Gabby considering her a friend.

Before Alli could sit down, Kaspar brought a hand out and pointed it toward his father. "And this, Alli, is my father, the Wolf."

The Wolf didn't rise, but he brought his head up and inspected Alli. A flare of her power flew up inside her—a seemingly automatic precaution against the Wolf's power. Then she felt something touch her mind, but Alli put up blocks of magic to shield herself.

The Wolf's serene face didn't seem to hold any danger, but his eyes bored into hers with more intensity than his son's had earlier. He was also more broad of shoulder than Kaspar, but Alli could see the family resemblance.

After the stretching scrutiny, the Wolf nodded his head toward Alli. "Welcome, Allison. Good of you to join us today. My wife is out of town on business in Tillimot. I am sorry that she won't be able to meet you."

Alarms screamed inside Alli's head. He had called her *Allison*. Did the Wolf know who she really was or did he just guess at her full name? Her hands had instinctively moved toward her knives.

"No need for that here," the Wolf said. "You are not in any danger at the moment."

Alli breathed in deeply and readied herself for whatever might happen next.

Gabby looked to her father and shook her head. "Don't be so intimidating, Father. You know how you scare people with your seeing." Gabby furrowed her dark eyebrows at her father, but her lips held a hint of a tease.

Then her father let out a loud, booming laugh and slapped his hand on the table, making the crystal goblets shake and spill a few drops of juice onto the table mats. He turned to Alli once again. This time, his expression held amusement and genuine kindness.

"Please excuse my manners," he said. "In my position, I am not used to dealing with young people so much. I must protect the king from those who would harm him. Please sit down. Let's enjoy our meal, and you can tell us what you are doing here, so far away from home."

Alli let out a long breath and did as he had bid her, sitting in the high-backed chair next to Gabby. Gabby smiled genuinely at Alli, and servants began to dish out a meal for the group. For the next few minutes, Alli concerned herself with fried cakes and syrup, fresh fruit—she was told it was mango and pineapple—and spiced pork. She finished her plate and then looked up.

All three of her hosts were looking at her, and Alli blushed.

"Quite an appetite, for a young girl," the Wolf said, his eyes holding secret thoughts behind them. "You must expend a lot of energy to stay so thin."

"I exercise a lot," Alli said. Food always helped her to feel better.

"Maybe a little sparring after our meal?" Kasper said to her. "What is your weapon of choice?"

Alli smiled broadly. Weapons were definitely a subject she was well versed in. "Pick your best, Kaspar. I am familiar with short or long swords, knives, or the staff."

Kaspar raised one of his dark eyebrows. "Oh, a challenge, huh?"

Gabby laughed, and Alli turned in her direction.

"Don't encourage Kas, Alli." Gabby rolled her eyes. "He thinks he's the best at everything."

Kaspar blushed only slightly and turned to his father as if for help.

His father only shrugged. "You brought this on yourself, Son. Possibly being king someday doesn't mean you have to be the best at everything."

Kaspar struggled for words for the first time since Alli had met him.

"And I have a feeling," the Wolf said, "that our dear Allison here might be quite a master of weapons." He looked intently at Alli once again.

Alli turned back to her plate, trying to find one last scrap of food there to distract her. That man, the Wolf, definitely knew more than he was saying.

Servants came in and cleaned up the meal. Then Kaspar stood up, and Gabby told Alli that she would escort her to a changing room and then to the courtyard, where the sparring would take place.

Before they could leave the room, the Wolf called Alli back to him. So, leaving Gabby at the door, Alli walked tentatively back to the man.

Approaching the Wolf, Alli realized how tall the man was and took a step back to keep from needing to look up so high. Keeping a hand close to her knife, she mentally rehearsed where all the exits of the room were. She had to be prepared for trouble.

As the Wolf placed one strong hand on her shoulder, Alli tensed her muscles.

"Be careful with my son."

Alli nodded, not knowing what to say. Was he threatening her?

"And, when you are done with Kaspar, I would like to see you inside my office in the castle," the Wolf continued. "And bring your dragon rider friend with you."

Alli blushed, despite trying to keep her composure.

"But how…?"

"It is my job to know what happens in this city," the Wolf said as his dark eyes bore down on her.

Then Alli realized something. "You are not just the Minister of Trade—or, at least, that is mostly a front, isn't it?"

"I see that you have a sharp mind, Battlemaster."

Alli held her mouth in a tight line. The man did know more than he had let on. Was *he* behind the trouble brewing in the city?

"Then, why let me spar with your son?" she asked.

The Wolf's eyes twinkled, and he grinned broadly, showing the same straight, white teeth as his son's. "Because it's good for him to get beaten once in a while."

"You have high confidence in me, then?" Alli bantered back.

"Let's just say that rumors of the grace and power of the young Battlemaster from Alaris have been floating around here for the last few months. I do hope this was not exaggerated."

"I'll see what I can do to exceed your expectations, sir." Alli smiled.

The Wolf laughed once again and shooed her out of the room.

This should be fun! Alli thought, for she had been itching for some exercise.

CHAPTER FIFTEEN

When Breelyn had first arrived at the Raleez castle, she'd been taken to a room and been promised a meeting with General Trevis—the man left in charge while Solshi's kings traveled south, to Quentis. That was two days ago, and she had still seen nothing of the man. The servants had treated her well, though with some trepidation. And Breelyn had spent her days reading in their library and communicating with Miriel, who had stayed outside the city walls.

This morning, Breelyn walked down the main thoroughfare of the city to visit the market district. Elves, in general, were patient, but Breelyn felt all bound up inside and couldn't stand much more waiting. This was her first visit to Solshi, but she didn't think the mood here was normal. The city seemed quieter than it should have been. People talked in whispers. And vendors were not as aggressive in calling out their wares.

Standing outside of a dress shop, she overheard two women talking a few paces from her.

"My husband says that shipments of food from the North have slowed," said the one who was more plump than the other.

"That's where most of our beef and lamb come from," said the second woman, whose voice was higher than the first woman's. "My brother travels there every spring to oversee some of the birthing. He has been told not to come this year."

"We might have to trade with Alaris," the plump woman said.

The second woman gasped. "I don't want to have anything to do with those people. They locked themselves up for one hundred and fifty years and now want to just traipse in and start being our friends."

"I hear that their Citadel is recruiting young people from here—wizards."

"Why wouldn't they just go to Quentis, to the Sanctuary, like they always have?" the thinner woman asked.

"I hear there is unrest there too. That's why the kings have gone there."

The two women moved out of earshot, and Breelyn continued down the street. Walking by a knife shop, Breelyn stopped for a moment and looked at some of the blades in the store window. A dark one caught her eye and pulled her inside the shop.

"Good day," the shopkeeper said. He was a broad-shouldered man, a dozen years older than Breelyn. When he glimpsed her ears, he tried to hold back a gasp. "What can I do for you?"

"The dark blade in the window." Breelyn pointed.

"Ah. That one is only for display. It's not for sale. It is a black obsidian blade."

"How did you come by it, then? You didn't make it?" Breelyn asked, moving toward it.

"It comes from the plains of Turg, in the North, and has gone through many owners, most having met with bad luck after they possessed it," the man said, frowning as he spoke.

"Bad luck?" Breelyn said.

"*Cursed* they say it is," the shopkeeper continued. "A man pleaded with me, a few years ago, to trade it for a proper metal knife. And I was intrigued, so I did." He paused and then added, "I carried it on me once…"

"And what happened?"

"I lost my wife that day," he said. "A cart turned over and fell on her."

Breelyn was intrigued. She put her hand on his arm, and he jumped.

"I am sorry for your loss, sir," Breelyn said. "But surely a blade cannot cause a cart to turn over." Breelyn could feel the blade calling to her. "I would like to hold it."

"No, no, no," the man reiterated. "It is cursed, I told you. Death follows in its wake."

Breelyn grew angry. "Then why put it in your window to tempt buyers? Let me see it."

The man took a few steps, trying to place himself between Breelyn and the display window. Then he looked down for a moment in embarrassment. "I keep it there to draw people inside. It is a good conversation piece. Then I sell them other knives and swords. I know it isn't very honorable, but I have to make a living somehow."

Breelyn felt the darkness begin to creep into her vision once again. Its familiar taunting pushed her toward the knife. Maybe it is why she came to Solshi. The black blade was beautiful and soaked in all the light around it. So she reached for it.

The shopkeeper grabbed her wrist and said, "Please stop."

But Breelyn shook the man's hand off of her arm and grabbed the knife. She squeezed the handle in her left hand and closed her eyes. It was a perfect fit. The knife sang to her, and the darkness brought peace to her heart. The blackness around the edge of her vision seemed to wrap itself in comfort around the knife.

When the man gasped, Breelyn opened her eyes. The man was staring at the bottom of her hair, which hung down her sides. Breelyn glanced down. It had turned black.

Such a nice look on me, Breelyn thought to herself.

"How much?" Breelyn asked him.

The man backed away, saying, "Take it. It's yours. But never bring it back here again. I warn you one last time, that thing is cursed. If you take it, it is yours. I don't want you back in my store ever again." He pushed her toward the door with his meaty hands.

Exiting the store, Breelyn still held the blade in her hand. Onlookers peered at her with questioning looks. So she stuck the blade through a sash she had tied around her waist. She could have sworn that the sash had been white when she had put it on that morning, but now it was black as night.

Then she continued up the street. Before turning at the corner, she heard the voices of a few men talking, so she paused instead to listen in.

"He is sending all of us out of the city, but it doesn't make sense," said a man with a high voice.

"Who knows what makes sense, with nobles," a second man said, his voice lower and quiet.

"But the general isn't a noble," a third man said. "At least, not that my sister says. She works for one of them, and he just showed up a few months ago. It's not right."

"But what can we do?" said the man with a high voice. "Food is already becoming scarce. I have to take care of my family."

"We can fight back," the third man said.

"Fight against who?" the quiet man said. "The kings are gone, many of the nobles have disappeared, and now soldiers are being sent east. There won't be anyone left to fight against."

"Maybe we can get Alaris to help us," the third man said. Then his voice began fading as they moved away. "Or those dragon riders I have heard about…"

Breelyn turned the corner and tried to follow the men without being noticed. She pulled up her white cowl, draping it over her face to cover her pointed ears.

The first two men laughed, and the quiet one voiced his thoughts. "Dragon riders? You have got to be kidding me. There are no such things as dragons."

"Oh, you are wrong, my friend," the first man said. "My cousin works at the city gate. One landed there the other day. The thing was the largest yellow and orange monster he had ever seen."

Breelyn bristled at hearing her dear dragon being called *a monster*. She picked up her pace and found her hand holding the obsidian knife once again. Walking a few feet behind the men, she reached her bladed hand forward.

Suddenly, an overhang above the shop she was in front of made a loud cracking noise. Looking up, Breelyn noticed the boards beginning to crack. Seeing this also, the three men jumped forward, out of the way, and Breelyn jumped backward. Then the overhang crashed to the ground between them, the shopkeeper running out to see what had happened.

Breelyn studied the knife, still in her hand, and thought of the curse the shopkeeper had warned her about. She shook her head and thought, *Coincidence.*

Stuffing the knife back into her sash, Breelyn tried to remember why she had been holding it in her hand in the first place. She shook her head to clear her mind. But she couldn't remember the last few minutes.

Turning across the dirt roadway, she headed back to the castle. Her strides grew longer and more purposeful, her cowl slipping back down onto her back. Citizens of Solshi moved out of her way like animals fleeing a fire. She would march straight through the city to see General Trevis. Nothing was going to detain her any longer. She needed answers now.

In the back of her mind, Breelyn felt Miriel, lazily lying around the edge of a lake to the north of the city. Through the bond, Breelyn pulled more power into her soul, until that, along with her own Elvyn powers, flashed out of her pale blue eyes— almost like fire.

Reaching the top steps of the castle, a guard moved to detain her. Instead, he found himself thrown backward, against the wall of the castle. Then, with a wave of her hand, the immense doors opened on their own, and Breelyn strode into the entry hall.

Other guards and servants stopped and stared, but she didn't care. She knew where the throne room was and headed that way. A small servant girl dropped a tray of dishes in front of her, but Breelyn scarcely noticed.

Two burly guards in red stood in front of the throne room doors.

One bowed his head to her and said, "Dragon Rider, welcome back."

"Get out of my way!" Breelyn said, her voice echoing down the hall. Her long hair, still tinged with black, floated around her as if alive. Her right hand rested on the hilt of the obsidian knife. And power coursed through her veins. She had never felt so powerful before.

She tried to pull more power from her dragon, but Miriel resisted.

Dragon Rider, what is wrong? Miriel asked, her alarm spreading through the bond. *What are you doing?*

This is what needs to be done, Miriel, Breelyn said, flashing a thought back in mere seconds while waiting for the door to open. *These people think they can keep putting me off. But I need to find the cure for Lan and deliver my message from Bakari.*

I don't think this is what Bakari meant, Miriel said.

Her dragon was being argumentative, so Breelyn ignored Miriel and turned her attention back to the two guards.

"The general is not in the throne room at the moment," the taller guard said, eyeing the dagger in her hand.

But she thrust her other hand out, and the door flew open. "Then I will wait here until he arrives," she said as she entered the room. "And you may tell him that I won't wait much longer before something drastic occurs."

"Yes...yes, Dragon Rider," stammered the shorter of the two guards, and he took off running down the hall. The taller guard stayed at his post, but he wouldn't look Breelyn in the eyes now. Then the heavy doors closed behind her.

Somewhere in the back of Breelyn's mind, alarms were going off, reminding her that this wasn't how a dragon rider should be acting. The role of the riders and their dragons was to establish peace, not cause havoc.

"What I am doing will bring peace," she justified with a mumble. The throne room was as ornate as the grand throne rooms in the Citadel or in Cassian, all of which being much more formal and gaudy than the Elvyn hall of the kings. The elves were less concerned with making a show of their wealth or power.

A golden throne with red cushions sat atop a dais, a few feet above the floor. As Breelyn walked single-mindedly toward it, she hardly noticed the tapestries, golden vases, and jewel-covered ornaments. Those meant nothing to her. Reaching the throne itself, she paused momentarily.

Someday, Lan would be king of Elvyn—if he survived—and she would be his queen. *Queen of the elves.* A much simpler and peaceful people than all these barbarians to the west of their borders.

She turned her head to the side as a flutter of blackness seemed to dance on the walls. Nothing was there. Another flash, to the other side, had her turning again. The sunlight that had been streaming through the windows now darkened. A passing cloud? Or something else?

I wonder how it would feel? she thought to herself as she ran her hand lovingly over the ornate arms of the throne. Backing up to it, she sat down on the throne and leaned her head back. A slow grin covered her face. In many kingdoms, sitting on the throne was punishable by death. But who would kill her here? There was no one powerful enough to stop her in these two pathetic kingdoms.

CHAPTER SIXTEEN

Breelyn was still enjoying the feel of the throne around her body. She wasn't sure how much time had passed since she had entered the room. But she had been thinking about how it would be to rule over a kingdom.

Breelyn, I am coming, roared Miriel in Breelyn's mind. *You are in danger.*

What danger? Breelyn asked. *There is no one here. I am more powerful than all of them.*

He is coming. I can feel him. Her dragon's mind was frantic as she added, *Hold on!*

Breelyn didn't know what had got into her dragon. The silly animal was still so young. There was nothing of danger here—except for maybe dying of boredom!

Breelyn heard a sound from outside of the throne room, and then the doors slowly opened. A man took a step inside, and the room darkened.

But this meant nothing to Breelyn as she thought, *This must be General Trevis, the man two entire nations fear.* Well, she was an Elvyn protector, a dragon rider, and a mage of considerable power. Nothing could frighten her.

The man took slow steps toward her, his gray cape flying around his broad shoulders. His heavy, black boots echoed on the marble floor. A dark hood covered his face—which was bearded, from what Breelyn could tell.

Still lounging in the throne, Breelyn felt a brief spark in her mind, encouraging her to stand up. But she pushed it aside.

The man stopped a dozen feet away in front of her, his face still shrouded in shadows. "My dear, are you comfortable?" he asked. His voice was not as Breelyn had expected. It was low and soft and inviting. "We can work on making that permanent, if this is what you like. My name is General Trevis."

The voice echoed in her mind as much as it bounced off the walls of the throne room. Breelyn breathed in deeply and reached her mind out. The general had power—extreme power—an influence that she recognized. It brought up the dark shadows around her. Looking down, she found herself holding the knife once again in her hand, and darkness had now spread up one sleeve of her robe.

Breelyn felt the man's supremacy over all the power she had. She was humbled in his presence. If any man had the power to help her, he was the one.

"What do you want, Breelyn Mier?" the man asked, still not showing his face. "Why are you here?"

Breelyn stood now. "I want my king to live," she said with fire and determination. An underlying feeling of her love for Lan spread through the faraway recesses of her mind. She wondered briefly if what she was doing was right.

The general took a long step forward. "I have the power to cure your king, and so do you now. But what are you willing to do to let him live? How far are you willing to go?"

Breelyn didn't understand the general's meaning. She took two steps down the dais and stopped, now only a few feet in front of and above the man. "What do you mean?"

"To save the one you love, are you willing to change your allegiance?" the general said as his voice grew more raspy and heated. "Join me, Breelyn."

Breelyn watched the general put his hand forward. She was drawn to it. The dark shadows flew around her, comforting her, making her feel needed and wanted. She would give up anything for her beloved Lan. Lan was so much better than her, and his wisdom was needed to guide the elves.

So, taking the last step down the dais, she paused in front of the man who had called himself General Trevis. But she knew now that he was so much more than just a general.

A whisper escaped her throat as she said, "Who are you?"

With slow hands, the man reached up to his hood and threw it back behind his head. Then he brought his face up and peered into her eyes.

His brown eyes blinked and then turned a golden color. She had seen those eyes before. They had been the eyes of the man that had stood right in front of Lan.

"The Chameleon?" Breelyn asked.

The man now laughed—a booming sound that rocked the walls. "Oh, no, my dear elf maiden. That one is my brother. He hides and slithers around, taking on the forms of others. I am simply known as *the General* now, one who is building an army to crush all those that oppose us."

"Us?" Breelyn squeaked out.

The General's mouth grew into a wide smile. "Yes, there are three of us. My oldest brother, the Sentinel, gathers power for us on an island in the Realm. My second oldest brother, the Chameleon, which you have met, sows discord now in the Sanctuary of Quentis. And I, the youngest, am consolidating power in the western lands. I will march my army through each land until all bow to us."

"To what end?" she asked.

"We will conquer the entire Western Continent and then give it all to our father, who we will rule forever and ever."

"Your father?" Breelyn's mind finally began to think on its own. What had she done? She felt drawn to the General's dark power but knew now that it wasn't right—but, was it too late?

"Our father was the last wizard king of Alaris over one hundred and fifty years ago. He began to raise an army, with plans to take over all the lands around Alaris." The General brought his hands out to his sides, and then disgust crossed his face. "But wizards from Elvyn and Mahli and other kingdoms fought back, killed my father, and, with the power of the Dragon Orb, put a barrier around Alaris for all these years. Now that the barrier is down, we can bring him back."

"Bring him back from the dead?" Breelyn asked, taking a step away from him, horrified at the thought. "You can't do that."

"Ahh, but we can. Once we control the powers of the dragons and Cremelinos—the power to bind—we will bring his soul back from the darkness and into the world once again. It will be glorious!"

"But the dragon riders will never allow it," Breelyn said as she began to think clearly again. She could feel that Miriel was coming closer. "We will fight back. You can't control us."

The General laughed again, a low, menacing laugh. "We can't control *you*? Think again, you puny, pathetic elf. Your power is nothing compared to ours. Look at your hair, your clothes, your knife, and your heart."

Breelyn looked at them all and then gasped. All of these were almost totally black now. "No," she said. "What have you done to me?"

She reached out with her magic. But before she could do anything, the General flashed his hands in the air, and a thick, black fog enveloped Breelyn, choking off her powers. She gasped for air and then crumpled to the floor.

The General leaned over her and said, "You can fight me and lose all your powers, girl. Or join with me and save your precious king. I might even be benevolent enough to allow him to continue to rule Elvyn under me. We will need good administrators to do our bidding."

Breelyn lay on the floor, her powers totally gone, her bond with her dragon only barely there, in the back of her mind. All she could feel was the power in the obsidian knife. She could throw it at the General, kill him right now, and be freed from his evil plans. But what would happen to Lan? Lan meant more to Breelyn than her own life, and the king of Elvyn meant more to their people than one of his protectors.

She lifted her head off the floor, tears streaming down her face, and said, "You will save Lan? You promise?"

The General kneeled down in front of Breelyn and brought his hands out in front of him, grabbing a hold of hers with a soft touch. He stared into her eyes, golden flames dancing around within his own.

"If you join me, Breelyn Mier, dragon rider and Elvyn protector, I will spare your land from the destruction that is to come, and your king, Lanwaithian, will rule for a long, long time."

As Breelyn came up onto her knees, still holding the General's hands, her soul broke, but her tears stopped.

"I will do it," she said. With these words, power flooded back into her. Not the power she had been born with or the power of the dragon bond but a dark, awesome, destructive power—the power of hate.

The General stood and smiled. Tuning back toward the throne room doors, he began walking away, the click of his boots fading down the long room. As he put his hand on the doors, he turned back to Breelyn and said, "We will speak again tomorrow, for we have much to do. I need to let my brothers know."

With that, he exited the room, and then Breelyn crashed to the floor. "Oh, Bakari, my Dragon King," she whispered. "What have I done?"

Just then Breelyn heard a loud, wailing roar from outside the castle walls. She knew who it was, but she couldn't sense her dragon inside of her anymore. She only prayed that Miriel would leave her alone here and return to safety. Eventually, Breelyn closed her eyes and fell asleep on the cold throne room floor.

CHAPTER SEVENTEEN

Roland didn't know how much time had passed since his body had collapsed. Sometimes he was conscious, and other times, not. His soul or spirit floated in another realm—next to or in or around the stream of magic. He couldn't tell for sure. He glanced down and studied his own appearance, holding out his arm in front of himself. He still wore his golden cloak, and his flesh seemed solid enough, although it glowed and was slightly—ever so slightly—translucent.

He ran his hand down over his chest and stomach and back up again. He *felt* solid. It wasn't as if he could move his hand through his body. He jumped up a little and floated a bit higher than usual before alighting back down to the ground with a soft landing.

Where am I? he thought to himself, but his thought carried outside of himself, echoing off of some unseen walls. Looking around himself, Roland squinted and tried to determine what he was seeing. A dark gray mist obscured his vision. But, as he walked, spots of light flashed around him at times.

"Hello?" he called out, not really expecting an answer but deciding that he needed to do something.

He thought back to what had happened at the Citadel. The wizards from Quentis were nothing but pawns of the real darkness—The Chameleon and his brothers. But someone else crept through the realm of magic also. A greater evil than even the three of them. As Roland had lain hidden, he had felt that evil presence lurking around and searching for him. So far, Roland had stayed unnoticed.

As Roland walked forward, another gleam of light flashed closer to him. With hardly a thought, he reached out to it and grabbed hold. Light flared up inside him and encompassed him, shutting the darkness away for a moment.

Whether only in his mind or actually in his spirit, Roland was suddenly transported someplace else. Looking around himself, he tried to figure out where he was now—a cobblestone courtyard, with palms and other large, leafy plants standing in groupings around its edges. Tall, white walls with opened windows surrounded the courtyard. The slight scent of an ocean breeze tickled Roland's nose.

Looking around, he saw two people, who seemed to be fighting at the far end of the space. Without actually stepping forward, he moved closer. He arched his eyebrows in surprise.

"Alli!" he said out loud, but neither Alli nor the man she fought seemed to hear him. Roland watched for a moment and then realized that the two were only sparring. But he was mesmerized by their forms.

Alli, as usual, danced gracefully around her opponent—a man with an olive complexion and dark hair. The man's eyes held Alli in his gaze, and a smile of joy filled his face.

A low growl erupted from Roland's throat. Who was this man?

Alli laughed and lunged underneath a sword stroke, then somersaulted across the cobblestones past the man's feet.

Coming up behind him, she knocked his head with the hilt of her sword.

Roland smiled. He wished she had hit the man harder.

With one swift motion, the man turned and grabbed Alli's arm, pulling her in closer. As he stared into Alli's eyes, Alli froze for a moment in his gaze. Then, slipping a leg around hers, the man brought Alli to the ground. A grunt of frustration came from Alli. But it was not like her to be taken in so easily. The man was distracting her.

Alli stood up, her back a few feet from one of the walls. The man smiled, and Roland frowned again. It was not fair for someone to look so good. The man walked steadily and slowly toward Alli.

Alli could be infuriating, he knew, but, over the past six months, he had developed a deep friendship—if not something more—with the young Battlemaster. She was fierce in battle, but sensitive to a fault to those that needed her help.

Roland could see Alli's chest heaving with exertion, and he wondered if she would be taken in again. But a last-minute glimmer in her eye told him otherwise. A glimmer that he had seen many times.

At that moment, her nose wrinkled up slightly, another sign that Roland had learned to love. It meant she was having fun but was about to finish things off.

"Ready to end this, Kas?" she asked.

The man laughed, deeply and full of joy. "You are yielding to me, Alli?"

Now it was time for Alli to laugh. She jumped into the air and landed on the edge of a huge fern pot, balancing on the toes of her right foot. Then she leaped to the side, taking two steps along the wall, and jumped again, somersaulting in the air, to land behind the man she had called Kas. She reached around him with bare her hands and grabbed his sword from his hand. Spinning him around to face her, she brought her sword up to his neck and held it tight.

Roland smiled, for the man appeared to be in fear of his life.

"Yield?" Alli's eyes twinkled with amusement.

The man submitted. So Alli pushed him back playfully and lowered her sword arm.

"I don't know how you did it," the man said. "No one beats me like that."

"And I didn't even use my magic."

Kas laughed. "Mercy, Alli. You are a dangerous woman indeed."

"Only if you oppose me." Alli grew serious. "Now, I need to leave."

"Leave?" Kas walked closer to Alli. "Leave where?"

"You father wants to see me," she said.

"My father?" Kas furrowed his dark brows. "Why would he want to do that?"

Alli smiled again and shrugged her shoulders. "You'll have to ask him." She gave Kas a short bow and said, "Thanks for the exercise, Your Highness."

Your Highness? Roland thought. The last that he knew, Alli was in Quentis. Who was this Kas?

Then the scene started to fade around him.

"Alli!" Roland called out. "Alli!"

Alli cocked her head to one side and turned around as if she had heard him, but then she shrugged her shoulders, and the scene faded away.

Roland stood once again in the darkness, the flash of light floating away from him.

Seeing another light flash in front of him, Roland reached out for it. This one didn't flash as brightly as the last one. But the same thing happened as before. The darkness faded away, and he stood once more in the light. He instantly knew where he was—the throne room in Cassian.

Roland had lived there for two years, prior to coming back to the Citadel. He had trained in Cassian as a counselor apprentice wizard. He smiled at the familiar surroundings. Mericus, king for the last few months, had changed very little, only there was now an actual throne in the room—one that hadn't been there when the Chief Judge had ruled Alaris—a throne that Mericus now sat on.

Suddenly, Roland figured it out. The flashes of light in the darkness must be wizards. The brighter the light, the more powerful the wizard. A few thoughts came to him at once. He could find Tam and see what was happening in the Citadel or search for Bakari and ask for his help—again. Roland frowned a bit at that. He had always been so much more powerful than his timid scholar wizard friend, who was now a dragon rider. But Roland had seemed to need his friend's help more often than the other way around these days.

He walked around the throne room of Cassian a bit more, watching Mericus deal with a trade delegation from Tillimot. The sea-based nation had plenty of new types of food to sell to their northern neighbors. Since the barrier around Alaris had fallen, many of the neighboring nations were clamoring for new trade provisions—an opportunity for many merchants to become rich through trade.

Roland willed himself back out of the vision, and soon he stood again in the darkness of the magic stream. He was beginning to learn the rules of this place. His thoughts ruled here.

So he thought about the Citadel, and he traveled once again without moving his feet. Dozens of lights flashed around him. That made sense, since the Citadel housed many wizards and apprentices at any time.

Now to find the right light, he thought as he reached his mind out.

Opening his mind, Roland felt the different magical signatures of each of his wizards and apprentices. Finally, he focused on Tam: a young wizard that had served him well.

Tam's light came to Roland, and he grabbed it. As before, he was pulled into the light and found himself in a room that was dimly lit. Glancing around, Roland almost jumped. this was his room. His own bedroom in the Citadel. Tam stood before him in the dark.

What was Tam doing in his room? Was Tam moving in already, with Roland barely gone?

A woman opened the door and walked in. It was Selena, a promising scholar apprentice. Tam looked up at her, and Roland noticed the bags under his friend's eyes.

"How is he?" the woman asked in sympathy.

Tam motioned Selena to join him, and they walked over to Roland's bed. Roland followed them, curious as to what they were doing in his room. Then he followed Tam's gaze to the bed.

"Whoa!" Roland said out loud, for he stood staring down at his own body, lying still on his comfortable bed. A warm quilt was pulled up to his chin, and his head sat on a fluffy pillow—his favorite one. A small tube sat over his mouth, attached to an accordion-like box that was pumping up and down.

Roland shook his head back and forth. *This is freaky!* He didn't want to see himself lying there like that. *Am I really dead?*

"Tam?" Roland yelled at the wizard. "What is this?"

Tam brought his head up and glanced around. "Did you hear something?"

"No." Selena appeared concerned. "You stay here too long, Tam. You need rest." She put a hand tenderly on his arm.

"I can't leave him, Selena. What if he wakes up?" Tam reached over and touched the apparatus next to Roland's body. "What if this stops working? It's all that's keeping him alive."

"Others can watch over him. The council needs you," Selena said. "I have heard that some of the older wizards are already trying to take power for themselves."

Roland grunted. *Figures.* Wizards were drawn to power. And Roland's absence had left a power vacuum to fill.

Tam just shook his head. "What will Alli do to me if Roland dies while she is gone?"

Selena smiled. "You may be right. I wouldn't want to face that. She is fiercely loyal to him."

Roland frowned, remembering the recent scene of Alli fighting—and maybe flirting—with the beautiful man in Quentis. Was Alli thoroughly loyal to Roland and the Citadel? His heart hoped so.

Selena gave Tam a small peck on the cheek, and Tam blushed.

Roland grinned. When had that happened? Were these two now an item?

Selena closed the door behind her as she left, and Tam stood in front of Roland's body again.

"Roland, High Wizard, are you still alive somewhere in there?" Tam asked.

"I'm here, Tam," Roland said.

But Tam did not react.

So Roland reached out tentatively to touch his own body. He wondered if he could. Slowly, he moved forward and ran his fingers over the top of his own head. When he did, a small light flared up around the body lying on the bed.

Tam jumped back. "What was that?" he said. "Roland, is that you?"

Roland smiled. Maybe he could get back into his body again. He took his own head on the pillow and held it between his two spiritual hands. Light flared up again, and he felt a connection.

"Tam," he said to the wizard.

Tam considered Roland's face. "Are you really there?" Tam asked. Then a big grin spread across his face. "I knew you weren't gone. You are too powerful—or maybe just too stubborn for that."

At that moment, Roland felt a darkness move across the scene. He was being pulled back.

"No!" Roland screamed.

He stood halfway between the two worlds, and a deep voice called out to him, saying, "Roland Tyre, come to me!"

The voice was powerful and deep, but the power it held was almost overwhelming. He felt his spirit-self wanting to move away back into the darkness. But he kept his hands on his physical head to maintain contact with the real world.

"You cannot hide forever," the deep voice said again.

"Who are you?" Roland called out.

"I think you know who I am."

Roland wasn't sure how it all worked. But the wizards from Quentis had talked about the father of the Chameleon. Was this him? Could Roland withstand his power? He realized that, as long as he kept his hands on his physical head, he must be hidden from the evil man.

"I already have Breelyn," the voice said, and Roland's hold on the physical world slipped. "And soon I will have Bakari and Jaimon. With the dragon riders on my side, nothing can stop me from coming back into the world."

The voice hadn't mentioned Alli. For that, Roland was thankful. Also, Roland knew that there were other powerful wizards in each of the lands. He had felt them. And, wasn't Bakari going to find another dragon rider?

Roland decided that he would have to fight this evil man himself—holding him off—until the others succeeded. That was his duty. He would have to wait for his body awhile longer.

Roland grabbed his physical head once again and pressed his hands to it with force, saying, "Tam, keep my body alive. I will return." He heard his voice come out in his bedroom as only a soft whisper.

Tam gasped and said, "I will, Roland. I will." The man had tears in his eyes.

Then Roland let go of the physical world and felt himself rushing back into the darkness.

"Aaah, there you are," the deep, dark voice said as it came closer through the darkness.

Rather than a flash of light, Roland now saw a dark spot, darker than anything else he had ever seen. It absorbed all the light around it. But Roland stood his ground and pulled all the magic at his disposal into himself. Then he reached his mind out to find the lights and pulled power from each one of them, for he had to hold off this evil.

Out of the darkness swirled a man, taller and broader than Roland, dressed all in black. The man's face was shadowed, and tendrils of black power snaked around him and reached toward Roland.

"High Wizard," the man said as he nodded his head, "we meet at last in person." This statement was followed by a mad laugh. "Well, at least, as much *in person* as this place affords us."

Roland could hardly move. The slime of evil power flowing off of the man was the hardest thing Roland had ever borne. The days Roland had spent locked in the room below the Citadel were easy compared to this. But there was one thing that Roland had now that he didn't have then. His magic.

"I am Rodric Ekhart, the rightful wizard king, the last true king of Alaris," the voice boomed. "And the Sentinel, the Chameleon, and the General are my children. They are preparing the world for my return."

Roland shivered and pulled in more power. In this magic realm, there was no limit to what power he could hold. Each speck of light that his mind touched gave him power—he instinctively knew who each one was, and he took from them what he needed now. Roland hoped they didn't mind. There was Bakari, Alli, Tam, Mericus, King Darius of the Realm, Emperor Alrishitar from Gildan, and High Wizard Danijela Anwar of the Wizard Conclave in Arc. He had pulled from all of them and from so many more—all his wizards and apprentices at the Citadel. Then Roland felt Breelyn and lost his concentration for a moment.

Her magic is dark now. He pushed this thought to the back of his mind. A problem for another day.

Roland began to glow in the darkness, his magic spreading out from his body.

Rodric put his hand up to block his eyes, "It's not possible," the wizard king said. "You can't be that strong here. It's just not possible."

"Well, I am!" Roland pushed out his power toward the darkness, illuminating the area around himself.

"No!" Rodric yelled and pushed back at Roland.

Roland's brightness dimmed momentarily, but he pulled more power into himself. Then voices came to him—of wizards that he had pulled from—warning him, pleading with him to not take any more. And Roland realized that he had now reached a limit. To take more power would hurt his friends. His current power wasn't strong enough to vanquish the darkness, but maybe it would be enough to buy some time.

Rodric screamed in a low wail and said, "How can you be this strong?"

Roland smiled and pushed all the power he held toward the dark apparition. As it hit the ancient wizard king, the man howled with an eerie, nonhuman sound that tore into Roland's being. Roland pushed harder, and the darkness began to recede. It faded back into the single point of darkness, getting smaller and smaller.

Now, in answer to the man's question, Roland cried out, "Because I AM MAGIC!" And, with that, Roland threw the last ounce of his magic at Rodric, and the black point blinked out.

Roland sank to his knees, all his magic depleted. He scooted backward, trying to get farther away, but he knew that physical location had no meaning here. He stopped moving and reached back into his mind. His magic had all been exhausted. He hoped it would be enough for now.

Reaching farther into his mind, Roland saw a small spark, and he smiled. His magic wasn't altogether gone—because he was magic.

CHAPTER EIGHTEEN

After surviving the ordeal out at sea, Bakari needed a day of rest to recover. Governor El'Han had bidden him farewell earlier that day, with the reiterated promise of getting King Darius to help. Bakari was sad to see the governor leave. He had been a good friend.

Now Bakari sat across from Breanna and Liam at a corner table in the library at the White Island Wizard School. The twins had been gracious enough to give him a tour of the facilities earlier that day. Then Bakari had requested to meet with the headmaster, but the twins had not been able to discern his whereabouts.

Liam furrowed his dark brows in concern as he said, "Headmaster Penrose has been gone a lot lately." He looked over at Breanna, and Bakari noticed her shaking her head at Liam.

"What, Breanna? It's true. Something is going on here," Liam said.

"Nothing is going on, Liam." Breanna tossed her long, brown hair to one side. "Don't bother Bakari with your delusions."

"Was that thief stealing books imagined? Or, were those missing Cremelinos imagined, Breanna?" Liam's face was red.

Turning to Bakari, Liam continued, "No one takes me seriously. Just because…because…"

Breanna put her hand on Liam's shoulder, and he stopped trying to speak.

"I am sorry, Liam," Breanna said. "I didn't mean to upset you. I know you see things that some of us don't see. It's just…we have known Headmaster Penrose our entire life. He's a good man."

Liam took a deep breath and then said, "He is a good man, and that's the point. He has not been acting like himself lately."

"I wonder if it could be him," Bakari wondered out loud, his mind racing with the possibilities.

"Who?" Breanna asked.

Bakari glanced carefully around the library, wondering how much he should tell them. His eyes lingered on the tomes longingly. It was quite a collection, almost as big as the Citadel's. But the Realm had not been closed off from the rest of the world for the last one hundred and fifty years, so Bakari was anxious to look through them.

"I'm on a quest," Bakari began. "There is a dark magic in the southern kingdoms that we need to find out how to combat. A man called the Chameleon takes on the appearances of others and has caused trouble in multiple kingdoms. Just last week, the Chameleon hurt the new king of Elvyn and took our magic away for a time."

Bakari stopped short of mentioning his own need to find the new dragon and its rider. He had the impression that he was looking across the table at the rider himself.

Liam leaned back in his chair and blew out a long breath as he turned to his sister, as if to say, *I told you so.*

Breanna smiled and shook her head. "All right, Liam. You win again. Tell him what you have seen."

Liam opened his mouth to speak. But something strong intruded upon Bakari's thoughts. His mind was immediately seized by something not of his own doing. He grabbed his head and moaned softly.

Breanna reached across the table, placing her hand on Bakari's arm.

"Bakari, what is it?"

"My head. Someone is trying to pull power from me." Bakari opened his eyes in a squint and glanced up.

"I'm going to look around," Breanna said and was instantly on her feet looking around the room.

Liam was just as alert as Breanna, but he stayed seated. Then he mumbled under his breath, "I guess I'll stay here and keep an eye on our new friend."

Even in Bakari's painful state, he could feel Liam's sadness at not being physically able to join his sister. Earlier, on their way around the school compound, Liam had ridden around on his Cremelino so as not to slow them down with his lame foot. And, inside the buildings, he had used a crutch to help himself along.

A new wave of pain crashed into Bakari and sent his body slumping back in his chair. Someone was pulling more power from him. How was that possible? Bakari closed his eyes and drew more power to himself—but the more he pulled in, the more that was taken away from him.

Bakari heard Liam yell out. He tried to make sense of things, but his mind began to grow fuzzy, and he couldn't think clearly. Putting all his efforts into it, Bakari tried to push himself deeper into the stream of magic. Finally, he was there, in the dark. Far ahead was a bright golden light standing in front of a dark presence.

It was Roland. What was he doing?

Bakari's body began to shake. His magic was leaving him at an alarming rate—being sucked out of him and toward Roland. He tried to breathe, but even that was hard.

Roland, stop! You're going to kill me.

A brief lightening of the drain helped Bakari to be able to concentrate once again. With a sudden flash, he felt the presence of Jaimon, the youngest dragon rider. Jaimon was far to the south. Another brief flash, and he saw Alli in a room he did not recognize. As the head of the dragon riders, Bakari had a special connection to the riders, but Alli was strong, and her presence always showed up in the stream of magic also. Bakari didn't know what that meant.

Roland. No more! he yelled out in his mind, and he saw the bright light of Roland flood out and engulf the blackness in front of him.

As soon as that had ended, Bakari felt a small bit of his strength return. With his physical eyes still closed, he looked around the magic stream. Maybe he could find Abylar. Bakari was so exhausted, but he pushed on anyway. He tried looking west, the last place he had felt his dragon. And he thought he felt a brief spark of the bond.

Abylar!

Dragon Rider! said the familiar voice in his mind. *Help me!*

Bakari felt the pain from the pull to help Abylar, but before he could do anything else, he was swept farther south and away from his dragon.

No! he yelled in the darkness.

"Bakari!" Liam said, trying to wake him.

Bakari tried to open his eyes, but his power was still so weak that he couldn't seem to escape the darkness, so he just flowed along with wherever it was that had taken him.

Seeing that a small spark of light stood in front of him, Bakari instinctively reached for it. It had a familiarity. Without warning, he found himself inside an ornate bedroom. Looking around, he gasped as he saw the back of a woman's head.

I shouldn't be in a woman's room! Bakari thought to himself.

The woman was standing in front of a tall mirror, but her body blocked Bakari's view of her face. She was almost as tall as him, with mostly black hair—only a small spot of blond sat on top. Her dress, too, was black on the bottom and up one arm, with the rest a dull white that continued to darken further, right before his eyes.

Bakari felt something familiar from the woman. He knew he shouldn't be in her room, but he took a step to the right to see her face more clearly in the mirror.

Breelyn! he gasped. No, it couldn't be.

The woman tilted her head to one side and turned around, as if hearing Bakari's voice. Her once beautiful and flawless face now held a dull and stern look, and her blues eyes were now black and hard.

Oh, Breelyn! Bakari stepped up and tried to touch her arm. He couldn't connect with anything solid, but a blackness flared up around her as he grew near.

Breelyn's eyes refocused for a small moment, and a flash of blue ran across the black.

"Bakari?" she asked, her voice almost a whisper, pleading.

Before Bakari could do anything more, a man walked into the room without knocking. The man's eyes sent a shiver down Bakari's spine, and he stepped backward.

"Are you ready, my dear?" the man asked, his voice deep and commanding. "Ready to gather our army?"

"Yes, General." She nodded and began following the man out of the room. With one hand still on the edge of the doorframe, she turned back. A lone tear dripped down her face.

Bak? she whispered so soft that Bakari hardly heard it before the door closed.

He willed himself out of the scene and stood once more in the darkness of the stream of magic. He tried to find his way back to his body. But, after walking aimlessly for who knows how long, he stopped and dropped to the ground. He was so weak.

"Bakari!" called a faint voice.

Bakari brought his head up. Who had called him?

"Bakari?" the voice called again.

It was Liam. He was sure of it. So Bakari stood back up with renewed hope. A light grew brighter in front of him, and he walked toward it. In the brightness, he saw the outline of Liam, who stood before Bakari with a look of surprise on his face. Liam reached his hand out toward Bakari's. When their hands touched, Bakari felt a mental connection with the young man, feeling and knowing all that Liam felt and knew. The transfer of information happened in mere moments.

Then, suddenly, Bakari was back in his body again. He opened his eyes. He was lying on the floor of the library, next to the table they had been sitting at. Breanna had a look of concern, and Liam just stared at him with astonishment in his eyes. Then Bakari motioned for them to help him sit up.

As Breanna helped him back up, she said, "Are you all right?"

Bakari sat up and leaned his head against the wall to gather his wits. "I'm fine now. Just weak."

"I couldn't find anything in the library causing problems," Breanna said.

Bakari grimaced. "I know. It wasn't here. It was my friend Roland, pulling power from me."

"Some friend," Liam said, still staring intently at Bakari.

"He had a good reason, but still—not much control." Bakari moved to stand up, and Breanna and Liam helped him to his feet and back onto the chair.

Everyone sat quietly for a moment, allowing Bakari to collect himself. He still felt incredibly weak. He could barely hold his eyes open. Almost all of his magic had been drained from him, and then his vision of Breelyn had hurt him deeply.

Oh, Breelyn! What happened?

He glanced up at Breanna and Liam. Liam was staring at him with questioning eyes. Bakari smiled as he realized that whatever connection Bakari had made with Liam upon their contact—all the knowledge and feelings he had felt from

Liam—the same must have happened in reverse. He wondered how much Liam had learned before their connection was severed. Bakari had been taught to shield his thoughts from others at an early age. Without Liam's help, though, Bakari didn't know whether he could have escaped the magic stream or not.

"Thank you, Liam," Bakari said. "That was amazing. I didn't know you had that much power."

"Me either." Liam smiled. "I just kept going deeper. I guess, since we are both wizards of the mind, we connected easier."

That made sense to Bakari, but he supposed there was another link also.

"Is it true?" Liam asked, looking intently at Bakari.

"Is what true?" Breanna said. "What do you mean, Liam?"

Liam ignored his sister and asked Bakari again, "Are you a dragon rider?"

Breanna gasped and covered her mouth.

Bakari felt he could trust these two, and he needed their help, so he said, "I am not only a dragon rider, I am the Dragon King."

CHAPTER NINETEEN

The next morning, Bakari sat up in bed in the private room he had been given. He supposed that, for Liam and Breanna, being the children of the king afforded them some privileges. Though, judging by their personalities, Bakari guessed that they didn't push it very often. He eyed a table by the wall with a full platter of food on it. The mixed scents of breads and sausage wafted by his nose, and he found his stomach grumbling.

Bakari took stock of himself and discovered that he felt refreshed from the second ordeal in as many days. Being drawn into the magic stream by Roland had brought more questions than answers: What kind of trouble was the High Wizard in? What had happened to Breelyn? And was Abylar all right? The questions seemed endless, but the answers were even more elusive.

Getting out of bed, Bakari walked over to the platter of food and grabbed a few sausages, popping them into his mouth. They were still warm, but not hot, and tasted delicious. He poured himself a glass of a sweet-smelling juice and grabbed a few slices of a bread smothered in frosting.

Looking down, he noticed that he was in different clothes. He hadn't remembered changing. He blushed, wondering who had changed his clothes.

A few minutes later, Liam knocked on the door before poking his head into the room.

"Good. I see you are awake," Liam said as he limped in, holding a cane at his side.

"Thank you for providing all of this. How can I repay you?"

"No need for that. Rank does hold a few privileges." Liam smiled. "Speaking of rank…"

Bakari knew what Liam was referring to. He supposed Liam had a multitude of questions regarding Bakari declaring himself the Dragon King. He knew that Liam had seen into his mind, but he didn't know how much Liam had seen. Too much knowledge too quickly could be overwhelming.

Ignoring Liam's implied questions for now, Bakari implied one of his own: "You were about to tell us about the headmaster yesterday. You seemed to have reservations about his recent actions."

Liam scowled for a moment, as if knowing that his questions were being brushed aside. But Liam had received enough training, Bakari guessed, to be diplomatic about it. Much more training than Bakari had ever received about court etiquette.

Liam limped back out into the hallway and looked right and then left. Then he crooked his finger at Bakari and said, "Come with me."

Bakari grabbed a blue cloak that was lying on a chair by the door. The color reminded him of Abylar. He took a deep breath and calmed his mind, then followed Liam down the hall.

At the end of the corridor, they turned and soon came to a significant-sized gathering room.

"See?" Liam said quietly.

People—mostly young men and young women—stood around in small groups. The room itself held groupings of chairs and tables. And a few shelves of books stood off to one side. Everything here appeared to be in order to Bakari.

"I don't understand." Bakari furrowed his eyebrows as he spoke.

"This room is the main gathering place for the university," Liam said. "It is usually full of people and laughter. It's where all the flirting, visiting, and bragging occur."

"But it's so quiet," Bakari observed.

"Students have been disappearing," Liam said. "And those that are left seem to walk around with distrust of others."

Bakari nodded and took in the room once again. He spied two men in dark robes walking around at the far side of the room. Reaching out his senses, Bakari gasped and took a step back, behind a pillar.

"You felt them, didn't you?" Liam asked.

Their magical signatures seemed to be in line with what he had felt from Breelyn the previous day. It was the same thing that he had felt from the Chameleon.

But how could that man be here?

"Who are they?" Bakari asked Liam.

"They showed up about two weeks ago—at about the same time that our headmaster disappeared for a while. When he reemerged from his supposed sickness last week, these two were his right-hand men. That is when wizards began to disappear." Liam pulled Bakari back out of the room and then added, "I have tried to ask about the missing wizards, but all I have been told is that they are *needed elsewhere*."

"Have you told your father?"

Liam hung his head low. "No. I wanted to figure it out myself."

Bakari felt bad for Liam. He was sure Liam's physical deformity had made growing up more difficult.

"I did tell Breanna," Liam said. "But she didn't believe me."

"Where is your sister?" Bakari asked as the two of them continued walking down a long hallway.

Liam stopped. A look of horror covered his face. "I haven't seen her since last night. Usually, she meets me for breakfast, but there was a note saying that she had an errand to run this morning. What if she was taken?"

"I'm sure she is fine," Bakari said.

Liam began to hobble forward faster. "I can find out."

Bakari gave Liam a questioning look.

Soon they came to a different part of the wing. It looked like more of a dormitory. Then Liam directed Bakari into a room.

"My room." This was the only explanation Liam offered as they walked through the doorway. Liam sat down on his bed and looked up at Bakari. Liam's eyes looked afraid, and his chin trembled. "I can reach out to her with my magic."

"Like you did to me?" Bakari asked.

"No, no. That was the first time that has ever happened to me." Liam said, rushing his words. "Through the Cremelinos, we have been able to communicate with each other since we were born."

Liam closed his eyes, and Bakari stood watching him. Liam's face scrunched up as he tried to concentrate. Mere moments later, Liam opened up his eyes, and tears formed around the edges of them.

"She is west of here," Liam said. "She must have been taken to the mainland. Who would do that? Who would take Breanna?" Liam stood back up from the edge of his bed and, taking a step, tripped on his lame foot and almost fell down. Bakari managed to grab him at the last possible instant.

"Stupid foot!" Liam screamed. "That's probably why they don't want me too—I'm broken."

Bakari's heart went out to the young man. What could he do to help Liam? At the same time, a flare of magic rose up in Bakari. *The new dragon!* He felt the pull for the first time in a while. It was farther north, but it was getting close to the time of its emergence. And he now knew, more than ever, who needed to be the next dragon rider. He was looking right at him.

"What?" Liam said defensively. "You think I'm a freak too, don't you?"

Bakari shook his head. "Oh, no, Liam. Quite the opposite." He couldn't tell Liam yet, and, obviously, Liam hadn't seem this in Bakari's mind either. He couldn't tell riders ahead of time because it was always the dragon's decision—he would have to wait.

"Whatever," Liam said. "I need to find my sister."

Bakari was torn—he also needed to get to the dragon egg. "I want to help, but..."

Liam started to hobble away. "Don't worry about me. I can do it myself."

"Liam," Bakari said as he tried to call Liam back.

Just then, a guard came down the hall and stopped in front of Liam.

"Sir," the guard said as he bowed. "Headmaster Penrose would like a word with you."

Liam's previous frustration turned into fear. He turned toward Bakari.

"I will go with you," Bakari said firmly.

The guard looked at Liam's guest and shrugged his shoulders. Then he motioned them down the hall, toward the headmaster's office.

Before entering the office, Liam whispered to Bakari, "Be ready!"

Bakari nodded. He didn't know whether Liam was over exaggerating things or not. The young man did seem to get frustrated easily, and his mood shifts were worse than those of anyone Bakari had ever met. But Bakari still readied himself with his powers.

CHAPTER TWENTY

When Bakari had followed Liam and the guard into the headmaster's office, the room had appeared darker than it should have been in these morning hours. Heavy, red drapes covered the windows, and only a few candles were lit in the sizable room. A sturdy desk sat in front of a bookcase on one side. A fireplace was lit on the other side, in front of which sat a leather couch and three chairs, grouped around a low maple table. And upon the couch lay a man.

They were ushered over to the headmaster, and then the guard removed himself from the room. Without words, the headmaster motioned for the two of them to seat themselves. Bakari regarded this man, who was supposed to be headmaster of a wizard school. He didn't look well. He looked like he used to be bigger. Flesh sagged around his face, and his hair was thinning. He had a thick blanket over his body, but Bakari could tell that it too was most likely too thin. *This* was the headmaster of a university of magic? Something indeed had happened.

"Liam," the headmaster croaked. "Who is our guest here?"

"This is Bakari," Liam said carefully. He sat on the edge of his seat, his eyes darting around the room. "Bakari is a wizard from the southern kingdoms."

The headmaster opened his eyes wider.

"From Alaris, sir," Bakari explained. "Well, I grew up in Alaris, but my heritage is Mahlian."

"Aaaah," the headmaster whispered. "The famous Alaris barrier. We wizards have been trying to figure that one out for a long time. Tell me, young man, how did it come down?"

Bakari was saved from answering this by an interruption from Liam.

"Headmaster Penrose, can you tell me where my sister is and where all the wizards have gone?"

The headmaster's eyes flashed brighter momentarily, then he closed them, grabbing his head with one of his hands as a painful groan escaped his thinning lips.

"What is wrong, sir?" Bakari asked.

The headmaster's eyes grew clearer for a moment. Turning back to Liam, he said, "Now, I may only have a few minutes, Prince, but you must listen."

The two of them leaned closer.

"Things are not good here," he admitted.

Liam looked at Bakari as if to say, *I told you so*, but he only nodded to the headmaster.

The headmaster sat up a little on the couch. "I am not well, as you can see."

"What happened?" Liam put a hand on the headmaster's shoulder.

A knock came at the door, and a guard stuck his head in and said, "Sir, your advisors are here."

Fear crossed the headmaster's face, and his eyes darted around. "Tell them I will be a few minutes." Turning back to

Bakari and Liam, he continued, "I must be quick, before he returns."

"Before who returns?" Liam's eyes flared. "What is going on, Headmaster?"

"A man...a sinister man with dark powers. He takes control of me and does horrible things."

Bakari grew more worried. This seemed different than the Chameleon. The Chameleon took on the visage of someone else but wasn't exactly that person. But Roland had warned Bakari about someone else.

The headmaster's eyes flashed yellow. He grunted and closed his eyes, saying, "He's coming again. I can't stop him. Listen to me." When his eyes opened, they were brown once again. "I have sent your sister and the others away, to be safe. You must trust me."

"Safe from what, sir?" Bakari asked.

"He is trying to take over the school, take power for himself. He wants to control wizards in order to control the Cremelinos." He rushed the information out without pausing. "He wants to rule the kingdom and free someone from the dead." The headmaster shook all over. Then his eyes flared bright yellow once again, and a loud growl escaped his lips.

Bakari stood and walked over to the headmaster. He placed his hand on the man's forehead and dove in with magic. As soon as he had, his hand felt stung, and he brought it back. Then the man's arm fell out of his blankets, and Bakari saw black tendrils snaking up his skin.

"Get back!" Bakari yelled.

Liam stood up and stepped back a few steps.

"Headmaster, come back to me," Bakari said with power in his voice—the authority of the Dragon King. "Shake it off and return."

Headmaster Penrose's eyes rolled around for a moment. Then he blinked and became lucid again. "Run," the headmaster said through clenched teeth. "Run away. Quick."

"We can help you," Bakari offered.

"No. No one can stand against him," the headmaster cried out. "He is too powerful." That last word came out as a roar, so Bakari stepped back. Yellow eyes flashed out at them, and the man began to sit up.

"Who are you?" Bakari asked, ready to strike the man at any moment.

"I am one of three determined to free the one true king."

Liam turned to Bakari, but Bakari shook his head. He didn't know what the man was talking about, but his magic was similar to the Chameleon's.

"You are not the Chameleon." Bakari didn't know how he knew this, but the Chameleon shape-shifted and took on another's look, while this man seemed to have possessed the headmaster instead.

The headmaster was still trying to fight off the possession, but the evil entity was winning. "I am not the Chameleon; I am his brother, the Sentinel, as is the General."

Bakari groaned. He remembered the man he had seen with Breelyn. Bakari and his allies hadn't figured out how to combat their magic yet.

"Liam, we need to do something." Bakari turned to the prince.

The headmaster's eyes flashed yellow again, and his hands came up in front of him. He was now sitting up on the couch, black magic pouring like fog out of his fingers.

"I know you now, Dragon Rider," the headmaster snarled. "I will kill you all, and we have your dragon."

Immediate anger came into Bakari. He reached out and grabbed the collar of the man. "Where is my dragon?"

"Pitiful dragon rider. Can't even find your dragon." The man hacked and coughed and then laughed. "My father watches him."

"Your father?"

"The last true wizard king of Alaris. He is readying himself to return. We will bring him back, and he will rule all the lands on this side of the Blue Sea." The headmaster's eyes lost some of their shine, and he began to slump back down onto the couch.

Bakari had only this one chance. He reached into the headmaster's mind and tried to take control as he had done before, with animals. There was so much darkness there, but a spark of the headmaster still remained.

Bakari grabbed this part—this clean, coherent part—and said, "Headmaster, where did he take my dragon?"

"I don't…" the man mumbled, and he fought against the evil in his mind and against Bakari's control.

"Tell me!" Bakari ordered in the man's mind.

"Bakari, what are you doing?" Liam yelled. "Compulsion is unlawful."

The headmaster's eyes became clear for a moment as he said, "He is in a cave in the Superstition Mountains, close to

Denir, a place of long ago—a place that blends the physical and magical realms."

Then the man's head slumped forward.

"How can I find him?" Bakari said forcefully once again. He grabbed the headmaster's chin and pulled it back up. If there was any hope of finding his dragon again, he must find out how.

"The Cremelinos...the dragons...they can help you reach him. The power to bind." The headmaster fell to the side, and Bakari pulled out of his mind. He reeled with this new information.

The headmaster slumped on his couch, passing out for the moment.

Turning around, Bakari saw a look of horror and shame covering Liam's face.

"I did what I had to do," Bakari said, his voice deep and forceful, brooking no argument. The power of the Dragon King flowed through him. "Sometimes a king must make hard choices."

Liam nodded as if he understood and asked, "Now what?"

A knock on the door interrupted Bakari's answer. Then one of the headmaster's guards poked his head through and said, "The advisors are still waiting."

"The headmaster is tired and resting once again," Liam said. "Please inform his advisors to come back later."

The guard nodded and closed the door.

"That won't satisfy them for long," Liam said.

"We need to leave the island. Quickly!" Bakari said. Turning to Liam, he asked, "How do we do that without being caught?"

Liam thought for a moment and then motioned Bakari to another door in the room. Opening it carefully, they moved inside, shutting it behind them. They found themselves in a narrow walkway.

When Bakari lifted up his eyebrows in question, Liam let out a short laugh.

"My father had this place built," Liam said. "I've been coming here my whole life, off and on. As a young child, I discovered quite a network of hidden passages. Just follow me quietly."

Bakari followed behind Liam's staggered steps. He kept his ears open for sounds of being followed, but nothing out of the ordinary sounded behind them. Fifteen minutes later, they opened another door and emerged into the muted light of day.

"A stable?" Bakari asked, peering around.

"The Cremelino stable," Liam offered in explanation. "I need mine. And Cremelinos are the fastest way to get to the harbor."

As they took a few steps forward, a man in his late twenties or early thirties stepped up to the duo. He was taller and thinner than Bakari but had the look of one who worked hard every day. A beautiful white male Cremelino followed a few steps behind him.

"Prince," the man said as he nodded his head to Liam in respect. "Nice to see you, as always."

"Jakob, could you get my Cremelino for me?" Liam asked. Then, turning to Bakari, he added, "Jakob Widing is the head caretaker of the Cremelino herds for my father. Jakob, this is Bakari. He is from the southern kingdoms."

Jakob bobbed his head in a nod toward Bakari but then spoke to Liam. "Prince, your Cremelino is all ready."

"But…" Liam said.

Jakob smiled with a broad grin. "You know these horses; they have minds of their own."

Liam laughed. "Don't I know it."

Jakob waved his hand toward the white Cremelino and said, "And this one insisted on coming with me today. I suppose he is for your friend here."

Bakari opened his eyes in surprise and was about to ask how the caretaker knew, when a voice came into his mind.

I am here for you, Wizard.

"Amazing!" Bakari said out loud.

Liam motioned Bakari toward the horse and said, "He spoke to you, didn't he, sir?"

Bakari nodded. "As has Crystal, Breanna's Cremelino."

"I remember my first time, as a young kid. It still is amazing," Jakob said. "I am blessed to be the head caretaker, as were my fathers before me."

"It's softer than a dragon, but similar," Bakari said before he realized what he was saying.

"Dragons?" Jakob said, his eyes as wide as saucers.

Bakari looked from Jakob to Liam and back to Jakob. "I am a dragon rider."

"Mercy." Jakob put his hands up to his head. Turning back to Liam, Jakob said, "I suppose you have quite an adventure ahead of you, then. I remember those days with your father."

Just then, Liam's Cremelino came up to them.

"His name is Liberty," Liam said before mounting.

Bakari had read about the fabled Cremelinos in an old book in the Citadel, when he was but ten years old. The information was scanty, but he did know that a Cremelino had to choose its rider, similar to the dragons.

The Cremelino that Jakob had brought out went down on his forelegs, in what could only be called *a bow.*

You honor us, Dragon King. You may ride on me.

"I've never seen them do that before!" Jakob exclaimed to Liam. "It's almost like he is bowing to him."

Liam smiled. "They are, Jakob. They are."

Bakari put his hand forward and stroked the nose of the spectacular horse. Then he climbed on his back.

The horse stood up and neighed loudly. *Hail the king!* he proclaimed in Liam's and Bakari's minds.

Liam's horse neighed also, and a look of surprise came into Liam's eyes.

"Hail the king," Liam whispered.

Jakob looked startled.

So Bakari reached a hand over and patted the man's shoulder. "Caretaker, you do a great thing here in caring for these magical animals. I appreciate your discretion in this matter."

Jakob seemed a little confused but, with a glance to Liam, nodded his head. "Of course. If the Cremelino chose you, then

I am the one who is honored to meet you, sir." He gave Bakari a long, low bow.

"Did he bond with you?" Liam asked Bakari.

Bakari shook his head. "Not a full bonding—no. But we can communicate." Bakari felt the presence of the Cremelino in his mind.

What is your name, mighty Cremelino? Bakari asked.

You tell me, the horse said with a hint of humor.

Bakari thought, then said out loud as he hopped up on the horse, "Flash. I will call you Flash, as we need to get somewhere very quickly."

With that, Liam and Bakari, on the two Cremelinos, began to trot, then gallop, then run. Bakari was amazed at the horses' speed. The ground flew by in a blur underneath them. They were five times as fast as the quickest horse he had ever ridden. The Cremelinos' strong legs burned across a field of late spring grass, then sped into a small forest of trees, taking a small, winding path.

Liam seemed to know where they were going, so Bakari just let his horse follow. Soon they turned right and came out a few dozen feet above the sea again. Looking down, he saw a small town with ships anchored in its bay. Liam pointed to a narrow path down the cliff, and the Cremelinos took it—surely and swiftly.

Coming up to the harbor, Liam carefully dismounted , took a small cane from his pack, and walked stiffly toward a small ship. Taking a few minutes to speak to a man beside the ship, Liam then motioned Bakari forward.

"This ship will take us to Mar," Liam said.

Bakari was amazed how quickly they had secured passage.

Liam must have guessed his question, for he said, "It does help to be the son of the king."

Bakari smiled. It was easy to forget sometimes that Liam was royalty. Liam didn't fit the pompous molds Bakari had read about within royalty.

It took the rest of the morning for the captain to gather his crew, who were enjoying a day of rest in the small town. And, just as the ship's sails rose and they began to move away from shore, the headmaster's advisors appeared on the dock.

As Bakari stood at the back of the ship, looking at them, one stuck his hand out, and a tendril of blackness snaked its way toward the ship. Bakari reached out with his own power, but a brighter light came to his mind.

Pull back, Wizard. It was the Cremelino, Flash. *Your wizard power will not work on them… I will take care of it.*

Bakari watched as a bright light emerged from the ship and headed out over the water, colliding with the dark tendrils. A flash occurred, and he watched as one of the advisors fell to the dock. Then their ship picked up speed as it moved out of the bay.

Moving around to the front of the ship, Bakari could already see the mainland of the Realm. They would be in Mar soon. He felt a tug in his mind once again, pulling them north.

CHAPTER TWENTY ONE

As Alli left the city and entered the tunnel back to the Sanctuary, she tried not to think of all the seawater above her. She proceeded then to the back of the complex where she and Jaimon were staying on the Sanctuary grounds—protected by the Followers of the Dragon. Alli rolled her eyes a bit, thinking of the group. Low-level wizards, most of them, with a fanaticism about dragons that made Alli doubt their sanity at times.

After giving a specific knock on the door, she was let into a dim room. She walked down a maze of hallways, in a part of the Sanctuary that was little used, and stopped when she came to a particular room. Jaimon stood by a table inside, examining small carvings and artifacts shaped like dragons. Three Followers of the Dragon, a man named Devin and two women, stood around him.

Jaimon turned to Alli as she entered, holding a small jade carving in front of him. "They say these all have some type of magic in them." His eyes sparkled with excitement.

"These draw power from the dragons," Devin said. "Each of these figures and artifacts will accentuate a dragon rider's power when needed. You must be very careful with them. In the histories, we have evidence of many artifacts. In fact, I have read—"

"Well then, Jaimon, you better grab a few of them," Alli interrupted as she tried not to roll her eyes—for the second time in the last few minutes—as she cut off the dragon fanatic. "Because you and I have been invited to the castle."

Jaimon blinked rapidly, and the others in the room stopped what they were doing and turned to Alli.

Devin laughed uncomfortably and said, "You can't just *take* the artifacts, Battlemaster."

Alli glared at Devin. But, before she could tell him that she could and would take whatever she wanted—if it would help them, Jaimon spoke up.

"Where exactly have you been, Alli?" Jaimon asked with authority in his voice. "Are we in trouble?"

Alli cringed only slightly, then put a serious look on her face. She didn't answer to Jaimon—well, she kind of did, through Bakari. Oh, it was so confusing.

She knew that Jaimon was intimidated by her. But he was a good young man, and she had tried to stay patient with him. Besides, he was a dragon rider, and Alli didn't want to get on the wrong side of Cholena.

"I met someone." Alli crossed her arms in front of her. "And I kind of *ran into* the Von Wulf's."

A multitude of gasps filled the room.

"The king?" Jaimon's eyes opened wide.

"Not him, specifically, but his son." Alli paused to take a breath. "And Kaspar."

Jaimon slapped himself in the forehead and laughed. "The famous Kaspar Von Wulf, second heir to the throne? His abilities with the sword are a legend already—second only to his looks, I have heard."

A few women in the room blushed, and Alli felt her own cheeks burn. She tried to divert attention with a cough. "He wasn't that good with the sword." But thoughts of Kaspar's perfect visage still heated her face. The man was too beautiful for his own good, however. She tried to think about Roland's face but had a hard time concentrating on it at the moment.

Jaimon took a step toward Alli and asked, "You didn't fight Kaspar, did you? Please tell me you didn't, Alli."

Alli stuck her chin out. "I *sparred* with him. And, yes, I beat him—and I didn't even use my magic."

Gasps sounded around the room again.

Alli didn't care. She shouldn't hide her talents. Just because she was a woman and was small didn't mean she couldn't do anything these arrogant men did. She was the Battlemaster!

Then Jaimon actually laughed. "Well, no wonder we've been invited to speak to the Wolf."

"He knows who we are, Jaimon," Alli said. These words had their intended effect on the group. They sobered the others and gave Alli the floor.

"The Wolf and his son have some type of magic," Alli reported. "I don't think they are wizards, but they can tell things about people—it felt like they were looking into my soul. So we need to be very careful," Alli said. "On my way here, I heard that the two kings of Solshi are arriving to talk to the king of Quentis. The castle will be guarded well. But, if we are being invited in, we could have an opportunity to find out what is going on. Rumors are the king is sick, but I think it may be otherwise."

Jaimon nodded. "The Chameleon is still around. I can feel him, but not as close as he was yesterday. I think he is in the city."

Devin stepped forward reluctantly and shoved some of the artifacts into Jaimon's hand. "Take these, Dragon Rider. You might need them."

Jaimon nodded his thanks, and Alli raised her eyebrows at the man. He wouldn't give them to her, but Devin would trust them in the hands of a dragon rider. She wondered if they would even do any good. Alli would trust her own abilities before trusting some inanimate object made of ivory or stone or wood.

Then a few of the Followers of the Dragon walked with Jaimon and Alli to the tunnel. And the two of them began their walk back toward the city.

Alli was getting tired of this trek and wished they had opted for using a boat instead. But they were being searched for, so the tunnel seemed like the best course for the time being.

Jaimon turned to Alli. "Truly, you met Kaspar? What is he like?"

Alli tried not to blush, but she couldn't prevent the color from creeping up her pale cheeks.

Jaimon laughed. "That good, huh?"

"Shut up, Jaimon." She slapped his arm playfully. "It's hard to take Kaspar seriously. It's really not fair..." Alli added, trailing off as she thought about Kaspar's smile.

"Watch out, Roland might get jealous." Jaimon's eyes crinkled.

But Alli was still lost in her own thoughts. Then she said, "For a moment, I thought I felt Roland there, when Kaspar and I were sparring. It was strange." She shook her head. "And then, a short time afterward, I felt someone trying to drain my powers. It gave me a horrible headache."

Jaimon opened his eyes wide and said, "As did I. But what could do that?"

"I am not sure." Alli shook her head and gave a slight scowl. "But I swear that boy gets into trouble every time I go away."

"What boy?" Jaimon asked.

"Roland," Alli said.

Jaimon laughed. "Oh, I didn't know we were still talking about him. I thought we were discussing the headaches and our loss of power."

Alli only grunted in reply.

Soon they emerged from the tunnel and began the short walk to Margarid. Entering the gate was easy, and they soon found themselves walking down one of the city's main streets. Shops lined either side of the broad street, their colorful flags hanging off of sturdy awnings, which were erected to block any storms coming off the Blue Sea. The shops were still open, but there were not a lot of customers about.

"Kind of quiet," Jaimon said.

Alli nodded her agreement. In her experience, when things were too quiet, trouble was afoot. So she placed her hand on her sword and heightened her wizard senses.

Soon the shops thinned out, and the large, multi-storied homes of the nobles began to take their place. Alli made sure to stay off of the Von Wulf's street. She didn't want to run into Kaspar again, for she needed to stay focused on the task at hand.

"Do you feel anything?" Alli asked Jaimon.

"Yes. We are getting closer to him," Jaimon said. "Alli, what do we do if we see the Chameleon? He neutralized your power last time."

Alli nodded. She, of course, remembered that. It was horrible to be without her magic. She had felt lost and empty inside for the next few days following their encounter in Elvyn with the Chameleon.

"*When* we find him," Alli said. "Then we will report back to Bakari, and he will let us know what to do."

"I don't know if we *can* communicate with Bakari anymore, Alli."

As Alli flipped her head around, her growing hair flew around her face and she said, "What do you mean?"

"Cholena said that she can't communicate with Abylar anymore, and Breelyn and Miriel seem to be in trouble too." Jaimon looked worried. "So we might be on our own."

"Well, we are not without our own powers. I am the Battlemaster, and you are a dragon rider. That might have to do." She smiled, trying to reassure the young man without showing her own concern. The Chameleon was the first person Alli had ever met that had truly scared her.

Soon they arrived in front of the castle gates, where they were stopped by a guard. Alli decided to play up who they were, now that they were at the castle.

"Battlemaster Allison Stenos and Dragon Rider Jaimon Schafer to see the Wolf."

These titles had the intended effect, for the guard stood up straighter. "Yes, ma'am," he stammered. "We have been expecting you." With a short bow to Jaimon, the guard ushered them through the gates, where a set of two other guards fell in beside them.

"Quite a parade," Alli said to one of them. But he ignored her and continued walking straight ahead. It seemed they had no sense of humor. Then Alli noticed they were turning away from the main castle doors and heading toward a door on its south side.

So, even the Wolf doesn't necessarily want to parade us in front of others, Alli thought. She guessed that, here, like everywhere, information was power.

After entering the immense building, they soon arrived at a waiting area, where the guards motioned for Alli and Jaimon to sit.

As they waited, Alli turned around and realized that this building was ancient: much older than the castle in Cassian—maybe it rivaled the Citadel for its history. The gray stone walls showed signs of age and held tapestries and paintings from all over the Western Continent.

Alli rubbed the smooth wooden armrest of the chair she sat in and wondered about what would happen. What did the Wolf want with them?

Then the door opened, and a woman ushered the two of them inside.

The room was significant in size but was furnished more reasonably than—and not as gaudily as—the waiting area had been. Behind a serviceable, dark desk sat the Wolf. Motioning the woman out, he stood and approached his two visitors.

Turning first to Jaimon, the Wolf bowed, with his hands clasped in front of him, and said, "Welcome, Dragon Rider."

Jaimon appeared nervous, but he held himself together well. "Thank you, sir."

"And, nice to see you again, young lady," the Wolf said, his tall frame rising way over Alli's head. "I hear that you gave my son quite the beating."

Alli shrugged. "He tried his best."

The Wolf laughed and motioned them to a grouping of chairs around the desk. After they were seated, the Wolf looked at each of them in turn before he started talking. "It seems we have a slight problem here."

Alli raised her eyebrows but waited to see what this problem was before saying anything.

"Both of you were seen entering the Sanctuary," the Wolf continued, "but have not presented yourselves to the commander yet, and he seems to think you have been hiding there." The Wolf smiled, but Alli could tell that there was a dangerous undertone to what he was beginning to imply.

"We were not informed that the commander was available to see us," Alli said, holding her voice firm.

The Wolf waved his hand in the air. "That is beside the point. The dragon rider's stay there can be excused; he is one of us at least. However, it seems you stayed rather hidden while you were there. Having a Battlemaster from our northern neighbor—one with which we have had no contact until recently—hiding in the Sanctuary cannot be excused."

Alli stood, resting her hand on her sword, which, surprisingly, had not been taken from her. "And, what is the point of your threats, Minister of Trade—that is the role you play in this government today, isn't it?"

The Wolf glared at Alli. And, once again, she felt his eyes prying inside of her.

"Get out of there!" Alli yelled and brought up a ball of fire in front of her.

"Alli!" Jaimon yelled as he stood up. "What is going on?"

"He's trying to see inside my mind—he has powers," Alli said to Jaimon. Then, turning back to the Wolf, she said, "You have no right to invade my privacy."

The Wolf stood and took a step forward. "I have all the right. You are a foreign Battlemaster on my soil."

Alli realized that the man had a point, but she still had to save face. So she turned the conversation back on him. "You don't seem like a wizard."

The Wolf guffawed and sat back down. "You are correct, young lady. I am not a wizard, but the power of *seeing* runs in my family."

Alli grunted and then said, "I remember your son trying to do the same thing."

The Wolf waved for Alli to sit back down. "As I said, it runs in the family. My father had it also."

"Had?" Alli asked.

"That is none of your business," the Wolf snapped, not seeming too happy with where the line of questioning was going. "Now, tell me why you are here."

Alli took a deep breath. She didn't know if she could trust the Wolf, so she had to be careful about what she said. "Jaimon is here on the order of Dragon Master Bakari, and I am only accompanying him. We are searching for a man who has caused disruption in both Elvyn and Alaris, and we have reason to believe he may have come here."

The Wolf turned and stared at Jaimon for confirmation of Alli's story.

"That is true, sir," Jaimon said. "We would never do anything to jeopardize Quentis. It is my home."

"But you did not come and present yourself at the Castle or to the Sanctuary commander when you arrived." The Wolf leaned forward in his chair.

Sweat formed on Jaimon's brow. Alli knew he was not used to politics. Until recently, Alli herself had not been either. But, with the barrier coming down and the fighting between the judges and king-men the previous year, she had been thrust into politics on many occasions.

So Alli pulled the Wolf's attention back from Jaimon to herself. "Sir, do you deny the right of the Dragon King in this matter?"

The Wolf turned pale—the first sign Alli had seen of a weakness in the man. Or, was this awe at the mention of the Dragon King? He covered this up with a quick cough, but he took a moment to think.

The afternoon sun sent a ray of light into the room. It landed on Jaimon, giving him an altogether otherworldly look. The Wolf had seen this also, and he poured himself a drink before answering.

"I do not deny the right of a dragon king, if there is one." He seemed to gather strength again as he spoke. "But he would need to present himself to my father, the rightful king of Quentis, for any acknowledgement."

"We can arrange that, can't we, Jaimon?" Alli said.

Alli's statement made the Wolf search again for his words.

"When the time is right," he finally added.

"You mean, when you are king?" Alli said. "I've heard your father is sick."

The Wolf stood up and, in two long strides, stood directly in front of Alli. "I don't know what game you play here, Battlemaster. Your future sits in my hands. How dare you talk of my father in that way. He is a great king and has ruled in peace for years—at least, until the barrier around Alaris came down. Now, nothing but problems have arisen."

Jaimon and Alli stood up, both seeming small compared to the Wolf's stature and anger.

"Sir, Alli didn't mean anything by it," Jaimon said, trying to smooth things over. "We are just concerned for the king's health."

Alli opened her mouth to retort, but Jaimon shook his head at her, and she relinquished her words—this time.

The Wolf paced a few steps toward the window, then back again. His anger seemed to subside before he spoke again.

"Your timing is not good here. The kings of Solshi are arriving today."

Alli had to be bold now. She had to discover whom to trust. "We would like to present ourselves to the king, then. As a dragon rider and an official representative of the Citadel of Alaris."

The Wolf took a few more paces before he answered, "He has been spending a lot of time with the Sanctuary commander."

"Great," Alli said. "Then we will see them both—we weren't able to find the commander available at the Sanctuary."

"Now?" the Wolf asked.

Jaimon looked nervously at Alli.

She just shrugged her shoulders nonchalantly and then smiled sweetly. "If that works best for your schedule, sir. You must have trade meetings to attend to."

His anger seemed to recede, and he barked out a laugh. "My, my. Your tongue is as sharp as your sword."

Alli just smiled and cocked her head to her side. "You have no idea of all the powers at my disposal, Minister." She felt a slight probing of her mind once again. But, like a fly before a giant swatter, it was batted away with the use of her magic.

The Wolf glared at her harshly for a brief moment, without betraying any of his thoughts, then motioned the two of them to the door. "I am sure the Sanctuary commander will be overjoyed to meet you. Let's go and see my father. Maybe they are together."

Walking behind the Wolf into the wide hallway, Jaimon and Alli were soon joined by half a dozen guards at their backs.

Jaimon leaned over and whispered, "We are getting closer to him, Alli."

"Closer?" she whispered back.

"To the Chameleon," Jaimon said quietly, with a nod of his head in the direction they would be walking.

Alli's hands went to both of her swords, and she put up all the barriers around her mind that she knew of. "Ready your dragon, Dragon Rider," she whispered. "This may get exciting for us."

CHAPTER TWENTY TWO

Once the Wolf, heir to the throne of Quentis, had led Alli and Jaimon down a multitude of hallways and up two flights of stairs, they arrived at an ancient double door. Alli tried not to be distracted by the opulence of the castle and the views of the bay from the windows this high up. She wiped sweat from her forehead. The afternoon humidity was getting worse. Breathing in deeply, she tasted salt in the air.

"I'll be back in a moment, and I will arrange the meeting." The Wolf stepped inside the room.

Turning to Jaimon once the Wolf was gone, Alli noticed the young man shaking. By putting a hand on his arm, she tried to assure him that it would be all right.

"Is he here?" Alli asked.

Jaimon cocked his head to the side. "He is close. He could be in the room. It's so hard to tell sometimes. I don't know how accurate I can be." He hung his head down low. "I would feel better if Cholena were here."

"How far away is she?" Alli's attention was on full alert.

"Not far. Just north of the city," Jaimon answered. "But even a few minutes away could make a difference." He brought out one of the artifacts and held it in his hand.

"Do you think they work?" Alli moved closer to look at what Jaimon held. It was a small crystal carving of a dragon—its wings held out in flight.

Jaimon shook his head. "I don't know, but at least it's something to hold on to. I'm not gifted like you are."

"Don't worry." Alli smiled and flipped her hair to the side of her face. "We just need to find out where the troublemaker is."

"Do you trust the Wolf?" Jaimon asked, changing the subject.

Alli laughed. "I don't trust many people, Jaimon. That's why I am still alive." She paused and thought for a moment. "It's not that I distrust him, I just think he is hiding something."

Before anything more could be said, the door opened and, instead of the Wolf, a servant stepped out, closing the door behind himself.

"The Wolf will be detained for a while." The servant's face was passive. "I will escort you to a room where you may have some refreshments and rest." He motioned for them to follow.

"We don't need to rest," Alli informed him.

The servant stopped with a jerk, obviously not expecting resistance.

"We have things to do," Alli said. "We would like to see the king, or we will leave and come back another time."

"You cannot leave," the servant stated. "That would not do."

As three soldiers came toward them from the other end of the hallway, Alli's hand went once again to her sword hilt. They would be easy for her to handle.

"We must insist you remain in the castle," the servant said, his expression turning harder.

The man's stance suddenly didn't look like a servant's anymore, and Alli wondered who he really was. The three soldiers stood behind him and glared at Alli and Jaimon.

"Something is going on here," Alli said. Then, with viper-like speed, Alli reached for the door handle and began to push it open. But, before she could, two of the soldiers grabbed her arms.

Jaimon took a step back in surprise.

Alli kicked the chin of one of the guards, knocking him off balance and freeing one of her arms. The third guard stepped forward but found the point of Alli's sword at his throat.

"Back off," Alli sneered at all of them. Jaimon had moved next to her and had his own sword now pointed at one of the other guards.

Then Alli noticed that the servant wasn't in front of them anymore. From behind, she felt two strong arms grab her arms and twist them back behind her. Before she could react, something cold and metal was snapped onto her wrists and all her power drained away—both physically and magically.

"What did you do?" she tried to scream, but her voice only came out as a whisper. She sank to her knees, unable to stand.

To Jaimon's credit, he reacted with his newly trained instincts as he jumped out in front of Alli—but not before almost tripping over her. He put his hands on her shoulder, to steady himself and then, with a quick move to the side, sliced one of the guards' arms, drawing a line of blood and a loud scream from the man.

Another guard came forward, but Jaimon parried his sword also and almost had him, when, from behind, the third guard knocked Jaimon on the head. Jaimon dropped the sword, and then the young dragon rider slumped to the floor, unconscious, next to Alli.

She struggled with the contraption on her wrists but soon found her energy waning substantially. The man who had played the servant grabbed her roughly and pulled her up from the floor.

"Take her to the dungeon," he said and then pushed Alli into one of the guards that wasn't hurt. "I will take the dragon rider with me. The commander will want to see him first."

"No! Jaimon!" Alli screamed. "Jaimon, wake up!"

But Jaimon stayed slumped on the floor as the guard lifted Alli up to her feet.

"Get going!" the rough guard spat at her. "You can walk."

She tried to walk, but she felt like she had been drugged. So the guard had to practically drag her down a hall to the top of some back stairs, which were probably used by the servants.

As they went down the stairs, the only thing that kept Alli going forward was the thought that if she fell, it was a long way down—and most likely would be fatal. The effort to get down even one level was painful and tiring.

"I need to rest," she said, pleading. She hated doing this, but she was just so weak. Once again, she tried to reach out for her powers. Her magic was there, close by, but she couldn't quite get it to obey her wishes.

"Get up!" the guard said as he dragged her back to her feet.

Without thinking, Alli's instincts took over, and she bashed her forehead into the guard's nose, hearing a crunching sound. Noticing that and the smell of blood in the air, she didn't wait any longer to try and kick out at him. But, instead, she fell back against the stone stairway.

The guard stood above Alli and glared at her, his hand over his nose. Blood dripped through his fingers. Then he kicked her hard in the side, and she grunted and tried to roll away, but her senses felt dulled, and her body didn't respond.

"You barbarian witch!" the guard roared as he kicked her again.

Alli tried to roll into a ball, to protect herself. "I'm not a barbarian," she grunted.

The guard laughed wildly. "Stuck behind that barrier for one hundred and fifty years. You are a backward, hopeless people. It is time for Quentis to rule the lands, and we won't let you little girls from Alaris get in our way."

From down the stairwell, Alli heard voices. Maybe someone would help her. She screamed as loud as she could, but it wasn't very loud. However, soon two male servants came up the stairs. They stopped short and stared at the scene. Blood was dripping down the guard's face, and Alli was trying to stand up. A look of horror flashed across their faces, and they began to back away.

"You two will help me," the guard said, then grabbed a cloth from one of the servants and held it to his bleeding nose.

"But...but..." one of the servants stammered. "We are needed upstairs."

"You are needed here now." The guard was large and angry and brooked no argument from the two servants. "Now, lift this assassin up, and follow me to the dungeons."

"Assassin?" Alli croaked. "You are the one trying to kill me."

"Shut your mouth, Witch," the guard said as he slammed his fist into the side of her jaw.

Alli did all she could not to cry out in agony.

The two servants looked ready to bolt but did as the guard had ordered. Carrying Alli down two more flights of stairs, they went into the underground floors of the castle. Soon they came out of the stairwell and walked along another hallway. The rock walls here looked more roughly hewn in the dim light. A solid wooden door stood at the other end.

The guard knocked, and they all waited.

Alli was trying to keep from blacking out as she looked around and gathered as much information as she could. The door opened, and another guard met them, this one wearing chain mail and carrying a sword on one hip and a hammer on the other.

"This traitor is to be imprisoned," her guard said.

The new guard glanced down at the manacles on Alli's wrists and smiled. "I have just the cell for her."

The servants continued to carry her forward, clearly not wanting to be there. The scents of blood, human waste, and rot made Alli gag, but she stopped short of vomiting. A dozen cells, with thick metal bars, filled each side of the walkway. Two other guards were stationed there. The door guard ordered the two servants to take Alli to the end of the row of cells. Opening a door, the two servants laid her on the ground, and one backed away.

Before leaving her, the other servant leaned over and whispered, "Hail the Dragon" so softly that Alli didn't know if she had actually heard it.

Alli almost laughed. The fanatical Followers of the Dragon were here too. They knew who she was. Maybe there was some hope after all.

Her pain was almost unbearable. She closed her eyes and heard the barred metal door close behind her. Receding footsteps echoed down the walkway as the guards and servants all walked away.

Lying motionless for who knows how long, Alli tried to think of what to do next. Her entire body ached, and the manacles were cutting into her wrists. Rolling onto her back, Alli tried to sit up. Once she did, she scooted backward, toward the closest side of her cell. She bumped into the bars but felt something else behind them. She brought her head up and tried to look behind herself. It was difficult, with her wrists still chained behind her back.

When she did look behind herself, she gasped. Standing in the next cell was a grimy man with long, dirty hair and an unshaven face.

He leaned down closer to her, his head in line with hers. Pushing his face as far as he could between the bars, he said,

"Hello, Wizard!" His voice was deep and raspy, as if he hadn't spoken in a while.

His foul breath almost made Alli gag again. And she tried to breathe through her mouth as she scooted away from the bars and glared back at the man. "How do you know I'm a wizard?" she finally asked.

A deep laugh ensued, followed by a series of coughs. "Who else do they put these manacles on?" he asked. He held out his arms, and she noticed, for the first time, that his wrists were also manacled. Although, his were held in front of himself, rather than behind his back, like hers.

"How long have you been in here?" Alli asked. She didn't want to end up looking like him. The man appeared to be half crazy, and his clothes hung loosely over his thinning frame.

"How long? How long?" the man asked. "A day is too long, in this place." He then paced away from the bars and back again. "How long can you survive is the better question."

Alli gasped. She could usually hold her own, but, without the use of her hands or her magic… Panic began to rise inside of her. She needed help to get away, and this man might be her only hope. She looked him up and down and wondered what he had done to get such harsh treatment. *Probably some low level wizard found pilfering goods or cheating at cards.*

Pushing herself back up, onto her feet, she walked closer to the bars. She tried to show more confidence than she faced the man in front of her.

"Who are you?" Alli asked.

"Ah, that is the question, isn't it?" The man laughed again. "Your mind must be wondering what petty crime afforded me these luxurious accommodations." He proceeded to push his manacled hands through the bars and toward her right shoulder. "You are probably thinking that you must be stronger than some pathetic man in the cell next to yours, right?"

She wanted to back away, but she steeled her mind to not be intimidated by the filthy man. His dark brown eyes bore into hers, and she couldn't look away. There was power behind his gaze, a power that was trapped as much as her own power was. Was she mistaken in her earlier assessment of his strength and crimes?

She still couldn't look away as he said, "It's nice to see I still have a little power left." His voice was growing stronger the more he used it.

Alli might not be able to use her power, but that didn't mean she didn't have her own steel inside of herself. She reached inside and stilled her fear, asking him the same question one more time.

"Who are you?"

The man put his face up to the bars and said, "I am the highly esteemed and most powerful commander of the Sanctuary of Quentis. I am Commander Tobias Bruel." With that, he pulled his hands away from the bars, stepped back, and gave a flourishing bow.

CHAPTER TWENTY THREE

Breelyn stood on a hill just west of the capital city Raleez. After several days of recruiting—or rather, intimidating—the group at the bottom of the hill, it was now growing big enough to be considered *an army*. A small one—but an army nonetheless.

Turning to a young servant next to her, Breelyn said harshly, "Tell the captains to meet me in the command tent as soon as possible."

The servant was barely thirteen, but she was fast and did Breelyn's bidding. She sprinted down the hill to find Breelyn's captains—or, were they General Trevis's captains? Did it matter anymore? They feared Breelyn now as much as they feared him.

Standing still and taking in her surroundings, Breelyn rung her hands tightly. Looking down at them, she noticed the black leather bands around her wrists. The General had given them to her. Running one hand over the band on the opposite wrist, she felt power rise up within her once again. Closing her eyes, Breelyn breathed in deeply and let the black power wash over her, calming her down. At the very edges of this power, a spark tried to push its way in, but Breelyn pushed it back out.

The dragon!

For the first few days after Breelyn's agreement with the General, Miriel had tried to visit—had tried to break through the new barriers in her mind—but Breelyn had pushed her out. It was for Miriel's own protection. A part of Breelyn knew that what she was doing now was wrong, and she didn't want harm to come to her dragon, so she had blocked Miriel out and had tried to will her away. With the dragon obviously farther away from the area now, it was easier not to think about what she had done.

The young servant returned and bowed to Breelyn. "They will meet you momentarily, Mistress. Would you like an escort to the tent?"

Breelyn knew that, behind her back, they called her *Mistress of Dark*, but she felt no concern. She had sold her soul for a reason: to protect her homeland and its king. Both of which she probably would never see again.

Steeling her nerves, Breelyn shook her head at the servant. "I can manage myself."

Lifting up the hem of her black dress, Breelyn walked down the hill, toward the command tent. On the way, the ragtag soldiers—men and women—bowed to Breelyn while averting their eyes from her scrutiny. She walked with her head held high and paid them no attention. She could crush them all with a moment's thought.

At the tent door, two servants held the flaps open for her and the captains. Upon entering, she motioned them all to sit. Soft pillows had been arranged around the edges of the spacious tent. Then she walked around the tent, with long strides, staring each one of the five captains in the eye. Finally, she returned to her starting point and sat down with them.

"How is training going?" Breelyn asked.

No one spoke. They seemed to be doing anything they could not to look directly at her.

Her anger growing, Breelyn slapped her hand on the ground and sent tendrils of black smoke into the air, heading toward one of the men. At seeing that, he looked up at her and tried to back away. But the tendrils wrapped themselves around his throat, and choking sounds ensued.

"Can someone answer my question," Breelyn said, "before Captain Argos faints?" Breelyn glared around at the group.

Captain Leeds nodded his head and looked over at her, saying, "Please, Mistress, let Argos go. He is a good captain."

"Very well." Breelyn waved her hand in the air, and the black tendrils receded into her black bracelets. "Speak, Captain Leeds."

"Mistress," Captain Leeds said and then began his report. As Leeds began to speak, Breelyn saw Captain Argos holding his hand to his throat as he sucked in air. She didn't like threatening people, but the General had told her it was the only way these simple folk would learn to obey. And, during war, a general could not have his captains and soldiers not obeying.

"More recruits come every day," Leeds continued. "But Solshi is a spread out kingdom: it is taking time to get the word out."

Breelyn nodded and said, "I don't like excuses, but I appreciate the honesty."

There, that should help them to relax.

"And, the training?" she said as she turned to Captain Willis, a woman in her late twenties, who appeared ready to fight back. "Do they know how to fight?" Breelyn asked.

The woman stiffened in front of Breelyn but said, "The professional soldiers do well—though there hasn't been a war in a long, long time, Mistress. With the barrier up, we didn't have anyone to fight. We kept up good relations with the other bordering kingdoms."

The captain pushed a stray hair out of her eyes, swallowed hard, and then continued, "The new recruits are awkward and clumsy. More of them get hurt in practice than seem to learn anything from the exercises."

Turning back to Captain Argos, Breelyn asked, "Argos, do you agree with their assessments?"

"Yes, Mistress." The man still held his throat with one hand but bobbed his head to her, nonetheless.

"And, what do we do about this?" Breelyn asked Argos and then let her eyes wander over the entire group.

The captains looked back and forth between each other, and Breelyn's displeasure began to rise once again. She pushed it back down.

Why do I get upset so easily now? I'm still an elf. I was born in patience.

But she knew she had always been short on patience—even while in her homeland—and now it was scarcer still. But she had to prove her worth to the General so that he would heal Lan.

Breelyn raised her hands into the air again. Did these captains need another reminder?

Just then, the tent flap opened. A male servant, seeing Breelyn's hands in the air, ready to strike, began to back out of the tent.

"Why do you disrupt me?" Breelyn called out.

"The General, Mistress; he is coming." The man's eyes bulged wider when he saw Breelyn's reaction. Could he tell that she was afraid?

"Here?" Breelyn asked. "Why was I not informed earlier?" Breelyn found herself brushing her dark hair down with her fingers. Realizing what she was doing, she scowled and berated herself. The General held some sort of sway over her, for she felt compelled to please him and didn't know if this feeling was natural or not.

"Very well," Breelyn said with a wave of her hand to dismiss the servant. Turning back to her captains, she rose to dismiss them also. "We will meet again in the morning. And I better get stronger reports on the men. It will be time to march soon."

Rising to their feet, the captains had turned to leave, when Captain Willis turned back to Breelyn and said, "Mistress." She bowed low to Breelyn. "You asked us what could be done. Well, we don't have enough for the soldiers to eat. The General has curtailed food production and transportation. They won't be strong without enough food."

The captain had been bold to speak up, but she bore the truth of the matter: Their soldiers needed food to maintain their strength. The General had been shortsighted.

"I will discuss it with the General," Breelyn said, then ushered them out of the command tent.

The General would be there soon. She knew that he could pop in suddenly almost anywhere he desired. Somehow, his dark powers allowed him to move about quicker than his legs or a horse could carry him.

Not faster than Miriel.

This brief thought, of the speed of her dragon, seized her breast, and Breelyn leaned over and placed her hand on the edge of a table.

Her dragon!

Out of all that she had recently lost, that loss still hurt Breelyn the most: The bond and comfort of feeling another so close. It angered Breelyn to think about it. That was not her life anymore.

Before she could straighten back up, the tent flap opened. Breelyn glanced up. Unnaturally yellow eyes flashed at her. The General's shaggy, dark hair hung down to his broad shoulders, which sat higher than her eye level. Looking up at his face, she shrank back for only a moment.

"Something wrong, Breelyn?" the General asked, cutting through any pleasantries. "Not having second thoughts, are we?"

Breelyn stood up straighter and shook her head as she said, "No, General." All thoughts of her dragon were buried deep once again. "I was just meeting with my captains…"

"*Your* captains?" The General took a step closer and loomed over her head. "This army is not yours, Elf."

Breelyn berated herself for making such a mistake. Bowing low, she groveled in front of the most powerful man she had ever met.

The General put his strong fingers under Breelyn's chin and lifted her face back up. He ran one finger up her jaw line; his thumb gently touched Breelyn's lips and then caressed her cheek. Reaching up with his other hand, he stroked her hair down its long length and said, "You grow more beautiful every day, Elf Maiden. Black becomes you."

Receiving praise from this man of power lifted Breelyn's spirits. How could she ever have doubted the man's wisdom or her position with him? He was more powerful than anyone. His dark touch sank deep inside her and buoyed her soul back up.

"Thank you, Master," Breelyn said.

"Now, about the army." The General brought his hands back down, and he was all business once again.

Breelyn groaned inside at the loss of his touch, but she quickly remembered what her captains had told her. "The men need more food, sir."

The General's face turned red, and he opened his mouth to reply in apparent anger, but Breelyn pushed forward.

"We cannot expect a strong army if they don't eat enough. They need the strength from sufficient food. We need more. Then they will be ready." She didn't tell him about the deserters. That would earn her his displeasure.

The General nodded his head. "I will cut food delivery to the city, and the army can have their food."

Breelyn nodded her head but felt a small stab of pain for those that would now suffer in order to build the army's strength.

"We must all give up something, mustn't we?" The General tilted his head and smiled with his teeth. "You should know that most of all."

Breelyn kept her expression neutral but felt her face redden.

I hate him! she thought to herself.

The General brought his hand back up to her face, and it took all that she had to not pull back. "Don't hate me, Breelyn. Hate Alaris. Hate the men that killed my father and put up the barrier. Hate the wizards of the aggressors."

Breelyn nodded and remembered: She thought of Roland and his pompous strength. She thought of Bakari and how he had brought down the barrier that had protected them all from Alaris. She thought of Kanzar, Onius, and Mericus and the lives that had been lost as they fought for control of Alaris.

And then she smiled. This time it was genuine. She leaned her face into the General's hand and relished his power and wisdom. How had she ever felt hate for the man?

"You are right, as always, General." Breelyn smiled up at him. "We will crush Alaris."

CHAPTER TWENTY FOUR

Roland sat in a corner of the magic stream—well, he didn't know if it was truly *a corner* or not, but he pretended it was. The vast emptiness of the place seemed to stretch out forever. Some areas were darker or lighter than others. But that and the flicker of lights representing the wizards were the only things to look at in this dreary place.

So Roland was bored. That was the easiest way to describe his current mood. He was also concerned—very concerned. The day before, Alli's light had all of a sudden blinked out. He had been watching it, wondering if he should intrude again, and then it had just gone out.

Hours later, Alli's light had come back but was so dim that it was hard to know if he was actually seeing her light or just wishing he were.

Breelyn's light had also dimmed. Roland had reached out to touch it once, but he had jumped back from the evil taint he felt there.

Roland shook his head now and worried about the beautiful elf maiden and what she had done to deserve such darkness.

The evil wizard king—at least, that is what Roland had named him—hadn't appeared again. But Roland wouldn't mind another bout with him just now…it would give him *something* to do.

Standing back up, Roland ran as fast as he could, watching the starry lights around him race past. But no other scenery changed. It was infuriating. How could he get out of this place?

Then Roland's scattered and melancholy thoughts brought him back to Bakari's light. It wasn't hard to miss, for the *Dragon King* outshined most other lights in this place. That thought made Roland wonder what his own light might look like to others. And he wondered if he appeared as bright as Bakari.

Reaching Bakari's light, Roland decided to see what his friend was up to. Touching the light with his hands, his mind was taken into the light, and he found himself standing on a bustling street corner. Brilliant colors surrounded him: banners hung from vendors' awnings in bright colors, and the people around him wore clothes of the most colorful designs. The women's dresses were cut lower on the top and higher on the bottom than was considered proper in Alaris, but it was the swirls of color that took most of his attention.

Turning to the side, Roland saw Bakari, walking next to a brilliant white horse, while another young man rode on a similar horse next to them. Roland was mesmerized by the horses' auras—they exuded immense power.

"They're beautiful," Roland exclaimed.

The horse next to Bakari turned its head, as if it had heard Roland speak. And its bright blue eyes looked directly at him. Roland swallowed hard and wondered how much power they had.

"Bakari, where are we going?" the young man asked.

Yes, Bak, Roland wondered. *Where are you going? I'm stuck here, in a magic void, and you are out for a leisurely stroll through some exotic marketplace.*

"Do you feel anything through the bond, Liam?" Bakari said to the young man next to him.

Liam nodded his head. "She is here somewhere."

Bakari nodded and looked around. Then Roland noticed a more distant and tired look in his friend's expression. Looking up in the sky, Roland searched for Bakari's dragon, Abylar, but didn't see him. This thought set off some alarms. Roland knew that the wizard king was after the dragon riders. So Roland needed to warn Bak. But how?

Roland followed them through the marketplace, then into a poorer district of the city. Soon the cobblestone streets turned to dirt, and the buildings became more run-down. A few street urchins scattered in front of them as they continued deeper into an obviously seedier part of the city.

"I can feel her close by," Liam said.

"Do we need help?" Bakari asked.

Liam appeared to be concentrating on something. Turning back to Bakari, he said, "I could go to Governor San Ghant, but, as the son of the king, I don't want to cause too much commotion. This needs to be done quietly. And we both are wizards."

Bakari nodded his understanding.

Roland still wondered where they were. The scent of the sea was strong, but that only meant that they were somewhere on a coast. The accent of the young man was not much different from theirs, only slightly more formal in its pronunciation.

Soon Liam stopped and dismounted, and Roland saw that Liam limped on one foot and struggled to move forward quickly. Then the young man motioned for Bakari to follow him around the side of a dirty, white building.

As they came around the corner, a group of hands came out and grabbed both of them. Without thinking, Roland brought his hands up to protect them, intending to form a ball of fire. But nothing happened.

"Stupid place!" Roland yelled.

Bakari tried to lift his own hands. Getting one free, he threw a punch of air at his attacker that pushed the man back, onto the ground. Liam struggled and seemed about to unleash his own magic, when a female voice cut through the uproar.

"Liam! It's me, Breanna."

The fighting stopped, and Liam limped forward to embrace Breanna. Then, pulling away, Liam asked, "What happened?"

"Come inside," she said.

She directed them near a small door at the side of the building. Then, looking up and down the street, she opened it and told them to hurry inside. The horses followed the young men, with Roland just behind them.

The room looked to be an old inn. Wooden chairs sat broken on the floor with a few tables still standing nearby. It was filled with young people. One young woman was tending a small fire in the corner. Everyone in the room stopped and watched as the group entered.

Liam turned his head around. "They're all here? All of the students?"

Breanna nodded and smiled, her brown hair framing her heart-shaped face. "The headmaster helped us to escape, and the governor gave us this place."

"Not much of a place," Liam grumbled. "You could have done a lot better."

"Not if we want to stay hidden," Breanna said. "We are protected here from a growing evil at the school."

Bakari nodded as if he understood and said, "We talked to the headmaster—in a moment of clarity for him—and know that he is being manipulated by one who calls himself *the Sentinel*."

Roland was having a hard time following what was being said, but he did understand enough to know that trouble was brewing in this land, as it also was in the others. He needed to talk to Bak. So he thought hard of how he could do it.

He called out, "Bak! Bakari!"

But there was no response.

It would be easier, Roland assumed, *if Bakari was asleep.* But that would occur too much later in the day.

"Hey, Dragon King!" he tried.

No response came from Bakari, but Roland did notice one of the beautiful horses looking his way. Maybe that was how he could talk to his friend.

Moving closer to one of the horses, Roland put his hand out and tried to touch it. He couldn't feel it physically, but there was a change in the magic.

You must be a powerful wizard, said a voice into Roland's head.

Roland jumped away in surprise. Then, putting his hand back on the horse, Roland reached out with his mind and said, *Was that you who just talked to me?*

Yes, it was I. Who are you?

I am Roland Tyre, High Wizard of the Citadel in Alaris.

Nice to meet you, young wizard. And you are friends with the Dragon King?

Yes, me and Bak—um, I mean, the Dragon King and I are good friends, Roland said. Talking to a horse seemed very strange.

A powerful wizard your friend is. More powerful than he even realizes. He needs to bring peace to the land once again.

Roland laughed and replied, *Don't I know it. I need his help also. Could you arrange for me to speak to him, most noble creature?* He was hoping that flattery would work on the...*the Cremelino*—that is what Liam had called it.

It moved over closer to Bakari and nudged his arm.

"Looks like Flash has taken a liking to you," Liam said to Bakari.

Bakari laughed. "He is persistent. What does he want?"

"Go with him," Breanna said. "He wants something from you."

Following the Cremelino across the room, Bakari reached out and touched Flash on the nose. Instantly, Roland felt Bakari's presence.

Bak! Roland said.

Roland? Bakari asked. *How did you do this?*

I am a powerful wizard, remember? Roland laughed. It felt good to talk to his friend again. It felt good to be doing *anything* again.

Where are you? Bakari asked and then laughed.

Roland felt himself become more solemn. *That's what I need to warn you about. There is an evil wizard: the last ancient king of Alaris. He died long ago but is trying to return to life. He has three sons, or some kind of descendants, that are helping him.*

The Chameleon and the Sentinel! Bakari said.

Yes, and another one, called the General.

That's who Breelyn is with, Bakari said. *But what about you? Where are you, Roland? How are you able to do this?*

Roland was quiet for a moment. He hated having to confess embarrassing things to Bakari.

Roland? Bakari said. *What did you do?*

Do? Roland said, repeating the question to delay answering. *Well, I might be dead. I'm not sure.* There, he had said it. He was dead. That must be what had happened. His spirit was caught between the living and the dead.

Stop playing games, Roland. This is serious.

I am being serious. I am a spirit floating in the stream of magic, Bakari. My body lies in the Citadel. Tam and the other wizards are keeping it alive magically, but I don't know how long that will work or how to get back out of this place.

Bakari let out a long stream of air, and his eyes dropped to the floor. When he looked back up, his mouth was held tight and his eyes were watery. *You can't be dead, Roland. I can't handle that right now. If you are talking to me, you can't be dead.* Bakari wiped at his eyes.

You're the scholar, Bakari. I'll trust you if you say I'm not dead. But I am trapped here.

Roland, I can't help you right now. I need to get to the other dragon. It's time for another rider.

Roland sighed. *I understand. The weight of the world falls upon your shoulders, Dragon King, so why would you help out an old friend?*

That's not fair, Roland, and you know it. Don't you, the mighty High Wizard, have any ideas? Bakari said back, as a bitter retort.

As anger had filled Bakari's voice, Roland had smiled, for he knew that his friend still cared for him.

Ouch, Bak. I didn't mean that. It's just so infuriating here, all alone.

Roland heard Bakari take a deep breath. Then Bakari said, *I'm sorry too, Roland. It's just that everywhere I turn, I feel like we are being defeated by something that we don't understand: Abylar is missing. Breelyn is in trouble...*

And Alli has lost her magic—at least, the use of it, Roland added.

Bakari was silent for a moment.

Bak?

I'm thinking.

Roland waited a few moments longer. He was about to say something more, but then he felt something else tug at his mind.

Oh no! Roland groaned. *He's back again!*

Who? Bakari asked.

The evil wizard king himself. He roams the stream as I do, looking for havoc to cause. I need to run again.

We'll figure this out, Roland. I need to find the other dragon egg, then go after Abylar, Bakari said with haste. *There has to be a way for you to get back out—or for us to get in.*

That last comment got Roland thinking. Maybe, if he couldn't get out, he could instead find a way for other wizards to get in—to help him defeat the wizard king here, before he entered the world again. That was something that Roland could put his mind to.

Breaking his contact with Bakari, Roland glanced around the grayness of the magic stream. There, in the distance, the blackness was creeping closer once again.

Time to go!

With only a brief thought, Roland pictured himself somewhere else, and his mind or spirit—or whatever it was—jumped there. He had to endure several long moments of darkness, then brief dizziness. When this stopped, he marveled at what was around him. The place was brighter and, somehow, in front of him, stood a woman. She was twice his age, pale-skinned, and shorter than himself, with short, blond hair. She stood with her hands on her hips and a stern look on her face.

"Who are you?" she said.

Roland was taken aback. She was the most substantial form he had ever seen in the magic stream. The woman stared up at him, power radiating from her. Here was someone with abilities that even outpaced Roland's. And he knew it.

Giving her the deep bow that she deserved, he answered back, "I am Roland Tyre, High Wizard of the Citadel in Alaris."

The woman nodded as if she already knew this.

"And who are you?" Roland asked tentatively.

The woman seemed to relax and smiled. Roland saw a fun-loving excitement in her.

"I am Danijela Anwar, High Wizard of the Wizard Conclave of Arc. We have much to discuss!"

* * *

Bakari opened his eyes and found everyone in the room staring at him.

"What?" he asked out loud. He put his hand to his head, feeling a growing headache. How had Roland done that?

Liam limped over and asked, "Were you communicating with the Cremelino?"

Bakari nodded, then shook his head and said, "Well, not really. I was speaking to my friend Roland Tyre, the High Wizard of the Citadel in Alaris. Somehow, he used the Cremelino here as a conduit for us to talk through. It was quite amazing!"

Bakari ran his hand over the Cremelino and thought about what Roland had done. His mind was already searching for ways to use that ability to defeat the evil powers that were still growing. While touching the horse, Bakari felt a growing sense of urgency to find the next dragon egg.

"Liam, we need to leave," Bakari stated.

"What?" Liam threw up his hands. "What do you mean, *leave?* We just got here."

"Breanna and the rest are safe for now."

"For now, maybe. But what if that evil impostor finds them?" Liam seemed to be growing angry. "I won't leave them."

Breanna walked over to them and put a hand out to either one. "Liam, we can fend for ourselves." She softened that statement by adding, "But I do thank you for finding us. That was very brave of you."

"Don't patronize me, Sister. You know I would do anything for you."

Breanna smiled and looked at her brother proudly. She touched his arm with her hand and lowered her voice as she said, "I know, Liam. I know that. That is why you need to go with Bakari."

Liam held his lips tightly together and appeared to be thinking about what to do. After a moment, he turned to Bakari and asked, "And where do we go that is so urgent?"

"To find the next dragon egg," Bakari stated firmly.

The group in the room gasped and moved closer to hear the conversation. One young woman stepped forward and said, "Are there really dragons again?"

Bakari nodded. "Yes, and I am a dragon rider." He didn't mention the part about him being a king. "And there are two others." He pursed his lips, thinking about what Roland had said and what he had seen. Bakari felt a stern responsibility for Breelyn and Jaimon. But he hadn't heard from either one in some time.

"Where is your dragon, then?" A young man a few years older than Bakari stepped forward. His arms were folded over his chest, and his chin had jutted out with his question.

"Hush, Davis," Breanna said. "Bakari is separated from his dragon for now. Don't pester him with your questions."

Bakari nodded his thanks to her, then turned toward Liam, waiting for an answer. Liam ran a hand over his Cremelino and seemed to be deep in thought.

"Liberty says I need to go; there is something waiting for me." Liam gave Bakari a questioning look.

Bakari smiled back. "There just might be. You'll have to wait and see."

Breanna hugged Liam. "I will send a messenger to Papa. He will protect us, Liam. Go with Bakari. This is the right thing for you."

Both of the Cremelinos nudged Bakari and Liam.

"Time to go." Bakari motioned with his head to Liam. "We will pick up a few supplies on our way out of Mar."

"Where are we heading?" Liam asked as he walked out of the front door with Bakari and the Cremelinos. The rest of the group waved at them and bade them good luck.

Breanna ran up and gave them a few blankets. "To drape over the horses," she said. "It will hide their identities—well, at least somewhat—until you are out of the city."

Once they were outside, they laid the blankets over the horses and both Liam and Bakari mounted their respective Cremelino. Liam glanced over at Bakari with a look that repeated his earlier question.

Bakari took a moment to reach deep inside his magic. As Dragon King, he could always feel the faint presences of all the dragons and their riders. After reassuring himself, he turned back to Liam.

"We ride north," Bakari said.

"North?" Liam groaned but picked up his pace. "Nothing is north but the Mountains of Gold and the Forgotten Lands."

"Yes, I know," Bakari said with sudden excitement. "Dragons like mountains."

CHAPTER TWENTY FIVE

Kharlia sat in a chair next to King Lanwaithian Soliel, who was resting on a reclining couch. A light breeze fluttered the leaves and blew through the open-air room, high up in the treetops of Lor'l, in Elvyn. The day had dawned bright, and a tinge of salt hung in the air.

But, even though the weather was cheery, the mood in the room was not. It had been almost two weeks since the king had been attacked, and he wasn't getting any better. Kharlia noticed that the blackness had crept up his arm again, ever so slightly but still more than a few days before.

"Drink this, Your Highness," Kharlia said with compassion, bringing another concoction to the king's lips.

The king drank this and then rolled his eyes at her. "Kharlia, I know you mean well, and I understand that you have learned a lot here, but none of these mixes of herbs is ever going to work on me." He breathed out an exasperated sigh.

"But, sir…" Kharlia began to explain.

Lan reached his good arm out toward her. "Kharlia, no need to be so formal here. Call me Lan."

Kharlia blushed at the attention. Who would have thought that she, the fifteen-year-old daughter of a healer with only a modest home in Alaris, would ever be sitting high up in a tree and waiting on the king of the elves? *The elves!* A race that magical stories had been told about around the evening fire back home.

"Well then, Lan," Kharlia began again. "Just because something doesn't work doesn't mean we stop. All it takes is for one thing to work. Here, drink this." She handed him a silver cup with a light blue liquid inside.

The king sighed again and gulped it down. Making a sour face, he handed the cup back and said, "With all the magic and healing around here, you would think we could make things taste better, wouldn't you?"

Kharlia stifled a giggle. "You are not a very good sick patient, Lanwaithian." She gave him a mock scowl.

"Kings aren't supposed to get sick—at least, not like this. I am still young. I need to be out leading my people."

"You lead them well enough from here. Your advisors carry out your commands, and everything is running smoothly."

Lan pouted. "Then maybe they don't need me at all."

Kharlia stood up and placed her hands on her hips. "King Soliel," she began formally. "What you need is to get out of this bed and walk around, so the people can see you."

The king opened his eyes wide at her boldness.

So Kharlia continued, with her tone a little softer, "You need to see how much they love you…"

"And how much I love them," Lan finished for her with a nod of his head. "You are very wise, Kharlia. You must have spent too much time with that dragon rider of yours."

Kharlia blushed again and then lowered her eyes. "I hope Bakari is safe. It's been almost two weeks since he has left."

The king moved his feet from the couch to the floor. "One thing I know about that boy is that he is smart and brave and will make things work out."

Kharlia nodded. "But I do miss him, Lan."

"Of course you do," Lan agreed. He sat forward on the couch, as if readying himself to stand up. "We all are missing those we love."

"Oh, Lan," Kharlia gasped. "I didn't mean to put my own loss before yours. You must miss Breelyn also."

"Yes, I do." Lan sighed. "And I am more worried about her than about Bakari. She is young, for an elf, and impetuous. So she thinks with her heart before her head sometimes."

Kharlia moved over to Lan's side and helped him stand. Then she said, "She will be back soon, I am sure."

Pulling on a dark green cloak, Lan took a few steps.

"You look grand, my lord," Kharlia said.

They walked out onto a balcony overlooking the tree city of Lor'l. Kharlia watched Lan breathe in deeply and smile for the first time this week. The king cradled his bad arm and kept it wrapped up tightly in the cloak.

A progressive hush filled the city until all were silent. Kharlia saw heads poking out from various trees, houses, and even looking up from the ground. In reverent awe, they watched their king for a moment, then bowed their heads to signify their love.

Kharlia watched Lan from the side. His jaw was held firm, and his dark hair hung behind him, pulled back in a golden band. As his eyes took in everything, a tear slipped down his face.

"There is so much love here," he whispered so that only Kharlia and a few guards nearby would hear him. "How can such an evil exist in this beautiful world?" he said, clearly referring to the Chameleon and the darkness that was spreading in himself.

Kharlia kept a hand on his back to keep him steady. With the pain the king must be feeling, it was an amazing feat for him to even be standing there like he was.

Taking a few steps toward the lift, the king said more loudly, "I need to see my people."

One of his healers stepped up closer and said, "Sir, you are still not well. You need to rest."

"No, my people need to see their king," Lan said firmly, implying that he would brook no debate in the manner.

"It is still spreading, Your Highness," Kharlia whispered next to him. "Moving around too much may make it spread farther."

As the king turned to look down at her, Kharlia felt so small in his presence, and not just physically. The king was one of the most regal people she had ever seen, and his aura filled the small area where they stood.

His eyes were hard, at first, and then softened. "Thank you for your concern, Kharlia. But I cannot just think of myself in this," the king said with a gentle voice. "My people need to know that things are going well. This has been a challenging time, since the barrier came down, and they need hope and strength. This is my duty."

Kharlia nodded. She knew all of the things that Bakari did out of duty. Fulfilling one's duty was a heavy burden sometimes, but one that forged strength.

"Then let me walk by your side," Kharlia offered.

The king raised his slanted eyebrows at her, and she blushed.

"I promised, to Breelyn and Bakari, to take care of you." She gazed directly into his green eyes and added, "I, too, take my duty seriously."

"Well said, young healer." The king laughed and added, "We'll make an elf out of you yet."

A group of guards and one other healer joined Kharlia and the king as they descended to the ground on a wooden lift. The quiet hush in the city turned into whispers and then into many excited voices as the people saw their king coming to them.

Reaching the ground, the new king strolled along slowly, but regally, through the shaded paths, greeting each elf he saw by name.

Kharlia still marveled at the elves. A beautiful race with fine features and clear eyes—some blue, some green. Their hair, whether dark or light, hung down their backs, and many of them had headbands on, holding the silky hair back behind them, their upswept ears showing on either side of their heads.

As others came down from the trees, they walked toward the king, soon forming long lines, winding throughout the grounds beneath the tree city. Loose robes in bright colors hung on most of them, with a few pants and tighter clothes being worn by the tradespeople and warriors.

There were no poor or rich among them, no anger or hate. They reverenced the king with a common, unanimous support that brought tears to Kharlia's eyes. So she stepped a few paces back to let the king have this moment with his people.

"Greetings friends... So nice to see you... Be at peace" were some of the things the king said as he greeted them, offering hope and strength to each elf individually. As the children approached, the king kneeled down and took their small hands in his larger ones and gave them encouragement in their studies.

As people left him, to return to their duties, Kharlia heard their expressions of love and concern for their beloved king. She smiled and thought of how wonderful it would be if all lands were governed this way. But the elves had achieved something that no one else had.

"You are wondering how all this happened?" asked an elf that came up next to Kharlia.

Kharlia glanced up to find the healer that she had worked with so often in the past week. "Halleema, how did you know?"

The middle-aged elf smiled—although, for an elf, being *middle-aged* was probably quite a bit older than it would be for an Alarian.

"Your thoughts were written all over your face, Kharlia."

"It's truly amazing," Kharlia said. "Have you ever been outside of Elvyn?"

"No." Halleema shook her head. "No, I haven't. I have heard stories, though..." Her face clouded over.

"It is not like this," Kharlia continued. "There is so much hate and pride and greed in the world. How did the elves move past all that?"

Halleema patted Kharlia on the back and said, "Now that is quite a story. We were not always the peace-loving people you see today. Back in the old land, across the sea, the elves were a strong race of warriors."

Kharlia raised one eyebrow. "That is hard to believe."

"Yes, but true nonetheless. There were multiple cultures of elves, and not all believed as we did," Halleema said.

"We?" Kharlia asked. "You mean, there are other groups of elves?"

Halleema laughed, and the sound reminded Kharlia of Breelyn. "Aren't there different lands, kingdoms, cultures, and even colors of humans?"

"I never thought of it that way before." Kharlia was surprised at this news. "It does make sense, I guess."

"Just as the southern elves, in Mallek, are different from us, there are others, farther away, that are different from us also." Halleema's face saddened.

"Do you know where they are?"

"Far, far away, I suppose," Halleema said. "We left a thousand years ago."

Kharlia wanted to know more—this was fascinating—so she said, "Tell me about it."

But Halleema looked toward the king, and worry spread across her face. Kharlia followed the healer's look. The king's face was pale, and he was now sitting down on a wooden bench—an extension of a nearby tree that Kharlia did not remember being there before.

"The king needs to rest," Kharlia said.

Halleema nodded. "The story will have to wait until later."

Kharlia understood. She walked up next to the king and put her hand on his shoulder. He tried to smile at her, but she could see the pain he was hiding. Only a few elves remained, and the king greeted them briefly, then his guards circled around him.

"We must get you back to your tree." Halleema motioned.

The king tried to stand up but stumbled. Before he had fully slumped to the ground, two guards each took an arm and held him up.

"His eyes are dilating," Kharlia said in concern. "He's about to pass out."

"There is no time to get him to his tree," Halleema told the group. "Follow me," the healer said as she moved off down a smaller trail.

Kharlia had to run to keep pace with the long-legged elves. Then part of the king's cloak slid down, and Kharlia gasped. The blackness was on his shoulder now. Looking up at the king's face, she saw that his eyes were closed and his breathing was labored.

"Halleema, hurry," Kharlia said. "He's passed out."

An onlooker saw the procession, and compassion covered his face, and a soft song escaped his lips. Soon another voice joined in, and then another.

Halleema turned to Kharlia and said, "The song of hope."

More voices joined in as they lead the king farther down the narrowing path. The voices joined, turning into a harmonious chorus, filled with a range and depth of voices that brought tears to Kharlia's eyes.

"Where are we going?" she asked, hardly able to bring the words forth. Her voice sounded harsh and unpolished in comparison to the singing that filled the forest.

"There is a healer's hut on the ground close by here," Halleema said. Then she turned her face up and joined in the song.

They sang of a people from long ago, a people who were persecuted in a faraway land. They sang of their hope and faith and love and of how these people didn't give in to their brothers' and sisters' hate and greed and pride. They sang of a people who stayed pure, escaped in ships, and then sailed across the sea for many weeks, eventually landing in a beautiful land full of trees, greenery, water, and food—a land they named Elvyn.

Kharlia cried as the song tore at her heart with this brief history of the elves and their struggles and their triumphs. She felt truly blessed to be there that day and to have learned from them. As the song rose to its crescendo and then moved to its finish, Kharlia felt something stir within her soul—an infusion of power—and she gasped out loud.

Arriving at the healer's hut, Halleema opened the door for the guards, to bring the king into the hut, and then continued to hold it open while Kharlia entered.

"You felt the power, didn't you?" Halleema asked Kharlia. "Not many outside of our race have heard that song before. It is very powerful; you have been blessed today, Kharlia."

The guards laid the king down tenderly on a small pallet of colorful blankets while Halleema moved to the fireplace and started a fire. Kharlia looked around the room—it felt *alive*. She could sense the life in the wood. She didn't know if this was a power from being in this room specifically or was the residual power from hearing the joyful Elvyn song.

Moving over to the king, Kharlia felt his forehead and almost jumped back. He was so cold. She rummaged in her satchel for something that could help. She took out the vials of cinnamon and ginger, mixing them together with a few tablespoons of water. Then she brought a small cup of this mixture up to the king's mouth and poured it in.

He did not open his eyes or say anything, but he did swallow down the concoction.

"It is spreading," Halleema said, pointing to the blackness that was now creeping up to his neck.

"I won't let this happen, Healer," Kharlia said forcefully. "I made promises that I intend to keep."

Kharlia thought about what other herbs she could use— nothing was stopping it. Tears came to her eyes as she thought about the love Lan had shown his people. About the hope he had given them, even knowing it was killing him. About all the knowledge that the elves had and the many years of study that their healers went through.

Then, turning to Halleema, Kharlia's face reddened with anger as she said, "Why can't you heal him? Why can't you heal your king?"

Halleema didn't rise to Kharlia's anger but instead put a hand softly on Kharlia's arm as she said, "We work with the natural forces around us, Kharlia. We can heal normal ills or pains and even broken bones and deep wounds of the flesh. But this is magic—dark magic. This is not something we have been trained in."

Kharlia felt ashamed about lashing out at one of these peaceful people, but something had to be done. "I have seen evil in this world, Halleema: Men wanting to be king by stepping on others' backs while having no thought for their lives. Barrier beasts having evil hearts. And the Chameleon unleashing his evil powers on us. But their powers came from somewhere. Both Bakari and Roland have taught me that power is not evil or good, only the intentions of those wielding it can determine how it is used."

Halleema nodded her head in understanding. The two guards still present looked from Kharlia to Halleema and then to their king. Lan's coloring was slightly better now, but he still lay unconscious.

He is dying!

Kharlia breathed in and tried to channel the energy of her anger into thinking like Bak would think. She tried to remember all she had been taught by her mother about herbs and natural healing. She remembered the feeling of uselessness she had experienced when she couldn't heal her mother's sickness. But she had more knowledge now. And she had studied with the elves for the past week—a short time, to be sure, but she had learned things!

She closed her eyes and steadied her breathing. Echoes of the beautiful Elvyn song still floated on the air, and Kharlia breathed them in. Then the herbs, the natural healing of the elves, the power of their song, and the memories of things she had seen Bakari and the other wizards do all came together in her heart. She felt a power grow there—something new, but not frightful; something powerful, but hopeful.

Without opening her eyes, Kharlia placed her hand on the king's forehead and used all the knowledge and power that she had felt to reach inside of him. The evil taint almost forced her hand away. But, with determination, she gritted her teeth and dove in deeper. She was a healer. That is what she had always been. And now, the elves' magic infused her with clarity and precision.

She felt the king's good heart and his love for his people, and tears ran down her face.

Kharlia—little one—how are you here? the king's voice said in her own head.

I don't know, Your Highness. But I had to do something. Kharlia choked back a sob. *How do you stand the evil stain inside you?*

I try not to think about it, the king said, and Kharlia felt the king wince in pain. *The love of my people sustains me.*

With Kharlia's new clarity of thought, she found the cinnamon and ginger she had given the king earlier, urging these deeper into his system, and felt the king's skin warm under the touch of her hand.

His body also had natural abilities, and she suddenly understood these. Reaching out, she somehow formed a barrier between the king's strong heart, filled with his love for his people, and the evil taint that had crept up his arm and onto his neck. She couldn't take the taint away, but she could stop it from getting worse. She knew she could.

Kharlia! "You are amazing!" the king proclaimed, his voice moving from within her head to a vocal praise of her abilities.

Kharlia opened her eyes and peered into the clear eyes of the king. Glancing down, she saw that the black tendrils had retreated slightly, staying now at the top of his arm. But sweat beaded on her own forehead, and her legs felt weak. Kharlia grabbed the side of the pallet, to keep herself from falling over. Then Halleema grabbed her and led her to a nearby chair, to sit down.

"Kharlia," Halleema said, her usually slanted eyes wide with wonder. "What did you do?"

Kharlia smiled. "I honestly don't know. But something had to be done." Her head pounded, and she felt weak, but the power of healing still soared through her soul.

"Are you sure you do not have Elvyn blood, my dear?" the king said in a soft voice from his pallet.

Kharlia just shrugged her shoulders. "I'm just glad I could help."

"You have done more than help, Kharlia. You are a true healer," the king said. "A true Elvyn healer and a friend of the elves forever." Lan sat up on his elbow and motioned Kharlia back over to him.

Kharlia stood up and steadied herself for a moment. She was so tired. She laughed inside as she remembered how tired Bakari was, at first, after merging with another animal. Then she took two steps over to the king's side.

He placed his slender, pale hand on her smaller, dark one and said, "My guards and Halleema do witness this day that I name you Elvyn-friend, an official distinction that few have ever been named to. Kharlia, you will be honored in the long history of my people. Your name will be added to the song of hope. Today, you have given of yourself that which is the rarest and most powerful—you have given your love and have used that power to heal me. You will be welcome across Elvyn and will be afforded anything you desire. Kharlia, you will always have a home among the elves. With this decree, you are now blessed with all Elvyn knowledge. As a king of the elves, I, Lanwaithian Soliel, do now decree this as an unalterable and binding promise for all time."

Kharlia gasped as power flooded into her from the king's hand. It made her feel as if she had been born again. The air around her brightened, and the trees and flowers *spoke* to her. She felt the souls of the small animals scurrying by the hut. Her mind was bright, and knowledge filled it immediately. Her heart expanded, and she felt a love for all around her.

With tears in her eyes, she gazed into Lan's face. "Thank you, Your Highness. You honor me far beyond what I deserve. It was only my intent to help you."

"And that is why you are being so blessed, Kharlia. Your motives were pure, and your love for a king that is not even your own king showed your true heart. A heart that is now Elvyn."

As Kharlia, Halleema, and the two guards bowed their heads to the king, in reverence, all was silent for a moment.

"And now," the king said, breaking the silence, "I must ask more of you, my new Elvyn-friend."

Kharlia looked back up at him with curiosity.

"I need you to go and find help for my beloved, Breelyn. I fear she may be in trouble and may need a friend."

CHAPTER TWENTY SIX

For three days, Alli had seen no visitors, except for the occasional servant, bringing small morsels of bread, and the person who periodically changed the chamber pots. None of these servants spoke to or looked at Alli. Her wrists were still held in the manacles that cut off her wizard powers, though she had been able to maneuver them to the front of her now, rather than behind her back. Her physical strength had returned after the first day, only to begin to diminish again with the lack of food and exercise.

Alli had discovered that Tobias, the Sanctuary commander, had been held there for over a month. Putting the time frame together in her mind, Alli had determined that the Chameleon had been in Quentis, sowing discord, before arriving in Elvyn. He had, most likely, now resumed the periodic role of the commander and was having a negative influence on the King of Quentis.

While sitting on the floor in the back of the cell, she heard a door open and soft voices approaching. Figuring it was another servant, she didn't even bother to look up.

"Allison Stenos," a strong voice said, "you have a visitor."

The mention of her own name brought up Alli's head. There were two men standing in the shadows of the cell wall.

One was smaller than the other. She stood up and walked forward, her curiosity winning over her weakness.

As a light flared in the hand of the taller man, she gasped. It was a duplicate of the Sanctuary commander. So, her notion had been correct. In the next cell over, the real commander shuffled forward.

The other person with the false commander was none other than Jaimon. From the young man's body language, he appeared cowed and fearful.

"The dragon rider wanted to see his treacherous wizard companion one last time," the false commander said with authority.

"One last time?" Alli asked. "What are you going to do to him, Chameleon? He has done nothing wrong."

The man laughed. "Good, good. You know who I am. But you misunderstood me. It is *your* last time, Battlemaster. My dear dragon rider will denounce his other allegiances and will join with me. You, on the other hand, will be executed."

Alli stared at Jaimon, who had yet to meet her eyes. "Is this true, Jaimon?" She couldn't believe he would give in, but he was young. She laughed at that idea. Jaimon was just a year younger than she was. It was just that he was so much more naive about the world.

Jaimon brought his head up slowly, and his eyes pierced hers. Alli held back her joy at seeing that the young man had indeed not defected. His eyes were steeled, and Alli knew that he had not given up at all. She was quite surprised, though, that Jaimon had fooled the Chameleon so well. This told her that the Chameleon had a weakness—most likely his vanity or his lust for power.

"The commander here," Jaimon said, moving a hand to refer to the false commander, "and the king of Quentis have asked for my help in securing our land. I cannot turn down a direct command from my king."

Alli had new respect for the young dragon rider. He was playing his part well, and so would she.

"They want to control your dragon, Jaimon. They will use it to conquer other lands. You know what the Chameleon wants."

The Chameleon stepped closer. "You have no idea what we want, Battlemaster."

Alli raised her eyebrow in question. He had used the word *we* rather than *I*. Was the Chameleon not working on his own? That information would be helpful to know.

"Like all brutes and bullies, you want to control everything," Alli lashed out.

The Chameleon laughed heartily. "Oh, you are so wrong, my dear. I don't want to control everything, only a part of it. My brothers and I will carve out the western lands and will rule under my father, the rightful wizard king!"

Alli was confused. "Your father?"

"My father was the last wizard king of Alaris. His kingdom and ambitions were taken from him before his designs were accomplished."

"But he is dead." Alli couldn't believe what she was hearing. She glanced at Jaimon, and his eyes told her that he didn't understand either.

The Chameleon moved toward the bars, putting his head up close to them. It was unnerving to see both him and the rightful commander in the next cell over.

"We will bring him back from the dead, and he will rule all!" the Chameleon said through the bars. "All will bow then, especially those arrogant elves. They will be the first to scrape our boots with their tongues."

The real commander took that moment to voice his first words since the Chameleon had entered with Jaimon. "I will kill you!" he screamed. "You are crazy!"

The distraction caused the Chameleon to turn away from Alli. As soon as he had, Jaimon brought his fingers up to the bars and grabbed Alli's fingers. She began to pull away in surprise, but then Jaimon slipped something into her hand.

The Chameleon turned back around and pushed Jaimon's hands away from the bars as he said, "What are you doing?"

Jaimon turned, looking frightened, to the Chameleon commander. "I wanted to see her manacles closer. Their power must be amazing."

The Chameleon frowned and took his meaning incorrectly. "Don't worry, Dragon Rider. The manacles won't harm you— only wizards."

"So they won't work on dragons?" Jaimon asked.

The Chameleon grabbed Jaimon's arms. "Of course not, stupid boy. They are made to stop wizards like her. She will never feel power coursing through her veins ever again."

Alli hated the Chameleon's pompous attitude. "Afraid that my power is greater than yours, Chameleon?"

The man's veins pulsed in his neck, and he pulled Jaimon away from the cell with him as he said, "Your power is nothing, Wizard. Already we have converted Breelyn, and now Jaimon will follow us. Their esteemed leader has lost his dragon and soon will come to our side as well. You cannot stand up to the dragons and their riders."

Alli put her face to the bars and growled at the false commander, "We will see about that!"

A guard joined the Chameleon and Jaimon as they were exiting the room. But, before the door closed, the Chameleon turned back toward the cells. He was only an outline in the now dimmed light as he said, "You won't be *seeing* anything, girl. You will be executed tomorrow, for sneaking into Quentis and trying to incite rebellion. The Wolf has already signed the decree."

The door closed, and Alli stepped back from the bars of her cell. "The Wolf?" she whispered under her breath.

"Seems you have gained high enemies quickly." The real commander cackled from the next cell.

Alli ignored him. Would the Wolf actually kill her? She didn't think Kaspar would let him. But, would his son know about it? She fingered the item that Jaimon had slipped into her hands.

"What have you got there?" Commander Tobias asked, moving as close as he could against the bars.

"A figurine, from the dragon rider." She walked closer to the high, barred window. With its meager light, she was able to see that the figurine was a small statue of a dragon, carved in jade. It felt smooth and cool to the touch. "It is from the Followers of the Dragon."

"Those incompetent fools?" the commander mumbled. "They have been looking for a dragon for centuries."

"Well, there is one here now. So, maybe their fanaticism was not so misplaced," Alli said as she held the jade dragon in her hand. She closed her fingers into a fist around it and then closed her eyes.

Why did Jaimon give me this one?

She reached inside of herself and tried to find her power. It was there—but still held at bay by her manacles. She searched harder and then felt another flicker at a far corner of her mind—another kind of magic—different from her wizard powers. She struggled to grasp it. But, finally, in the darkness of her mind, she saw a green flare and dove into it.

Wizard! said a surprised voice. Alli had never actually heard this voice before, but she had an inkling of who it might be.

Cholena?

Who else? We girls need to stick together, remember?

Alli laughed with delight. *I hope you have a plan to get us out of here. I am imprisoned in the dungeon, and Jaimon is being manipulated by the Chameleon.*

My rider is not being manipulated as much as you think—he did get you the dragon artifact.

Alli had to agree with Cholena, but Alli knew that the Chameleon could be ruthless.

Help will arrive soon, the dragon said into Alli's mind. *I cannot get down to the dungeons.*

Who? How? Alli thought back. *I am to be executed tomorrow.*

My Followers will help you. Don't despair, the dragon said. Then her presence faded away from Alli's mind.

Alli tried to reach out again, but it was useless—the dragon was gone. Her *followers*? Did Cholena mean that ragtag bunch of fanatics, as the commander had called them? Alli was glad they had found and kept the artifacts, but she didn't think they were organized enough or powerful enough to get her out.

The rest of the day had nearly passed, when a servant delivered an evening meal—if you could call it that—of beans and water. Later, a hazy moon shone through the high window. And, at some point in the night, Alli fell asleep into disturbing dreams of her impending death.

As Alli woke up the next morning, a new despair began to settle in her breast. But she held it at bay. There had to be a way out...there always was. But Alli had always had her powers to get her out of bad situations. She knew that both her fighting and her wizard skills were far beyond what most people could bring against her.

But now she sat alone in a cell, without the use of any of her abilities. She had never thought much about dying. But, now that she was starting to, she realized that she wasn't nearly ready. She was still not even sixteen. She wanted to live. And she would!

She still had her mind, so she put it to work, thinking about how to escape. Looking down at her manacles, she tried to figure out how to get them off. She leaned back against the stone wall and thought hard.

Even without her powers, Alli knew that she could fight. When they came to take her from her cell, that's what she would do. She would fight and try to get away and find Jaimon or Cholena or even Kaspar. Her face warmed as she thought about him. So she mentally slapped herself back to focus. Would Kaspar even help her?

The morning had dragged on, but then she heard the wooden door open and footsteps approach.

Probably the next meal, she thought, becoming more alert in waiting for any possibility to escape.

As had happened every day since Alli had been put into the cell, three people approached: a guard and two servants, usually women. One servant brought the food, and the other removed the waste. Alli turned her head to the side, not wanting to look at her final meal. She would rather go without eating.

Then a whisper came from the cell door, "Alli."

Alli whipped her head around. Never had a servant spoken to her—let alone known her name. With suspicion, Alli walked to the cell door. Then the servant pulled her hood back from her face.

"Gabby!" Alli exclaimed. "What are you doing here?" The youngest daughter of the Wolf, Kaspar's sister, stood in front of Alli, with a huge grin on her face.

"I am one of the Followers," Gabby said.

"Followers?" Alli was confused.

Gabby glanced around for a moment and then said in a soft voice, "Of the Dragon."

Oh, those Followers, Alli thought. Maybe she had dismissed the group too harshly.

"We need to go, Miss." The guard nudged Gabby. Then he pulled out a ring of keys and unlocked Alli's cell door.

Gabby turned to the other servant woman and said, "Change clothes."

"What?" Alli asked.

"You are switching places," Gabby said.

Alli shook her head as she watched the other woman remove her outer clothes. "I can't let her do that," Alli said. "They will kill her."

"No, they won't," Gabby said. "By the time they figure out she is the wrong person, you will be gone. They will not kill a servant. And she will pretend that she was forced to do it."

Alli didn't want to put someone else in danger, so she hesitated.

"I know what I am getting into," the other woman said. "Hail the Dragon."

"Hail the Dragon," the guard repeated softly.

"Please, Alli," Gabby begged and placed a hand on Alli's arm.

Alli felt something there and looked up into Gabby's eyes. Was this girl—the daughter of the Wolf—a wizard?

Gabby moved her head in a barely perceptible nod.

Alli smiled warmly and thought, *The world needs more female wizards.*

In the next cell over, Commander Tobias came to the bars. "Let me out too!" he yelled. "I'm going to kill that pretender."

"Who is that?" Gabby asked and took a few steps closer. "No, it can't be. I just saw the commander this morning, walking through the halls to see my father."

Alli slipped on the other woman's clothes and then walked over to the commander, saying, "Shhh. You will alert the guards." Then, turning to Gabby, she said, "This is the real commander. The other one is an impostor, a man called *the Chameleon*."

"I don't take orders from you," the commander said, getting louder. "Let me out, now!"

Alli put the cloak around herself and pulled the hood up over her face. "I will come back for you, sir. I promise."

The man's eyes opened wider. "You mean, you really are not letting me out?" he said, his voice rising in anger. "How dare you!"

"There is more at stake here than you realize, Commander," Alli said. "We can't have you charging in and messing things up."

The commander started to yell again.

"He's going to alert the other guards," the other woman said as she moved into Alli's cell.

Gabby nodded her head to her guard, and he walked over and grabbed the commander through the bars. Bringing back his other fist, he then punched him hard. The man fell to the ground in a heap.

"Well done, Micah," Gabby said.

Alli looked back and forth between Micah and Gabby, feeling surprised.

Gabby laughed. "My family oversees the Followers."

Alli almost choked. She had not seen *that* coming. "Jaimon's dragon told me you were coming. How is Jaimon?"

Gabby frowned. "We need to get you out of here first and then worry about him. He put his own life on the line for you to get out, Alli—by bringing the artifact to you."

Gabby went into Alli's cell and picked up her bucket of waste and handed it to Alli.

The smell made Alli's nose wrinkle up.

"The guards will stay away from you, with this in your hands," Gabby said.

"But my manacles…"

"Just hide them under your cloak while holding the bucket. We will get them off later."

Alli nodded and then followed Gabby and Micah to the large wooden door. Exiting through the door, three other guards eyed them, one nodding his head to Micah. When Alli approached, they backed away, not even bothering to look at the face under her hood.

Soon they were down the hall and were about to open another door, when two other guards almost fell through it as Micah opened the door. Alli hung back a few steps, not wanting to be questioned.

"Where are you two going in such a hurry?" Micah asked the two guards.

"To get the prisoner," one of them said. "Execution is today. The commander wants her all cleaned up and looking pretty."

Alli's heart raced. It was too soon. They wouldn't have enough time to get away before she would be discovered.

As the men moved to walk past, Alli pretended to trip, spilling the waste from the pail all over the two guards.

They both screamed and tried to swat Alli away, but it was too late. The waste dripped down the front of their clothes.

"Stupid woman," one of the guards said and moved closer, his hand raised as if to hit Alli.

But Micah grabbed the man's hand before it could strike her. Honestly, Alli wouldn't have minded a little scuffle. It had been a few days since she had gotten into a good fight.

"It was an accident," Micah said. "Go change. You two stink," he said as he waved a hand in the air and plugged his nose. "I'll find two others to bring the prisoner."

The two men grumbled, but they moved out of the hallway and went back the way they had come.

"That will buy us some time," Micah said. "But not much."

Gabby directed them down another hallway and around a corner. There, three familiar men approached them, and Alli almost stumbled. Gabby pulled Alli's cloak farther over her head, and they moved forward as if nothing were wrong. But, coming toward them, down the wide hallway, was the Wolf; his son, Kaspar; and the Chameleon commander.

Alli's heart beat so loudly that she thought for sure they would hear it. Would they recognize her? She hoped that the Chameleon's magic wouldn't notice hers.

The two women walked with their heads down, the remaining waste in the bucket still smelling up the air around them. Micah moved out in front of them and, as the three passed, bowed his head low.

Walking past, Alli let out a small sigh and felt both the Wolf and Kaspar poke her mind. They knew what Gabby was doing. "Guard, where are you heading?" the commander said as he turned around and then eyed the three of them.

"These two were serving the prisoner, sir," Micah said. "They got turned around, and I am escorting them back."

The Chameleon wrinkled up his nose. "Well, that will be the last waste you have to pick up from there. The spy from Alaris is to be executed today."

"Very well, sir," Micah said and bowed once more. "Health to you and your family."

With that, the three men turned and left. Receding boot clicks faded down the hallway and around a corner.

Then Alli let out a bigger sigh. "That was too close. I need to get out of this castle."

Two doors later, they took a servants' flight of stairs that circled around the back of the castle and then exited out into the bright sunlight. Alli squinted, and the other two covered their eyes with their hands. Then Gabby continued to lead them through the grounds and around to a small door in the castle's walls. This opened out into an apple orchard.

Putting the pail down, Alli flipped her head to throw back the hood of her cloak. She took Gabby's hands in her own manacled pair and felt the spark within Gabby once again.

"Thank you so much, Gabby. That was very close."

"Now we need the dragon," Gabby said.

Alli was confused. "No, we need to get Jaimon first. He can talk to Cholena."

"So can you," Micah said.

"With the figure Jaimon gave you," Gabby added.

Alli pulled the jade dragon out of the pocket of her new clothes. She had kept the figure in her hand as she had exchanged clothes earlier with the poor woman now in her dungeon cell.

Grasping the jade dragon tightly, Alli reached her mind out again. She tried to access her own powers but grunted with the realization that, with the manacles still on her wrists, she could not yet.

This time, it was easier to reach Cholena. So she called out to the dragon.

Can you get to the north of the city: where we first landed? Cholena asked.

Alli relayed the request to Gabby, who nodded her head.

Then what? Alli asked.

Then we save Jaimon and crush those who took him, Cholena said, and Alli felt a powerful force echo within her mind.

Alli smiled and said, *Ah, time for a little fighting.*

"What about my manacles?" Alli asked Gabby out loud.

Gabby frowned slightly, making her seem even younger than she was. Then she said, "My brother's working on that."

CHAPTER TWENTY SEVEN

Moving with quick steps, Gabby and Micah led Alli through the orchards to the back door of a tall, whitewashed brick building. Micah pulled the heavy door open and motioned them to enter. Alli surveyed the dark room, trying to get her eyesight back. Blinking a few times, she began to see the outlines of a group of people who were standing around a long, rectangular table.

The Followers of the Dragon.

At their head stood Kaspar—tall, dark, and handsome. He smiled at Alli, and she barely controlled her blush this time.

I'm glad Roland isn't quite that perfect.

The thought surprised Alli. Why did Roland always seem to pop into her mind at the most strange times? But she did wonder how he was doing.

Looking around the room once more, she thought she felt Roland's presence nearby, as she had once before. *I'm getting paranoid,* she told herself. *And, just because I feel something for Roland doesn't mean I can't notice the beautiful man in front of me.*

"Alli," Kaspar said. "I'm glad to see you."

"Do I have you to thank for my rescue, Kaspar? Are you the leader of these Followers?"

Kaspar fidgeted for a moment. "Well, technically, my father is, but I do run things for him from time to time," He smiled, and his teeth shone, bright white in the dim room. "We need to leave now."

"But your father was the one that gave me up." Alli felt her face turning red with her anger. "*He* sent me to the dungeon."

Kaspar shook his head and said, "No. That was the commander's order. My father didn't dare intervene, for he is in a dangerous position."

"And I wasn't?" Alli retorted.

"We don't have time for this right now," Kaspar said. "You don't understand the politics here. My father stalled the Commander as long as he could to allow us time to help you escape and for me to get back here."

As a woman gave Kaspar a bundle of clothes and weapons, Alli gave him a questioning look.

"For you," Kaspar said. "But first, we have to get those manacles off."

"Now would be a good time for that," Alli said, holding her hands out in front of herself.

Kaspar's face reddened. It was the only time Alli had seen the young prince look embarrassed.

"I don't know how yet," he said. "But we have to go."

Two guards came up next to Kaspar, and they motioned Alli to follow them as they went out of a back door.

"North of the city, by the river," Alli informed them. Through the figurine, which she still held in her hand, Alli knew exactly where Cholena was.

In about thirty minutes, they were clear of the city, and then, a short walk later, they came over a small hill. Alli spied the dragon. Cholena was next to the Mahli River, where the river fed into the Bay of Ghazi, her green scales glistening magnificently in the sunlight.

As they approached her, Cholena roared a greeting, green fire emanating from her growing maw. *Glad to see you safe again, Battlemaster,* the dragon said to Alli's mind as Alli reached her side.

You are looking beautiful today, Cholena, Alli said. She moved her hands out, to touch the dragon, but the manacles got in the way.

"Kaspar!" Alli turned on the prince. "I need these off now!"

Kaspar thought for a moment, and Alli felt his influence push against her mind.

"Stay out of there, Kas," Alli said and then held her jaw clenched. What was he trying to do?

"Sorry—old habits," Kaspar apologized. "Just trying to find a way for those things to come off."

Alli sighed and then paced around while Kaspar continued in thought.

Finally, he called out to her, "I got it. The dragon!"

"*The dragon* what?" Alli was getting tired of this. She needed her magic and her hands.

"She can bite them off."

Alli halted in her pacing and thought, *It might work.*

Using the figurine, she held her hands up to Cholena and asked, *Can you take these off?* The dragon brought her heavy head down, close to Alli's petite body.

As Alli held her hands up in front of her, the dragon moved her mouth over Alli's hands. Gleaming white teeth, at least six inches long, sat in front of Alli. What if Cholena missed and bit off Alli's hands instead?

Hold still, little one, Cholena scolded. *I'm not going to eat you— at least, not today!*

Cholena, don't joke like that, Alli said. *You dragons have a strange sense of humor.*

Alli could feel the warm fires of the dragon's belly escaping through Cholena's mouth and onto her hands. Then she saw Kaspar and the two guards step back in fear.

As the dragon crunched down over one hand, Alli held her breath and closed her eyes…then she felt the manacle drop from her wrist to the ground. The dragon repeated that same action over Alli's other hand and then backed away with what could only be described as *a smile* on her fearsome face.

Alli ran her left hand over the wrist of her right. The cuts and scrapes from the manacles stung, but her wrists were serviceable still. Bringing her hands up in the air, she formed a ball of fire and threw it, off toward the river.

"It's back!" Alli laughed in delight. "My magic is back."

With the figurine in one hand, Alli reached her other small hand up and rubbed Cholena's hard, green scales, saying, *Thank you, my friend.*

Kaspar brought Alli the bundle that the two guards had carried. "I suspect that, before the day is over, you might need a little more freedom in your movements."

"You mean, a fight is coming?" Alli took the clothes from Kaspar. Moving behind the dragon, she told the men to turn around. Soon she had slipped on some tight, black pants that stretched easily, a black tunic, and a long, black cloak, which finished the outfit.

Much easier to move around in, Alli thought to herself.

When Alli came back around from behind the dragon, Kaspar handed her two swords and two knives and asked, "Will this help?"

"For starters," Alli said with a smile, cocking her head to the side.

Kaspar laughed. "You are a tease, Battlemaster."

Cholena shook her wings in apparent anxiousness, so Alli gripped the figurine and heard Cholena say, *Climb aboard, Alli!*

Without Jaimon? Alli asked, feeling surprised. She had never flown on one of the dragons without a dragon rider aboard.

Yes, you are worthy, Cholena said to Alli. *And you may bring the others also.* Cholena kneeled down on the ground so that the group could climb up onto her back more easily.

Alli mounted and then motioned for the others to climb aboard.

They hesitated a moment, as if unsure of flying on a dragon.

Cholena growled, *Tell them to hurry. We must save my rider.*

"Hurry," Alli said.

Soon Alli and the three men were sitting in a line on Cholena's back. Before lifting up into the air, the young dragon unfurled her wings and stretched them out to each side. Then, with a few great flaps, they took off, high into the sky, and raced across the short distance, toward the city.

The dragon took them up very high in the air—higher than normal eyesight would notice. They flew over the city and then landed on the top of a flat building, to be away from prying eyes. Alli dismounted and moved to the edge of the building and looked down.

A crowd had gathered in the courtyard of the castle. Alli spotted a hooded figure in black being escorted toward a platform. She inhaled sharply as she realized it was the woman who had replaced her in the dungeon cell. The guards that had taken her from the cell obviously hadn't known what Alli looked like. They must have assumed she was Alli and just escorted the woman to her impending death.

"I can't let her die for me," Alli said out loud.

"She knew the risks," Kaspar whispered from behind her. Alli hadn't heard him dismount from the dragon.

"No, Kas. No one dies for me," Alli said. Looking over the rest of the crowd, she spied Jaimon up on a stand next to the Wolf, the false commander, and a man that, she knew instantly, had to be the king of Quentis. He was an older version of Kaspar and his father. Same olive skin and dark hair, but the man's face looked thin and sickly, and his body appeared to be frail.

Then Alli felt someone's attention on her, and she peered down into the upturned eyes of the Wolf. She felt him push against her mind with thoughts of relief. Alli decided to send her thoughts out. She didn't know for sure if the Wolf could understand, but she tried anyway.

You hide behind layers and layers of secrecy and play a dangerous game here, Alli thought.

I am the Wolf.

This was the only reply back. It made Alli smile for some reason. Then the Wolf moved over closer to Jaimon.

Alli! Jaimon's voice said to Alli through their current mutual connection to the dragon. The rider still kept his eyes forward, watching the procession, so as to not give away the presence of the dragon or Alli.

"It's up to you and the dragon, Alli," Kaspar said. "I can't get involved—at least, not yet. There is a precarious balance right now."

Alli understood. As long as the Chameleon pulled the strings in Quentis, Kaspar and his father would have to be careful.

The two guards joined Kaspar, and they moved to the back of the building while Alli remounted.

Ready? she asked Cholena.

They timed their appearance to the perfect moment to save the woman that had taken Alli's place, lifting up off the roof again and flying above the crowd. The hooded figure now stood on top of a platform, and one of the executioners moved forward to remove her hood.

At the exact moment the hood was removed, Cholena flew low over her, and Alli reached down and with the strength of a Battlemaster wizard picked the woman up, throwing her back behind her. The dragon emitted a loud roar and spewed fire from her mouth, blocking the guards from reaching them.

Careful, my friend. There are also good people down there, Alli cautioned the dragon.

My Rider! Cholena roared and flew toward Jaimon.

On the way there, Cholena stopped quickly to allow Alli to drop off the woman at the side of the crowd.

Flying back up into the air, Cholena soared over the group. Alli stood up on the back of the dragon, her cloak floating out behind her, and removed both of her swords from her side. She jumped through the air and landed on a dais where the dignitaries sat. Cholena continued to her rider, and Jaimon grabbed a hold of her neck, swinging up to take Alli's place on the dragon's back.

"Protect the king," Alli yelled to the Wolf.

The Wolf nodded at her. This was her way of keeping them both safe and of keeping his other allegiances secret. He grabbed the king and pulled him back to the castle.

"Kill her!" the Chameleon commander yelled at the guards.

Three guards approached her, and she backed up—as if afraid of them—until her back hit a railing on the dais. Then one of the guards lunged for her, and Alli jumped up, balancing on the railing with her right foot as she leaped into the air, kicking the guard away with her left foot and landing back on the platform.

As the other two guards rushed forward, Alli brought her two swords up in the air and began spinning them faster and faster, infusing them with magic. Flames spewed forth, forcing the guards back.

Behind her, she heard a swooshing sound and turned just in time to see a ball of wizard fire racing toward her. Leaning quickly back, almost parallel to the ground, the young

Battlemaster let the fireball scream over her stomach and into the two guards that had been attacking her.

Hearing a grunt behind her, Alli turned to see Jaimon and his dragon knocking down the wizard who had unleashed his power at Alli. The dragon was also clearing the courtyard quickly.

Alli looked around the dais for the Chameleon and couldn't find him. She yelled in frustration. Out of the corner of her eye, she noticed another man racing toward her. He was the biggest giant Alli had ever seen—over seven feet tall. The man was swinging a ball of spikes around his head, with black tendrils of power flaring out from it. Looking into the giant's eyes, Alli saw the Chameleon looking back at her.

"I told you that you would die today," the Chameleon bellowed as he advanced on Alli.

Alli couldn't let the black tendrils touch her. She had seen what they had done to Breelyn and to the Elvyn king. Somehow, Roland had used that power without damaging himself, but he was special—a thought Alli would never admit to that arrogant man.

She dug deep inside of herself and pulled up all the magic she could gather, flinging it in one hot stream of fire at the Chameleon. His body was engulfed in flames, but he walked out of them unscathed.

"Your powers are puny compared to my father's." The Chameleon was still swinging the ball of spikes and its chain, faster and faster, the black tendrils moving around it with an increasing speed. "He gives me power from the other side. Dark powers of death."

Alli shook her head and tried not to get distracted by the Chameleon's rantings. Then she remembered the figurine. She had moved it into the pocket of the new clothes that Kaspar had given her.

Dropping one sword onto the ground, Alli grabbed the figurine with that free hand and concentrated on it. Power flared up inside her.

Alli! said Cholena's voice.

Now that Alli had her own wizard powers back, she could pull more power from the figurine—a new power, a different power, the power of dragons.

Be careful, Battlemaster, Cholena warned Alli.

Alli could hear the dragon and Jaimon finishing up the rest of the fighting behind her. So it was now down to her and the Chameleon.

"Die!" the Chameleon yelled as he jumped forward, spinning the spiked ball and chain, its black tendrils reaching like fingers toward Alli.

Time slowed down for Alli as she pulled more power from the jade dragon carving in her hand, moving past the power of just Cholena.

Who pulls my power? said another voice from afar. Another dragon.

I am the Battlemaster, Alli said. *I need power to fight the Chameleon.*

Take it, the voice replied. *I am Miriel.*

Alli heard the roar of the second dragon in her mind. Using her own power and that of both Cholena and Miriel, Alli struck out and time resolved itself.

Black tendrils clashed with the pure white light emanating from Alli's outstretched hand. Then the white light formed the visage of the jade dragon Alli held. It grew in size until it was almost double Alli's height and then opened its mouth, consuming the dark tendrils by sucking them into the white-hot magic.

"No!" the Chameleon yelled and then slumped over.

Alli advanced on the Chameleon. But, with all the distractions around her, she had not seen the figure now racing toward them. Turning, she saw the real commander, a crazed look in his eyes, his manacled hands outstretched. He had no magic power and very little physical strength left. Alli didn't know how he had even escaped.

"He is mine. All mine," the real commander said as he raced toward the Chameleon, who now stood back up, resuming the guise of the commander as his own face.

"You cannot kill me—I am you," the Chameleon taunted.

"I will die trying then," the real commander said. He seemed to pause for a moment and tried to gather in his strength. Alli supposed that, as commander of the Sanctuary, he had been very powerful once.

The commander's manacles glowed bright, and sparks came forth.

As the Chameleon reached out his fingers toward the man he had replaced, the familiar black tendrils came forth and began to encircle the rightful commander.

"No. No." The commander threw himself into the Chameleon, and they both fell over the railing and off the dais with a loud thud.

Alli raced over to that side and looked down the ten-foot drop. On the ground lay one man—only one. She could guess who that would be. She picked up the sound of footsteps, off to her right, and jumped off the platform herself, landing in a comfortable crouch. Then she stood up and raced after the running figure.

The crowd from the planned execution earlier had been pushed back, out of the square, but still hung around outside the castle walls. So Alli found herself looking into a sea of people. Trying to find something to give herself some height, she jumped up the side of a tree and clung to a low limb.

Surveying the crowd, Alli knew that she wouldn't be able to find the Chameleon. He could be anyone by now: the guard at the corner, the merchant escorting his wife away, or one of the tradespeople, gathered together and talking.

Cholena flew over the receding crowd and landed next to Alli. She dropped down from the tree, and Jaimon jumped off of his dragon and joined her.

"I almost had him," Alli spat.

"What did you do up there?" Jaimon said, pointing toward the dais. "Where did that white fire dragon come from?"

"I pulled from the powers of Cholena and Miriel, and I almost had him." Alli stopped and thought for a moment. "If I could have pulled from more dragons, I could have done it. That's it, Jaimon! That's how we can defeat the Chameleon. We need to pull all the dragons' powers together."

Jaimon nodded, and his eyes sparkled with excitement. "Yes, that might work. The manacles and his powers earlier never blocked the power of the dragons!"

"The power of the spirit—the power to bind," Alli said. "We need to let Bakari know!"

Alli heard quick footsteps and turned around. In the shadow of the castle appeared Kaspar and Gabby. Alli and Jaimon approached the pair carefully, making sure others didn't notice.

"Are you all right?" Kaspar asked Alli.

Alli nodded. "I found out how to defeat the Chameleon's evil. It's the power of the dragons."

Kaspar smiled. "That's what we have been protecting for thousands of years, Alli. The Followers of the Dragon protect the power of the dragons, to be used only when there are no other choices. There are rumors of others that are searching for more artifacts. The histories do say that there used to be more. But the figurines are powerful—and could be devastating in the wrong hands."

"I understand, Kaspar," Alli said. "But we will need to take these few with us."

Kaspar furrowed his eyebrows. "You have to be careful." He looked away from Alli and said to Jaimon, "Dragon Rider, who will wield this power to defeat the darkness?"

Jaimon turned to Alli, and she gave him a small smile. They both knew who it had to be.

"The Dragon King," Jaimon said. "Bakari, the Dragon King, will use the powers of the dragons. That is his right."

Kaspar clapped his hands, and Gabby squealed in delight. Then they both turned and looked back at the castle. Deep in the shadows stood the Wolf and the king. The Wolf stood close to his father, holding the king up on his feet. They both nodded their heads to Kaspar and Gabby and then turned and retreated back into the castle.

Kaspar turned back to Alli and Jaimon. "The Dragon King it is. That is what we were hoping to hear. It is for him that we have protected the artifacts. Hail the Dragon."

"Hail the Dragon," whispered Gabby.

CHAPTER TWENTY EIGHT

Bakari and Liam had spent an afternoon in the twin cities, stocking up their supplies for their trek into the Gold Mountains. Bakari did not feel good about bringing the Cremelinos into that rough mountain terrain, but Liam couldn't walk that far on his own. An urgency filled Bakari's heart to the point that it was hard for him not to bolt away on his own toward the dragon egg, for they needed to be there before it hatched.

That morning, Bakari had felt something disturb his magic. He had reached out in his mind somewhat but hadn't had time to go deeper. He thought he sensed the movement of dragon power—the power to bind—being used somewhere to the south. The only explanation he could think of was that someone needed power and was pulling it to them.

He would have normally guessed it to be Roland, but Bakari thought that Roland was probably still stuck in the magic stream and didn't have the knowledge of how to pull on a dragon's magic. That left Breelyn, Jaimon, or possibly Alli. Breelyn was in trouble the last time Bakari had seen her, and Jaimon didn't have magic powers of his own. So, with a small smile, Bakari guessed that it was probably Alli.

"Why the smile, Bakari?" Liam mumbled. "These mountains look impossible to cross over, especially on our horses."

"Oh, Liam, didn't I tell you?" Bakari said with a grin. "We aren't going over them; we are going under them!"

"Under?" Liam stood by his Cremelino and almost looked sick now. "You mean *through the mines?*"

"Yes. It's the fastest way there." Bakari mounted his horse. "I've asked a couple of the miners to lead us through."

"I bet my father put you up to this, didn't he?" Liam's horse kneeled down for him to make mounting easier.

Bakari checked the straps on his packs and made sure they were secure next to him on the horse. "I don't even know your father, Liam. I have never met him."

Liam just growled, and Bakari motioned him and the two miners forward. It took all Bakari had not to lash out at Liam sometimes. He didn't think he had ever been around someone who complained about and looked at things in such a negative light as Liam did.

Bakari tried to have compassion on Liam because Bakari knew it must have been hard to grow up in a royal household with a lame foot. But Liam was now at an age barely less than Bakari's. And Liam needed to grow up. Bakari guessed that getting on a dragon would help with that, and he grinned again.

Liam's horse trotted up next to his. "You're smiling again, Bakari."

"Maybe I'm just happy, Liam," Bakari snapped at the young prince. "Did you ever think of that? Maybe some people are just happy and like smiling."

Then Bakari noticed the looks that the miners were giving him. Liam was their prince, after all—and Bakari had just yelled at him. Bakari took a deep breath and steadied his mind.

Oh, seeing Liam fly on a dragon was going to be fun. Real fun!

Bakari tried to keep his face looking complacent, but he couldn't. So, to not raise Liam's ire any further, Bakari sent a mental image to his Cremelino and jumped out ahead of the group.

Soon they entered the mouth of the mine. Bakari had been told by the mining captain that a tunnel lead all the way through the mountain and out on the other side, though not many had ventured so far. Rumors of wild animals and strange people being in the Forgotten Lands had kept many people away, except for the miners, who didn't have time for such long expeditions.

One of the miners, Emory, turned to Bakari and said, "If you don't mind, sir, my father said men looking like you came and worked these mines about sixteen years ago."

Bakari almost fell off his horse. He turned to Emory and asked, "What did he say about them?" Bakari's heartbeat picked up pace.

"They had braids like yours, sir, but longer," Emory said. "And they worked hard but were looking for someone."

They stopped for a moment as they reached a crossroads in the mine. Frederic, the other miner, motioned them to the right. The torches inside the mine were getting farther apart now. Bakari turned to Liam with questioning eyes, as if to ask if he or Bakari should bring forth a mage light. He would rather not draw any more attention to himself; though, riding a

Cremelino probably already had the villagers thinking he was a wizard of some sort.

Liam brought forth a flame, then turned it into an oval mage light and pushed it out in front of the group a bit. The miners nodded their thanks.

Turning back to Emory, Bakari continued questioning him. "Do you know what they were looking for?"

Emory shook his head. "No, I don't recall, though I know they helped move around our mining machinery and then would disappear, for days at a time, deep into the tunnels."

"They were looking for some kind of king," Frederic butted in. "Those were the days when King Darius, Liam's father, first visited the mines—the day our lives became better." Turning to Liam, Frederic continued, "Did you know I met your father?"

Liam raised his brows, and Emory mumbled, "We've heard this story before."

"He saved me from being whipped or killed," Frederick said.

"And why would you have been treated so?" Liam asked, his eyebrows furrowed.

Frederick laughed. "I was caught stealing, down at a village. My father was sick and could hardly work in the mines. The king saved me that day and changed how the miners were treated. You father has a good heart." Frederick gave a short nod to Liam.

Liam nodded his head in return, and a small grin replaced his normal scowl as he said, "He does have a good heart."

Bakari was glad that the subject had moved away from the visit to the mines years ago by the men of Mahli. The mention of *a king* always made him nervous. He knew that he had declared himself one a few times already, but he was still hesitant to proclaim himself a king and would be until he had gathered all the dragons and established peace throughout the land.

Thoughts of the dragons pushed him forward more quickly now. "We have to hurry." Bakari motioned to the others to step up the pace of their horses.

* * *

Hours later, they had long since passed the last of the miners working in the mine, and the group was now traveling through smaller, rough-hewn tunnels that wound their ways through the Mountains of Gold. Stopping only periodically, to feed and water the horses, the four hurried forward as fast as they could. But the tighter tunnels and lowering ceilings sent a somber mood through the group.

At one point, they heard a loud wail off in the distance in front of them. Liam and the two miners turned to Bakari for direction.

"We push on," Bakari said and motioned with his hand.

A few minutes later, the wailing sound came again, this time from much closer. Soon they came to a fork in the tunnel. The miners studied some markings on the walls and talked in quiet tones between themselves while Liam moved over closer to Bakari.

"Why are you pushing us forward so hard, Bakari?" Liam asked.

Bakari sighed. How could he make Liam understand all the pressures he was under?

But before he could say anything, a strange beast burst out of the tunnel to their right, knocking Emory over. The creature was about the size of a pig, with gray spikes like a porcupine. Emory yelled out, and the creature turned back toward him. Putting its snout up in the air, it sniffed at the men and horses.

Bakari brightened their mage light, and the creature shrieked and backed away, clawing its feet against dirt and the stone floor of the tunnel.

"It's afraid of the light," Liam said.

"They must live in the dark," Bakari guessed.

Emory had jumped back up to his feet, and he and Frederick backed up until they were behind the two wizards. The Cremelinos had stayed calm, but the miners' two horses were acting spooked. Bakari reached his mind out to comfort them.

"Kill that thing!" Emory shouted.

Liam turned to Bakari. "I'd hate to kill it. We are intruding into his lair." Liam scrunched up his face in thought. "In fact, its life here, in the dark, would be an interesting study."

Bakari smiled. "I agree with you, Liam, but we don't have time right now. I can't afford any delay."

Bakari motioned the two miners to get back up on their horses. For the time being, the creature was keeping its distance from them, so Bakari said, "Which way?"

Frederick shook his head. "I'm afraid we don't know, sir."

"The beast came from the right," Emory said. "Maybe we should take the left."

"What would these creatures eat in here?" Liam wondered out loud.

Bakari closed his eyes and reached his powers out, trying to sense the direction of the dragon egg. Finally, he opened his eyes and said, "We go right."

A series of groans ensued from the two miners and Liam, but Bakari motioned them on nonetheless. As they proceeded, the creature stayed back behind them and caused them no more harm. Soon the tunnel thinned again, forcing the group to ride single file. Bakari kept light contact with the horses' minds, sending them thoughts of comfort.

After another hour of walking, a dim glow appeared ahead. Buoyed by the hope of going back outdoors, the travelers hurried ahead, entering a substantial cavern. All four gasped at the same time, with the miners also bringing out their swords.

"What is this place?" Liam whispered.

Bakari shook his head and glanced around. The walls were full of some type of gem that filled the cavern with a green glow. Taking the walkway that sloped down in front of them revealed plants and shrubs interspersed between several small, crude dwellings. The creature that had followed behind them squealed and ran past, joining others of its kind.

Slowly, the four travelers continued to descended into the cavern. A rustling in the leaves to their right caught their attention, and Bakari brought forth a second mage light. Running across their path was a young, dark-skinned boy with not much on but a cloth wrapped around his waist.

Liam looked at Bakari and said, "People down here? I've never heard of this from my father."

"We might not even be in the Realm anymore, Liam," Bakari answered.

A few steps later, a small group of men and women moved out onto the path in front of them. Bakari, who was in front, held his hand out in front of Liam and the miners.

"Be careful," Bakari whispered. "We are the visitors here."

In front of the travelers stood three men and two women. The men were as dark-skinned as Bakari, but quite a bit taller. Their dark hair was braided like his, and their eyes, although also brown, had a milky white film over them. The two women were lighter-skinned but also had dark hair. All five wore simple robes that hung down to their knees, and they put up their hands to block the light from their eyes.

Bakari dimmed the mage lights and moved them off to the side. Then more men and women appeared, moving around and behind Bakari's group. And youths, barely younger than Bakari or Liam, joined them and stood with spears and rocks ready to throw at his group.

As Emory raised his sword arm up, all the locals, both in front and behind, moved closer.

Bakari put his hand up and said, "No, Emory. We are visitors here." He knew that these men and women were no match for his or Liam's powers. If it came to fighting, swords would not be needed.

Emory lowered his arm.

Liam rode up next to Bakari and spoke first to the crowd. "I am Liam DarSan Williams, son of Darius and Christine

DarSan Williams, king and queen of the Realm. We come in peace on a mission of much urgency."

Bakari was actually quite impressed with Liam's short speech. The young man could be diplomatic if needed, it seemed.

A man with long braids stepped forward. He appeared to be in his forties and had the bearing of the leader of the group. He bowed his head slightly and said, "We have heard of the great heart of the king of the Realm."

Liam nodded his head in thanks.

"Please dismount and follow us," the leader said.

"But we are in a hurry," Liam said, voicing his opposition. "If you could just show us the way outside, we will be on our way."

The young men behind them moved closer. One moved his spear out in front of him and poked Frederick's back.

"Hey!" Frederick turned around, looking at the young fellow.

"It seems we have no choice," Bakari said to his fellow travelers and then proceeded to dismount.

Liam looked down at Bakari with a frown. Bakari knew what Liam was probably thinking. So Bakari helped him down, and Liam grabbed a walking stick from the side of his Cremelino and then took a few steps forward.

It's close, Bakari's Cremelino said, speaking to Bakari for the first time since they had entered the cave. *Can you feel the power?*

Bakari nodded and replied, *You're right. It is close by. We must be close to the outside too.* He grew excited. He wondered what color this dragon would be.

The four visitors walked forward, surrounded by the villagers. Bakari kept the mage lights out front, but he dimmed them considerably more. But it was quite light in the room, once his eyes had adjusted.

Soon they were taken to a group of benches that could only be described as the town square and were told to sit down. Food was brought out to them. A strange mixture mostly of plants with some type of meat that Bakari wasn't sure he wanted to know what it was. The people were quiet, yet hospitable. As a few more had joined them, now about two dozen locals were sitting around and looking at the travelers.

Bakari stood, and some of the young men tightened their hands on their weapons.

"We mean you no harm." Bakari spread his hands to the side. He had to gain their trust. He didn't want to hurt them. "Tell me what brought you here?"

The men and women relaxed at hearing Bakari's interest. Then another man, about the same age as the first that had addressed them, stepped forward. He motioned Bakari to sit back down.

The man's voice was low and gruff and held a slight accent, but Bakari still understood his words as he began his story. "Sixteen years ago, three of us left the kingdom of Mahli—a kingdom to the south—in search of our prophesied king: the Dragon King."

Bakari smiled and relaxed, for these were his people.

CHAPTER TWENTY NINE

Bakari listened intently as the man talked about many searchers leaving Mahli to find their prophesied king. Three of them had worked the mines. But something had pulled them deeper into the tunnels. And, one day, they had found this spot. The strange gems had given them enough light, and, with an underground stream, plants bloomed and grew in abundance in the cavern. They had tried to find their way back to the entrance of the mines, to return to the twin cities, but they could never find the way out.

"We explored farther north and found a way out of the mountains," the man continued. "By this time, though, we had been gone two years from Mahli. We had lived on what this cavern had provided us. Our eyesight had dimmed. And our skin was not prepared to live in the outside world again. People in a village close to the tunnels treated us well and supplied us with the food and clothes that we needed, in exchange for some of the gems."

Bakari turned and glanced around the cavern, marveling at the story. Then his heart began thumping louder as he realized where the dragon egg was.

The man continued, "We felt something draw us back to this cavern each time we were away. We felt a need to protect what was here. Over time, we married women from the village and had children. We still interact with those living in the village, but we spend most of our time here—where we are more comfortable and where we are needed."

"Needed for what?" Bakari asked, sitting forward on the edge of his seat. He knew the answer, but he wanted to hear it from them.

The man looked at the other villagers. Some nodded their heads, while others shook theirs. "We feel that you are here in peace, but this is something sacred to us."

Bakari nodded his understanding, then offered words of encouragement by saying, "You have done a great service here, men and women of Mahli. I know of what you speak. It has grown lately, hasn't it?"

A few of the younger men jumped forward, anger crossing their faces.

One poked his spear out in front of Bakari and said, "How would you know about that?"

Bakari stood and brought the power up within himself. Then, with only a short wave of his hand, he pushed the spear back and, with a thrust of air, softly threw it away from the group. As Liam and the two miners stood up next to him, the group of men and women backed away.

"We mean you no harm," Bakari said, letting a slight glow surround him. "Look at me. What do you see?" He now had the attention of the entire group. "I am one of you. I am from Mahli. I was born a little over sixteen years ago."

The milky eyes of the villagers opened wider, as if they were realizing what Bakari's words meant.

Bakari turned and walked down a path with Liam, the miners, and then the group of locals following him. No one tried to stop him as he went down a winding path and over a small creek. Then he pushed aside enormous fern fronds until he came to a mound in the cavern.

It stood a few feet taller than Bakari. It was covered with a thin layer of dirt, but the whiteness under that began to show through, glowing brighter as Bakari and Liam approached it.

He decided to explain before touching the mound. So Bakari turned around and faced the group. "Do you know what this is? Do you know what you have been protecting?"

"We do not know what it is," the leader said, "but, as you say, it has grown lately. We have almost seen something inside it. Do you know what it is?"

Bakari nodded. "It is a dragon egg."

Liam's gasp next to Bakari joined in with the gasps of the group of locals. Then many people started talking at once.

Bakari put up his hand to silence them and then said, "Years ago, you went searching for the one prophesied to bring peace to your land. I am he. I am the one you went searching for. I am a dragon rider."

Bakari took a deep breath, unsure whether to admit the rest. But these people had spent their lives looking for him—they deserved the truth.

"I am the Dragon King."

Tears came to the eyes of the original three men from Mahli, and then, as one, they fell to their knees. Bowing their heads to the ground, they wept with joy, and the rest of the villagers followed.

"I am Gethii, sent by the regent of Mahli sixteen years ago," said the leader of the group. "I have now fulfilled my duty. I have seen the prophesied one. Hail the Dragon King."

As one, the villagers lifted their heads and said, "Hail the Dragon King."

Tears came to Bakari's eyes as he realized what others had struggled with to find him. "Please rise," he said. "I appreciate your sacrifices. Today, you shall see what you have protected."

Bakari turned back to the egg and then called Liam to come closer to him. So the young man hobbled over.

"What are you feeling, Prince of the Realm?" Bakari asked.

Tears fell unashamedly from Liam's eyes. "It can't be, Bakari. It can't be."

Bakari nodded his head and said, "Touch the egg."

"I am not worthy," Liam said, and anger crossed his face. "I am broken."

Bakari put his hand on Liam's arm. "I know you have suffered, but you have a good heart. Your physical abilities do not define who you are. You are so much more than your body, Liam."

Liam reached his hand out to the egg, and it brightened as he brought his hand closer. The soil began dropping away. Then Bakari took a step back as Liam placed both hands on the egg. It flared bright white in the previously dark cave, and the villagers shielded their eyes.

Liam turned his head, back toward Bakari, tears still streaming down his face. "What do you mean, I am more than just my body, Bakari? What am I?"

"You are a dragon rider!" Bakari said loudly.

The egg under Liam's hands cracked open, and Liam took a step back. Small pieces of shell fell to the sides as a hole grew larger in its center. Soon a dragon's head popped out, followed by its two wings, and then the rest of the egg shattered.

Standing before them was a beautiful, dark red dragon.

"He's beautiful!" Liam exclaimed, clapping his hands in front of himself. Back in the small village square, the two Cremelinos neighed loudly. "It is a he, isn't it?" Liam asked, looking back at Bakari.

Bakari nodded his head.

"I name you Ryker—you will be my strength!" Liam said to the dragon.

The dragon stretched his neck proudly and gave out a small puff of smoke.

Liam turned and took a step toward Bakari. Then he got down on one knee and bowed his head. "Though I am a prince of the Realm, I give my first allegiance to you, Bakari, Dragon Rider, Dragon Master, and the Dragon King. I will go where you direct me and do what you command. You have given purpose and strength to my life. I follow you above all others."

Liam's head stayed bowed until Bakari stepped forward and touched it. He motioned for Liam to rise and said, "Welcome, Dragon Rider!"

And everyone clapped and hollered with joy.

"When do I get to ride him?" Liam's face was full of excitement.

Bakari laughed. "Well, unfortunately, they do take a week or so to get strong enough to ride on."

Liam frowned. "What will happen to Liberty, my Cremelino? I have never been without her."

"Do you still sense her in your mind?" Bakari asked.

"Of course I do," Liam said without hesitation. "Since the day I was born."

"Then, Liam, you have the privilege of being bonded to two powers of the spirit: a dragon and a Cremelino."

Liam laughed. "You're right, Bakari. I can feel both bonds." He stood still for a moment, as if thinking. Then Liam said, "Oh, Bakari, I never thought I would be someone special. Thank you again!"

"I didn't choose you," Bakari said. "A dragon chooses its rider."

Liam turned toward his dragon. "Well, Ryker, let's get you some food."

The dragon gave a small roar and then walked tentatively on his legs toward his dragon rider.

"You know, he will not fit in the tunnels, to return the way we came," Bakari told Liam.

"I will stay with him until he can fly."

Gethii walked up to them. "And we will care for him and his dragon. We will feed them and make sure they are strong before they leave here. The dragon can stay in the village outside the tunnels. There is room for him to grow there."

Liam's eyes gleamed brightly. "I will never leave him."

Bakari nodded, but he held his mouth tight. He felt happy for Liam, for he knew the feeling of the dragon bond—at least, he used to know it.

"I will go back with Emory and Frederick," Bakari said, "and will take the Cremelinos."

Liam's expression turned serious. "Oh, Bakari, I am so sorry. I was so caught up in my own joy that I forgot about your needs. As I said, I am yours to command. What do you need from me?"

"To get your dragon strong and then fly south. I will be searching for my dragon, Abylar, in the Superstition Mountains. I can't very well be a dragon king without a dragon, now can I?"

CHAPTER THIRTY

Time drifted by for Roland Tyre. In the never-ending expanse of the stream of magic, time had little meaning—and direction, even less so. At times, he found himself just sitting in a daze, waking up and wondering how long he had been sitting there. Other times, he would walk and walk and walk, never seeming to get anywhere. The dull gray hue of the space seemed to crush down on his nerves. He wasn't hungry—but he felt a strong desire to taste something. His senses were being dulled.

Oh, to taste, smell, touch, or hear something! he thought to himself.

The only thing that helped, sometimes, was when Roland felt or saw the presence of the evil wizard king, trying to find him. The man must be as trapped as he was. Roland didn't actually want to confront him, but, in a twisted way, it gave him something to look forward to.

Roland's mind churned with ways to escape his imprisonment or to defeat the evil that seemed to be spreading throughout the western lands.

He had met and talked quite considerably with Danijela Anwar, head of the Wizard Conclave in Arc. She had shared a few insights, about the spreading evil, and had promised to help Roland find a way out. Currently, she was heading south from

Arc to try and meet up with Bakari, for she had voiced the concern that Bakari was the only person that could truly vanquish this evil.

Roland had also glimpsed Alli's escape in Quentis and her use of the dragons' powers—which, he had to admit, had made him jealous. And that man that had stood by Alli at the end—the prince of Quentis—was Roland jealous of him too?

It was all so infuriating. He was not meant to be caught in this maddening place; his destiny was to be the most powerful wizard in the land. He had to get out.

Feeling frustrated, he began to run. He knew it didn't do any good in here, but he wasn't in his right mind anyway: his thoughts wandered too much. So he ran in a straight line as far and as fast as he could go. The gray hue around him lightened and darkened in areas but never ended.

He actually *wished* for the evil king to jump out at him then—anything to latch on to, anything to do. So he ran harder.

Without his physical body, Roland didn't tire. He could run forever and ever, never getting anywhere. Seeing some bright lights ahead, he ran toward one, feeling drawn to it. Before touching it, Roland knew who it was. Mericus deGrande, King of Alaris.

Grabbing hold of the light, Roland was sucked into Mericus's world. He found himself standing in the castle in Cassian. Mericus sat on his throne, dressed in all his black finery. The man was too polished and too sure of himself. Roland was more powerful than Mericus. Maybe he should take the throne from him.

Where did that last thought come from? Roland asked himself. He had never thought of taking the kingship before.

Off in the distance, an evil laugh rolled through the stream of magic. Roland placed his hands on either side of his head. He was going crazy. This place was changing him.

Steadying himself, Roland looked at the scene around him.

"I don't believe it!" Mericus was saying to one of his generals. "Why would Breelyn be leading an army into Alaris?"

The general shrugged his shoulder. "Maybe the dragon riders intend to take over, sir."

Mericus slammed his hand down on the plush armrest of his throne. "What is that Dragon King up to?"

A woman stepped forward and said, "Your Highness, there also seems to be trouble at the Citadel. Something has happened to the High Wizard, but they are being very tight-lipped about it."

Roland smiled. He bet they were. How would they explain that the High Wizard's body lay on his bed, but his spirit was gone elsewhere?

"We will deal with that later." Mericus stood up and walked down the three steps from his throne to stand in front of his advisors. "How close is Breelyn? And how many troops does she have with her?"

The general spoke again. "She is a few days from the border, with at least five thousand."

"What of her dragon?" Mericus asked.

"No sign of it," another advisor said and then shook her head. "And, sir, the elf has changed, they say."

"Changed?"

"Her hair has turned dark, and she wears only black."

Mericus smirked as he glanced down at his own black attire and said, "That doesn't mean anything. But I want to know what her intentions are. Send scouts ahead—only wizards. I don't know what powers Breelyn has." Mericus paced and then added, "And find the Battlemaster. I need her here by my side."

Roland frowned. What right did Mericus have to send people to bring Alli to him?

Maybe I should do away with the man, Roland thought. *No!* he told himself.

This place was making him crazy. He had to get back to his body. Every man Alli met was making sweet eyes at her. Something had happened to Breelyn, and she was marching to Alaris. And Bak was busy on his own quest. So Roland was done wasting time in this infuriating place.

Popping back out of the scene, Roland found himself once again in the dreary stream of magic. He was done running—done being the hunted. He would be the hunter now. This place was making him go crazy—and, if that had happened to Roland in just a few short weeks, what had one hundred and fifty years of this done to the evil wizard king?

The man must be truly demented by now, Roland thought. *And demented, evil men could be toppled.*

"I'm coming for you!" Roland yelled out into the grayness. "Do you hear me? I am coming for you."

Nothing answered him back, but it made Roland feel better anyway.

He reached his mind out. He could get all the magic he wanted now. This place was magic. He just needed to become one with it. So, trying to leave his friends' lights alone, Roland pulled other lights to himself—and the power built within him, stronger and stronger. He would become one with the magic— he would be the magic.

A low laugh sounded again in the distance. But it was coming closer now, and Roland didn't care. He gathered power to himself and became a beacon of light and magic. He was going to get out of this place—either alive or dead—but he would leave and return to his body once again.

* * *

Kharlia entered the castle in Cassian with two Elvyn guards at her side. Not taking the time to change, she asked for an audience with the king. Now, sitting in the waiting room with the two guards, she wished she had taken a few minutes to freshen up. After days of riding, through the Elvyn Forest and across the Dunn River, she must look horrible.

Using her fingers, Kharlia brushed through her dark hair, and then she took a few deep breaths. Looking around her, she was awed by the opulence of the castle. Having grown up in a small home—one that would fit in a corner of the room she now sat in—she realized that she had come a long way in the past year. Not even sixteen yet, she wondered what the rest of her life would hold for her. Being an emissary of one king, visitor to another, and a friend with the Dragon King himself…well, she hoped, more than just his friend.

"Are you all right?" asked Gloron, one of the Elvyn guards. "You are flushed. Do you need some water?"

Kharlia berated herself for thinking of Bakari in such a way. "No, no, I am fine. Just tired from the trip."

Soon a steward walked in and invited Kharlia and the two elves into the throne room. As they were walking in, a group of men and women walked out, who didn't look very happy. Looking to the front of the throne room, Kharlia saw Mericus, standing in front of his throne. He appeared deep in thought, and a frown covered his face.

"Kharlia Attah, emissary from the elves, Your Highness," announced the steward.

Mericus looked up and blinked twice, then covered his previous thoughts with a generous smile. "Welcome, Kharlia. Good to see you again. Your help in healing after the war was greatly appreciated."

The man is smooth, that's for sure, Kharlia thought.

She bowed her head to him, as was appropriate for his station, and said, "My King, I bring you tidings from the elves."

The king's face clouded over for a brief moment, but it returned to a smile before Kharlia could say anything.

"Come and sit. You must be tired." Mericus motioned the three over to a side table, which was set with pastries and drinks. "Please take some."

After sitting and taking a few bites and a drink of cool water, Kharlia proceeded with introductions. "This is Keryth and Gloron, members of the Elvyn guard."

Mericus nodded his head at the two elves. "I have heard of the famous Elvyn guard; though, I must say that, with the barrier up for the last while, my knowledge is limited to books and stories from over one hundred and fifty years ago."

"My King," Kharlia continued, "I am sure you are aware of King Lanwaithian's condition."

Mericus nodded.

"It has grown worse, but I have contained it for now," Kharlia said.

"*You* contained it?" Mericus raised his eyebrows, and the corners of his lips turned up in a small grin.

Keryth turned to Mericus and, in a soft but serious voice, stated, "Kharlia is an Elvyn healer and has been named Elvynfriend."

Mericus waved his hand in the air. "I meant no offense, Keryth, but Kharlia is quite young to be an Elvyn healer, isn't she?"

"Discussing my age is not the purpose of this meeting," Kharlia said hotly. "Evil is spreading throughout the western lands. And the dragon riders are off trying to find a way to contain it—"

"Are you sure that is what the dragon riders are doing?" Mericus interrupted in a raised voice. "Are they really trying to contain it? Or, are they using it to their advantage, to take over the kingdom?"

"What are you talking about?" Kharlia said, voicing her surprise. "Bakari is finding another dragon rider and gathering knowledge. He would never take your kingdom."

Mericus opened his mouth, but before he could continue, Kharlia plunged forward with the real reason she was there.

"I am here at the Elvyn king's request, to find his betrothed, Breelyn Mier."

Mericus opened his mouth and laughed. "Oh, this is rich."

"I assure you," Gloron said, "there is nothing funny about this request. Kharlia has the full weight of the king behind her quest."

"Oh, I have no doubt about that," Mericus said, his hands flat on the table in front of him. A vein bulged in the side of his neck. "But, what is the king's endgame? Does *he* want my kingdom also?"

Kharlia gave a questioning look to Mericus. "What do you mean, my lord? Why do you think everyone is out to take Alaris from you?"

Mericus stood. "Because Breelyn Mier, your Elvyn king's betrothed and famed dragon rider, is at this very moment leading an army from Solshi toward the borders of Alaris. What other meaning can I take from this aggression?"

Kharlia opened her mouth to retort, then closed it again. She didn't know what to say. Leaning back in her chair, she let out a deep breath. Mericus slumped back in his chair and took a deep drink from his goblet.

Mericus smirked. "Quite a mess, isn't it?"

Kharlia nodded, still unsure what to say.

Mericus leaned forward, across the table, and said in a softer voice, "I hold no animosity for you, Kharlia—and Bakari has been more than fair with me—but you might be in over your head here. More is going on than others are telling us."

"I trust the elves, sir," Kharlia finally said.

Mericus nodded his head to the two Elvyn guards and then said, "No offense to present company, but I have an elf marching an army to my borders. What am I supposed to think? Are we being played here?" He peered intently into Kharlia's eyes. Then he lifted his arm, pointing a finger at Kharlia, and said, "Or, are *you* being played here, young healer?"

Kharlia felt like she had been slapped in the face. *Being played?* No. She was sure of it.

"There must be an explanation," Kharlia said. "Breelyn would not send an army to Alaris without a reason."

"She may have changed." Mericus sat back in his chair. "It is said that her dragon has left her and that now she supports a usurper to the Solshi throne."

Kharlia put a hand to her mouth and then said, "No." What would she tell Lan? This news would break his heart.

"I am sending scouts to the border, to find out her intentions," Mericus said. "But I will not allow an army to invade my land."

"We will go with the scouts," Kharlia said. "And I will deliver the Elvyn king's message to Breelyn. Maybe it will help."

Mericus nodded his head. "Let's hope so." He stood up to go, but before he left, he added one more thing: "And I hope that dragon king of yours comes back soon. He may be the only one able to fix all of this."

Kharlia smiled inside. *Her* dragon king, Mericus had said. She hoped Bakari was all right. She missed him terribly.

"My steward will escort you to the scouts," Mericus said and motioned to the man by the throne room door. "They will be leaving shortly. I'm sorry that you will not have any time to rest."

Kharlia and her two Elvyn guards bowed their heads to Mericus as he walked off, most likely to another meeting.

"Oh, Breelyn," Kharlia said and then sighed. She knew about the taint Breelyn had received when the Elvyn king was attacked. Based on what Mericus had said, things may have become worse.

CHAPTER THIRTY ONE

Atop Cholena, Alli sat behind Jaimon as they flew north, over Westland. Jaimon kept the dragon artifacts in a small bag tied to his waist. It was harder than Alli had thought it would be, to give up the figurine and lose contact with the dragon. She thought now about all the power she had held when calling forth the powers of the dragons. It was thrilling, but it had also frightened her that someone in the world could have such power. If the figurine fell into the wrong hands—like the Chameleon's or his brothers'—its power would be devastating indeed.

"Can you tell where Bakari is?" Alli asked.

"No, not yet," Jaimon answered. "It's strange, but Cholena says there is a spark of something far, far north."

"We need to get him the artifacts and then find all three of those brothers." Alli shifted a bit on the dragon. They had been flying all day.

"I agree," Jaimon said. Then he paused and cocked his head to the side, as if listening to something. "Miriel is joining us."

Alli looked around and then spotted a speck to the west. It grew quickly in the bright sky, and Breelyn's beautiful dragon came into view. However, Miriel wasn't so bright and yellow anymore. Her wings were tipped with black.

"What happened?" Alli asked.

Jaimon was silent for a moment and then began to repeat to Alli what he had learned. "Breelyn has been infected by the dark magic of the Chameleon's brother, a man called the General. She has taken up his cause now and has shut out her dragon. It's killing Miriel. A dragon feels lost without its rider."

"We need to find Bakari!" Alli insisted again.

Looking west again, Alli noticed dust rising in the distance. She bumped Jaimon in the back. "Fly over there," she said as she pointed.

With Miriel behind them, Cholena turned west. In a few minutes, Alli recognized the cause of the dust as an army of men and women. Thousands of them. Riding a strong, black horse in the front of an army was a woman dressed in black, with long, flowing hair blowing behind her in the wind. The top of her head still held a hint of blond, but the remaining hair was as black as her clothes.

"It's Breelyn!" Alli couldn't believe it. What was she doing with an army? "Get closer."

Flying lower, Cholena brought Jaimon and Alli toward the head of the army.

"Breelyn!" Alli shouted.

Breelyn turned her face up—her eyes were black, and she didn't seem to recognize Alli for a moment. Then, with a tightening of her lips, she said, "Battlemaster, you shouldn't be here."

"And where else would I be, if not here, protecting the land I love?"

"You should leave," Breelyn said. "I hold no animosity toward you, but my master, the General, will destroy all who oppose him."

Jaimon yelled out, "Your master is Bakari, Breelyn! You are a dragon rider."

Miriel flew over the troops and roared, fire flowing from her jaws.

Breelyn put her hand up, to stop the army, and then rode out in front of them a few dozen feet. "I have a new master now," she said. "It is the bargain I made."

Alli could see moisture glistening at the corner of Breelyn's eyes. "What kind of bargain, Dragon Rider?" Alli asked. She had used Breelyn's title in the hope of bringing her round.

"I am not a dragon rider!" Breelyn shrieked.

As Miriel roared in pain and dove down over the troops, many dropped to the ground in fear.

Alli couldn't believe what she was seeing. Breelyn was the first elf Alli had ever met. She had helped Bakari from the first, been there when Abylar emerged, and helped to establish peace in Alaris.

"What bargain, Breelyn?" Alli asked.

Breelyn looked down and mumbled something that Alli couldn't hear.

"What did she say?" Alli grumbled to herself.

"She said she bargained for Lan's life," Jaimon said.

"How did you hear that?"

"The dragon's power supplements my senses, makes them greater."

How could Breelyn bargain for Lan's life? Bakari or Roland or someone would find a cure for him.

"We have to do something, Jaimon."

"But what, Alli?" Jaimon said from in front of her. "We can't kill all these people. It's not right."

Alli nodded her head. Before she could think of anything else, however, someone rode up from the back of the troops—a man on one of the tallest horses that Alli had ever seen. A dark, smoky substance swirled around him. The army parted to let him pass.

Fear and anger boiled up in Alli at that same time. This was one of the Chameleon's brothers. His evil, she had learned, they couldn't fight without the powers of the dragons.

Breelyn looked back at the approaching man and then yelled up into the air, "Jaimon, leave now. Please. I don't want you or the dragons hurt."

"What about all the other innocent people you will kill with this army?" Alli screamed down at her.

The General approached and came up next to Breelyn. "There are no innocent people in Alaris," he yelled up at Alli. "They took my father's throne one hundred and fifty years ago, and now he will have it back."

Even though Alli didn't know if it would do any good, she gathered a lightning strike as quickly as she could and threw it down at the General. With a flick of his hand, the General made the lightning dissipate into his tendrils of blackness and reappear again a few feet away before it hit the ground.

"How?" Alli said out loud but more to herself.

The General threw his hands into the air, and blackness raced from them toward the dragons. Cholena had barely maneuvered to the side before the darkness slid by her into empty air.

"We can't fight him like this, Alli," Jaimon said. "We need more help."

Alli hated to leave but knew that Jaimon was right. "The Citadel. It's not far away. There are more than enough wizards there to stop this army."

Jaimon directed Cholena up higher. Before the dragon turned around, Alli saw Breelyn's face. Conflicting emotions seemed to almost immobilize her.

"Remember your master!" Alli yelled down at her, not knowing for sure if she would hear. Though, a split second later, Alli thought she saw a brief and tiny nod of Breelyn's head.

Cholena, with her two riders, and Miriel headed east to the Citadel. Alli and Jaimon would rally Roland and his wizards, and they would stop the army together, before it invaded Alaris.

* * *

In the few hours it took them to fly to the Citadel, it had grown dark outside. When they finally arrived, the gates to the city were closed, and very few individuals were outside. Landing in a courtyard, Alli and Jaimon jumped off the dragon. The late spring air was still warm, but Alli rubbed her arms anyway. Something here was not right.

A few guards met them in the courtyard and nodded their respect.

"Battlemaster," said Arcon, one of the guards Alli knew. "Welcome back."

Turning to Jaimon, they greeted him as well.

"Seems quiet around here for this time of evening," Alli noted.

Arcon turned to the other guard before responding. "Things have happened here, Battlemaster."

"What things?"

Arcon waved his hand toward the building. "Come and follow me. I will take you to a member of the Council."

"I would like to see Roland—I mean, the High Wizard."

But Alli almost had to run to keep up with Arcon's long legs. Jaimon trailed behind her.

"I have important information for him," she added.

Arcon was silent and just continued walking next to the other guard. So Alli decided that she wouldn't be getting any answers from this bunch and would have to wait to see Roland to find out what was going on.

Entering the front doors of the Citadel, Alli and Jaimon were greeted with quiet stares. No one would meet Alli's eyes. What was going on?

"Where's the High Wizard?" she asked.

Just then, Gorn, her old mentor, came walking down the hallway. She realized how old he now looked. He had never fully recovered from the ordeal in Celestar, when so many of the guardians were killed.

"Gorn!" Alli ran up to him and hugged him. Looking back up at him, she noticed a heaviness in his eyes that hadn't been there before.

"Alli," he said. "So good to see you." Looking over to Jaimon, Gorn nodded his head. "Dragon Rider."

Jaimon nodded back and walked up next to Alli.

"What is going on here, Gorn?" Alli asked.

"Come with me" was all that Gorn would offer. He led Alli and Jaimon up the stairs and down the hall. Alli recognized this as a way to Roland's private rooms.

Without thinking about it, she ran her hand over her hair and tried to straighten her clothes, the dark ones that had been given to her by the Followers of the Dragon. She was suddenly aware of how tight they felt, and she blushed, thinking about meeting Roland in them.

"Is this place always so somber?" Jaimon asked Alli.

She was glad for this diversion. "No. Especially since Roland has been in charge. There are usually people bustling around, laughing, and talking—you know Roland."

"But...?"

Jaimon had started to ask something, but right then they had reached Roland's rooms. A soldier stood at attention in front of the door. Nodding his head to Gorn, he stepped aside. A sudden foreboding filled Alli's heart. Had something happened to Roland? Why hadn't he met them down below? She steeled her emotions and willed Gorn to open the door quicker.

Gorn put his meaty hand on the knob and then waited a moment, as if he didn't want to go in. Finally, he pushed the heavy wooden door open. The parlor was dark, with only a few candles lighting the room. Tam was sitting on a chair by the bedroom door. But he stood up when they approached.

"Tam, what's wrong?" Alli was worried about him too. "You look like you haven't slept in weeks."

Tam held his mouth tight. Tears gathered in the corners of his eyes, and he tried to blink them away. "I've tried my best, Alli. I really have." His words were thick with emotion.

"You're scaring me, Tam." Alli's defenses went up, and she turned her head, in quick motions, to survey the room. She still didn't see Roland anywhere. Her heartbeat picked up as she realized something was very, very wrong. "What is going on?"

Tam beckoned her and Jaimon toward the bedroom door, while Gorn stayed behind. Opening the door, Alli saw Selena and another wizard by the side of the bed. At the sight of Alli, their eyes went wide.

"Selena." Tam motioned for her and the other wizard to leave the room.

As she moved past Alli, Selena whispered, "I'm sorry."

Sorry? About what?

It was dark in the room, but Alli could see someone was lying on the bed. She stepped closer and gasped.

"No, no." Her hand flew to her mouth, and tears filled her eyes. Jaimon grabbed Alli from one side and steadied her from falling. She took a step closer. Lying in front of her was Roland. His head sat on a pillow, his blond hair brushed perfectly around his light face. His eyes stood closed, and a tube was fitted over his mouth.

Alli rounded on Tam. "What have you done to him?"

Tam stood and took it, tears streaming down his own face. "Oh, Alli," he groaned, then pulled her into his strong arms and held her until her tears stopped.

Finally, she pulled away. She noticed Jaimon sitting on a chair on the other side of the bed. He stared at the floor, his head held in his hands. He looked up as Alli moved back toward the bed again. Then Jaimon stood up and joined her, looking down at Roland.

"What happened?" Jaimon asked.

"Wizards from the Sanctuary in Quentis came here," Tam said, in control of his emotions once again. "They attacked him with a dark power."

"From Quentis?" Jaimon asked, looking at Alli.
She nodded.

"The Chameleon's followers," Jaimon said. "He's infecting everything."

"Roland isn't...?" Alli couldn't say the word.

"Dead?" Tam shook his head. "No, not really. But..." Tam glanced around nervously.

Alli reached her hands up to Tam's shoulders. "Tell me, Tam. You were as close to him as anyone. You put this contraption on him. For some reason, you think he isn't dead."

"It's crazy, Alli," Tam began. "When they attacked, Roland and the rest of us held out as long as we could. Then, at some point, Roland seemed to make a decision and just blinked out. His body collapsed. But, before it did, his spirit left it. His spirit is still alive," Tam said, becoming more animated. "It sounds crazy, Alli, but I will tell you. I felt him here, in this room, just days ago. He spoke to my mind. His soul is still alive."

Alli nodded but stayed quiet.

"That does sound like a tall tale, Wizard," Jaimon said. "A body can't live without its soul. It's not natural."

Tam hung his head. "I know. I just keep hoping."

"Hoping that he will come back?" Jaimon asked.

"Yes." Tam brought his head up. His eyes were bloodshot.

Alli put her hands on Tam's arms. "I believe you, Tam. I do! I have felt Roland twice this past week. I know he was with me, watching me. Somehow, his spirit is trapped somewhere."

"Yes." Tam nodded and grew more excited. "Yes, that is what I keep saying. But the longer he lies here like this, the less and less others believe me."

"Alli?" Jaimon questioned.

"Jaimon, you don't know Roland like I do. He is stubborn and flashy and incorrigible at times, but he is powerful and brilliant when it comes to magic. If anyone can find a way back out, it will be him. One more reason to find Bakari."

"Where is the Dragon King?" Tam asked.

Alli shrugged her shoulders.

"North," Jaimon said. "He is north."

Alli looked at Jaimon with a question in her eyes.

"Cholena and Miriel can feel him to the north," Jaimon said. "There is a bond there, but not with his dragon—with another animal. He is now riding south through the kingdom of the Realm to try and find Abylar, who is lost somewhere in the mountains there."

Alli smiled and said, "Go to him, Jaimon."

"You're not coming with me?"

"My place is here." Alli nodded toward Roland's lifeless body. "I need to be here to help him return. I am his Battlemaster."

"And his friend?" Tam said in a teasing tone.

Alli blushed. "And his friend."

Jaimon nodded. "I will take both Cholena and Miriel with me."

"Miriel?" Tam asked. "Then the elf is with you also?"

"Oh, no!" Alli said. "I forgot all about that. That is why we came here—to get help. Breelyn is leading troops to attack Alaris."

"But you need to stay here, Alli—with him." Tam nodded toward the bed.

"I know." She smiled. "Gorn?" She called the elderly battle wizard in from the sitting room, where he had stayed. "You up for one more battle?"

CHAPTER THIRTY TWO

Bakari had been riding hard for three days, and he was exhausted. The kind folk in the twin cities had sent him with a pack of food, along with a bag of oats for Flash, the Cremelino he rode. He had ridden as far as he could each day and then found a copse of trees to sleep under. Flash was true to her name and ran with boundless energy along the road from the twin cities west to Sur. He and Flash had then turned south and were now entering Tean, a smaller city in the western part of the Realm.

You need to rest, Wizard! Flash said to Bakari's mind.

I will rest when I find my dragon.

The Cremelino slowed her run to a trot so as not to attract as much attention in the town.

We will rest here tonight, Flash said.

I can go farther, Bakari tried to argue. Though, he knew in the end that it was a losing battle. The Cremelino was right, and Bakari wouldn't be any good to Abylar this way.

The guards nodded their heads to him and let him pass without stopping him. But the Cremelino's presence drew attention from onlookers as they continued down the main thoroughfare of the city. From what Liam and Breanna had taught Bakari, the herd of Cremelinos had increased in number the last few years, but they were still considered rare, and not all wizards had them. So Bakari presumed that the citizens of the city figured that he was one of their own wizards.

Better off that way, he thought, *than knowing I am the Dragon King, without a dragon.*

We will find your dragon, Flash encouraged him. *We feel something in the mountains south and west of here. There is power growing—both good and evil.*

"Abylar," Bakari said out loud with a deep sigh. Oh, how he missed his dragon.

Soon Bakari found himself a nice inn. He paid extra, to make sure his Cremelino was taken care of, and then he sat down in the common room, for a hot meal.

The common room was fairly crowded, but he had been able to find a small table, alone at the edge of the room. Other patrons kept glancing his way, but he didn't know if it was due to his color, his age, or the Cremelino he had come in on—or to a combination of all three. But he was too hungry and tired to get overly concerned about it.

A nice servant approached and gave him a warm smile. She wasn't much older than Bakari himself. "We have stew and bread tonight, or, if you would like, we also have some lamb chops left over from yesterday."

Bakari smiled back. "The stew sounds wonderful—two bowls, please."

The servant laughed. "You don't look like you could eat that much—though, it wouldn't hurt, to put a little more fat on those bones of yours."

Her teasing brought a small laugh from Bakari, and he relaxed a bit more and said, "I've been traveling a long way."

The young woman nodded but didn't ask any more questions. She brought Bakari a small loaf of bread and some water, which he devoured and drank quickly, before his stew had even arrived.

Finally, it did. Taking an overflowing spoonful of the stew, he gave a small yelp.

A few men at a nearby table laughed at his outburst.

Then one of them leaned over, closer to Bakari, and said, "Take your time, kid. Nobody's going to take it from you. This inn has got some of the best food in town. Enjoy it!"

Bakari felt embarrassed and nodded his head at the man. Turning back to his stew, he took another spoonful, but this time he blew on it a few times before stuffing it in his mouth. He tasted warm beef, carrots, tomatoes, and onions.

"Mmm."

After the first bowl, Bakari did slow down for the second. About halfway through it, he wondered if he shouldn't have ordered so much. He sat back in the chair and took a deep breath. For the first time since sitting down, he listened to the conversations close to him.

"I tell you, something's happening, Hans," said a man that appeared to be in his thirties. "I hear there are problems at the wizard school. Young wizards are leaving."

A man with a deeper voice spoke up. "I agree." Then he lowered his voice, and Bakari strained to hear. Bakari missed the enhanced hearing he had before, when he was with Abylar.

"And, Kade," Hans said, "have you felt your powers weakening lately?"

There was a pause in the conversation as the young serving woman refilled their glasses.

When she was gone, a third man spoke up. "I feel it too. My powers are weakening. It's like someone is draining them away from me." He took a sip of his drink, then continued, "Someone is attacking the wizards. We need to gather together and make a plan."

"Do you think the king knows?" Kade asked. "He is the mightiest wizard in the land. We should go to him."

"Aye," said Hans with his deeper voice. "You are right, Kade. But, in the meantime, we should bond together and fight back."

Bakari wanted to ask them what was going on, but he didn't want to draw any more attention to himself than needed. Were the Chameleon and his brothers attacking the wizards somehow? Bakari hadn't felt any recent drains on his powers— other than the exhaustion he was feeling.

Finishing his second bowl of stew and downing another glass of water, Bakari left money for the serving woman and headed upstairs to the small room he had rented. The room had one small bed and a table with a chair next to it and a pitcher of water and a cleaning bowl on top. Washing his face, Bakari turned back to the bed and lay down on it.

Before drifting off to sleep, he thought about Kharlia and was glad that she was safe, back in Elvyn. He hoped she was learning a lot and doing well. He missed her company and encouragement. He knew that he had a tendency to get down on himself for not living up to the expectations of the Dragon

King, but Kharlia always lifted him back up and supported him. She was a good woman.

And, with that last thought, Bakari drifted into a deep and dreamless sleep.

* * *

Kharlia and her two Elvyn guards were riding on horseback with a small group of military scouts, who Mericus had sent to the border to see what Breelyn and the army behind her were doing. Rather than going straight across to Westridge, they were told to go north to the Citadel first and elicit some help from Roland and his wizards. But the group of scouts had treated the Elvyn guards with quiet reservation and had seemed to only tolerate the presence of Kharlia among their ranks.

A few days after leaving Cassian, they approached River Bend. This brought back happy and painful memories for Kharlia: happy, because she remembered being there with Bakari, and painful, because it reminded her that he was most likely thousands of miles away now and busy with his own quest.

"Why not just go straight to the Citadel?" asked Keryth, one of the Elvyn guards.

Kharlia shrugged her shoulders. She hadn't traveled far from her own small town outside of Cassian until Bakari had needed her help the last year.

Then Conway, one of the few scouts that had befriended them, turned to the three from Elvyn and said, "The fields between Cassian and Whalen are farmed and soft—it is harder for the horses. The road to River Bend and then to Whalen, even though longer, saves us time and is easier on the horses."

"Thank you, Conway." Keryth nodded his head. "There is much about this land that we do not know."

"We are used to the trees," Gloron said. "All of these open spaces are strange to me."

"Where do you grow your food?" Conway dismounted with the other scouts.

Kharlia and her two Elvyn guards followed suit and began to lead their horses into the town. Unlike the last time she was in River Bend, children now ran in the streets, and vendors were taking down their tents for the day. The city appeared to be thriving.

Through the trees, Kharlia could see riverboats being tied off for the evening. These held large cuttings of trees—wood to be shipped south to Corwan and down to Mallek in the southern desert of Elvyn and even to Tillimot, now that the barrier was down.

Gloron moved closer to Conway to answer his question. "The land provides for our needs. Roots and vegetables grow under our great trees, and there is some farming done along the coast. For other goods, we trade with the kingdoms to the north and south."

"I would like to visit there someday." Conway had a dreamy look in his eyes—before he bumped directly into his commanding officer, the captain of the scouts.

"Watch what you're doing, Conway," the captain said, a man with a permanent scowl on his face. "For all we know, these elves are behind the army being on our western border.

They may be preparing to sandwich us between their two forces."

Kharlia stepped forward and glared up at the captain of the scouts. He was a good foot taller than herself. Putting her hands on her hips, she prepared to give him a piece of her mind. "The elves are not attacking us. They are peaceful. And I was sent by their king to help him find his betrothed."

The captain stopped moving and peered down at Kharlia. "What does a little girl know about such things as war?"

Gloron and Keryth moved up next to Kharlia, one on each side. Their muscles were held taut, and their faces looked solemn.

"Kharlia is Elvyn-friend and has honor among us," Keryth said, holding his bow ready in his hands. "You will do well not to speak to her so."

The captain put his hands up in the air and said, "I want no trouble here. I will honor the king's request to escort you three, but leave my men alone." With that, he motioned his men to come away with him.

Conway looked back over his shoulder and mouthed that he was sorry.

Kharlia guessed that these old hatreds—built during the one hundred and fifty years of Alaris's solitude—would take a while to be reconciled.

Walking their horses to a nearby inn, they handed them all off, then headed inside. After a hot meal, the entire group headed to the rooms prepared for them. And Kharlia drifted off to sleep, wondering what Bakari was doing right then.

* * *

Around noon, three days later, Kharlia, the two Elvyn guards, and the scouts from Cassian entered the gates of the Citadel. The mood at this home of the wizard school appeared somber as the group was greeted by three guards at the gate and then ushered inside.

Soon Kharlia heard the door of the Citadel open, before they had even climbed the steps, and Alli came running down, taking two steps at a time.

"Kharlia!" Alli exclaimed. "What are you doing here?"

"Alli, I could ask the same of you." Kharlia laughed. She had become friends with Alli over the past six months and enjoyed seeing her again now. Alli's dark hair had grown longer and now hung down below the top of her shoulders. Her grin was infectious, and Kharlia turned to introduce her to the rest of the company.

The captain stepped forward and said, "Battlemaster." He nodded his head to Alli.

He obviously knew who Alli was. Most people in Alaris did. Alli had made quite a name for herself throughout the battles of the last year and the new buildup of the Citadel.

"We are here on urgent business from the king," the captain continued. "He specifically sends his greetings to you."

Kharlia watched as Alli tried to hide her blush by motioning them toward the Citadel doors and saying, "I can guess what this is about. Please come in."

"Will the High Wizard be joining us?" the captain asked as they entered through the ancient doors.

Kharlia glanced up at the high walls and curving staircase. She had been here a few times before, but each time it had awed her—the history of this building and the power it held.

Power! I can feel its power! Kharlia thought, wondering how that could be. She was not a wizard.

"Kharlia?" Alli asked. "Are you all right?"

Kharlia realized that she had stopped walking and stood as if in a daze. So she nodded her head to Alli and said, "The power is almost overwhelming."

Alli opened her green eyes wide and round. "You feel it? You feel the power? But…"

Kharlia put a hand on Alli's arm and said, "I am a healer now."

Gloron stepped forward and bowed low to Alli. "I am Gloron, and this is Keryth." He motioned to the side. "I am pleased to greet you, Battlemaster. We have heard much about you in Elvyn." A smile spread across his face. "It is said that your dance is as graceful as an elf's."

Alli blushed again and laughed. "I'm afraid I don't dance, sir."

This time both Keryth and Gloron laughed, their voices filling the air with the most pleasant sound.

Then Kharlia explained for Alli. "They mean your fighting, Alli. You fight with the grace of an elf."

"Oh, thank you," Alli said. "But what about the power?" she asked, returning to her previous question.

"Kharlia Attah is now Elvyn-friend and a healer of great renown among us," Gloron said. "She possesses the elves' ability to heal."

Alli looked like she didn't know what to say, and, before she could say anything, the captain spoke up again.

"This little reunion is all well and good, Battlemaster, but we have urgent business with High Wizard Roland Tyre. Will you please inform him that we are here at the king's request?"

Alli glanced down for a moment. When she looked back up, her eyes were hard. "I am sorry to inform you, Captain, that the High Wizard is not available to meet with you today. However, our other Council members would be most pleased to do so. I am sure you are here to discuss the building up of an army on our western border."

The captain frowned. "Where is the High Wizard?"

"That information is not available to share with you, Captain," Alli continued. "Needless to say, we are prepared to talk with you about the army and will do all we can to help you prevent them from marching into Alaris."

Tam joined Alli now and motioned to the captain and his men as he said, "If you will follow me, sirs, you can meet with Battle Wizard Gorn. We are planning a trip to the border, and you may join us if you would like."

The captain nodded his head, but he still didn't look very happy. Then he and his men followed Tam to another room while Kharlia and the two Elvyn guards stayed with Alli.

After the scouts had left, Alli turned to Kharlia. "I need you to see something." Then she motioned them to follow her upstairs. "Maybe there is something you can do, to help Roland. He's gotten himself into a bit of a problem."

Kharlia wondered what was going on, but she dutifully followed Alli upstairs, Gloron and Keryth on their heels.

CHAPTER THIRTY THREE

Bakari arose early the next morning. The late spring air was cooler this close to the Superstition Mountains. After waking the stableboy from his sleep in the hayloft, Bakari retrieved Flash and was soon on his way. The sun had not yet risen, but an orange glow in the east promised a warm and clear day. The Cremelino seemed to know the direction to go, so Bakari let the horse run free down the road leading south.

They soon passed the road that went east, to Anikari, the capital of the Realm. Bakari wanted to see the city, but he couldn't spare the time. There was a current of urgency in the magic stream. Forces were building for good and bad, and he would need his dragon and the strength that Abylar brought to him.

As Bakari rode the Cremelino, he let his mind wander—not in a lackluster way but letting his scholarly mind try to figure out everything that was going on around them from the bits and pieces he had received from Roland in the magical stream, from a few words he had received from the High Wizard of the Wizard Conclave in Arc, and from what Liam and Breanna had shared with him. Soon a clearer picture was forming in his mind of what must be happening.

The last wizard king of Alaris had escaped into the magic stream or had been stuck there somehow—Bakari wasn't quite sure which. Either way, the man was in the stream of magic and was trying to reenter the world of the living, to take control of the land once again.

Three of his children, or descendants—the Chameleon, the General, and the Sentinel—were wreaking havoc on various parts of the Western Continent. Each held the power of darkness in himself, which could not be combated completely by the current powers of wizards. All the surrounding lands were in danger of falling under their influence.

Bakari knew that the dragons were the key, but as yet he couldn't figure out how. That's why he needed his bond with Abylar back.

Sometime after noon, Bakari had Flash slow down and take a small trail off the main road, to rest for a few minutes. Bakari needed to stretch his legs, and both of them needed to eat and get a drink. While Flash wandered a bit farther away, to a small meadow of grasses and spring flowers, Bakari set off to a nearby stream.

Kneeling down on one knee, he reached into the stream and brought up a handful of cool water, then splashed it over his face. Before leaning back up, he heard his Cremelino squeal loudly, and a scream flashed through his mind.

Bakari moved to stand up. But, with only a moment's warning, he heard someone behind him. Before he could do anything, a hard object smashed against the back of his head, and he slumped to the ground.

The last thing that Bakari heard was the Cremelino's frantic voice in his head, saying, *Help is coming. Spring is coming!*

What a strange thing to say, Bakari thought as he tumbled fully into the darkness.

* * *

The next thing Bakari knew, he was hearing voices. His hand automatically moved, intending to rub his sore head, but both his hands were tightly manacled behind his back. He gritted his teeth in frustration.

Why couldn't anything be easy?

Opening his eyes, Bakari tried to look around himself. He saw a group of men, sitting around a small fire, and then noticed the smells of roasted rabbit filling the air. His mouth watered.

The brightness of earlier that day was now growing shadowed. The sun had dropped behind the immense mountains, signaling evening approaching. Moving his head a few inches, he saw Flash, the Cremelino. His heart lurched. The poor animal had chains around his feet and his neck was tied to a tree.

Bakari's first thought was to bring forth his powers—he was a wizard, wasn't he? But, even though he knew his powers weren't gone, he wasn't able to access them. He didn't know if that was from being hit on the head or from the strange manacles his hands were secured in behind his back.

"Ah, the wizard is awake," said a bulky man that had muscles bulging under his leather vest. His light brown hair was cut short, and he walked over with a sneer toward Bakari.

"Surprised you, huh?" the bulky man said.

Bakari didn't say anything.

The three other men, none as large as the first, stayed huddled around the fire. But one of them called out, "Llew, come back to the fire and eat. He's not going anywhere."

Llew snorted and returned while Bakari tried to figure out what to do. Then Bakari ventured a question.

"Who are you?"

One of the thinner men laughed. Holding a piece of roasted rabbit in his hands, he licked his lips and said, "Just doing some trade, good wizard."

"Shut up, Madoc," Llew said. "He doesn't need to know anything."

"What does it matter?" pushed Madoc. "We will be long gone with the Cremelino before he gets free of those things." The man glanced at Bakari's manacles.

"Where did you get these?" Bakari asked.

"From a man in Mar," continued Madoc, much to the disapproval of his comrades. "He is offering good coin for these magical horses."

Another thin man punched Madoc in the shoulder and said, "The boy doesn't look much like a wizard."

All four of the men laughed and then turned their attention back to eating.

Bakari grunted. They were right. He didn't look—or feel—much like a wizard.

Help will be here soon, the Cremelino said into his mind once more.

Bakari almost jumped in surprise. *Flash, you can still talk to me?* He had figured the manacles that obviously blocked his magic would also block the Cremelino's speech.

The power of the spirit is hard to contain, Flash said as a cryptic answer. *Your dragon is the same way.*

Then why can't I feel him? Bakari screamed inside his own mind, and he tried to pull off the manacles that secured his hands and pull away from the rope that held him to the tree.

Try.

The request was so soft that Bakari wasn't sure he had even heard it. He didn't have anything else to do at the moment, so he closed his eyes and reached outward with his senses. His magic was blocked. He tried to work around it, but nothing happened. So he breathed deeper and let his mind relax. Then he tried to move it to the same level of how he spoke to the Cremelino.

Flash?

Yes, I am here, Dragon King.

The reply surprised Bakari.

Pretend you are speaking to me, Flash suggested, *but reach out farther.*

Bakari went deeper into the wide expanse of his mind. It wasn't the familiar magical stream—as his normal powers were not available—but it did have similarities. Then, all that he had read or learned in his life began to flash before him. He never forgot anything that he saw or heard. Libraries full of information were stored there. A power in and of itself.

Aahhh. Something had dawned on Bakari. His capacity to remember—a unique ability, as far as he had heard of—was in itself a power. A power outside the reach of the manacles stopping his wizard powers.

Then he felt it. A brief spark to the southwest. Not far away. Up in the mountains. He tried to grab hold of it and bring it closer. Then more thoughts and feelings came to him. A dragon's thoughts. Abylar's thoughts!

I found him, Bakari said to Flash.

I feel him through you, the Cremelino said with awe. *A powerful presence.*

Abylar! Bakari said.

But nothing happened.

What had so taken his dragon? Without thinking, Bakari pulled some of the Cremelino's power to himself and found that his own abilities were amplified.

Abylar, Bakari said again.

This time there was a stirring. A recognition.

Master? came the weak thought.

Abylar, it's me, your rider.

Dragon King! Help me! Abylar said, and then his voice faded away once again.

But now Bakari knew where Abylar was.

Now I just have to get out of these things. Bakari flexed against his wrists again. He opened his eyes and saw the men looking at him. They shrugged, laughed, and returned to eating.

Spring is almost here! Flash said to him.

Why do you keep saying that? It doesn't make any sense, Bakari thought, feeling frustrated. Had the Cremelino gone mad? It had been spring for months.

What are you talking about? Bakari asked Flash.

Then there was a flaring light in the bond, and another voice said, *Dragon King, don't despair.*

Bakari looked around, trying to figure out who it was that had spoken to him. The voice sounded familiar.

Suddenly, Bakari heard a loud noise through the brush and trees.

Here comes Spring, Flash said with joy.

Bakari turned his head, and through the trees came another beautiful white Cremelino with a small woman on its back. She wore a white robe over a blue riding skirt. Her blond hair was short, and her flushed face held much youthfulness, though she was probably at least twice Bakari's age.

"Hello again, Dragon King." She nodded her head at him.

"Danijela!"

The High Wizard from Arc rode up next to him. The four men around the fire scrambled to their feet, and soon the sounds of four swords being drawn rang through the air. Then the men began to encircle the newcomer.

They didn't get very far, though. With a small flick of her wrist, Danijela sent the swords flying. Before the men could run, she circled her arms in the air, and the ground beneath their feet rose around them. Suddenly, a ditch appeared from nowhere, and water from the nearby stream flowed into it and mixed with the dirt and rocks. And soon the dirt around their feet began to form into blocks.

"It's the earth wizard!" Llew yelled.

"We're dead now!" exclaimed one of the others.

With a gust of heat from the fire, Danijela hardened the blocks of dirt and rock around the men's feet. In a matter of a few minutes, she had made sturdy walls—as tall and well-built as a house—around them, until only the tops of their heads could be seen.

The men yelled out in fear and tried to push against her walls, but these held firm. There was no door or window in the walls. Madoc reached his hands to the top of the wall and pulled himself up. And Bakari could see the fear in his eyes. Madoc opened his mouth to say something, but Danijela waved her hands again, and a sudden gust came forth, carrying thick branches from the tall pine trees. Soon the branches flew down onto the top of the building, forming a roof. Then mud crept up the walls and flowed over the branches.

Then Danijela brought a stick from the fire up over the top of the building and set it on top. This began drying out the mud and hardening the room. Then the pine greens began to smoke.

"We can't breathe!" yelled one of the men, but Bakari didn't know which one.

As Danijela blew out a breath, the fire went out and the smoke stopped. She threw her hands forward again, and a small hole was punctured through the structure toward the top.

Bakari just sat there in amazement. He had never seen such control over the forces of the earth. Being a wizard of the earth in Arc was equivalent to being a battle wizard in Alaris. But, where someone like Alli controlled the battle around her with forces from the earth, this earth wizard controlled the earth itself. It was marvelous to behold.

I need to study this more, Bakari thought to himself.

"There, now you have air to breathe," the High Wizard said. "It's most likely more than you deserve for trying to capture a Cremelino and a wizard."

With the men whimpering inside the newly created building, Danijela now turned her attention to Bakari.

"Please, free the Cremelino first," Bakari begged.

Danijela smiled. "I'm glad to hear you say that." She turned to Flash and, with a flick of her hands, removed the chains from his feet and the rope from his neck. "Many people that are not even wizards would put their animals before themselves."

"Flash is more than just an animal," Bakari said. "The Cremelinos and the dragons have the power to bind, the power of the spirit. We will need them to help us destroy the evil that is consuming our kingdoms."

Danijela untied Bakari from the tree. Then she frowned. "I'm sorry, I do not have the ability to remove those manacles, Dragon King."

Bakari grunted. "Seems like one roadblock after another. Either way, I know where my dragon is now."

Danijela smiled and clapped her hands. "Well then, let's ride. Flash won't let you fall."

It was a little tricky, mounting the Cremelino with his hands tied together. But the two of them were able to get his hands from behind his back to the front, and, with a boost from Danijela, Bakari balanced atop of Flash.

Danijela motioned her hand forward and said, "Lead the way."

Bakari took off back toward the road. They would head south for a bit more, before heading up into the mountains. Nightfall was coming soon, and, hopefully, they would find his dragon by the next morning.

As they rode with the speed of the Cremelinos, Bakari turned to Danijela and asked, "How did you learn to do what you did back there?"

"Oh, that?" A sparkle came to Danijela's bright blue eyes. "That was nothing. I've been doing that since I was fifteen."

Bakari shook his head and mumbled, "I'm glad you're on our side."

"And, is Roland Tyre on your side also?" she asked with a frown.

"Yes," Bakari said hesitantly. "Why? What did he do this time?"

Danijela laughed. "Well, it's good to know that you are not surprised that I would call his actions irresponsible and reckless."

Bakari shook his head. What had his friend done now?

"Roland is trying to pull all wizard power to himself."

"What?" Bakari asked. Doing that was crazy. But he remembered the conversation he had overheard at the inn in Tean. The wizards there were talking about their powers weakening.

"What do you think he is up to?" Danijela's blue eyes squinted as she thought. "Does he have a plan?"

Bakari smiled in exasperation. "Probably not. But I'm sure he means well." He paused as Danijela gave him a questioning look, and then he added, "He is a good man."

"Good man or not, that boy is going to burn himself out!" Danijela sped up. "Let's find that dragon of yours and then find out what's going on."

Bakari agreed, and the two sped even faster down the road. The trees raced by them in a blur, the forest growing darker and darker as night descended.

CHAPTER THIRTY FOUR

Eventually, they'd had to stop for a few hours of sleep. Then Bakari continued to lead Danijela west, into the Superstition Mountains. The traveling became more difficult, now that they were off the main roads. But the Cremelinos were hardier than he had anticipated, and they still made decent time.

The manacles were rubbing Bakari's wrists raw, but a growing sense of urgency filled his mind and heart. Trying to keep his mind focused on Abylar was difficult, with the distractions of the terrain. But, trail by trail and crevice by crevice, they were getting closer.

Darn dragons! Why do they feel the need to be up so high? Bakari thought, not intending his thought to go any farther than his own mind.

We rule the ground, and the dragons rule the skies. That's the way it has always been, Flash said to Bakari's mind.

"Dragon King," Danijela said with a smile, "what are your plans once we find the dragon?"

"Why do you always call me Dragon King?" Bakari asked. "Bakari is fine."

A small laugh escaped from Danijela. "Because, if I call you that enough, you might finally begin to believe it!"

Bakari grunted. "I am the Dragon King. I do accept that—at least, in name. I just don't have a dragon right now, and I don't know what I am king of."

"Fair point," Danijela conceded.

Bakari slowed a bit, riding on a wider trail next to Danijela.

"How long have you been a wizard?" he asked her.

Danijela raised her light brown brows. "About fifteen years—officially, that's when my mentor, High Wizard Sallir, took me under his tutelage—though, I had been doing magic in secret quite a few years before that."

"I've been a full wizard for only two years and a dragon rider for less than six months."

"And, your point?" Danijela said seriously. But before Bakari could answer, she put her hand up and said, "That was rhetorical. I know your point. Did you know that, at fifteen, I knew and did things that wizards dozens of years my senior didn't know how to do?"

"Sounds like Roland or Alli but not me," Bakari said. "I am just a simple scholar wizard."

"A scholar wizard who rides on and talks to and pulls power from dragons, Bakari." Danijela shook her finger at him. "The king of the Realm and I were the most powerful wizards on the Western Continent—at least, until the barrier around Alaris came down and revealed some powerful teenagers there."

Danijela smiled and then continued, "Between the two of us, we can move earth, control the weather, heal horrendous injuries, tell what people are thinking or if they are lying, destroy entire armies, and ride like the wind on our bonded

Cremelinos. But, you know what? Neither I, the High Wizard of Arc; Darius DarSan Williams, the king of the Realm; Mezar Alrishitar, the emperor of Gildan; Tobias Bruel, commander of the Sanctuary; the kings of the elves—past or present—nor Roland Tyre, the High Wizard of the Citadel in Alaris, ever bonded with a dragon, pulled from their magnificent powers, or flew on one over the Western Continent. None of us have, Dragon King."

Bakari bowed his head, feeling the censure.

"I don't say this to make you feel bad, Bakari." She smiled at the use of his name. "But to build you up and to tell you that you are one of the greatest wizards to live, in centuries. You are here for a purpose, right now, at this time. Your age or experience means nothing in your powers as a wizard. But your heart does. You have a generous heart—or you wouldn't be traveling thousands of miles from home. You are destined to bring peace to a fractious land and to destroy the evil that is growing there. You and the dragons will do this! You are the Dragon King."

Bakari smiled at her lecture. But she was right. He had moped around long enough. It was time to find his dragon and set things straight.

* * *

An hour later, they reached a plateau, high above the ground. Bakari could see for hundreds of miles in each direction. Climbing off his horse with difficulty, Bakari walked a few steps into a grouping of thin pine trees and then yelled to Danijela.

"A cave," he said as he ran back out toward the high wizard. "There's a cave here. And Abylar is inside."

They left their Cremelinos outside and made their way into the cave. Danijela lit a mage light in front of them as they moved deeper into the huge cavern. It was large enough for Abylar to walk into it, and Bakari wondered what it was originally used for.

"This is a place of power," Danijela said. "By the size of it, I would say that it was an original roosting spot for dragons."

Long side trails crisscrossed the main cavern, but the two wizards continued forward, moving deeper into the cavern. The mage light lit the way in front of them, but the height of the ceiling was lost in the darkness.

Then Danijela stopped and put out her arm in front of Bakari. The High Wizard stood about nine inches shorter than Bakari, so her arm hit him in the gut. He turned to look at her.

"There is evil here, Dragon King," she said. "Can you feel it?"

Bakari tried to reach out his senses. "A little. Maybe the manacles are blocking it."

"That might be a good thing." Danijela moved forward with more caution.

Soon they heard the lapping sounds of water in front of them, and Bakari remembered the vision he'd had of Abylar, right before the bond had been lost. Bakari remembered feeling the dragon's eyes closing as he had shouted one last time for

Abylar, and then, just before the dragon's eyelids closed, Bakari had seen a light that flared within the water.

They moved more slowly and glanced around with careful motions. The cavern had narrowed before, but now it opened up again, into a vast underground hall. Danijela brightened her mage light, but they still couldn't see the other end of the room. A lake of black water lapped against the stones near their feet, and out in the middle of the water, almost lost in the darkness, sat a large rock.

Danijela turned to Bakari. "Well, where is he?"

Bakari focused inward and searched for his dragon. He closed his eyes to help himself concentrate and felt himself merge easily with the stream of magic this time.

A hoarse laughter sounded off in the distance across the water. "Welcome wizards," a voice said.

Bakari felt a jolt of magic with the voice, but he kept his concentration firm and dove deeper into the magic stream.

"This could be dangerous, Dragon King," Danijela said as she joined him in the stream of magic.

"If I cannot find and free my dragon, I am not worthy of being the Dragon King," Bakari said in a tone of soft determination.

Bakari felt the presence of two great magics in the stream: one good and one evil. He ignored them both for a moment and tried to reach out to his dragon.

Abylar! he called, projecting his thoughts outward.

Master? came a low reply. *You came for me.*

Of course I came for you, Abylar—I am your rider and your friend. Where are you?

He tricked me, Abylar said. *The evil king tricked me, and I can't escape.*

Bakari felt Abylar now more than before. With Bakari closer to Abylar, physically and magically, their bond was beginning to heal. In the cave, Bakari felt the churning of the black water. He opened his eyes but kept his contact with the magical stream at the same time. In front of Bakari, the rock in the middle of the water began to move and lift up, taller and taller.

"Abylar!" Bakari yelled out loud.

Dark water fell, dripping off of Abylar's beautiful and sleek blue dragon scales. Bakari was so excited that he almost lost contact again. Something was still impeding the full revival of the bond.

"Dragon King," said a voice of pure hatred. Its words echoed in both the cavern and the stream of magic. "You have come to take my dominion from me once again?"

"You have no place here," warned Danijela with a push of power out from her side. "Leave this place now!"

The ground shook, and Danijela and Bakari were pulled into the magic stream once again—this time with the evil presence from the cave—the sounds and sights of the cave fading around them.

In front of Bakari stood an apparition of a heavy, well-built man. His dark hair cascaded down to his shoulders. He was wearing the robes of a wizard and had a crown on his head, but the man wasn't quite solid, and Bakari could see through his body.

"My rule was cut short by those who were unfaithful to me," the man said. "So I am coming to take it back again."

"Rodric Ekhart?" Bakari asked.

The man smiled. "I see you know your history, Scholar Wizard."

"I know that you were deposed for a reason," Bakari said. "You were trying to take over other kingdoms." Bakari looked down at his own hands and noticed that, in the magic stream, he didn't have the manacles on.

"And now I will, and no one will stand in my way!" Rodric said.

"Why do rulers always get hungry for more power?" Danijela asked. "A wizard should know better than that. We are here to protect and help others."

"We are here to rule!" Rodric screamed out in the magic stream, echoes of his words filling the never-ending darkness.

"Not if I can help it!" a voice called out, from behind Bakari and Danijela.

Bakari turned around and smiled. It was Roland, striding toward them. Light gathered around Roland so brightly that it was hard to look his way without squinting.

The old king took a few steps back and shielded his eyes. "No, you young whelp," Rodric said, his voice filling the area around them. "You will not stop me now. My three sons have been gathering power and preparing the way for me. Your wizard schools are in disarray, and I've felt the wizards' powers weakening."

Bakari looked toward Danijela, and she, in turn, looked at Roland with a glare that said she knew that he was the guilty one who had been taking power from the other wizards.

"What?" Roland said to Danijela, with his hands out to either side.

"You are taking too much, Roland," Danijela said sternly. "You will burn yourself out. You do have limits."

"I don't," Roland said, his eyes smoldering. "Why is everyone trying to stop me from using my powers?"

"Good, good," Rodric said and then laughed. "Now you know how I feel, Roland Tyre. Everyone tried to limit me too. They said I should be happy with ruling just Alaris. But my power was so much more. I needed to rule all the lands. And I would have. I would have been a good king."

Roland glared at the old king, but Bakari saw a bit of empathy in Roland's eyes for the man.

"No, Roland." Bakari pulled his friend's attention back to him. "Don't listen to him."

Bakari, Abylar said in the back of Bakari's mind, *I need your power to release me fully.*

Bakari was starting to have a hard time splitting his attention between Abylar and Rodric and Roland. He needed to figure out what to do to end this evil.

He was about to turn more of his attention and power back to Abylar, when three more apparitions joined them in the magic stream.

The three beings stood next to Rodric, their bodies barely visible in the magic stream. But black tendrils of power outlined their persons, so Bakari could see who they each were. And bright yellow eyes flashed from each one.

"My sons, you have done well in sowing confusion and distrust on the Western Continent."

All three men bowed to their father, their eyes full of adoration.

Then Rodric spread his hands out to his sides and said, "It is time now for me to reenter the world of the living."

CHAPTER THIRTY FIVE

B akari and Danijela found themselves standing alone in the empty darkness of the magic stream. Rodric and his sons had vanished, and all had been quiet for several minutes. "We need reinforcements," Danijela whispered to Bakari.

In a matter of moments, two men popped into the stream of magic and stood by Danijela's sides. She turned to Bakari and introduced them. "Dragon King, meet Darius DarSan Williams, king of the Realm and wizard of the heart, and Mezar Alrishitar, emperor of Gildan and wizard of the mind. They are two of the mightiest wizards in the land."

Bakari nodded his head at the two newcomers. The emperor had slanted eyes, light brown skin, and black hair, which he wore down his back, pulled together with a golden band. The king looked like an older version of Liam: medium brown hair to his neck, gray eyes, and broad shoulders.

"I have met your son, sir."

Darius nodded. "My daughter sent me word. Where is Liam now?"

Before Bakari could answer, a rush of dark power plowed into him from behind. He fell down and then turned to look back up.

The Chameleon's yellow eyes were gleaming brightly. "I should have taken care of you earlier, Dragon Rider. Your kind has caused me nothing but trouble." Then Rodric and his other two sons appeared again.

Roland stepped forward and unleashed a wave of bright, flashing light at Rodric and his three sons. The hit should have taken them by surprise, but the power just wrapped itself around them and did them no harm.

In retaliation, the brothers threw out tendrils of black power toward Bakari and the wizards with him. Off to the side, Bakari saw Danijela, Darius, and Mezar holding their hands high in the sky, their magic forming together—becoming a brilliant glow of multiple hues.

"Just like old times." Danijela smiled at the two.

Bakari didn't understand her reference, but he could tell that the three of them had a longer history together than he knew about. He stepped back, allowing their combined powers to grow. Then Roland stepped forward and joined them. Adding his power almost brought Darius and Mezar to their knees.

"It's too much, Roland," Danijela screamed. "We won't be able to control it."

Roland pulled back some of his power, and Danijela, Mezar, and Darius threw a powerful bolt at the four evil apparitions. A boom sounded in the air, and the colors flashed across the magic stream.

But no harm came to the four men.

"What kind of magic is this?" Darius yelled.

"Evil magic," Bakari whispered. "Pure evil."

Bakari watched Roland gather power again. His spirit glowed brighter, almost pure white.

"Stop!" yelled Rodric.

Before they tried to attack, everyone turned to look at Rodric. The old wizard king waved his arms in a circular motion, and all of them were moved rapidly through the magic stream. Then dots of light appeared around them, and, in the blink of an eye, Rodric had grabbed one.

"I think you recognize this one, Roland Tyre—don't you?"

Roland gasped and then said, "Stay away from her. She is of no concern to you."

Rodric laughed.

Suddenly, they were pulled into a room. Glancing around himself, Bakari realized that Darius and Mezar had not followed them. Then Bakari recognized that they were in a room in the Citadel. The window opposite himself showed that it was late in the evening, and two people sat on a couch in this well-decorated room.

"It's Alli, Roland!" Bakari yelled out to his friend. "What is she doing there?"

Rodric turned to the Chameleon with a glare and said, "Yes, Son, what is she doing there? I thought you had things taken care of in Quentis."

The Chameleon's eyes opened wider, and he couldn't find words quickly enough. So Rodric sent a wave of black power into the Chameleon, and he leaned over and screamed.

"Do not fail me again," Rodric bellowed, "or your brothers will inherit without you."

"It was the Followers of the Dragon, my lord," the Chameleon said. "They freed her and the dragon rider boy."

Rodric growled and turned back to the group around him.

Bakari rubbed his head. This place was confusing. It was as if he was now in three places at once. His body stood in the cavern with Danijela, his spirit was in the magic stream with those around him, but now, through tapping Alli's aura, they were also in the Citadel.

"It is time," Rodric said, repeating his words from earlier. He led his three sons into the next room, and Bakari and the others followed them.

Then Bakari stared down at a form on the bed in front of them and gasped. Turning to Roland, Bakari stated the obvious, "Roland, that's you!"

"I will use Roland Tyre's body!" Rodric yelled. "What would be better than a High Wizard of the Citadel to rule the lands?"

"Oh, no you don't." Roland turned quickly toward Rodric. "You're not having my body. It's way too good-looking for you."

No one laughed.

"Alli, is there any change?" a young woman said from the other room.

Bakari whipped his head back around and took a few steps. "Kharlia!" he exclaimed. "What is she doing here?"

Danijela stepped up next to Bakari and nodded her head, as if she was understanding something that he was not. "An Elvyn healer," she said. "Interesting."

Bakari turned to Danijela and said, "She's not Elvyn. She's Kharlia, my...my..." He didn't quite know how to characterize their relationship. "My good friend," he finally said, though he knew it sounded lame.

"Bakari," Roland sighed from behind him, "I don't think women want to be referred to as just your friend. *Girlfriend, sweetheart,* or something more official would be the best."

Bakari blushed.

Behind them, a swirl of black power began to build. Roland ran over and pushed the apparition of Rodric, but nothing happened. Not being in the physical world, they couldn't actually touch each other.

Tendrils of black began to pour darkness into Roland's body that was lying on the bed. Roland stepped forward and, with a flick of his wrist, brought forth a powerful white light. His light met the black power head-on, but the white light couldn't penetrate it and eventually dissipated.

"I hope Jaimon finds Bakari soon," Alli said in the other room.

Bakari kept moving his head back and forth, for it was hard to keep track of what was going on between the physical world and the magic stream.

"You said that the artifacts were the only way to defeat the Chameleon?" Kharlia asked Alli.

These words were heard by those in the magic stream. The Chameleon stepped away from Roland's body and towards the two young women.

But Rodric pulled him back. "No, I need your power now," he ordered. "Worry about killing them later."

Both Bakari and Roland turned to Danijela.

"Our wizard magic can't work against them," Bakari said to his group. "We've seen it before. Their powers absorb our magic."

"But the power of a dragon might work," Danijela said. "Bakari, can you reach your dragon? You have to try again. It might be the only way."

Bakari concentrated, trying to put more of his focus on being in the cave, back where Abylar was standing in the dark, underground cavern.

Abylar, come to me, Bakari ordered.

He felt the cavern floor rumbling around him and saw the lake churning again. Abylar stood taller and took a step forward.

Abylar, as your master, I order you to come to me now. Bakari reached into Abylar's mind and dug deeper. He could feel the poisonous compulsions of Rodric's powers there. But, with the old king's attention elsewhere, Bakari was finally able to break through these.

With one last push of thought, Bakari directed Abylar out of the dark water and back onto the dry ground of the cavern floor. To Bakari's surprise, the dragon brought his huge jaws down over Bakari's wrists and bit the manacles off with one snap of his teeth.

I am the Dragon King!

Power raced through Bakari as the bond came back—this time, more powerful than ever. Abylar's deep roar thundered through the cave, and colors of power swirled around him. Bakari felt alive once again. His hearing, sight, and other senses were all amplified.

So Bakari focused his attention on the others, moving through the magic stream and back into Roland's room at the Citadel.

He brought his arm up, to confront Rodric with all the power coursing through him.

But Roland shouted, "No," stopping Bakari just before he would have released his dragon powers.

"Too much of him has entered my body now," Roland explained. "If you kill Rodric, you will kill me."

"But, Roland…" Bakari begged. "We can't allow him to take over your body."

"I have an idea," Roland said.

"Roland, you already hold too much power," Danijela warned. "Be careful."

"Aren't I always careful?" Roland smirked.

"Roland, focus!" Bakari commanded.

Roland walked toward the other room and called forth, "Alli! Alli!"

Alli stood up from the couch and glanced around. "Kharlia, did you hear someone call me?"

"No." Kharlia shook her head. "You're tired, Alli. Get some sleep. I'll watch over him. Anyway, Tam will be back shortly."

"Alli!" Roland yelled again, putting more of his power into his voice. The others in the room cringed at its intensity. And Rodric's sons faltered.

But Bakari noticed a euphoric look on Rodric's face. Looking over at Roland's body, he saw his body begin to twitch.

"Roland, whatever you are going to do, do it now!" Bakari yelled.

"Alli, please come to my room," Roland said, trying to coax her.

Alli turned toward the room. "I need to check on Roland," she told Kharlia.

Kharlia followed, then gasped. "Alli, look!"

When the two young women looked at Roland's body, it began to twitch again.

"He's alive!" Kharlia exclaimed.

Alli moved over to the bed and touched Roland's cheek tenderly. She pulled back with a hiss. "It's hot. Too hot!"

"I'll get some water," Kharlia said, and she ran out of the room.

Alli pulled back the blankets a bit and yelled out, "His arms are turning black—just like Lan's did."

Bakari turned to Roland and asked, "What are you doing?"

Roland gazed at him, with power in his eyes, but then a tear dropped out of the corner of his eye. "I was wrong. This is the only way, Bakari."

"What is the only way? Roland, what is your plan?" Bakari asked.

But Roland turned back to Alli and said, "Take out your sword."

Nothing happened.

So he yelled again, putting more power into his voice, "Alli, Take out your sword."

Alli pulled her sword out from its scabbard as Kharlia came back into the room.

"What are you doing, Alli?"

Alli turned to Kharlia. Tears filled Alli's eyes as she said, "He's here, Kharlia! He's here. I can feel him and hear him. He needs me."

"Why the sword, then?"

"I don't know... I don't know," Alli began to cry.

Roland's body convulsed and shook as Bakari watched the last of Rodric's powers enter it. A look of glee spread across Rodric's sons' faces as Rodric's apparition totally dissolved into Roland's body.

"No, Roland!" Danijela screamed. "You can't do this."

Bakari fully put together what Roland intended. "Why, Roland?" He moved to stop his friend. "There must be another way."

Before anyone could answer, Roland's body sat up in the bed. He blinked a few times, then turned and stared hard at Alli. His eyes were black, and his smile looked wicked. Then he opened his mouth to say something.

Roland turned to Bakari and said, "Tell Alli that I loved her and that I don't blame her."

"Blame her for what?" Bakari asked. "For this."

"No. Roland!" Danijela yelled out.

As Bakari watched, Roland's spirit glowed with the brightness of thousands of wizards. Then Roland's spirit broke the barrier between the magic stream and the Citadel, and he stood in the room with Alli and Kharlia.

"Kill me!" Roland's spirit yelled out. "Alli, kill my body now!"

Alli peered up at Roland's spirit then back to the body on the bed. Black tendrils crawled up his body's arms and neck.

The mouth opened, and a loud, evil laugh came forth. Alli looked at Roland's apparition one last time, then brought the blade through the air.

"No, Alli. Don't!" Kharlia had said, to try to stop her. But Alli's instincts were legendary, and she had brought her sword up and back down in one swift stroke across Roland's body.

"Nooooo!" An evil wail screamed out of Roland's possessed body. The body thrashed around, then it stopped moving, and the black tendrils of darkness faded away into the air around them.

The three brothers in the magic stream glared at Roland's spirit in horror.

"He entered me fully and became mortal. Now he is dead!" Roland's spirit yelled out. Then he fell to the ground in the magic stream, power blinking out from him.

Bakari rushed over to his friend. "Roland, what have you done to yourself?"

Danijela was soon by Bakari's side. "He sacrificed himself to rid the world of the evil king."

"Why would he do that?" Bakari felt tears sting his eyes. "We could have found another way." Turning to Roland he continued, "How will Alli feel? She killed you, Roland. You made her kill you!" Anger mixed with the tears, and he hit his friend on the shoulder—but of course in the magic stream his fist just slid through Roland's spirit.

Roland opened his eyes weakly. "I did what I had to do, Bakari. It was the only way. Our magic wasn't working, but a sword can kill just as easily as magic can—sometimes even more deftly."

Bakari was briefly aware of Kharlia rushing to Alli's side in the Citadel room.

"Move over, Alli," Kharlia yelled as she jumped up on the bed to try and keep Roland's body alive.

But Bakari knew it was too late. He had seen Rodric's spirit fly away. He was dead. After one hundred and fifty years the evil king was finally dead, and the body of Bakari's best friend had died with him.

"Now what will you do?" Bakari said to Roland's spirit, though he was mad at his friend. "Your spirit is still here, in the magic stream. Are you going to roam the stream like he did, going more and more mad, until you try to return again?"

"I don't know." Roland smiled. "I don't know. But please, Bakari, don't hate me."

Bakari didn't know what he felt. He had never imagined Roland dying like this. He felt his own body fall to the ground in the cavern. Abylar curled up next to him and tried to comfort him.

"I don't hate you, Roland," Bakari said, feeling himself fading out from the magic stream. "You are my best friend. As pompous and bragging and arrogant as you were, I still knew there was good in you."

"I finally did something for someone else, Bakari. You were right. I did have some good in me."

Danijela and Roland began to fade away, and Bakari found himself, once again, in the cave, next to Abylar. Danijela sat next to them.

"Thanks for believing in me," Roland said from the magic stream. . His voice sounded a soft echo off the walls of the cave.

Bakari turned to Danijela. Tears flowed freely from his eyes.

She reached over and held his hand. No words were said or needed.

CHAPTER THIRTY SIX

Bakari lay down on the hard cavern floor for a few moments, trying to gather his thoughts. Then the black water in front of them began to churn again. Bakari sat up, and Danijela flashed a mage light over the water.

In the deepest, darkest corners, a brief outline of three men stood above the black water.

One of them pointed a black finger directly at Bakari and said, "We are coming for you, Dragon King. First, though, we will destroy all you know and love."

Bakari stood up and let out a loud wail. As he did so, he pulled the power of Abylar to him, and the wail turned into a roar. A dragon's roar.

His best friend was dead because of these men. They would pay!

The three specters laughed and then disappeared. Bakari was about to scream after the three brothers again, but he was stopped by a flash of acknowledgement through the bond.

"They're here!" Bakari yelled and began to run toward the cave entrance.

"Who's here?" Danijela asked as she used her short legs to try and keep up with him.

Abylar roared from behind the two, and a stream of fire shot by them.

"Hey!" Danijela yelled. "Is your dragon trying to kill us?"

"No, he's just excited to see his kin," Bakari said.

"His kin?" Danijela asked and then followed up, a brief moment later, with, "You mean the other dragons are here?"

Soon the three of them came out of the cave's entrance to view two dragons, circling in the air.

Jaimon waved down from his green dragon, Cholena. "Master! Glad we found you."

Miriel flew down lower, and her scales reflected light from the afternoon sun. She roared, and Bakari waved at her. Then he noticed Breelyn's absence and the black tips of Miriel's wings. A hollow pit formed in Bakari's stomach.

He gestured for Jaimon to land. Before Jaimon did, however, they heard another loud roar to the north. Stepping a few feet farther out, toward the ledge, Bakari shielded his eyes and looked north. Soaring down toward them was a bright red dragon.

Ryker dropped down lower, and Liam waved at Bakari and then at Danijela. "Auntie, how are you?"

Danijela was speechless.

"Surprised?" Liam asked.

Danijela shook her head. "I always knew you were destined for greatness."

All three dragons landed, and the two riders jumped off. After a few hugs, Bakari filled them in on what had happened. Jaimon was shocked about Roland's death but more concerned for Alli, as Jaimon knew Alli better.

Before the conversation went too much farther, Jaimon brought out a small knapsack and opened it on the ground. He pulled out half a dozen small objects—figurines of dragons in various poses.

Bakari looked down at him. "What are these, Jaimon? Toys?"

"Oh. No, Bakari." Jaimon smiled at him. "They are artifacts of power. A means of drawing more power from our dragons. Alli used one of them on the Chameleon. She almost had him, but then he got away."

"Alli used them to pull dragons' power?" Bakari was amazed. She wasn't even a dragon rider. She was powerful indeed.

"The Followers of the Dragon said these are for you," Jaimon said. "With these, we can call forth the power of the dragons—and then give all our power to you—to get rid of the Chameleon and his brothers once and for all."

"I'm in," Liam offered.

Danijela turned to Liam and smiled. "Settle down, Liam. We don't even know what we are dealing with here. I have shared a Cremelino's power before, but a dragon's…?"

"Well, Auntie Anwar," Liam shot back, "I am bonded to both."

Danijela's eyes opened wide, and she turned to Bakari.

"I'm in too," Jaimon said. "I saw Alli use the jade artifact. We can defeat them, Bakari. I know it."

"And save Breelyn?" Bakari asked.

The Jaimon shook his head. "I don't think so. I saw her. She's leading an army into Alaris. She's turned evil."

Bakari hung his head low. One friend dead, another turned evil.

When will this end?

"It stops now!" he yelled out loud and stood up.

"But we don't know where they are," Jaimon said.

"I know where they are in the magic stream. That is where I will go."

"But you need to rest, Bakari," Danijela said. "You've been through a lot today."

Bakari gritted his teeth together. He knew the High Wizard of Arc was right. "Are you always so pushy and matronly?" He grinned to take the edge off his question.

"Yes, she is," Liam answered with a laugh.

Bakari closed his eyes to feel his bond with Abylar, letting his dragon's powers and senses flow through himself. He thought about the best way to do this. They most likely would only have one chance. He thought about all he had been through to get to this point: the Orb, his dragon, the war in Alaris, his heritage in Mahli—

That is it! Mahli! My kingdom.

"We fly to Mahli," Bakari said. "From there, we will use the dragons' powers to destroy the Chameleon and his brothers." Then Bakari turned to Danijela and asked, "Will you join us?"

Danijela thought for a moment. "I would love to ride on a dragon, Bakari, but this task is for the dragon riders. I need to return and discuss these things with Darius and Mezar and the others."

"I understand." Bakari nodded. "Thank you for all you have done, Danijela."

She hugged them all, then began to lead the two Cremelinos back down the mountain trail. Before rounding a bend of the plateau, she turned back to Bakari, with a smile and sparkle in her eye, and said, "Don't give up hope, Dragon King. All is not lost."

Bakari gave Danijela a short bow and a wave before turning back to Jaimon and Liam.

"Mount up, Dragon Riders. We fly!"

* * *

Dragons fly fast. And, when they are urged on by the Dragon King, they fly even faster. The four dragons and three dragon riders followed the mountain range south, all the way to Mahli, stopping only briefly during the night to rest themselves. The dragons took this opportunity to catch a bit of something to eat—and even seared a few smaller pieces for the humans.

Early the next morning, the group arrived in Amar, the capital of Mahli. They landed in a field outside the city, and soon a group of men met the dragons and their riders there. The group was led by Zaire, Bakari's previous trainer.

As the dragon riders dismounted, Zaire took a couple of running steps up to where Bakari stood. "Welcome back, Dragon Rider." Zaire had an oversized grin on his face. His braids hung down to the middle of his back and swirled around as he turned to meet the other two dragon riders.

"Welcome, all of you," Zaire said.

As the men behind Zaire bowed low, honoring both the riders and their dragons, Bakari felt a better sense of acceptance this time. Then Zaire sent runners into the city ahead of the group.

"Come inside." Zaire motioned to the three riders. "I am sure the regent is anxious to see you again. He hoped you would return soon."

After a short walk to the city, Zaire led Bakari, Liam, and Jaimon into the small castle. As they entered the front hallway, a line of quickly gathered dignitaries met them. As the riders walked past, each person brought a hand from heart to forehead, then bowed in respect. At the end of the line stood the regent.

Regent Nagasi bowed low to the ground, touched his hand to his heart and then his forehead, and stood back up. His dark braids, showing signs of graying, framed his brown face. He wore his finest—red robes and a small crown on his head. The regent signaled to the side, and a woman brought out a blue silk cloak that she draped over Bakari's shoulders. Golden dragons were embroidered on the corners of it. The regent then motioned Bakari forward to the small throne.

As the two stood in front of the throne, the regent removed the crown from his own head and said, "As regent of Mahli, it has always been my duty to rule the land on a temporary basis, waiting for the king to arrive. As my fathers did before me, so I have done." A brief sadness flickered across the regent's face.

Bakari understood the meaning behind the regent's expression. The regent's son, Kolo, had wanted to follow after his father; however, Kolo had wanted to be more than just a regent. He had wanted to be a dragon rider and the king. By falling prey to the Chameleon's madness, Kolo had turned a dragon evil and had later died in the process of helping the Chameleon escape from the Citadel.

The regent cleared his voice. "Today, the regency ends." He lifted up the crown and motioned Bakari closer. Bakari took two steps forward and looked up a few inches at the older man's face. Bakari's heart was pounding.

"Today we crown a king of Mahli once again." The regent lowered the golden crown onto Bakari's head, pushing it down over his braided hair. Then he grabbed Bakari's hand in his and held it high in the air as he said, "Hail to the king of Mahli. Hail the Dragon King."

"Hail the Dragon King," the crowd cheered.

One by one, every man and woman present knelt down on one knee and bowed their heads to their new king. Liam and Jaimon were the last to do so.

"Hail the Dragon King," Liam said.

"Hail the Dragon King," Jaimon followed.

Bakari glanced over the heads of the crowd. It was hard to take it all in.

"Please rise." He motioned with his hand to his devoted subjects. "I am honored beyond all measure that you think I am worthy to be your king," Bakari said, his voice thick with emotion, and he tried to keep his tears in check.

He took a deep breath and felt the power of Abylar flow through his veins. He instantly felt a connection to all the dragons and their riders. Even Breelyn. There was still a small spark there. But her heart had been darkened, and Bakari didn't know if she could ever recover from that. Through the bond, he knew that she was at the border between Alaris and Solshi and that Gorn and an army of wizards and soldiers stood ready to battle against her. Bakari had to stop that from happening!

"I must leave you for a short time, my friends," Bakari began. "The other riders and I need to finish ridding the land of a great evil."

The regent turned to Bakari. "Surely you could breakfast with us first."

The pleading in his eyes and the eyes of those gathered warmed Bakari's heart. These were good people, here in Mahli. *His people.*

Bakari nodded his head to them. "Of course."

The people clapped and cheered, and the regent ushered Bakari, Jaimon, and Liam into a dining hall.

Bakari didn't know how they had put such food together so quickly, but he was happy nonetheless. Delicious smells of freshly baked bread, roasted meats, and sweet fruits filled the air around him. His heightened senses picked up everything at once—it was almost overwhelming—and he had to pause and try to control the onslaught.

Jaimon's stomach rumbled audibly next to Bakari, and the three riders laughed.

The regent smiled also. "Ah, young men. Always hungry."

During the meal, which lasted longer than Bakari had hoped, many people from the city came in to express their respect for Bakari and to wish him well. And Bakari found it hard to keep his eyes clear of tears through the morning meal. Their love and unconditional support for him were beyond anything he could imagine.

The only thing that would make this moment better was if Kharlia were there with him…and Roland. Bakari swallowed hard and tried to wipe his eyes without it being noticed. He had told himself that he had to be strong now and could grieve later, but it was hard. The love of his people in Mahli brought out strong emotions in him.

Bakari finally stood. "We thank all of you for your kindness. I will return soon, but we need to go and rid the world of a great evil once and for all. Please excuse us."

Jaimon and Liam rose with him. Together, these three young men from very different parts of the Western Continent wound their way through the people, toward the door.

All conversation stopped. Each person, in turn, stood up and then bowed in reverence. As the three riders approached the door, Bakari turned and looked back.

"Hail the Dragon King," said a lone voice from the back.

"Hail the dragon riders," said another voice.

Bakari put his hand in the air and waved. "Hail the people of Mahli. I will return."

The crowd cheered as the three young men walked outside. On the way to their dragons, they found throngs of people lining the streets, who cheered for their king and the other two dragon riders. Many people waved flags and brightly colored ribbons in the air or chanted the words to an old song about dragons.

"Quite a people!" Liam said to Bakari.

Bakari nodded. He and Jaimon had walked slowly so that Liam could keep up with them. Before they reached the dragons, a young woman no more than twelve or thirteen years old approached Bakari. She bowed low, then rose to meet his eye.

"Is it true that the Citadel is accepting new apprentices?" she said shyly, her brown eyes wide on her small face.

Bakari looked down at the young woman with compassion and asked, "Do you have magic?"

"I think so," the young woman said. She spread her hands to her sides and moved them upward. Three oversized rocks at the side of the road rose into the air.

Bakari laughed. "So you do. What is your name?"

"Izette," the young woman said.

An older woman, presumably her mother, came up and took Izette's hand and said, "Excuse her, Dragon King."

Bakari smiled. "She has remarkable talent. I will put in a good word for her at the Citadel. She will be welcomed there at any time."

Izette looked up at her mother with a big smile on her face.

Thinking of the Citadel reminded Bakari of Roland, and he gritted his teeth to keep his anger and sadness in check.

Soon they reached their dragons. Upon seeing the three riders, all four dragons, including Breelyn's dragon, roared loudly and sent fire—blue, green, yellow, and red—high up into the skies. The people cheered once again.

The three dragon riders mounted and soon found themselves flying high over the Mahlian countryside. Bakari led them forward, to one of the tallest mountain peaks on the southern side of Mahli, which overlooked Alaris. The tips of the peaks here still held a little snow, but, for the most part, each mountainside was green and lush. Birds sang, and wild animals ran through the forests and meadows in abundance.

"It smells wonderful!" Jaimon shouted. "Much like the mountains in Quentis. I can't believe I am flying."

"Me either." Liam's grin matched Jaimon's.

The two riders had become fast friends on their flight from the Superstition Mountains to Mahli. Bakari smiled at the two. He was barely older than they were, but he felt so much more so. A heavy weight settled on him: the weight of what he must do. Noticing a high plateau nearby, he motioned the others to land.

Soon all four dragons landed on the mountainside. Bakari took a few steps away from the group and walked out on the flat rock. Abylar and the other dragons stayed behind with the other two young men. He stared south and took a few deep breaths.

This is it.

He felt the cool wind on his face, his cloak blowing out behind him. Turning back to face Jaimon, Bakari motioned the young man toward himself.

"The artifacts?" Bakari asked.

"Right here." Jaimon opened the small bag and took out three pieces—one jade, one wood, and one stone of some sort.

Bakari took the wooden one and instructed Jaimon to take one and give Liam the other. Then the two younger riders sat on a rock by the dragons, and Bakari stayed where he was and closed his eyes. It was time to find the Chameleon and his brothers and destroy them once and for all.

CHAPTER THIRTY SEVEN

Holding the wooden dragon artifact in his hand, Bakari felt himself enter the magic stream. All was dark around him, a grayness that never ended. Sparks of light blinked in the distance. Bakari now knew those were wizards and other powerful men and women.

He drew upon his own wizard powers first, then augmented them with Abylar's power. He reeled for a moment at the increase of power that the figurine brought him with his dragon's powers. Then he reached his mind out to Jaimon and Liam and pulled their powers to himself also. The magnitude of power was almost overwhelming.

Steady, Dragon King, Abylar said. As his reassuring voice came to him, Bakari smiled. He knew now that his dragon would always be there for him.

Bakari filled himself up with more power than he had ever held before. He sensed that Jaimon and Liam were struggling to hold the amount of power they did, especially Jaimon, as he was not a wizard.

Don't take more than you can hold, Bakari warned them. Then he sensed Breelyn through the bond, but he would stay away from her until it was time to confront her.

He reached out to Abylar, Cholena, Miriel, and Ryker and made sure they were ready.

We are here to serve you, Master and King, Miriel said, echoing the thoughts of the other dragons, though Bakari could tell there was sadness in her tone. Miriel missed her rider terribly, so she said, *May you prevail over the evil.*

Now to find the Chameleon, Bakari said as he pulled areas of the magic stream to himself. Lights blinking around him now, he reached out his senses until he found what he was looking for. It was down in Quentis. Grabbing that light, he pulled himself into the castle there.

Standing before him, in a highly decorated room, were three men. One was only slightly older than Bakari himself, while the other two were considerably more so.

"My prince," said the oldest of the three men. "Your father is dying. You need to take the throne now. It is your duty."

"My duty is to care for my father," the second oldest man said. "He is still the king."

"I thought you were the Wolf!" the older man spat.

The young man stepped forward and said, "Be careful, Commander." His hand was on his sword's hilt.

Bakari stared at him for a moment. The young man had perfect features and olive skin, and he stood tall. There was a resemblance between him and the man called the Wolf.

Bakari, that is the Chameleon with the king's son and grandson, Jaimon said to Bakari through the bond. *The real commander of the Sanctuary is dead.*

Bakari readied his power. He had studied it out in his mind and had learned what had happened with Roland. Bakari needed to be quick and not hesitate.

Chameleon! Bakari yelled out from the magic stream.

The oldest man turned and looked around the room. "He is here."

"Who is here, Commander?" asked the Wolf.

"The Dragon King!" The Chameleon brought his hands up, and black tendrils of magic leaped forth.

Bakari drew all he could from the figurine and his dragons then. With a quick turn of his mind, he leaped physically into the real world in Quentis.

The Wolf and his son jumped back in surprise, but then they bowed their heads.

"My King!" the Wolf said in awe. "I never thought I would see this day."

The Chameleon attacked Bakari with his black magic, but the Dragon King was ready. As Bakari pushed out the power he held with the power of the three figurines the three dragon riders held, a dragon of bright light raced out from his fingertips and collided with the Chameleon's black magic.

The Chameleon staggered back. "Such power!" he shrieked and pushed out a stronger blast of black magic, which wound its way through the room and wrapped around the Wolf and Kaspar. Kaspar yelled and tried to bat it away with his sword.

"There will be no more killing, Chameleon!" Bakari yelled out and then unleashed a wave of hot blue fire—forming a blue dragon that stood next to the white one between Bakari and the Chameleon. "This ends now!" Bakari added.

As the Chameleon brought forth a new attack of dark magic, Bakari sent the blue and white dragons of fire racing across the short distance. They enveloped the Chameleon and his black tendrils of magic with their humongous, fiery dragon jaws. The Chameleon screamed and then dissolved into nothingness, his black power dissipating mere moments later.

Bakari drew back the dragons of fire and then fell to the floor, exhausted. The Wolf grabbed some water from a nearby pitcher and brought the cup to Bakari's lips. Bakari gulped it down and then rose to his knees.

Kaspar reached down and pulled Bakari up the rest of the way. The young man couldn't seem to stop smiling. "Greetings, Dragon King. We have waited long for you."

"Long?"

The Wolf turned to Bakari, standing a head taller than the Dragon King. "We are the Followers of the Dragon and have kept safe a few artifacts and books for you for hundreds of years...until they were needed."

Clarity dawned on Bakari. "*You* gave them to Jaimon?"

The Wolf nodded. "Yes, the few that we had. Some artifacts were lost long ago, and we haven't been able to find them."

Bakari frowned. If those fell into the wrong hands, they could indeed pose a problem.

"Will you meet my father before you go?" the Wolf asked.

Bakari needed to go after the other two brothers, for he was sure they would be warned somehow about what had happened here. But he couldn't turn down the Wolf's humble request.

"Quickly," Bakari agreed.

Kaspar led the way, out of the room and down the hall, with Bakari walking in the middle and the Wolf following him.

Walking behind Kaspar through the castle, with the crown on his head and power still glowing around his body, Bakari garnered more than a few stares. Soon they arrived at a door guarded by two men. The guards nodded to the Wolf and then let the three of them in.

Walking up to a bed, Bakari looked down at an old man with olive skin and gray hair. Bakari could see his resemblance to the other two men. The king opened his dark eyes and gave a brief smile to Bakari. Then Bakari felt something pushing against his thoughts, so he instinctively put up a barrier.

"Sorry," the king said. "It is a habit—or an ability—that we Von Wulfs have."

"Are you a wizard, Your Highness?" Bakari asked.

The king coughed and shook his head.

"We're not wizards," the Wolf explained, "but we have the ability to read others' thoughts sometimes. It's called *seeing*." He smiled.

Bakari glanced down at the old, dying man once again. "Your Highness, I cannot stay long."

The king opened his eyes wider. "I am honored that you would visit me, Dragon King, before I die." Bakari opened his mouth to say something, but the king kept talking. "Soon I will die, and my son will be king after me. We have protected the secrets of the dragon for centuries. It has been our duty here. Even with my last, dying breath, my order to my son will be to serve you. You are his king and overlord."

The Wolf nodded and immediately knelt down, with one knee on the floor. "Hail the Dragon King. I will serve thee for all of my days."

Bakari nodded. Then he felt a strange pull—back to the mountains above Mahli.

"I really need to go," Bakari said. And, with that, he refocused his mind and jumped back into the magic stream. Then he found himself staggering forward on the rocky plateau in the mountains of Mahli.

Liam limped toward Bakari, but Jaimon raced ahead. "You all right, Bakari?" Jaimon brought out a few slices of jerky and water for Bakari.

Bakari nodded and took a few bites and had a drink. "I need to go back in. One down, two to go," he said, then smiled and reached for the magic stream again. "Be careful." Liam whispered.

This time, Bakari pulled himself northward, to the wizard school on White Island.

He found himself standing in the office of the headmaster there. Two men were standing by the headmaster, trying to hold him up, as Bakari had suddenly burst into the room in physical form.

The two men gasped, and the headmaster lifted his head up. Then the two men brought up their other hands and threw fire at Bakari. But it was a measly attempt. Bakari moved a few fingers, and the two men went flying, twenty feet across the room, landing in a heap on the floor.

The headmaster stood up straighter and snarled at Bakari as he said, "Coming for *me* now, boy?"

The comment confirmed Bakari's suspicions that the Sentinel was possessing Headmaster Penrose's body.

"Leave this man's body alone," Bakari commanded. "He has done nothing to deserve this."

"Ahh, but he has," the Sentinel said. "All men have. All you wizards think you are better than everyone else. But you took my father's throne from him and—"

"Your father is dead now," Bakari said to cut him off. "Leave this man's body—by command of the Dragon King!"

Power shook the room and reverberated through the entire magic stream. Then Bakari sensed the presence of Danijela, Mezar, Darius, and other powerful wizards, with him, inside the magic stream. In front of Bakari, a black spirit separated itself from Headmaster Penrose's body, leaving the headmaster himself to slump down onto his chair, looking barely conscious.

The spirit of the Sentinel reached his hands forward, sending a black tendril of power toward Bakari. This time, Bakari immediately drew power from Liam and his dragon, Ryker, and a red dragon of fire came forth from Bakari's hand. The dragon opened its mouth wide and roared a deafening sound that rocked the building. Into its jaws it sucked in all the power of the Sentinel, leaving only the spirit to dissipate and disappear right in front of Bakari.

The headmaster sat up and nodded to Bakari, saying, "Thank you, Son. I don't know who you are, but thank you."

"I am Bakari, the Dragon King," Bakari said, his voice loud and strong.

Then, bringing the red dragon back to himself, Bakari pulled himself away from the wizard school and back into the magic stream. The spirit manifestations of many wizards stood around him there. They bowed their allegiance and gave him power, and Bakari nodded his thanks.

Feeling the dragons and his riders up in the mountains of Mahli still, he took a deep breath. This one would be the hardest, for he would have to confront Breelyn.

Finding he could now travel with only a thought to where he needed to go, Bakari raced south and eastward, to the border of Alaris and Solshi. As he pulled on the spark of a nearby wizard, he found himself looking at a battlefield. Evening was now falling, and men were setting up camp for the night. He could see two armies settling across the Mahli River from each other. And bridges and barges were being erected on the Solshi side.

Then he saw her! Breelyn Mier, Elvyn protector, dragon rider, and the Elvyn king's betrothed. Dressed in black leather, she sat atop a dark horse, her jet-black hair blowing in the wind. Breelyn barked orders to the men around her. Next to her, on an even larger black horse, sat a man. Bakari recognized his visage from the magic stream battle earlier. The General.

Bakari brought himself out of the magic stream directly in front of the General. With the two of them up on the horses and Bakari standing on the ground, the effect was not as great as Bakari would have hoped. But still they were surprised.

"Bakari!" Breelyn said with apparent astonishment.

"Dragon Rider." Bakari nodded to her.

"Not anymore," Breelyn said and lowered her head, refusing to meet Bakari's eyes.

"She is mine now," the General said from beside her. "I am her master."

Bakari shook his head. "Not for long, General."

Bakari gathered the dragons' power to him once again and used it to rise up into the air. He now stood level with the General and Breelyn, and green, blue, yellow, and red—the colors of the dragons—flowed around his body, swirling in the air.

Breelyn looked up and opened her eyes wide, but she stayed silent.

The General brought forth his dark and mighty powers quicker than Bakari had anticipated, and he threw a black thunderbolt at him. Bakari tried to dodge the thunderbolt in the air, but a black tendril hit his arm and sent him skidding backward in the air.

He righted himself and pushed forward. Using the powers of the dragons, Bakari drove any effects of the General's evil tendril out of himself.

"Attack him!" the General yelled out, and his guards drew their swords. But Bakari was too far away for them to reach. Then a group of archers stepped to the side, drew their bows, and fired at him.

Bakari put his arms up, and a shield formed around him, knocking each arrow down in turn. After two earlier battles, though, Bakari was getting tired and needed to end this soon. He floated back to the ground, landing with a gentle step, then walked up in front of Breelyn. He had to try to reach her.

"Breelyn," Bakari said softly. "What happened?"

As she peered down at him, a tear slid down her cheek.

"You don't owe him an explanation," the General said.

From the side, three men tried to attack Bakari. With a slight wave of his hand, first their swords and then the men themselves were thrown through the air.

"I did it for Lan!" Breelyn said. "I did it to save him."

"The General cares nothing for Lan," Bakari said.

"He said he would save the elves and save Lan."

The General laughed out loud, his deep voice filling the air. "See, Dragon King, your precious dragon rider is mine now."

"You have no intention of saving the elves," Bakari yelled at the man.

Breelyn looked over at the General with a question in her eyes.

The General laughed. "Whether I do or don't doesn't really matter now, does it?"

"But you promised," Breelyn said, her face contorting in pain. "You promised you would save him."

"I make all sorts of promises." The General shrugged. "Some I keep, and others I don't. We shall see."

Bakari was paying attention to Breelyn and the General's exchange, when he suddenly felt pain in his shoulder. He yelled out, and, for a moment, he could feel himself in Mahli, in the magic stream, and on the Alaris border—all at the same time. His physical form wavered briefly, then he brought it back more solidly. An arrow's shaft stuck out from his shoulder blade.

As Bakari clapped his hands together, a loud sound filled the air, and in front of him formed a beautiful yellow and gold dragon. He had formed it into as close of a replica as he could make of Miriel, Breelyn's dragon.

"No!" Breelyn yelled. "Don't do this to me, Bakari. I can't come back now!"

"Yes, you can, Breelyn!" Bakari yelled at her as the fire dragon grew in size. "The General will not help you."

"Either way, it is too late," Breelyn said. "I've done too much evil. I pushed Miriel away from me." Tears streamed down Breelyn's face.

But Bakari noticed something that the elf maiden had not—the blackness in Breelyn's hair had receded a few inches. He was reaching her!

"No!" Breelyn yelled, and she flung out her own powerful mage powers at Bakari. The attack surprised him, and he yelled out in pain as her fire had singed his arm. "I am dark now, Bakari. That's who I am. Leave here now."

The General laughed. "Looks like you lose, Dragon King."

Bakari wasn't going to let himself lose. He didn't fly across the Western Continent, destroy the ancient king and two of his sons, and watch his own best friend die just to be stopped here.

Bakari felt the other wizards at his side within the magic stream, while the other dragon riders' and the dragons' powers poured into him from Mahli. He gathered all the powers inside of himself—the powers of the mind, heart, and earth, together with the power of the spirit—and pulled them all into one. As he did so, the yellow fire dragon grew to the size of the real dragon in front of the army.

"Come forth, Miriel. Come to your master!" Bakari ordered the dragon in Mahli. With this command from the Dragon King, the dragon herself went into the magic stream and then came back out and appeared in the air as part of the fire dragon. The apparition and the real dragon merged together and breathed down fire from the sky.

The General brought forth a stream of black fire and threw it at Bakari, but Miriel intervened and swallowed the black fire. With a loud roar, she headed toward the General.

"Breelyn, Dragon Rider," Bakari said, his voice like the roar of a dragon. "Who is your master?" These last few words came out with such power and force that the soldiers nearby fell to the ground and covered their ears.

As Miriel raced toward the General, Breelyn sat by his side and glanced from Bakari to Miriel and back. Suddenly, with an inhuman quickness, Breelyn pulled a dagger from her belt, stood up in her stirrups, and using her magical powers jumped over to the General's horse, plunging the black dagger into the General's heart.

"You are my master, Bakari. The Dragon King is my master," Breelyn screamed, and her voice filled the battlefield.

The General wailed, his black tendrils swirling around him. Miriel reached him and opened her jaws wide. Breelyn jumped to the ground as the merged dragon let out a stream of yellow fire that disintegrated the General in front of his own army.

Miriel flew up into the air and roared, shaking the air around her with a mighty force. Then she disappeared, flying back into the magic stream to return to the plateau in Mahli.

Bakari collapsed to the ground, breathing hard. After a moment, he looked up and saw Breelyn standing back up. Her quick gaze seemed to take in the entire battlefield.

"Go home," she yelled. "Go home. This battle is over."

As she walked slowly toward Bakari, the blackness receded from her hair and clothes, shifting not back to white but to a soft silver. Reaching Bakari, Breelyn bent down and pulled him up to stand next to her. Tears fell down her face.

Bakari smiled through his own tears. "Welcome back, Breelyn."

She hugged him fiercely and wept. Then she turned Bakari around and pulled the arrow out of his back. He winced with the pain and moved his hand over to cover it. But she pushed his hand away and put her own hands on it.

Bakari felt a soft warmth on his shoulder. Then Breelyn removed her hands, and Bakari felt the area. It was healed.

"My powers are back again," Breelyn said. "My true powers. Maybe that means that I can heal Lan also." She smiled, then brought her head down low as she added, "Though, I doubt he even wants to see me, after what I have done."

Bakari flickered briefly, his body needed to get back to his physical form. "Oh, I don't know. I think that man loves you fiercely, Breelyn." He paused a moment, to concentrate on holding his body there for a minute longer. "I have to go now. My power is weakening. Go to the Citadel. They will provide you an escort back to Elvyn."

Breelyn only nodded. Then, before Bakari left, she knelt down and uttered, "Hail the Dragon King."

CHAPTER THIRTY EIGHT

Bakari found himself back in the magic stream, and Danijela and the others stood next to him.

"You did it!" Danijela smiled at Bakari.

He nodded and then smiled. "I did!"

"Truly a dragon king," Mezar said. "I look forward to meeting you in person someday." With that, he left the group.

"Take care of my son," Darius said and then smiled. "I am happy that Liam has found a purpose in life." He spread his arms out wide as he began to dissipate also.

Bakari gasped and looked at Danijela. "The joy Darius feels!"

"King Darius does have a flair for giving his heart to people," Danijela said.

After a moment, Bakari said, "Now what?"

The High Wizard of Arc smiled widely. "I have something to show you before you return to Mahli. Come with me."

She motioned for Bakari to follow her, and they flew through the magic stream, stopping in front of a significant group of lights.

Still holding the powers of the dragons, Bakari knew whose lights these were. They were all the wizards in the Citadel: The first home that he could remember having. Where he had been trained as a scholar wizard. Where he had first begun to read all the books he could.

"Who could have ever known that a five-year-old orphan boy would end up here today?"

Danijela nodded toward the lights. "You need to go inside."

Bakari felt torn. He knew that Kharlia was there. He craved to hold her again and feel her comfort and love for him. But he would also have to face the fact that Roland was gone.

"I don't know if I can right now, Danijela. I'm exhausted. I need time. I just can't…" Tears filled the corners of his eyes.

Danijela reached up and put a hand on his shoulder. "My boy," she said in a comforting but demanding tone, "you need to see this."

Bakari took a deep breath and then said, "All right." He grabbed onto a light—the one he knew was Alli's—and found himself inside Roland's sitting room. Grief almost overwhelmed Bakari once more.

"How is he?" Kharlia asked Alli.

"As stubborn as ever," Alli said with a laugh. "He wants to get up and run around already."

Bakari wondered who they were talking about.

"It wouldn't hurt him to get some fresh air," Kharlia said. "The healing worked well, but the rest will come from his own body."

Bakari looked back and forth between the two. What were they talking about? What healing? His heart leapt with the possibility that he only dared hope for.

From the other room came a male voice, saying, "Are you two ladies talking about me again?"

"Not everything is about you, Roland Tyre," Alli said with a laugh. "But, yes, we were."

Roland! But, how? Bakari thought. *Could it really be him?*

Drawing more magic to himself once again—it came easier now—Bakari popped into the room in his physical form. Knocking over a chair and a water basin, but, without missing a step, he ran into Roland's bedchamber, a surprised Kharlia and Alli on his heels.

Sitting up in the bed in front of Bakari was none other than his best friend.

"Roland!" Bakari yelled and ran over to him. He leaned over and gave the man a hug. "But, how? I saw you die. *You* saw you die."

Roland laughed and hugged Bakari back. "Where did you pop in from, Bakari? What kind of wizardry is this?"

"Dragon power!" Bakari said.

Kharlia grabbed Bakari from behind and turned him around, into her arms. "Oh, Bak!" She planted a long kiss on his lips.

"All right, you two!" Roland said.

Bakari smiled as he turned his head back to Roland, but he kept his arm around Kharlia. As he breathed in her scent, it filled and lifted his soul.

"Alli!" Bakari said and then nodded to her. She came over and hugged him too. Tears fell from Bakari's eyes, and he noticed that he wasn't the only one. "So, tell me what happened, Roland," Bakari said, "and none of your games, now, straight and honest."

"Me, play games?" Roland laughed. He brought his hand up and pointed to Kharlia. "It was all her, Bak. Kharlia saved my life. After we killed the evil king, she healed me, and then my spirit was able to come back."

Bakari looked down at Kharlia by his side. "How?"

She smiled up at him, her brown eyes holding his with her gaze. "I am an Elvyn healer, Bak." She laughed through her own tears. "Can you believe it? A real healer."

Bakari laughed with joy. He couldn't believe it! This was all more than he could ever have hoped for. Turning back to Roland, Bakari said, "I think the women here were talking about getting you outside for a bit. Seems like it might be time for you to get back to running things here."

Roland nodded and smiled. "I think they like having me here in bed and taking care of me. Makes them feel useful."

"Get up, you lazy wizard!" Alli said as she grabbed his arm roughly and pulled him up out of bed.

Roland stood on his feet, looking a little wobbly at first. But he steadied himself after a few moments and said, "So, Bak, what about the three brothers?"

"Gone," Bakari said. "It is finished. And Breelyn should be here in a few days. She will need some friends to help escort her back to Elvyn."

Roland opened his eyes wide. "Seems like I might have underestimated one skinny, young scholar wizard."

"Me, too," Bakari said and then laughed. Turning to all three, he said his goodbyes and then added, "I have to go back now. I need to go to Mahli briefly." He kissed Kharlia again and promised, "I will be back here soon."

"Don't stay away for so long this time," she said.

"Only a day or two. Abylar is fast." Bakari smiled and began to fade.

Then Roland reached his hand out and grabbed Bakari's arm. "Thank you for all you have done, Bak—I mean *Dragon King*." Roland knelt down on his unsteady knees and said, "I am still yours."

After only a brief disorientation, Bakari found himself in the magic stream once again, standing next to Danijela.

"Thank you," he said to her.

"I didn't do it."

"No," Bakari said, "but you helped me get there."

She nodded her head. "We are all here together for you, Dragon King. I will see you soon."

With those words, Danijela left, and Bakari jumped out of the magic stream altogether, going back to the other riders and the dragons in the mountains of Mahli.

As Bakari slumped to the ground, Jaimon and Liam came over to him. Bakari let go of all the dragons' magic and let the dragon figurine fall from his grasp.

Both young men gave him questioning looks.

But he smiled back up at them and said, "All is well. All is well, Dragon Riders."

CHAPTER THIRTY NINE

Six weeks later, Bakari was flying over the Elvyn Forest on the back of his dragon, Abylar. Kharlia sat behind Bakari, holding him tight. They had just returned from spending some time in Mahli together. The last few weeks had been busy, with Bakari visiting most of the kingdoms on the Western Continent and making sure that any damage done by the ancient evil king and his sons was fixed.

A warm summer breeze blew over him and Kharlia as they landed on the sandy beach between the Blue Sea and Lor'l. The sun had flushed their faces as they flew. Bakari noticed that the other dragons were already there. Boats filled the harbor, and thousands of people were walking around.

After landing, elves began to gather around them, offering to feed and take care of the dragon.

As long as they have some meat for me, Abylar said to Bakari. *I can't eat any more of those vegetables.*

Bakari laughed out loud and replied, *Still always hungry, I see!* The dragon had grown again in the last few weeks since his captivity in the mountains. So Abylar now towered over almost everything, except the enormous trees of the Elvyn Forest.

Bakari walked with Kharlia on his arm toward the Elvyn city. She wore a beautiful blue dress that contrasted nicely with her dark skin and eyes. It also matched the whites of his own eyes—which had stayed blue since using the full power of the dragons. Bakari himself wore dark black riding pants and a light shirt, with a small crown atop his head. Both were wearing matching blue cloaks. Bakari's was lined with gold, signifying his rank.

People from all over the continent were in attendance this day, for today was the day that Breelyn Mier would be wed to King Lanwaithian Soliel. Music and laughter filled the air, and Bakari's soul was lifted—except for one unpleasant task that he needed to do before the wedding.

As they entered Lor'l at the edge of the trees, elves bowed their heads to Kharlia.

She blushed and turned to Bakari. "I'm not used to this."

"Neither am I." Bakari laughed with joy. "So, you are Elvyn-friend? That is an honor indeed, Kharlia. You must have many friends here."

"I do," she said shyly. "But the friend I care about the most is right here, by my side, Bak."

Bakari peered down at her, and his stomach fluttered. Kharlia amazed him. Every day with her was the best day of his life.

Spotting Breelyn off in the distance, he turned to Kharlia and said, "I need to talk to Breelyn alone."

Kharlia pouted but then smiled. "Don't be too long, my dragon king. One of these elves may steal me away."

"I won't be long." He grinned. "I will find you."

He walked off toward Breelyn. This was the task he had dreaded. She saw him approach and walked away from the others near her.

They walked together for a few moments in silence. And Bakari noticed only a small band of black at the end of her hair; the rest was now a beautiful silver color.

"Lan is doing well," Breelyn offered as the first words of their conversation. "He is almost back to his full strength."

Bakari nodded. He had heard that, once he had killed the Chameleon, the evil magic inside of Lan had begun to recede. With some additional healing from Kharlia and the other Elvyn healers, Lan was expected to make a full recovery.

"But you are not here to talk about the king, are you?" Breelyn asked as she stopped next to a wide tree trunk.

Bakari let out a long breath. How could he tell her that she could no longer be a dragon rider? "Breelyn…"

"Bakari, once again, I am so sorry," Breelyn apologized for the hundredth time in the last six weeks.

Bakari waved his hand in the air. "I know, Breelyn. I forgive you. I have no problems there: you will make a great queen for Lan and do many wonderful things for the elves. But…"

"But…what?" Breelyn asked.

"You will not be able to be a dragon rider." The words he had dreaded to say had just rushed out of his mouth.

The two were silent for another moment.

Breelyn eased herself down onto a log and stared absently at a small group of wildflowers poking out of the ground in a spot of sun. She finally glanced back up at him. Tears filled her eyes—eyes that used to be bright blue but were now a light gray.

"I know, Bak." She nodded her head sadly. "I know, and it kills me to think about it."

"But you have Lan and the kingdom," Bakari said as he tried to reassure her.

Breelyn smiled at him and patted his arm. "But, to lose that bond and never fly over the lands ever again—" she said and then paused. "I will get used to it, and I hold no grudges, Bakari. I understand why. The power of the dragons—the power of the spirit—needs to stay pure."

Bakari nodded his head, but then his face broke out in a wide smile. "Who says you can't fly with one of us on a dragon every now and again, Breelyn?"

Breelyn jumped up and grabbed Bakari in a fierce hug. "Oh, Bak, how are you so forgiving and wonderful? Do you truly mean it?"

"Sure, why not?"

With that, the two of them headed back toward the festivities. They found Lan and Kharlia standing together. Both looked up at Bakari and Breelyn.

"Everything all right here?" Lan asked as he grabbed Breelyn's hands in his own.

Breelyn wiped a tear away, "Yes. Yes, I am fine."

"Well, everyone is waiting for us." Lan laughed. "Let's go and put on a show."

And quite a show it was. The two stood on a high platform at the edge of the trees, with dignitaries, leaders, and curious onlookers from most of the kingdoms on the continent watching from the ground. Bakari and a few other select friends sat on the stand with the bride and the groom.

Before the wedding ceremony began, Lan was publicly proclaimed as King of Elvyn, all to the cheers and smiles of his people. Then Breelyn joined him, standing up by his side.

The royal couple, dressed all in white, said their vows and then were married by one of the local Elvyn priests. At the end of the ceremony, the four dragons flew overhead, pouring baskets of white flower petals over the happy couple and the cheering crowd.

You owe me one, Dragon Rider, Abylar said to Bakari. *Throwing flowers? This is not a thing for dragons to do.*

I'll save you a few good chunks of meat, Bakari said back.

Grrrr, Abylar growled. *I want more than a few chunks. I want the whole animal.*

You're going to get fat, Bakari teased. *How will you ever fly me around to all the kingdoms we have to visit?*

You're just a stick; I don't need any strength to fly you around. Anyway, there is always food on the ground for me to eat.

What if we fly across the sea? Bakari asked. *Do you like fish?*

Big fish! Abylar said, and Bakari laughed.

Lan quieted the crowd and motioned for Bakari to approach. Bakari gave him a questioning glance, but Lan wouldn't give any hint of what was to come. But Bakari hadn't been told of any part that he would play in the ceremony.

Lan turned to Bakari and said, "Today would not have been possible without our friend here. He ended the war, freed my bride, and established peace in the lands once again. Today, I name Bakari Elvyn-friend."

Bakari smiled down at Kharlia, who nodded her head at him.

Then Lan continued by kneeling on the ground in front of Bakari. "I, Lanwaithian Soliel, King of Elvyn, do now give my pledge to Bakari, Dragon Rider, and do support him as the Dragon King. I follow him, bow to him, respect him, and..." Lan paused and stared into Bakari's eyes with tears in his own and swallowed hard a few times before continuing, "And name him my friend for as long as the both of us shall live."

Lan stood, hugged Bakari, and then turned to the crowd and said, "Hail the Dragon King."

Mericus deGrande, king of Alaris, came forward, then Darius DarSan Williams, king of the Realm, with Mezar Alrishitar, emperor of Gildan, next to him. Then others followed: The newly crowned king of Quentis, the Wolf, with his son, Kaspar, in tow. The two kings of Solshi and the kings and queens of Khazer, Turg, Cyrene, and the Kingdom of Arc all formed a line in front of the raised platform. Joining them were the leaders from all the magic schools in Quentis, the Realm, Gildan, and Arc. Roland, representing the Citadel, also came forward, with Alli at his side. Then Jaimon and Liam walked up behind them.

In one voice, they all yelled together, "Hail the Dragon King! Hail the Dragon King!"

It was a sight that Bakari knew he would never forget—well, he never forgot anything anyway, but it was one sight that would always have special meaning. All the leaders of the West bowed and pledged support to their high king, Bakari, the Dragon King.

The four dragons flew overhead and let out streams of colorful fire as the crowd cheered. Breelyn joined Lan and gave

Bakari a hug, then signaled for the unforgettable feast to begin. The celebration continued long into the night.

Late that night, Bakari left Kharlia for a few moments to check on the dragons. On the way there, he found Alli and asked her to join him.

They walked out under a full moon to where the dragons slept, at the edge of the sea. The dragons had been fed well so they didn't have the urge to fly anywhere for the night.

After watching them for a moment, Bakari turned to his side. "Alli, I wanted to thank you for all you have done this past year. The peace we have today couldn't have been achieved without you."

Alli smiled. "Turning into a politician now, Bak—I mean *Dragon King*."

Bakari laughed. "With so many roles to play, Alli, sometimes I miss being the old Bak, the boring scholar wizard. You know when that changed?"

Alli shook her head.

"That day you arrived with Gorn in Cassian."

"Hey, that's not fair." Alli furrowed her eyebrows.

"Coincidence, I am sure." Bakari laughed. "Either way, you have my thanks."

Alli nodded and said, "You're welcome."

"But, there is more."

"More?" Alli asked, appearing confused.

"Someone else wants to thank you also," Bakari said.

Behind the two of them, the dragons had stirred, and Miriel stood up and took a few steps closer to Bakari and Alli.

Her growing bulk vibrated through the ground. Then she brought her great head up close to Alli.

Alli put out her hand, to touch the dragon, but then turned and looked at Bakari before she did.

Bakari nodded to Alli that it was all right.

So Alli touched Miriel, and a broad smile came to Alli's face. "Oh, Bak!"

Bakari reached up and touched Miriel also and then said, "She has chosen you, Alli, to be her next rider. Will you join us as one of the dragon riders?"

Alli laughed for a moment, then stopped, and her lips turned downward. "What about Roland?"

"Roland?" Bakari asked and then laughed.

"He...he needs me," Alli said, stumbling on her words a bit, then blushed. "Well, maybe I need him too."

Bakari nodded his understanding. "I'm sure we can work things out. Having a dragon rider stationed at the Citadel would be a fine thing, don't you think?"

"Yes, it would. Someone's got to watch over that boy."

"That's for sure." Bakari smiled.

Hearing footsteps behind them, Bakari turned to find Roland, Kharlia, Jaimon, and Liam walking up.

"Were you two talking about me?" Roland asked, strutting forward.

"Why do you think we are always talking about you, Roland?" Alli said with her hands on her hips.

"Well, were you?" Roland asked, pushing his hair out of his eyes.

Bakari sighed. "Yes, we were, my friend. Yes, we were."

Roland gave Alli an I-told-you-so look.

Bakari pointed at the dragons and asked, "Anyone up for a midnight flight?"

"Ooooh," Kharlia exclaimed and then grabbed Bakari's hand. "Me!"

"Me, too," Jaimon said.

"I'm up for it," Liam said, "if I can get my sleepy dragon awake."

Ryker, Liam's red dragon, stirred on the ground and then opened up one of his big yellow eyes.

Roland looked at Alli, who smiled sweetly back at him and said, "I'm a dragon rider now, Mr. High Wizard. Want to take a ride with me?"

Roland's eyes grew wide for a moment. "I sure would." Then he winked at her and said, "As long as you don't let this go to your head. I'm still more powerful than you."

Bakari laughed and everyone joined in. Then he said, "Wake up, dragons. Mount up, riders. We ride tonight over a peaceful land."

Beneath the bright moon and clear skies, the dragons carried their riders and friends out over the Blue Sea. Then, banking back westward, they flew out over the Elvyn Forest, the dragons' wings rustling the tops of the massive trees.

"Hail the dragons!" shouted Bakari with a whoop.

"Hail the dragons!" echoed everyone else.

# # #

For More Adventures of Bakari, Roland, Alli and their friends, Read The Golden Dragon, Book 1 in The Dragon Artifacts.

How much wizard power is too much?
Some people are born with magical powers.
Others are not.
It's that simple.

Roland Tyre, High Wizard of the Citadel, has always wanted to be the most powerful wizard in the land and adored by all. But there is already someone else that vies for that title – Bakari, the Dragon King; one of his best friends.

While Bakari and the dragon riders race off to find the lost dragon artifacts and the mythical golden dragon, Roland discovers his own magical artifact that gives him the opportunity to increase his own powers and influence in the land.

Can friendships survive greed for power? And who will emerge as the most powerful wizard in the land?

A grand adventure awaits with powerful wizards, kidnappings, traitors, kingdoms changing hands, and of course dragons and other magical creatures.

Is the Golden Dragon real and if so, who will find him first?

Other Series By Mike Shelton

The Cremelino Prophecy

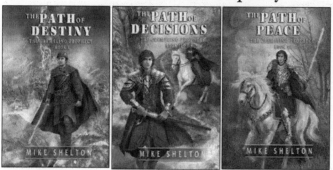

A Prophecy.
A Powerful Sword.
A Reluctant Wizard.

Darius San Williams, son of one of King Edward's councilors, cares little for his father's politics and vows to leave the city of Anikari to protect and bring glory to the Realm.

When a new-found and ancient magic emerges within him, he and his friends Christine and Kelln are faced with decisions that could shatter or fulfill the prophecy and the lives of all those they know.

Wizards and magic have long been looked down upon in the Realm, but Darius learns that no matter where he goes, prophecy and destiny are waiting to find him.

If you love magic, sword & Sorcery, arthurian style books, and wizards read this first book in The Cremelino Prophecy to find out what destiny awaits Darius.

Sign up on Mike's website at www.MichaelSheltonBooks.com and get a copy of the prequel novella e-book to The Cremelino Prophecy, **The Blade and The Bow**.
Follow Darius and Kelln in one of their more fantastic adventures prior to The Path Of Destiny.

About the Author

Mike was born in California and has lived in multiple states from the west coast to the east coast. He cannot remember a time when he wasn't reading a book. At school, home, on vacation, at work at lunch time, and yes even a few pages in the car (at times when he just couldn't put that great book down). Though he has read all sorts of genres he has always been drawn to fantasy. It is his way of escaping to a simpler time filled with magic, wonders and heroics of young men and women.

Other than reading, Mike has always enjoyed the outdoors. From the beaches in Southern California to the warm waters of North Carolina. From the waterfalls in the Northwest to the Rocky Mountains in Utah. Mike has appreciated the beauty that God provides for us. He also enjoys hiking, discovering nature, playing a little basketball or volleyball, and most recently disc golf. He has a lovely wife who has always supported him, and three beautiful children who have been the center of his life.

Mike began writing stories in elementary school and moved on to larger novels in his early adult years. He has worked in corporate finance for most of his career. That, along with spending time with his wonderful family and obligations at church has made it difficult to find the time to truly dedicate to writing. In the last few years as his children have become older he has returned to doing what he truly enjoys – writing!

mikesheltonbooks@gmail.com
www.MichaelSheltonBooks.com
https://www.facebook.com/groups/MikeSheltonAuthor/
http://www.Twitter.com/msheltonbooks
http://www.Instagram.com/mikesheltonbooks

73216292R00241

Made in the
USA
Middletown, DE